The
Promise
of *Dawn*

Books by Lauraine Snelling

UNDER
NORTHERN SKIES

1

The *Promise* of *Dawn*

LAURAINE
SNELLING

BETHANYHOUSE
a division of Baker Publishing Group
Minneapolis, Minnesota

Published by Bethany House Publishers
11400 Hampshire Avenue South
Bloomington, Minnesota 55438
www.bethanyhouse.com

Bethany House Publishers is a division of
Baker Publishing Group, Grand Rapids, Michigan

Printed in the United States of America

Library of Congress Cataloging-in-Publication Data
Names: Snelling, Lauraine, author.
Title: The promise of dawn / Lauraine Snelling.
Description: Minneapolis, Minnesota : Bethany House, a division of Baker
    Publishing Group, [2017] | Series: Under northern skies ; 1
Identifiers: LCCN 2016059755| ISBN 9780764219580 (cloth : alk. paper) | ISBN
    9780764218965 (trade paper) | ISBN 9780764219597 (large-print trade paper)
Subjects: LCSH: Domestic fiction. | GSAFD: Christian fiction.
Classification: LCC PS3569.N39 P78 2017 | DDC 813/.54—dc23
LC record available at https://lccn.loc.gov/2016059755

Scripture quotations are from the King James Version of the Bible.

This is a work of fiction. Names, characters, incidents, and dialogues are products of the author's imagination and are not to be construed as real. Any resemblance to actual events or persons, living or dead, is entirely coincidental.

Cover design by Dan Thornberg, Design Source Creative Services

Author is represented by Books & Such Literary Agency.

17 18 19 20 21 22 23   7 6 5 4 3 2 1

To longtime editor and friend, Sharon Asmus, who is now at home in glory, but I continue to reap the results of all her work on my books. She kept me straight on characters, plots, history, and made sure my time lines were accurate, for all the books we did together. Sharon, your life made big differences in so many lives. Thank you for love and laughter and deep caring.

Chapter 1

April 1909

M or, a letter from Amerika!"
Gunlaug Strand Carlson looked up from the loom where she was weaving a rug for her son Johann's wedding present. "From Ingeborg?" Her heart leaped. If only she had not lost touch in the years since her cousin Ingeborg married Roald and moved to North Dakota. At least she got bits of news from Ingeborg's mor.

Ivar, her youngest at fifteen, shook his head. "This is from Minnesota, so it must be your other cousin."

"Is it to me or your far?"

"It says 'Mister and Missus.' The writing is hard to read." Ivar handed her the letter.

"Takk." She studied the envelope and then smiled at her son. "So how was school today?"

"Better. There aren't as many absent, but some of those who came back are still coughing like to blow up their chests."

"Uff da." The schools had been closed for a week due to the influenza that seemed to come through every year. Every day she thanked God for keeping her family safe. Of all her children, Ivar loved school the most. He was already dreaming of college and becoming a schoolteacher. How they would ever pay for something like that was beyond her comprehension. She tapped the letter on the edge of the loom.

"Aren't you going to open it?" Ivar glanced at the clock. "Far will be home soon. What's for supper?"

"Ask Nilda. She's cooking for us tonight."

"Not porridge again?"

"Nei, Johann is bringing Solveig for supper to talk about the wedding. We will read the letter at supper."

"We could read it real quick and pretend like we didn't."

"Get on with you." She fluttered her fingers, shooing him on his way. "I want to get a few more rows woven before I have to cover it." She wanted the rug to be a surprise.

Ivar left the room, whistling. Besides being her most scholarly child, he also seemed the happiest. Like her cousin Ingeborg, Ivar saw the good in things; even as a baby he'd smiled and laughed. If only there were some way his dream of becoming a teacher could come true.

That night, with everyone gathered around the supper table, Gunlaug slit open the envelope and unfolded the one sheet inside.

"Dear Cousin Gunlaug and Thor,

"I hope all is well with you and your family. I am finally in a position to write to ask for help. As you know, Gerd and I have never been blessed with sons to help us here in the new land. The section of land I have purchased from a homesteader is covered with huge pine trees that we log and send to the mills in Minneapolis. The money from those trees has made it possible for us to build a home large enough to house a family. We farm what land we have cleared, but we need help. Gerd is not well, so we are asking if Rune and his wife and sons would be willing to immigrate to Minnesota. I would pay for their passage with the understanding that over time those funds would be paid back.

"We live near a small town called Benson's Corner, with the nearest big town being Blackduck, Minnesota. There is a school for the younger ones in the winter. Once the trees are felled and shipped on the local railroad spur to the northern mills, we will clear the stumps and plant crops. We have one cow now, but I have always planned on a dairy herd when the land is cleared.

"We are hopeful Rune will agree to come. This is indeed a land of opportunity. I know we are grateful we came here when we did.

"Yours truly,
"Einar Strand and Gerd"

Gunlaug laid the letter on the table and looked to her eldest son, who sat to her right. "What do you think?"

As she watched him ponder the news, she saw his slightly stooped shoulders stoop even more. His scalp showed through his thinning brown hair. *Oh, my son, I fear you are not built to be a logger. A farmer, yes, but . . .* It was the *buts* that hurt her heart. Her gentle son so far away. And his Signe? She looked frozen, like she might crack at any time. But she wouldn't. The light caught the gold highlights in her braided crown of long hair, but her lashes shielded her blue eyes. She sat erect, to scare off the fears Gunlaug knew were attacking.

Rune blinked in the kerosene lamplight. "Well, it is a surprise, but I have to say, I've considered emigrating more than once. But I planned to join the Bjorklunds in North Dakota. You know they've often sent letters asking for workers to come." He glanced at his wife, who stared down at her hands clenched in her lap. "What do you think, Signe?"

"I think we should say yes." Bjorn, their eldest at fifteen, could hardly sit still.

Rune frowned at him. "I was speaking to your mor."

Bjorn nodded slightly, but his excitement only dimmed rather than going out. He elbowed his brother Knute, to his right.

Nilda, the eldest of Gunlaug's three girls, set a plate of fritters on the table and went back for the coffeepot. "Warm-ups, anyone?" She nudged Johann. "Shame you don't have sons yet."

"Let us get married first, all right?"

"Well, I would go as soon as the ticket arrived." Nilda refilled Rune's coffee cup. "Come on, Signe, think of the adventure." She and Signe had been best friends since their school days and became even closer after Signe married Rune. Nilda had lived up to her reputation as a matchmaker.

Teeth clamped on her lower lip, Signe stared from her husband to Gunlaug and back. Shaking her head, she spoke softly. "If we go there, we will never see our families again."

Oh, you poor dear. Gunlaug patted her daughter-in-law's work-worn hand and nodded at her son. "I have always wanted to go find Ingeborg. How often I have wished we agreed to emigrate when they asked for more family to come."

"Why didn't you?" Nilda asked.

Thor interjected, "Because I have no desire to cross that ocean and then spend days on a train to North Dakota. I am content here in Norway." He looked to his wife, who shrugged. They never had agreed on this matter.

"Tante Ingeborg and her family have certainly done well," Rune commented. "At least that's what we've heard."

"Ja, they have." Gunlaug made sure her smile was back in place. No sense dreaming of what could never be. She looked at her children. "If you decide to go, know that it will be with my blessing and your far's also. Right, Thor?"

"Ja. If you want to go, so be it. But remember, not everyone who goes to Amerika does as well as Ingeborg and her family. There are heartaches aplenty there too." Thor nodded to Rune. "You must think and pray on this. You do not want to make hasty decisions and regret them later. Felling the tall trees is not only hard work but dangerous."

Gunlaug saw Signe shiver. Leaving her family—both families—would be especially hard on her, since she had already lived through such sorrow in her life. Her first husband died shortly after their son Bjorn was born. Nilda had brought her and the baby to live with the Carlsons and played a big part in bringing Rune and Signe together. Such opposites, she who loved to talk and he who made sure not one word was spent carelessly. He took after his father in that way.

How dear Rune and Signe's three sons were to the whole family. But tragedy had struck again and again as Signe suffered miscarriages. Then two girls died after birth, and after that, Signe began to believe she was barren. Sometimes life was harsh indeed.

And now that Gunlaug suspected Signe might finally be pregnant again, they might be leaving. Taking her grandchildren with them.

Gunlaug brought her mind back to the letter at hand. Einar had said Gerd was not well. Did that mean she was bedridden or just had a weak constitution? Either would mean a big load for Signe.

11

Rune looked thoughtful. "I know it is a big decision, but I am not afraid of hard work. Einar doesn't say anything about having land of our own. Does he expect us all to live in their house for the rest of our lives?"

"And what if we have more children?" Signe was frowning now.

"Did you know Einar and Gerd well when you were growing up, Mor?" Rune asked.

Gunlaug shook her head. "They didn't live close by. That family settled over on the mountain, and we hardly ever saw them. I never met Gerd. I know my mor stayed in touch with them, but she is so good about writing letters. That's probably where Einar learned you have sons. But surely he doesn't think Bjorn is old enough to fell trees. That's a man's job."

"I can handle a crosscut saw, can't I, Far?"

"Ja, but there is a difference between cutting up firewood and felling giant trees. Ach, we would have so much to learn. How old is Einar, do you think?"

"He was younger than I when they emigrated, probably in his late thirties. Just think—you can homestead in Amerika and earn your land free and clear."

Thor looked at his eldest son. "There are strict rules to be met. Remember Ole Sorenson? He gave it up and came back home. He said free land was all a lie. You might want to write Einar and ask him some of your questions."

Rune nodded. "Ja, that would be wise. Can we take the letter home with us so we have the address?"

"Of course." Gunlaug passed the envelope to him. "You might ask if there are any other family members near them. And when they would expect you to come."

"From the sounds of this, the sooner the better." Thor's scowl hadn't let up. If anything, the lines in his forehead had deepened.

"Remember, tonight we are supposed to be talking about our wedding." Johann raised his voice over the conversations breaking out. He smiled at his intended sitting next to him. "Do you have any questions?"

Solveig shook her head. "My brother Arne went to Amerika, then wrote back and asked for someone to send him a bride. He couldn't find a woman to marry over there and didn't want to be a lumberjack all his life. Even though he made enough money to pay for a ticket."

"And someone went?"

"Ja, he included a ticket, so the daughter of some friends agreed to go. As far as I know, they got married and now have a baby. Mail-order brides is what they're called, I think."

"I've heard of that." Nilda sat down in her chair. "Maybe that's what I should do, become a mail-order bride. After all, there are not many young men left in Norway."

"Don't be silly," Thor said. "It's not like you're an old maid."

"What a gamble." Rune rubbed his eyes. "I think we need to head home. You boys get your things together. Signe, I'm glad we got married when we did. Mail-order brides." Shaking his head, he tucked the envelope in his breast pocket and pushed back his chair. "When is the wedding to be, Johann?"

"Three weeks. You better not leave before then. You agreed to stand up with me."

Rune smiled. "We'll still be here, never fear. Solveig, how you'll put up with my brother is beyond me."

"My far said the same thing about me. I know I wouldn't mind emigrating to Amerika." Solveig looked at her intended. "Would you, Johann?"

"It bears thinking about." He slapped Rune on the shoulder. "You get us a place over there in a year or two, after we see how you do."

The next day, Gunlaug wrote Einar and Gerd a short, newsy letter—just a page—while Rune wrote a letter with his questions, the main one being when Einar would expect them to travel. To save postage, they sent both letters in one envelope,

Gunlaug worked long into the night in order to finish the rug, the monotony of throwing the shuttle and clamping the rug giving her too much time to think. If Rune and his family went to Minnesota, she would never see those grandchildren again, let alone her eldest son. Just like she'd never seen Ingeborg again. How could two cousins who were closer than sisters lose touch with each other this way? The break had happened when her far learned that the will of his younger brother did not deed any of the family land to him but all to Ingeborg's far. He'd forbidden them any contact with the family.

When the two families finally had contact again, it was not the same. Too much water under the bridge, as her mor would say.

She had written several letters through the years, but she'd not had an answer and had finally given up. Was it worth it to try again? That was the big question. Ingeborg did not even write to her own family very often. Mostly only when sending a request for help.

But Thor was adamant. He would not emigrate. The fact that he had so easily agreed to send Rune with his blessing was a shock.

She finished the rug a week before the wedding. After wrapping it in an old sheet, she tucked it away and restrung the loom for another rug, this one to go with Rune and Signe to Amerika. Even living in someone else's home, they would have a piece of her heart to lay by their bed. Einar must have a really large house to invite a whole family like this.

The day before the wedding, Rune and Signe brought the

answer from Einar to the house. "He wants us to come immediately."

Gunlaug clasped her hands over her heart. "And you will go?" She looked at Signe, whose face wore tear tracks.

Signe nodded.

"And your mor?"

"She is so disappointed with our decision that she can hardly speak to me."

Gunlaug gathered her daughter-in-law into her arms. "I am so sorry to hear that. But perhaps she will relent as the day draws nearer."

"Rune says I must be strong, but where do I find the strength?"

"The only place I know is in the arms of our God. If this is His plan for you, He will provide the strength."

"Easy to say," Rune grumbled under his breath.

Having lived under her far's edict all those years ago, Gunlaug well knew the pain this was causing Signe. How could she help her? What would it take to stiffen this young woman's spine enough to endure the voyage and a hard life in the new land? Not that life was easy here in Norway. Would that Gunlaug had had that spine years ago.

"So what will you do?"

"Answer him that we will be ready to leave within a week of receiving the tickets." Rune had obviously given this a great deal of thought. But he was the one fighting to support his family and keep food on the table in a land with few opportunities for the younger folk.

Gunlaug looked at the calendar. "How long did it take for his return letter this time?"

"Between two and three weeks. So I suspect we will hear by the first of June. Summer voyages are supposed to be much easier than winter ones." He looked at Signe. "Not so much seasickness."

Signe flinched, her sigh filling in the blanks. She obviously dreaded the voyage.

"If you send the letter by return post, then we will put this out of our mind for a couple of days and enjoy the wedding tomorrow. It's Solveig and Johann's big day, and it would not be fair to overshadow it with this news." Gunlaug hoped she sounded firm and positive and did not even hint at the cracking of her heart. Her oldest son and his family would be on the opposite side of the world. Somehow, reminding herself that they could write letters did not ease her sorrow.

After looking out the window the next day, Gunlaug stepped outside to enjoy the sunrise. It looked to be a clear day for the wedding, always a good omen. Johann was already out in the garden. With the extra-cold winter, it had taken longer for the soil to thaw out, which meant later planting.

"A good day for a wedding," she called out.

"Any day would be a good day for this wedding," he answered. "I've waited long enough."

She reached in the door for the shawl always hanging at the ready. Wrapping it around her shoulders against the early morning chill, she made her way to the outhouse and then to the garden. "Takk for your help."

"We all eat from this plot of ground." He leaned on the handle of the hoe. "I wonder if they grow the same things in Amerika."

"Most likely. I looked at a map. We aren't much farther north than Minnesota. But I hear in North Dakota the winters are worse than here, as there is nothing to stop or even slow down the wind off the northern plains of Canada. We have hills, mountains, and trees to protect us." *I want to go there!* The thought echoed in her mind like a trumpet call.

Johann walked to the fence. "When we go, Mor, we will take you with us. Both Solveig and I would go in a heartbeat."

"How you will save the money for that trip is more than I could do. I try to save against a rainy day, but something always eats it up." Last winter, when Thor had been without work because the cows were dry, had been a tough one. The porridge had been terribly weak at times.

"Ah, but we are young and don't have a family to feed yet. If the folks of Blessing—or in Minnesota—send out another call, I will go and send money back for a ticket for Solveig. Just the name of the town, Blessing, makes me want to go there."

"Why have you never said this before?"

"I've thought of it but never had someone else depending on me, like I will now. After today, I am no longer a free and easy young man. I will be a husband, a man with responsibilities." He laid his hand over hers. "But, Mor, I will see that you get to Amerika."

And find Ingeborg. But she didn't voice that dream, for after all, that was all it was.

<hr />

Johann's words dug in and took root in Gunlaug's mind as they prepared to send Rune and Signe on their way. Their two trunks were tightly packed, and each of the boys had a rucksack of his own. Gunlaug hoped that keeping busy would ease the heartache, but when the tickets arrived, she felt like Signe looked.

Realization dawned. She drew the younger woman into the bedroom.

"Signe, is there any chance you are with child?" It had been eight years since Leif was born, and she had figured, as did Signe, that her childbearing years might be over.

17

Signe nodded. "I have not told Rune yet, but if I have no showing next week, well, I feel sure . . ." She blew her nose. "If I lose this one on that horrible voyage, how will I forgive myself? Or Rune?"

"For forcing you to go?"

The shake of her head was barely perceptible. "He wants to do this, and I cannot keep him from it. If there is hope for a better life there, we must try. But the thought of him out cutting down trees gives me nightmares. He has no experience like that." She blew her nose again. "And Mor is barely speaking to me still."

Gunlaug clamped her teeth together to keep her thoughts back. Forgiveness might be preached in church, but too often those listening didn't heed the words. "I am so sorry, but I feel my job as a mother is to encourage my children to do what is necessary for the family. I wish your mor felt the same. I pray she will see the light before you go."

"Ja, it better be soon. I cannot worry about her, this babe I am probably carrying, and keeping my sons and husband safe on both the voyage and the train rides."

"Keeping you all safe is God's provenance, and He promises to never let us go. Do you believe that?"

"Ja, I try, but this is all so unknown."

"True, but hanging on to His promise to be with us always is what keeps my mother's heart from breaking right in two." Someday. Someday she would see them again, if Johann could keep his promise to her.

Waving goodbye when the wagon took them to the train tested Gunlaug beyond belief.

Chapter  2

JUNE 1909

The steamship dwarfed the other ships around it.

Rune and his wife turned to each other with their mouths hanging open. So many stories they'd heard had to do with sailing ships, but indeed, times had changed. Several gangplanks led from the Liverpool dock to various entrances on the ship. Their tickets said steerage. Signs above the gangplanks indicated the level of quarters.

"Ours is down there." Bjorn pointed to the steerage sign about halfway along the side of the ship.

Men and women dressed in the latest fashion strolled up the gangplank nearest them. Dockworkers wrestled trunks and other luggage onto the lowest level. The family followed Bjorn to the entrance to steerage. No one in fine clothing made their way up to this entrance, just people like themselves. Coats and shawls, carpetbags and knapsacks, women carrying babies and small children, everyone wearing hats of some kind, and most of them looking around, fear rampant.

19

A man at the dock took their tickets and spoke to them in English. He handed the tickets back to Rune.

Rune shook his head. The meager amount of English they had learned was not sufficient. He recognized *Duluth* and *Minnesota*, so at least they were at the right place. And the name of the ship matched the one on their tickets. "Takk. Sleep where?"

The man pointed, and they boarded the ship. They descended stairs. More stairs. Another man stood at the doorway to a long, narrow room. He pointed to their belongings and again spoke in English.

Rune shook his head and shrugged. The man muttered something unintelligible and waved an arm, motioning them in.

Stacks of bunks rose from floor to ceiling. Another man flagged them forward. He looked at their tickets and said impatiently in Norwegian, "You have three bunks. Come on, come on. Get out of the way."

Rune felt Signe cringe at the tone of his voice, her hand strangling his arm.

Signe sank down on the bottom bunk made of wooden boards, barely wide enough for one person, let alone two. Gaslights were set so far apart in the room that the dim light barely illuminated their features. She clutched her coat around her and closed her eyes. Rune realized how hard this journey would be for her. *Dear God, how do we get through this?*

The noise level rose as more people staggered past their bunks and claimed their own. Babies cried, some screamed, and small children yelled to be heard by parents so overwhelmed they could scarcely speak.

"Mor will have the bottom bunk," Rune instructed. "Leif, you will sleep with me on the middle one, and you two share the top one. We have our quilts and blankets, so spread them out and tuck your knapsacks in the corners."

"But there is no mattress," Knute moaned.

"I know. We will have to make do."

Signe looked near tears. "Rune, I think of the feather beds we left behind. And the down pillows."

"I'm sorry, but they took up too much room in our baggage."

"And the basket of food we brought is nearly empty already. When and where will the meals be served? Our tickets include meals."

While the section they were in had been chilly at first, with all the emigrants packed into the space, it was rapidly warming up. Who could they get to understand them well enough to answer their questions?

Rune told his boys to stay with their mother while he went to find someone who spoke Norwegian. But each time he heard people speaking Norwegian, none of them spoke English too. And no one knew whom to ask. The men working for the shipping line brushed him off and pointed him back to his bunk as they would be departing soon.

Rune heard the change in the engines growling beneath them. Someone was yelling orders, and the hatches slammed closed so that even less light entered the packed steerage section. Someone who could see out one of the small round windows called out in Norwegian, "We're underway." The floorboards shook beneath their feet.

"I want to see, go up on deck!" Bjorn muttered. "But they locked us in this—this hole."

They heard murmurs from those around them. Rune sat down and drew Signe to him with an arm around her shoulders. If only they had begun preparing for the trip earlier. Several people had told him to learn English, but with so much to do, there had not been time.

"We're out in the river!" the man at the porthole called back to the others. "And picking up speed."

Rune could tell that by the change in the tenor of the engines. It felt like the steam engines were right under their feet. So far they weren't hitting a lot of waves, or perhaps the ship was too large to be bothered by waves. He wondered how long until they met open water. He'd finally found a map and located Liverpool on the west side of England. It was a shame the man at the window didn't seem willing to share the view. Perhaps that would change too.

"How long do we have to stay in these bunk beds?" Leif asked from the top bunk. "I gotta go."

If only some of the signs on the wall were in Norwegian. If only he had learned to read and speak English. Rune took off his hat and scrubbed his fingers through his hair. Maybe he should have listened more closely and paid attention to what Signe had said.

Nei! he ordered himself firmly. *When we arrive in Amerika, these things will pass away. I know farming, and I have cut down trees up in our mountains. Perhaps not as large at those giant pines in Minnesota, but I will learn. We will have a new life with land of our own, eventually.* He settled his hat back on his head, patted Signe on the knee, and stood.

"Come along, boys. We will go find the necessary." All three boys scrambled down from their bunks, leaping and giggling.

"You find it and come back for me." Signe lay down on her side and tucked her skirts around her legs. "Do not get lost."

As if they could get lost on a ship.

After standing in line to use the head, Rune turned the wrong way, but thanks to Bjorn's unerring sense of direction, they found their bunks again. Signe lay sound asleep, the shadows cast by the lamps hiding her face.

"Can we go exploring, Far? We'll stay together." Bjorn spoke for all three of them as usual.

Rune heaved a sigh. What could be the harm in it? He nodded. "But don't be gone long. And be polite."

"Ja, we will."

He watched them disappear into the gloom down the aisle. Surely they would be allowed out of this crowded room once they were on the open ocean. He checked on Signe, but she didn't waken, so he made his way over to the group of men by the porthole. At least they were speaking Norwegian.

He learned that breakfast and supper would be served but not to expect much. They dumped porridge or soup in one's bowl and handed out a hunk of bread. Seasickness wasn't as rampant in the summer or on the steamships, compared with winter crossings and sailing ships of yore.

"Do any of you speak English?" Rune asked.

Most shook their heads, but one man nodded. "Badly, but better than nothing."

"Would you be willing to teach me and my family?"

"Ja, but I won't be much help."

"When? My boys will be back soon. My wife is not feeling well, so she is sleeping."

"You come find me when they return. We will start today. Bring a pencil and paper."

"What do you do for a living?"

"I was a schoolteacher at home and I hope to do the same in Amerika. But I have to improve my English too."

Rune returned to find Signe awake and needing the necessary, so he showed her where it was and waited until she finished.

"Uff da, that is worse than any outhouse. Don't they ever dump it?" She hung on to his arm as if afraid he might disappear again. When he told her about the English class, she didn't respond. "Where are our boys?"

"Gone exploring. I told them not to be gone too long." He sat beside her on the bottom bunk. "How are you feeling?"

"I have missed three cycles now, so I assume I am pregnant."

Pregnant! He covered the hand tucked through the bend in his arm. "God willing, you will carry this baby to term. Perhaps it will be the first of others to be born in the new land. When a baby is born in Amerika, it is an American citizen. The rest of us will have to pass a test to become citizens."

He watched her shake her head. "Signe, we will become Americans as soon as we can. No more being Norwegians. Americans."

"We must get there first."

She looked up as the boys skidded to a stop in front of them.

"Far, did you know we are locked in here? People on the other decks can walk all around the ship, but we are locked in!" Bjorn's face matched the horror in his voice.

"A man said that sometimes they will let us out to get some air and sun," Knute added.

Signe shook her head. "You can't know that for sure."

"When we tried to open the door, one of the sailors yelled at us."

"Didn't your far tell you to stay out of trouble? What were you doing?"

"Some other boys said there is a big place where we can walk around, and I wanted to see it. That's all."

"That man, he got real mad." Leif slid as close to Signe as he could.

Rune motioned to his sons. "Come with me, all of you. I found a man to teach us English. Signe, we need paper and pencils to write down the words."

"But that's like school." At ten, Knute had been the one most happy to miss out on school.

Signe dug in her bag to pull out one pencil and a small pad of paper and handed them to Rune. "You write down what he says for all of us."

At least learning English made the time go by faster. The schoolteacher gave them simple phrases and made them repeat the words. The boys learned them quickly, but Signe was either getting sick or . . . Rune couldn't pay attention to her and keep up with the lesson. She had to try, at least.

"I need to go lie down," she muttered with a tug at his sleeve.

"Bjorn, take your mor back to our bunks and return here immediately."

"Ja, I will come right back." He took her hand. "Come, Mor. Maybe you will feel better after we have some supper."

The lesson continued until Rune felt like his head was swimming. "We will meet again tomorrow?"

"Ja, and you must practice all these words and phrases. Each day we will speak more English."

Rune stared at the list that covered several pages. Ja, he had plenty of work ahead of him.

Signe tried to eat supper after they stood in line to get their bowls filled but finally handed Rune her bowl of soup or stew or whatever it was. "You share with the boys. Perhaps I can eat the bread a bit at a time."

"It's not very good, is it?" Leif muttered.

Bjorn made a face. "We fed our pigs better than this."

"Eat it and be thankful. You will not starve in six days." Rune forced himself to follow his own orders. Perhaps Signe was better off not eating. If this was a typical meal, they could be grateful the trip was no longer than six days. If only the light were strong enough to read by.

Signe started retching halfway through the night. He'd already heard others in the same situation. He dipped a bowl of water from the water barrel and, after pouring some in a cup, used the rest to wet a cloth and bathe her face. If only they had brought some peppermint for tea. That was his mor's antidote for an upset stomach. Would there be peppermint in Amerika? He finally fell asleep after she did but wakened a short time later to more of the same.

The stench grew stronger now, due to those ill with seasickness, even though the voyage was so smooth that he almost wondered if they were moving. The thrum of the engines assured him that was the case.

Leaving Signe sleeping in the morning, he took the boys for more English lessons. The buzz that passed from bunk to bunk said the door would be opened so some of them could get air. Not everyone could go outside at once.

The boys darted away as soon as they heard the announcement about the opening of the door.

"Wait!" Rune called. But they either did not hear or ignored him and disappeared into the gathering throng. "I will be back later," he told the schoolteacher. He tried to see his boys, but the crowding brought movement to a halt.

"Wait your turn!" The order penetrated the hubbub of languages, but no one could move anyway.

When Rune finally cleared the door, several boys darted past him, running around the open square, dodging the adults, most of them standing with their faces raised to the sun. Both the upper decks had walkways around the open area, and those were filling with the people in second class. Above that were the elite, the women with parasols to protect themselves from the sun—men and women dressed in the fashions of the day. Rune sucked in a deep breath of ocean air, heavily tinged by the unwashed bodies around him.

Cries of delight rang out as those on the upper decks tossed pennies and candy down to the children. Watching the children scrambling for the booty made those above laugh and shout comments. Three boys got into a fight over the treasure, and some of the younger ones cried because a coin was snatched out of their hands. Rune saw Bjorn running with some of the older boys, but where were Leif and Knute?

Staring up at the pointing fingers and laughing faces, he clamped his jaw. So now they were a source of entertainment to those above. Those who could throw pennies away. He forced himself to begin walking around the area, not only looking for his boys but also walking off the disgust that ate at him. He'd hoped things would be different in America, and perhaps they would, but on the ship, the classes were clearly divided. He felt something hit his hat, and a penny fell beside his feet, only to be pounced on by a boy who looked like he'd been through a war. The child scrabbled for the coin, but Rune stepped on it, ignoring the pitiful look on the boy's face. When the child left, he bent over and picked up the penny. He'd give it to one of his boys if they did not get their own.

The order went up for those in the open to return to steerage so others could have a turn. Signe was awake but lying in the bunk when he finally made his way back to her.

"Where are the boys?" Did her voice sound stronger?

He sat beside her and shrugged as he described the chaos outside.

"You let them go alone?"

Rune shook his head and growled. "They took off, and I only saw Bjorn once. You have no idea what a fiasco that was. Seems all the boys are towheaded."

"But . . . but where are they now?" She sat up, bracing her back against the wall.

"Signe, they know where we are. They will find us." He laid

27

his hand on hers, fighting to keep impatience out of his voice. "Did you manage to eat some of that bread you saved?"

"Ja. Hard as a rock, but it has stayed down. I think I'm feeling better. Could you please help me to the necessary?"

"If you can keep from vomiting again from the stench." He folded back the blanket covering her. "Come, the aisles seem a bit clearer." He guided her to the head and, making sure he breathed through his mouth, waited until she finished.

"Can we get some water on our way back?"

"If the barrel has been refilled. They did serve coffee with breakfast." He glanced down at her. "Nei, don't get your hopes up. The breakfast was like the supper. Not enough to fill a bowl and so watered down that the porridge was more like gruel. We soaked our bread in it."

Back at their bunks, Knute and Leif shifted from one foot to the other.

"Where is Bjorn?" Rune asked.

They both shrugged.

"Did he not come back in at the announcement?" They looked at each other and shrugged again. "He was supposed to watch out for you."

Knute dug in his pocket. "I got two pennies. Leif got a piece of candy, but he already ate it."

"I want to go out there again." Leif looked up. "How come those nice people threw pennies for us?"

Rune started to give his disgusted opinion but stopped. Why take away the little joy his boys found out there? He looked to Signe, who was still shaking her head. Instead he dug in his pocket. "Here, Leif, this one hit me, so you may have it. Signe, do you feel up to our English lessons?"

"Nei, but perhaps tomorrow. You can teach me what you

28

have already learned. Aren't you concerned that Bjorn could be in trouble?"

"What kind of trouble? He is either still outside or came in. He can't get off the ship."

"I suppose you're right." She slid down to lie flat again. "Perhaps if I sleep, I will wake up well again. How I would have loved to see the sunshine and the blue sky. To breathe clean air."

"Perhaps they will do the same tomorrow." He tucked the blanket around her. "Come, boys, our teacher is waiting." *At least I hope he is.*

Where, indeed, was Bjorn? And who was he with? Rune blew out a breath. Surely this was not a portent of life in America.

Chapter 3

Ellis Island was worse than anyone had warned them.

By the time they had waited in line to board the boat to the island, waited in line to enter the monstrous building, waited in line for the physicians to approve them, and waited in line to eat supper at real tables, they were given beds for the night, and Signe felt like a sleepwalker. Her ears ached from the constant noise. But the supper more than made up for the waiting, and cots with bedding seemed palatial compared with the board bunk beds on the ship.

She ordered the boys to remain right beside her after breakfast when Rune went to inquire about getting to Grand Central Station. There they would board a train for Buffalo, New York, where they would board a ship named *Juniata* for the final voyage to Duluth, Minnesota.

"We must hurry," he said when he returned. "We will have another line to board a ferry across the river, and then we will walk to the train station."

"What about our trunks?" Bjorn asked.

"They will be loaded on a wagon at the dock and then onto the train. That is part of our ticket."

Signe closed her eyes. Uff da! Was nothing going to be easy on this trip? "And we ride the wagon too?"

"Nei, we will walk. They say it is not that far."

She turned to her sons. "You will carry your packs, and you will stay right with us. There will be no stopping to look. I don't care what all you can see. Do you hear me?" She looked each of them right in the eye. "Bjorn?"

He nodded, staring down at his hands.

"Look at me!" When he did so, she continued. "There will be no running off like on the ship, you hear me?"

When had Bjorn grown taller than her five foot seven? Did he grow inches on that ship? He looked more like his far all the time, even to the cleft on his chin, which was not a Carlson trait. Already his body was growing into a sturdier frame than Rune's.

Again he nodded.

"You are all listening to your mor, right?"

All three nodded, but Signe caught the sideways look that Knute sent to Bjorn. "You can practice your English on the way, but if you get separated from us . . ." She shook her head. If only they had stayed in Norway. At least her sons were safe there. Bjorn had always been so dependable, but on the ship . . . Uff da did not begin to cover her feelings. Fear crouched like a lion, seeking to destroy at every opportunity.

Had she a rope, she might be tempted to tie them together in a line.

The sight of the skyline of the city as they crossed the river struck even more fear into her heart. Liverpool had been huge, but this? They docked and made sure their trunks were loaded for the train station, then set out at a brisk pace. There was no way they could walk abreast on the crowded sidewalks.

"You lead the way, Rune. I will follow at the rear." She'd much rather be next to him, but the crowds made that impossible.

At one point she almost lost them when he turned a corner and she got shuffled back by other people waiting to cross the street. Her heart thudded as if she'd been running until Bjorn, screaming her name, came pushing through the crowd and grabbed her hand.

Rune stopped and pointed to a huge domed building that covered several streets. "That is the station. The man on the boat said we couldn't miss it. It is bigger than our town at home."

They pushed through the swinging doors and walked down some stairs. Signs pointed to the ticket booths and down more stairs to the tracks where the trains waited. "To Buffalo," Rune said when they finally reached the window. "For five."

The man eyed their tickets. "You"—he said a few words in English Rune couldn't catch—"steamer to Duluth?"

Rune nodded, grateful he knew some of the words at least.

The man stamped their tickets and pointed to the stairs. "There will be signs in Buffalo for the docks for the ships."

"You are going to Duluth too?" a man asked from behind them in Norwegian.

"Ja."

"Can you speak English?"

"Very little."

"My name is Lindstrom." He held out a hand to shake Rune's. "I'm going to Duluth too, and I've done this before. Follow me."

Signe's first thought was relief, her second—could this man be trusted? But Rune waited, and the two men walked together, talking as if they'd known each other for years. The boys stayed right with their father so as not to miss a word.

Signe followed, praying their trunks would get on the train and then the ship, praying she could keep up. Her frustration grew with Rune, who seemed to be having the time of his life and forgetting his family. After all, he had vowed to watch out for her. Among other things. She jumped when the train beside the platform blasted steam. What was she doing? Why had she ever agreed to come on this horrible journey? Adventure, Rune had called it. Her head felt as if it might fall off and roll under the train wheels.

Rune at least waited to help her board their train. Bjorn beckoned them to empty seats, where they shoved what they could in the overhead compartments. The two men took the seats ahead of the four facing each other where she and the boys stored their things, and she dropped onto the scruffy, once-velvet seat. The grime on the windows made the world outside look dull and gray. She heard the conductor shout, "All aboard!" and the train jerked and screeched into motion. The boys glued themselves to the window, rubbing the grime off with their jacket sleeves. She wished she could watch the world go by too, but at the moment she needed the necessary. She tapped Rune on the shoulder, and he pointed to the end of the car.

The room was not much larger than she was, but at least it was clean. She washed her hands under warm running water. The ghost she saw in the mirror above the sink made her shake her head. Ja, that was indeed her. With dampened fingers, she tried to smooth some order into the dark honey hair braided and wrapped around her head. She repinned her hat, which surely was as disgusted with the trip as she. A knock at the door made her heart jump.

"I am sorry," she muttered as she hurried out. How did one even apologize in English?

The man tipped his hat and answered something. She nodded and moved out of the way, the lurching train making her grab for the wall. Uff da! Would this never end? Back in her seat, her stomach reminded her that they'd last eaten on Ellis Island, many hours before. The biscuits she'd tucked in her reticule would have to do. Did Einar send money for food on the train? At least once onboard the ship, meals would be included, and hopefully superior to those served in steerage. They wouldn't be of much use on the farm if they starved to death on the way.

Closing her eyes, she leaned back in her seat, the swaying of the train making her feel faint again. Oh, for even a moment of quiet.

"Mor, I'm hungry," whispered Leif.

"I know." How far would three biscuits stretch? She dug the napkin-wrapped packet from her bag and broke one in half. "You share this with Knute, but eat it slowly. It has to last." Until when, she wasn't sure. She gave half of hers to Bjorn with the same admonition.

"This is all we have?"

"For now."

If only she had thought to save more food. Rune had frowned at her when he saw her wrapping the biscuits as it was. But he didn't think of his sons, who needed to eat more often than he did.

Rune and Mr. Lindstrom kept on talking as if they'd known each other for a lifetime. Signe watched her boys, pointing out people on iron stairs that zigzagged up the walls of the brick buildings lining the track, or the wash hung on lines attached to those walls. Finally there were houses, then open country with trees and barns and cattle in the fields. They saw farmers on tractors or with teams plowing, even seeding. Would they ever have a farm like that? She shifted closer to the window so she could see better. They crossed rivers and creeks, the incessant clack of the wheels changing when on bridges.

The conductor came through after every stop, his voice announcing the next in metallic tones. The dining car was open for business. Someone had told her that eating in the dining car on a train cost more than a day's wages.

Leif leaned against her. "My stomach really needs food, Mor."

"When we get to the boat, we will have meals as part of the ticket. We'll just have to wait."

"How long?"

She shrugged. "I wish I knew."

As dusk drew a curtain over the entertainment out the window, the voice announced that supper was being served in the dining car.

Mr. Lindstrom stood. "Are you going for supper? I'm sure your boys think someone cut their throats by now."

"Uh . . . later," Rune replied.

"Did your relative not include money to feed your family?"

"He included some emergency money."

"Well, as far as I can tell, lack of food can constitute an emergency. Especially to growing boys."

Signe closed her eyes. Surely Rune could swallow his pride for the sake of his boys. She breathed a sigh of relief when he stood.

"I guess we could have a bowl of soup."

Knute started to cheer, but Rune gave him a look that worked like a hand clapped over his mouth.

Like ducks in a row, they all followed Mr. Lindstrom down the swaying coach and through a door that opened to a blast of hot air and the sight of tracks below their feet, the coupling of the cars shrieking metal against metal. Signe breathed a sigh of relief when the door closed behind her in the next car. At least the boys hadn't stopped to chatter about what they saw below them. Another glimpse of the railroad ties flashing past set both her head and stomach to churning again.

One more open stretch between cars, and they entered the

dining car, where white tablecloths covered all the tables set in front of the windows. They found two tables across the aisle from each other and pulled out the chairs. Surely this was too grand for the likes of them. Signe smoothed the tablecloth with an admiring hand. She had only one tablecloth in their trunks, and that for company, an extravagance she'd snuck in as a reminder that life would not always be hand-to-mouth living.

If that was possible. If they ever had a home of their own again.

A black waiter in a stiff white shirt and black bow tie stood at their tables with a pad and pencil. "Do you need menus?" he asked.

Signe could feel her eyes widen and looked to silence the boys. While they had seen people with dark skin on the ship and on the streets in New York, they'd not been this close to one. She glanced at her sons, who looked about to burst with comments. A barely visible shake of her head set them to staring at the white tablecloth.

Rune shook his head. "We'll each have a bowl of soup."

The waiter rattled off an explanation, and Mr. Lindstrom translated. "They have vegetable beef or creamed potato. Which do you prefer? And bread comes with that. Coffee or milk?"

Signe uttered a silent prayer of gratitude. Surely she could take some bread with them for the morning.

"The beef soup, please, and milk for the boys."

"I'll have the pork chops," Mr. Lindstrom added after giving their order to the waiter.

Signe sat at a table with her boys while the men were across the aisle. How the waiters managed to carry trays full of plates down the swaying aisle was beyond her. She could hardly walk without hanging on to the backs of the seats, and they carried the trays with one hand, above their shoulders.

"How do they do that?" Knute whispered from beside her.

She shook her head. "I have no idea. I guess they've had lots of practice."

She looked around the car. Most of the diners were dressed in fashionable clothes, with lovely fabrics in the women's dresses and fine wool in the men's coats along with starched white shirts. They were all fair of skin.

When one of the younger waiters set bowls of soup in front of them, she paused to inhale the fragrance. Her stomach told her to hurry, but she looked to each of the boys. "Bjorn, you say grace, please."

His wide-eyed look almost made her smile. He muttered the grace that they always used in a rapid-fire pace and lifted his head to her nod of approval. They were no longer in Norway, but some things they would carry on with. They dipped their bread into the soup, the food disappearing in one breath.

The older black man stopped at their table again. "May I bring you more soup and bread?" He motioned to their bowls.

"Really?" The word burst out before she could stop it.

"Yes, ma'am." He flashed a smile to both her and the boys. "Growin' . . . need . . . food." Even his voice was different, softer, and while she didn't understand all the words, she got the gist of it.

She called on her newly learned English to say, "Thank you."

All three boys echoed her words.

The man nodded and flashed them another of his bright smiles. When he returned, he set full bowls in front of them again, two baskets of crispy white bread, and a dish of butter pats lined up against each other. He also brought a pitcher and refilled their glasses with cold milk.

They said *thank you* in unison this time.

Signe ate slowly, not sure how much more she could hold. But there was no way to save the soup. She'd been sneaking bread into her bag, only allowing herself one piece so she could save more for the boys. Finally she asked quietly, "Would any of you care for the rest of my soup?"

Bjorn nodded immediately and swapped his empty bowl with hers.

When the waiter returned, he nodded and smiled. "I can . . . more." The *more* they understood. At their shaking heads, he asked again.

Signe looked to Bjorn, who shook his head too, mimicking stuffed cheeks. "Thank you. Nei—no."

The waiter gathered up the dishes. When they started to stand to leave, he shook his head and motioned them to sit. "Be right back." He returned with a basket of assorted cookies, set it in the middle of the table, and after refilling their glasses and her coffee cup, motioned to them to enjoy.

The basket was empty when they left the dining car. What they'd not eaten, the boys had tucked away in their pockets. Signe's bag carried more cookies, along with bread. Drinking water, at least, was free.

⁓⸜⁓⸜⁓

At last the costly train trip ended, and another ship journey began. Compared with steerage on the ship crossing the ocean, the second-class cabin they were assigned on the ship in Buffalo was a glimpse of heaven. Bunks with clean bedding, room under the bottom bunk to store their personal baggage, and posted on the back of the door were the serving hours of the dining room.

"Three meals a day." Bjorn spun to look at his mor. "Why is this ship so different than the other?"

"I have no idea. Just be grateful."

"Can we go out on the deck to watch us leave the dock?"

Signe looked to Rune, who nodded.

"Let's all go out there. Mr. Lindstrom said there are no restrictions on this ship like those on the other. We will stop in Chicago and some other ports, so I understand." He stared directly at each boy, his brow furrowed in a way that they understood. There would be no mercy if they went beyond the bounds. "You will not get off at any of the ports but our final one in Duluth. Do you understand?"

"But we can explore the ship?" Bjorn nodded as he spoke, his blue eyes sparkling in anticipation.

"Ja, but when a sign says *no*, you will not go there. No sneaking around."

All three boys nodded.

"Good, then we'll go on deck now. Signe, you want to come too?"

"Ja." She grabbed her shawl. There was sure to be a breeze, maybe even a real wind off the lake. Since she was not feeling any seasickness as on the first voyage, the idea of finding a spot out of the wind but in the sun sounded like a dream come true. She tucked her knitting into her bag and followed the others out the door into a narrow passage with stairs leading to the upper deck. They stepped outside to be attacked by the wind.

As they joined other travelers at the deck railing, they watched dockhands throw the hawsers to those on deck. The deckhands coiled the huge ropes into perfect circles of line. The timbre of the engines changed, and a tugboat helped ease the *Juniata* out into open water.

Signe wrapped her shawl around her head to hold her hat in place and clung to the rail with one hand as the docks and the shoreline slipped away and the waters roughened.

"Glad to see you made it out on deck," Mr. Lindstrom said as he joined them. "Some different from New York, isn't it?"

"Ja, that's for sure. That steerage, that horror—we treat our animals far better than that."

"Of course. You know, there are plenty of opportunities for fishermen in Duluth, if it doesn't work out with your relatives."

"Never been a fisherman, only ever farmed."

"Ja, that's Norway, but here in Amerika, no one is locked into doing what their fathers did. I know you're going to be felling trees and clearing farmland, but keep this possibility in mind. The boom in logging and lumber is past its peak, or at least that's what I hear. All those lumberjacks are going to have to find new work as the sawmills shut down. They're running out of the white pine in Minnesota like they did along the East Coast and the states in between." He pointed to a cargo ship heading east. "That ship probably has a hold full of lumber or iron ore. Both are shipped out of Duluth." He pointed out smaller boats. "Fishing boats. Right now this lake is calm, but a storm can come up faster than you can blink. More ships sink in these lakes than anywhere else in the world. They're called the Great Lakes, but you never want to take your attention off the water. Especially if you're in a fishing boat."

Signe looked around them but saw no sign of the boys. She studied the ship, looking for a place to sit. Benches and chairs lined the deck area, many of them already taken by others. She finally found one nearer the prow of the ship, and after telling Rune what she was doing, made her way to a chair in the lee of a large storage cabinet. She could see up and down the deck of the ship, watch people walking, and still look out over the lake. The shoreline was fading out of sight. She found it hard to believe that the lakes were so big that land could be over the horizon. As far as she knew, there wasn't a lake in the whole of Norway that large.

She took out her knitting but kept it in her lap, not wanting to miss a moment of deck life and the voyage. But the sweater she was working on—for Bjorn, as he'd outgrown almost all the clothes he owned—called to her, and she resumed her knitting, still free enough to watch.

A group of boys ran by, dodging among the crowd that had thinned out at the rail. Sure enough, all three of her sons were part of the dodgers. She looked around, searching for Rune. The boys dashed off with no sign of their father. What could he and Mr. Lindstrom still find to talk about? Rune had never been one to strike up conversations with strangers before. Perhaps all kinds of things would change now that they were in the new land.

The warmth of the sun in this protected place, the motion of the ship, along with the thrumming of the engines down in the bowels of the vessel—all combined to make her drowsy. With her bag tucked under her chair, she rested her head against the chair back.

She woke to someone shaking her shoulder. "Signe, wake up, it is almost past time to eat dinner."

Blinking, she stared into her husband's face. "Dinner? Already?"

"Ja, I let you sleep as long as I could. Come now."

"Where are the boys?"

"Here with me. Come along."

Getting to her feet, she trapped a yawn behind her hand. A nap during the day! She had actually fallen asleep during the day, and she wasn't even sick. That sweater certainly would not be done by winter if she kept sleeping on the job.

But somehow she didn't believe life in Amerika would stay like this for long.

Chapter 4

DULUTH

"W ill your cousin be meeting you at the pier?" Mr. Lindstrom asked.

"No, we are to take the train to Blackduck, and he will meet us there."

"I see. Then I will help you get to the train station."

"You have become a true friend." Rune clapped the other man on the upper arm.

"If you want, you could spend the night at my house. My wife would be pleased to have someone visit from the old country. Then we could take you to the station."

"Takk, but we agreed to come as fast as we could. But if you will give us your address, we could write and tell you we arrived safely." Signe couldn't believe she was offering to write letters. Rune could write but most likely wouldn't.

Lindstrom nodded. "I will do that. And remember, jobs are plentiful in Duluth, and your boys could go to school, probably easier than in the country."

They located their trunks in the dwindling stack of luggage, and Lindstrom commandeered a handcart to transport them. With him pushing the cart, they set off for the train station. Once they were onboard the train, he handed Rune a piece of paper.

"I'll be back on the boat day after tomorrow, but remember, you are always welcome at our house."

"Takk for all you have done."

"I've not done much but swap a lot of stories, but I hope I made the way easier." He nodded to Signe and tousled the boys' hair. They all waved as he made his way back to the station platform and then waved from the windows.

The train screeched and chugged slowly out of the station. Signe leaned back against the seat. Almost to the end of their journey. Onkel Einar was supposed to meet them with a wagon. There would be a logging train spur line, he said.

"Grand Rapids. Next stop, Grand Rapids," the conductor called. From her window, Signe could see that this was a sizable town. Would Blackduck be as large? *Silly. Why speculate? You'll find out soon enough.*

"Blackduck. Next stop, Blackduck," the conductor finally called as he swayed his way down the aisle.

Signe swallowed the lump that suddenly blocked her throat. The journey was almost over, and their new lives were about to begin. What if they had made a horrible mistake? What if they hated life here in Amerika? Would it really be that different from life in Norway? Hard work was hard work, no matter where one lived. In reality, life was just days of hard work, following one after another. The journey from Norway to Amerika, while difficult on her because of her pregnancy, had been a constant source of delight for Rune and his sons. Even the English-speaking classes had seemed much easier for him than for her. Would Tante and Onkel speak only English? Or only Norwegian? And Tante needed help because of her health. What was wrong with her? All questions Signe should have sought answers to before they left Norway. If only Rune hadn't been in such a rush.

They gathered their things and stepped down onto another station platform, Signe reminding the boys to stay right beside her and Rune.

A man came toward them, his face seeming to lack the ability to smile. "Are you Rune and Signe Carlson?" he asked in Norwegian.

"Ja, we are." Rune held out his hand, but the man hesitated before shaking it. "And you are Onkel Einar?"

"Ja. You are late. We still have several hours to home, and I wanted to be there before dark." He motioned to a team and wagon. "I suppose you have more baggage."

"Ja, those two trunks." Rune pointed down the platform to where the baggage handlers set their trunks, then leaped aboard the already moving train.

"Drag them over here, and we'll load them in the back. Signe and the boys will ride in the back wherever they can find room. I had to get some things at the store."

Rune motioned to his sons, and together they dragged the trunks along the worn platform to the wagon, then hoisted them in the back. Onkel Einar slammed the tailgate closed and climbed up to the seat.

Signe looked to Rune, who shrugged. *He never even said hello to me. As if I wasn't even here. Nor to the boys.* What kind of life were they going to have here?

Leif slipped in beside her when she found a place to sit on a bag of oats, leaning against a barrel of something. "Mor," he whispered, "how come he doesn't like us?"

What could she say? Had the man no manners? She shrugged and shook her head.

Dusk was falling when the team turned into a lane of two dirt lines divided by a line of grass, as wide as the wagon wheels. They could see a white house with a big red barn behind it.

"This is your place?" Bjorn asked.

"Ja, your new home."

Fenced pasture or hayfields lined both sides of the lane.

"You have more horses?"

"And cows?"

"Ja, and right away, I got to milk the cow. You know how to milk a cow?" Without waiting for an answer, he continued. "You boys will take care of the animals so Rune and I can get more trees cut. I already shipped out those felled during the snow. The big timber companies do most of their logging during the winter here so they can move the logs on the snow. I fell trees all year 'round. While we used to float most of our logs down the river, now we ship them on the train."

He stopped the team by the three steps leading up to the house's enclosed front porch. "Set your trunks by the door inside, and we'll get them upstairs for you later. You boys haul the food into the kitchen. Rune, we'll roll that barrel over to the cellar entrance and store it there."

Signe gathered their packs and carpetbags to one side. "Where will we put our things?"

"Upstairs, but you can do that later. Go in and introduce yourself to Gerd. She's not feeling well, so she will tell you what to make for supper."

Signe swapped looks with Rune. His shrug told her he was as surprised as she was. She'd known his wife was ailing, but not to have supper cooking when company was coming . . . Not that they were company, but still.

She climbed down from the wagon, picked up her bags, and mounted the three steps to the door. She held it open so Rune and Bjorn could hoist the first trunk up the steps and inside.

The other two boys carried their packs in and set them by the wall in the parlor, then scurried back out to help with the supplies. Signe set her bag down along the wall too and hung her coat on the hooks by the door. She unpinned her hat and looked for a safe place where it would not get squashed. Finally, she pinned it to her coat.

Walking into the kitchen, she saw a cookstove, sadly needing a scrubbing and blacking, that took up one wall. The other two were lined with cabinets both upper and lower. An open doorway led to a pantry, and a wooden table with six chairs claimed the space lit by two windows with no curtains. A sink with a hand pump divided the cabinets, lit by a window. One more door led to a bedroom, so she walked in that direction and tapped on the half-open door.

"Come in." The voice was hoarse, as if rarely used or the woman had a cold.

Signe stepped through the door to meet their Tante Gerd for the first time. Her long thin hair in a loose braid over one shoulder, the woman lay propped up by pillows, her skin almost as white as the sheets. Only her eyes seemed alive in a face of prominent bones. Her hands on the coverlet needed their fingernails cut, their restless motion showing either palsy or general fretfulness.

"Signe?" Tante held out one hand.

"Ja." Signe crossed to the bed and took the cold hand in hers. "Tante Gerd, I'm sorry you're not feeling well."

Gerd shrugged. "Ja. The pot. I need the chamber pot."

"I see. It is under the bed?"

"Ja, empty it now! Bucket is on the porch."

Signe knelt down to pull out the pot and almost splashed some of its contents on the floorboards. She rose carefully and carried the pot outside to dump in the bucket. What could she wash it out with? At the kitchen sink, she dipped water from the bucket beneath the pump, and after rinsing out the pot, dumped that water in the bucket on the porch. It too needed to be emptied. The smell made her gag, reminding her of the offal buckets in the steerage hold of the ship.

Back in the bedroom, she helped Tante Gerd out of bed and held her steady while she did her business, then helped her back into bed. Gerd lay down, exhausted. Surely there was a better way to do this if she was indeed bedridden.

"How long have you been like this?" The sheets were filthy, the floor needed scrubbing.

"Forever."

"Did anyone come to help you?"

She snorted. "Einar, but the animals always come first. I wasn't this bad when we first wrote. You took so long to get here. Now I can't get out of bed."

Where to start? Signe felt like an animal in a trap that was closing fast. "Is there something I can make for supper?"

"A haunch in the icebox. Canned potatoes in the cellar or whatever Einar brought back from town." Every word took effort. Gerd panted before adding, her voice growing weaker, "Part of the garden is planted but nothing to eat yet. Late spring."

Signe sucked in a deep breath. "Are there eggs?"

A nod.

"I can make noodles. Do you have rice?"

Gerd shrugged, eyes closed. "I-I don't know. Look in the pantry."

"Do you need anything before I start supper?"

"Coffee, if Einar bought coffee beans." She puffed. "Grinder in the pantry."

"Can you sit up in a chair?"

"Nei."

How long since you had a bath? Or clean clothes? "I'll start coffee as soon as I can."

The woodbox was empty, the stove cold.

She dug into the bags of supplies the men had left on the floor, finally discovering the coffee beans. Stepping to the outside door, she saw the boys with the men, unloading sacks of feed to store in the barn. She cupped her hands around her mouth. "Leif, Knute, I need you at the house." When they looked up, she beckoned with one hand.

Both boys came running. "What, Mor?"

"I need to start supper, and the woodbox is empty. I need kindling too."

"Where's the woodpile?" Knute asked, then shook his head when Leif pointed at the chopping block with an axe stuck in it. And several spools waiting to be split.

As the boys attacked the wood, she returned to the kitchen. What did they have for fire starter? At home they had kept a box with shavings near the woodbox, but here there was nothing. The box below the firebox grate was full of ashes. She pulled that out and headed back outside. Did they have a place to dump it?

Leif ran up to her. She handed him the ashes. "Go dump this."

"Where?"

"In back of the privy." Signe puffed out a breath, pointing to the small building about fifty yards out. Knute was already slamming the axe into the rounds to split them. "Then get enough wood in the house for me to make supper. Bjorn can split wood too."

"I can too."

"I know." She stared out at the giant trees that bordered a cleared area full of stumps. They had literally been carving a farm out of a forest of gigantic trees. No wonder Einar needed help. He dreamed of a dairy farm someday?

48

Knute paused in his splitting. "I found a chunk to cut off some kindling. Leif can bring that in too."

Leif returned the emptied ash box to her, then carried in armloads of wood as fast as Knute split it and dumped them in the woodbox.

Signe slid the ash box back into the stove and rattled the grate. She splintered the kindling Knute had cut even finer and found a box of matches on the warming shelf of the stove. Blowing gently on the flame so it caught the splinters, she added more kindling and several small pieces of wood before setting the stove lids back in place. Within minutes, she had the stove heating, adding larger chunks as she could.

Now the coffee grinder. She found it on a shelf in the pantry, which she saw also needed cleaning. Instead, she poured the beans in the grinder, closed the door, and turned the crank on top until she could hear that she needed to add more beans.

The coffeepot needed scrubbing too. "Uff da," she muttered. Was that man blind or what? Probably the *what*. Most men did not do well at keeping a kitchen clean, and Einar led the list. Surely they could have asked their neighbors or townspeople for help, or hired someone.

With the coffeepot on the hottest part of the stove, she shoved in more wood and left the damper straight up. The boys brought in another armload each of wood.

"Are there any spools left to split?" she asked.

"Ja, a few." Knute stepped closer as Leif headed back outside. "But the axe is so dull that Far will have to sharpen it."

"What is Far doing?"

"Bjorn is milking the cow, Far unharnessed the team, and Onkel Einar is fixing a fence. I'm supposed to feed the pigs, and Leif has to feed the chickens so they go in the chicken house, and then gather the eggs."

"I see." She nodded, chewing on her bottom lip. "Go tell Far about the woodpile and the axe and then do the chores you were told to do. Tell Leif to make sure the chicken house is locked up tight."

As he went out the door, she opened the icebox. There was the haunch of meat. Now what to put with it?

She went out the door and around to the cellar, grateful the doors set on angle had been left open. She found two quarts of potatoes and a jar of green beans. Along with biscuits, they would have enough food for supper at least.

With the canned goods heating, she mixed up the biscuits, cut them, and checked the heat in the oven. Not quite hot enough, so she stuck more wood in the firebox. The meat was already heating in the oven. Gravy from the pan drippings would be good.

"Do I smell coffee?" Tante Gerd's voice came plaintively from the bedroom.

"Ja, do you want cream?"

"Nei, black."

Signe poured the coffee, found a tray of sorts, and returned to the bedroom. "Can you sit up yourself?" A slight shrug was her answer. She set the tray on the foot of the bed and helped the older lady sit up, stuffing a couple pillows behind her. Setting the tray in Gerd's lap, she asked, "Can you drink this?"

"Ja." Gerd held the cup with both hands and sipped from the rim. "Hot, but like dishwater."

"You want it stronger?"

"That's what I said."

"Oh." Signe turned and headed for the kitchen. *A thank-you would have been nice.* She slid the biscuits into the oven on the lower rack, moved the kettles to the cooler part of the stove, and started going through the drawers, looking for dish towels and an apron. One dish towel in the drawer, the dishrag in the sink stank to high heaven, and the table needed scrubbing before she could even set it. At least the dishes were up in the cupboard and not filling the sink.

By the time the men came in, she had the table set and the meal ready to serve.

"Can Tante come to the table to eat?" she asked Einar.

"I take her a plate."

No wonder the sheet was so dirty. Dutifully she dished up a plate and took it into the bedroom to set on the tray. "Can I bring you anything else?"

"Jam for the biscuits . . . in the cupboard."

Signe found an open jar and scooped out a spoonful to put on the aunt's plate.

When she sat down, the two men had served themselves, and the boys were filling their plates. There wasn't much left when the bowls came to her. When she looked at Einar's plate, she could see why.

From now on she'd have to cook more food.

After supper, Einar and Rune went outside to split wood, the boys carrying it in as fast as they split. Bjorn split another box of kindling. As dusk settled into darkness, the two men sat at the table, enjoying another cup of coffee.

Tante Gerd had fallen sleep, and Leif was curled up on one of their quilts on the floor.

"How do we get upstairs?" Signe asked. She'd seen no staircase in the house. "Your letter said we would have beds upstairs."

"Oh, you pull down the ladder." The look Einar gave her asked if she had any brains.

"Ladder?" Signe sucked in a breath and stared at Rune. "We are to haul the trunks up a ladder?"

"Guess you better empty them first."

"Are there beds up there?"

"We figured pallets would be quicker."

"So no drawers or shelves either?"

"I just been too busy."

Signe could understand that. One man trying to do all his work and his wife's too—no wonder they were desperate for help. But still. She nodded. "And the ladder is where?"

"In the parlor." Einar stood. "I'll pull it down for you."

The attic was one empty room with a window in each end. A tall man like Rune would only be able to stand upright in the middle where the roof peaked. All Signe could see was a floor carpeted with dust. She backed down the ladder. "Do you have a broom?"

"Ja, on the porch."

Rune came to stand beside her. "Why don't we sleep in the parlor tonight and sweep up there when it is light so we can see better?"

Signe felt like collapsing into his arms and bawling against his chest. Tired did not begin to describe how she felt. "Maybe we'd be better sleeping in the barn. But then, there is no hay there, is there?"

"No, haying won't be for several months. The floor in here will be fine." He leaned closer. "At least it is cleaner than the attic."

"Ja, that is best for now."

Sometime in the night, she woke, her face wet with tears. Things had been hard in Norway, but at least they'd had beds to sleep in and a clean house. Right now, this house seemed bigger than a Norwegian mountain to conquer. And everything cried to be done at once. However would she manage?

Chapter 5

The rooster crowing sounded like home.

Blinking herself awake, Signe stared at the strange ceiling. With the second crow, she knew where she was. Not in a bed of her own but on the parlor floor of a filthy farmhouse in Minnesota. Caring for a sick woman along with scrubbing this house from top to bottom so she could stand to live in it. Where to start?

Rune snored beside her, and her three sons were bumps under the covers. There was no other sound in the house. Sliding her feet into her shoes, she pushed herself to her feet. How she had slept through the night without needing the outhouse she couldn't believe. She hurried out the back door and down the steps, lifting her nightdress to keep the dew from soaking the hem.

The outhouse desperately needed lime. One more thing to do. Outside again, she breathed in the fresh air and stared at the sky-tall trees beyond the barn. The cow stood waiting outside the barn door to be milked, a heifer right behind her.

The team of horses grazed in the pasture, and the rooster

crowed again from the chicken house. A crow rasped a good morning from the top of a much younger pine tree.

As she turned in a circle, she could see no other houses or barns. The lane led out to the road, and there was a cleared field on the other side of it. So there were neighbors somewhat near. Off to one side, she could see either the beginnings of a garden or a weed patch that had taken over.

Picking up her skirt again, she returned to the house to get dressed and start some breakfast. The cow bellowed. Wasn't it Knute who was supposed to milk the cow and Bjorn go help the men? As far as she was concerned, Knute and Leif would help at the house. At least the woodbox was full.

She was dressed, her family was getting dressed, and she had the fire going when Einar wandered out of the bedroom, stretching and yawning as he came.

"Good morning," she said.

He nodded and headed out the back door.

Rune smiled at her. "You're up early."

"Not really, but the sun isn't quite up yet." She dropped her voice. "Ask Einar if he has lime for the privy. The stench is horrible."

"He said last night that we'd start logging right after breakfast."

"Does he understand how little experience you have cutting down trees, let alone trees the size of these?"

"He'll have to teach us. Bjorn and I learn quickly."

"If his saws and axes aren't any sharper than the one at the woodpile . . ."

"I found a file and sharpened it last night. But he must have a stone around here someplace."

"I sure hope he's better at logging than cleaning a house." She pumped more water for the coffeepot and dumped in the last of the ground coffee, then set the pot on the hottest lid of the stove.

"What are you making for breakfast?"

She shrugged and went to search the pantry, returning from the icebox with eggs, flour, and buttermilk. "Looks like pancakes and eggs. Unless I cut off some of that haunch. But I don't know how long that needs to last."

When Einar returned through the back door, he rubbed his hands together. "I could smell the coffee all the way outside." He looked at Rune. "Get your boys on the chores. After straining, pour the milk directly into the flat pans in the well house. There's plenty of cream for churning butter. Sour cream too."

Signe looked up from mixing the batter. "Would you like that on your pancakes?"

"Ja. We have chokecherry jelly in the cellar if not the cupboard. Last year when she was stronger, Gerd did all the canning down there. The garden has gotten away from me. Your younger boys can set to weeding and hoeing today."

"When will Tante wake up?"

"Oh, she's awake. She did not sleep well last night, but that is not unusual." He eyed the stove. "Isn't that coffee ready by now?"

The three boys trailed into the kitchen, Leif rubbing his eyes.

"What are you making, Mor?" Bjorn asked.

"Pancakes and eggs. They'll be ready when you all come back from your chores."

Rune rubbed his chin between finger and thumb. "Bjorn, you split some more wood. Knute, you milk, and Leif, the pigs and chickens are yours."

"We need to drag another dry tree up to the house and cut it up. You boys know how to use a crosscut saw?" Einar stared from one to the other.

Bjorn and Knute nodded.

"Good. Then we'll drag that tree up right after breakfast." Signe took the largest cast-iron frying pan from the peg on the wall and set it on the stove. "Do you have a griddle for the pancakes?"

"Nei."

She took the next biggest frying pan down too and spooned bacon grease from the can on the warming shelf into both. "Do you like your eggs scrambled or . . . ?" She turned to look at Einar.

"Turn them over. The coffee?"

Fetching a cup from the cupboard, she filled it. "Black?"

"Ja." He sat at the table, and she set the steaming cup in front of him.

Once the grease sizzled in the pans, she cracked three eggs into one and spooned batter into the other.

"Could you please bring in the sour cream?" she asked Einar.

"It's in the icebox. There's cream out in the well house for churning. No butter. I don't have time for everything."

"No, I'm sure you don't." She located the sour cream and set it and the jam on the table, then flipped the eggs and the pancakes.

"Rune needs to eat with me so we can get into the woods."

Rune would make sure the boys knew where all the feed was for the animals and that they were doing what needed to be done. He'd always been a good teacher. She could hear the slam of the axe into the chopping block.

Setting a plate with a stack of four pancakes and the three eggs in front of him, she stepped back. "Anything else?"

He shook his head and spooned the thick cream over his pancakes, then the jam.

"If there is yeast . . ."

He shook his head and shoveled in the first bite.

"Then I need to start sourdough."

"Not going back to town. Brought back supplies yesterday."

Shame you didn't get yeast. Wonder what else I will find?

"More pancakes?"

"Ja."

I will make enough. One thing she had promised herself: When they got to the new land, her family would not go hungry. Perhaps there wouldn't be a lot of variety, but there would always be enough.

Rune stopped at the sink to wash his hands and sat down. "Do you have a grinding wheel anywhere?" he asked Einar.

"Ja, behind the machine shed."

Signe broke three more eggs into the sizzling grease and set a lid on the pan, then poured batter into the big skillet. She'd have to make more for the boys, and surely Tante would want pancakes too.

"I thought perhaps we should sharpen all the axes before we go," Rune said. "How long since you sharpened the saws?"

"They need it." Einar scraped up the last of his egg with a pancake.

She slid a plate in front of Rune, and he smiled up at her. "Takk."

"You're welcome. More coffee?" she asked Onkel.

"Ja." He dropped his voice. "Gerd likes hers thick enough to stand a spoon in. I just let it cook on the stove until she is ready to eat."

Signe gave a slight nod. "Who took care of her during the day?"

"She did. She sleeps a lot."

"Is she too weak to—to sit in a chair? Or come to the table?"

"See that chair in the parlor in front of the window? She used

57

to sit there and watch what was going on outside. She was still cooking then. I'm hoping with good food and care, she'll get stronger again."

"More pancakes, Rune?"

"Those eggs sure are good." Their hens in Norway didn't lay much in the winter, so eggs had been a treat, mostly used in cooking or baking.

"More?"

"More pancakes."

Bjorn came in carrying an armload of split wood for the woodbox.

"You sit yourself down and have some breakfast so we can get going," Einar said.

"Do you have more to split?" Signe asked as she pointed Bjorn to the sink to wash his hands.

"Ja, hopefully enough for today at least."

"Heating water for scrubbing takes plenty of wood." She pulled the two skillets back to the hotter part of the stove. She cracked two eggs into one and poured four round dollops of batter in the other, then nodded to the icebox. "Bring the milk jug to the table. There is no syrup for the pancakes. The men had sour cream and jam."

"Sometimes I traded butter and eggs for maple syrup," Einar said, setting his coffee cup down. "You drink coffee?"

"With half milk," Bjorn answered.

Signe flashed him a smile. When they had milk. Which they did now. She set his plate in front of him.

He looked up at her, his blue eyes dancing. "Takk, Mor. This looks so good."

"Well, eat up. You finished, Rune?"

"I could use a couple more pancakes."

Signe poured more batter in the pan, scraping out the mixing bowl. Get the men out of here, and she could feed the other two—er, three—in peace. When she set the pancake plate in front of Rune, she looked to Einar. "You have scrub brushes, mop and broom? Oh, and hoes for the garden?"

"Hoes are in the machine shop on the wall, rake too. The scrubbing things are on the shelves on the back porch, by the washing machine and tub. Should be soap out there too, but you gotta be careful with that. Don't have much fat to make more."

"You want I should start lists of things we need?"

"Ja. Help if we had something to trade, like butter or eggs."

While she talked, she mixed up more pancake batter and, without being asked, poured more for Bjorn. As she turned them over, Einar pushed his chair back. "Come on, boy, we got work to do."

"But—"

He shook his head. "You had enough. Come on." He clapped his hat on his head and paused at the door. "We won't be back until suppertime. You could send the younger boys out with dinner, if you have a mind."

Bjorn grabbed two pancakes on his way out the door.

She could hear Einar talking to Knute and Leif outside. Surely he was going to let them eat something. They both carried in an armload of wood as they came inside and dumped it in the box.

"Onkel Einar said we had to weed the garden today."

"You're going to help me scrub this kitchen too." She set plates in front of each of them. "The men had sour cream and jam on theirs. There is no syrup." She reminded herself to check down in the cellar. Perhaps Tante had made some fruit syrup.

"Can I have two eggs, Mor?" Leif grinned at her.

"Ja, but you better tell those hens to lay lots of eggs so we can eat some and still have enough to trade at the store in Blackduck."

"Blackduck. That's a funny name." Knute had already eaten half his food.

"I know." Signe finished the remainder of the pancakes and set a plate of them on the table. She had fried two eggs for herself, reminding herself that she needed to feed the baby growing inside her. They polished off the remainder of the pancakes, and she poured each of the boys another glass of milk and herself a last cup of coffee. Real coffee. What a meal. Breakfast had been porridge for so long. Their first real meals in ages had been on the steamship across the Great Lakes. They had even had dessert.

"Signe, help!" Tante Gerd called.

"Put your dishes in the pan on the stove and bring in more wood," Signe told the boys. "Coming." She entered the bedroom. "Good morning."

"The pot."

When that was accomplished, Tante collapsed back in the bed. "Coffee?"

"Would you like breakfast with that?" Signe tried to straighten the covers.

"What?"

"What is for breakfast?"

"Ja! That is what I said."

"I can fry you some eggs, and there is a biscuit or two from last night."

"I thought I heard pancakes."

"The batter is all gone."

"You didn't save me any?"

"I can toast the biscuit and—"

"You all had pancakes and now there is none for me." Gerd's eyes narrowed.

"I—I'm sorry. I can mix up some more. I wasn't sure what

you would like. Einar said—" She stopped. No sense blaming him. Did Tante always wake up this angry? "Would you like to come sit at the table?"

"No! I cannot walk."

"Not even with help?"

"Eggs and biscuits will be enough." Each word snapped like grease in a skillet.

"I will bring you coffee now and a plate in a few minutes."

"What are the boys doing?"

"Bringing in wood, and then they'll start weeding the garden."

"Make sure they don't pull out the vegetables."

"They know the difference between weeds and carrots and peas."

"Weeds are different here."

"Ja, I'm sure they are." Signe escaped before Tante could ask another question. Back in the kitchen, she inhaled a clear breath. That bedroom stank, almost as bad as the outhouse. How long since Tante'd had a bath and clean bedclothes, even clean clothes?

As she prepared the breakfast plate, she found herself shaking her head. Where to start? The kitchen or that bedroom or the wash?

With the plate and a fork on the tray, she returned to the bedroom. "I'll help you sit up."

Tante stared down at her plate. "Did you put salt and pepper on my eggs?"

"Ja, but not a lot."

"No pepper on my eggs. And I want butter on my biscuits."

"We don't have butter. If you want I will redo your eggs." Here it wasn't midmorning yet, and she was already biting her tongue.

"No. Just remember that."

"Are there any clean sheets? I will change your bed when you are finished."

"If we had clean sheets, they would be on my bed."

"I see. So where is all the wash?"

Tante pointed to a stack of clothing, sheets, and towels in the corner. Probably all that had accumulated over the winter.

"I will do the wash tomorrow."

"Be careful with the soap."

"Ja, Einar already said that. If we have fat, I can make soap." She left the room and, finding a wash boiler out on the back porch, set it on the stove and filled it with water. The water in the reservoir was hot enough to rinse dishes, so she set to doing that first while the scrub water heated.

"Take the plate!" The command came from the bedroom.

"Can I get you something else?"

"Take these pillows out." Gerd made a grab for one. "I will sleep now."

Good thing. Signe dumped the plate and cup in the dishwater. But when she started to put the clean dishes in the cupboard, she shuddered. Mouse droppings. Ach, the filth! If she had to use every bit of soap, she would get this place clean. And the people who lived here.

Chapter 6

Where to start? Signe stared around the kitchen. Inside the cupboards? The ceiling? Did they have a step stool somewhere?

The boys trailed in with armloads of wood.

"The chores are done, and this is the last of the split wood." Knute looked to his mor. "Where next? Inside or the garden?"

"Help me empty the cupboards onto the table, then you both work in the garden for a while before it gets hot."

"It's already hot in here." Knute threw open the windows and propped the back door open with a brick before heading through the house to do the same with the front door.

Signe handed the boys the dishes and cups out of the cupboards, then set a pan of hot, barely soapy water on the counter and started scrubbing. Surely there were mousetraps somewhere. If it was this bad in the house, what did the cellar look like? They needed a house cat. A hunter.

Leaving the doors open to air out the newly clean cupboards, she tossed the filthy water into a bucket so they could use it to water the garden, then attacked the second set of cupboards on the other side of the sink.

Had she known, she'd have brought bars of soap along. If they had to wait 'til butchering time in the fall to have fat for soap, she'd write it on the list. Had they butchered hogs last year? So many questions. Perhaps there was a crock in the basement with lard in it. Her thoughts kept time with her busy hands.

By the time the cupboards were washed and refilled, she gazed longingly at the coffeepot. At home, someone would have stopped by already, and they'd have coffee together. She should have made more pancake batter and fried the remainder to eat with jam and coffee. Thoughts of home made her sigh.

After shoving more wood in the firebox, she pumped water into a pail to refill the reservoir and dipped out hot water to scrub the outsides of the cupboards and the wall around them. The ceiling would have to wait.

"Signe!"

She dropped the cloth in the pan and headed into the dark bedroom. "Ja."

"The pot!"

A repeat of the early morning, the stink of the room not abating. "Would you like me to help you to the chair by the window?"

"Nei! Why?"

"I thought some fresh air might feel good."

"Coffee!"

Signe nodded. After settling Tante back in the bed, she pulled the coffeepot to the hot part of the stove, then changed her mind and took the pot outside to dump and scrub. The boys were chopping the weeds out of the rows, leaving the vegetables looking weak and forlorn. Some manure tea would give them a boost. One more thing to add to her mental list of tasks, all urgent. She paused and raised her face to the sun. A breeze stirred the hairs that escaped the bun at the back of her head. That same breeze wafted the stench of the outhouse her way.

Liming the outhouse moved to the top of her list. Would Tante know if they had lime and where?

"I want something to eat with my coffee," Tante demanded when Signe handed her the cup and saucer.

"As far as I know, there is nothing until I bake, and there is no yeast for bread."

"You made biscuits last night."

"They are gone."

Gerd's glare would have dropped a horse.

Signe strode to the window and pulled back the curtains so she could open the window.

"Nei!" The shriek jerked her back from inhaling the fresh air. "That hurts my eyes."

She closed the curtains.

"Shut the window. You want me to catch my death?"

Again Signe did as she was ordered.

"What are you doing out there?"

"Scrubbing the kitchen. The boys are weeding the garden." *Where I would far rather be than in here.* Without waiting for an answer, she left the room. Did she dare close the door?

What could she make to take out to the loggers? If she didn't get some sourdough started, she'd never make bread. Cringing at the filth in the pantry, she checked all the bins and tins. Cornmeal, flour, oatmeal, beans, rice. She should have started a pot of beans first thing this morning for supper. At home, they'd be eating porridge, if they were lucky. This looked like a wealth of stores compared with that.

If only she had some yeast.

After setting the pot of beans on to boil, she beat milk, water, and flour together and poured the mixture into a crock to set on the warming shelf as starter for sourdough. From the icebox she took the haunch of smoked meat to the now clean counter to cut the meat off the bone. Corn bread or biscuits to take to the men?

When she slid the corn bread pan into the oven, she drained the beans, keeping the hot water for the chickens or the pigs, and added the bone to the pot along with hot water from the reservoir. With that simmering on the back of the stove, she glanced in the bedroom. Snores told her Tante had gone back to sleep. How could she sleep so much?

The boys came inside. "Mor, can we have a drink?"

"Water or buttermilk?"

"Buttermilk. We really have buttermilk?" Knute grinned up at her. "You want we should throw the weeds in for the pigs?"

"The chickens too. Shame they can't run free like chickens should."

"Onkel said a hawk would get them."

Knute set the jug of buttermilk on the counter and reached for glasses. "They need a dog here to protect the chickens."

"Are there any cats down at the barn?"

"Ja." Leif already wore a buttermilk mustache.

"Any tame enough to make a house cat, a mouser?"

Knute glanced toward the bedroom door. "Would she allow a cat in the house?"

"Better than fifty mice. Before you go back to the garden, go down in the cellar and see if there are any mousetraps there." She glanced at the clock on the wall above the door. "I will have a basket ready to take to the men pretty soon. We'll have dinner with them."

The boys grinned at each other. "You haul the weeds down

in the wheelbarrow, and I'll split some more wood," Knute said to Leif. "Mor is emptying the woodbox as fast as she can."

They ran out the door, but it slammed behind them before Signe could catch it.

"How can I sleep with so much racket?"

How could Gerd shout so when she had a hard time breathing? Signe filled another pan with bits of soap and hot water and started on the pantry cupboards.

The clock had moved well past noon by the time the basket was filled with corn bread, sliced meat, boiled eggs, and pickles she had found in the cellar. "We are taking dinner to the men," she announced from the bedroom door, and left the house before Tante could demand anything more. Wisely, Signe left a hard-boiled egg and a square of corn bread to feed Gerd when they returned.

Knute swung the basket, and she carried a jug of coffee. Surely the men had taken drinking water with them that morning. The boys chattered about all they saw, as ever, full of a million questions, most of which she had no answers for. But her tiredness from the morning of scrubbing and fretting seeped away as the peace of the woods calmed her mind and spirit. They could hear axes ringing against wood, announcing where the work was happening.

"You stay by me," she reminded the boys. "You could get lost here real easy."

"I'd just follow the sound of the axes," Knute said with a grin.

Leif returned to her side. "How come Tante is so mean?"

"She is sick."

"I don't think she likes us."

I don't think she likes anyone. But living in a dark and dirty hole like that room would make anyone mean, like an animal trapped in a cage. "Wait for us, Knute."

"But they are right ahead. Hurry, Mor."

"You wait! They might have a tree about to come down."

His look argued with her, but he stopped at the edge of the trees.

Several big pines lay like fallen giants. Both men and Bjorn were chopping off branches but stopped when Knute yelled hello.

"Finally!" Onkel growled. "Over by the wagon."

Rune lifted his head and dried the sweat on his forehead with the rolled-up sleeve of his shirt. "I hope that is coffee in that jug."

"It is. You did bring water out?"

"Ja." He nodded toward the wagon. "Over there in the shade."

"Did you cut these down today?"

"Two of them. Bjorn has been limbing all morning." He smiled at his eldest son. "That's chopping off the branches," he explained before the question could be asked.

"What will you do with the branches?"

"Saw up the bigger ones for firewood." Bjorn met them at the wagon. "You can do that back at the house with the crosscut." He grinned at each of his brothers.

"We weeded part of the garden." Knute shook his head. "The weeds were really bad, but we found some peas and lots of beans. Corn too."

Leif joined the conversation. "The potatoes were up. I almost pulled out the squashes. I don't like squash much." He looked up and up. "These trees are huge."

"It sounds like the world is falling apart when one them hits the ground." Bjorn looked up at the trees as well. "Onkel said it is even worse when there is no open place for the trees to fall." He pointed to the tree that had only half its branches left. "I had to sharpen my axe already this morning. We used the smaller saw, since it goes faster for me."

"Let's eat." Signe motioned to the tailgate of the wagon, where she had laid out the meal. They all fell to as though they'd not had a big breakfast.

"We'll work out here until dusk." Onkel motioned with his corn bread, which held sliced meat in the middle. "There's a hen due for the stewpot. You can butcher a chicken?"

Signe gave him a look. "Ja, since I was a child." When she got no response, she continued. "You have lime for the outhouse?"

He shook his head. "Put it on the list."

"When will you go to Blackduck?"

"You can go. Just follow the main road." At the look she gave him, he shrugged. "I can draw you a map. Can't lose another day out here."

"You have another wagon and team?"

"I have an older mare and a cart. The boys can help you hook it up." He looked to Knute. "You know how to harness a horse?"

"Ja. Where is it?"

"Out in the pasture. We got eggs and maybe butter. You can take them to the store in trade."

Signe knew he meant if she got the butter churned. When she got back, she'd bring in the cream. She should have done that first thing so it would warm enough to churn more easily. She gathered the plates and forks back in the basket. "There's another piece of corn bread."

Onkel motioned to Rune. "You take it."

Rune shook his head. "Nei, Bjorn is still growing. He needs it worse."

By the time she and the two younger boys were back at the house, she'd given them their instructions for the afternoon. Setting the basket on the kitchen counter, she turned to the stove.

"Where have you been?" Gerd demanded from the bedroom. "I need the pot."

Signe sucked in a calming breath and picked up the pot she'd left outside to air. "I took dinner out to the men." Setting the pot beside the bed, she flipped back the covers, longing to open the windows. Hot and humid, along with stinking to high heaven—how could Tante stand this? "Are you hungry?"

"Ja, of course I am hungry." Gerd slumped back on the bed. "You could have told me where you were going."

"I did. I told you—"

"Nei! You left without a word. You can't leave me alone. That's why we brought you over, to take care of me and the house. I can't do any of the cooking or housework anymore." Her glare sizzled Signe's eyebrows. "Can't even use the pot by myself."

"I'll bring your food right in. The coffee should be hot again pretty soon."

After shoving wood in the firebox, she gave the beans a stir and pulled the coffeepot to the hotter part of the stove. The water in the boiler sent up spirals of steam, heating the room even more. At least she had the windows and doors open for cross ventilation—nothing like that bedroom.

After serving Gerd corn bread and meat with pickles, she asked, "Would you like some buttermilk while the coffee is heating?"

"Ja. If we have any left. We've been out of butter for a week or more."

What could they have for supper besides meat and beans? More biscuits? Signe stepped to the bedroom door. "I'm going down to the cellar. The boys are weeding."

"Coffee!"

"Ja."

After bringing up a jar of green beans and another one of pickles, she gave Gerd her coffee and returned to scrubbing the pantry. This time she used the wash water to scrub the floor and the back steps. At least she could be outside this way. How she would enjoy working in the garden. Pulling weeds sounded infinitely better than scrubbing walls and floors. In fact, while the floor was drying, she'd treat herself to some time in the garden.

When she went to fetch the dishes from the bedroom, Tante was asleep again, her mouth slack and her breathing somewhat labored. Surely the steam bath she lived in helped her breathing. How could she stand the covers over her?

Instead of having the boys bring in the cream, Signe crossed the yard to the well house and opened the heavy door to be kissed by the coolness inside. Several crocks and jugs nestled in the cemented rock trough of cold water. Water trickled in, thanks to the windmill, and flowed out to fill the stock tank. Pans of the morning milking waited on a wooden bench, with more crocks and jugs on the shelf underneath. After skimming the cream into a clean jug, she set that in the trough. She checked to see what was in each jug in the water, then carried the older cream to the house. Hot as the weather was, the cream should warm up quickly.

Back to scrubbing. It took two passes to get the painted floorboards clean. Leaving the floor to dry, she joined the boys in the garden.

"Almost milking time," Knute said when the cow bellowed from the barn.

"You two have done a good job out here." She leaned over to pull a handful of sow thistle and toss it on the closest pile.

"The pigs sure like us. The chickens too." Knute stared at his hands. "I got a blister. One on each hand."

"No leather gloves?"

He shook his head. "I saw Bjorn had some."

Chapter 7

So how are things going at the house?" Rune and Knute knelt on the edge of the garden after supper, setting snares for rabbits.

"Tante screams at Mor all the time." Knute dropped the cord and shook out his hands. "You make this look so easy."

"It will be for you too. You just need to practice. You'll need to check these morning and night, or something else will steal our supper."

"There's lots of animals here, aren't there?"

"Onkel told me about seeing a weasel the other day. They can be really mean and would happily kill all the chickens. Foxes, wolverines, and coyotes, sometimes even wolves, but them mostly in the winter." He patiently showed his son how to set the snare again. "Rabbit skins will make warm mittens for next winter, so we'll skin them and nail the hides to the barn wall to cure."

"There, I did it." Knute grinned at his father. "Does Bjorn know how to do this?"

"I don't think so. Set the other two, and we can get to bed." Dusk was settling around them, releasing a mosquito horde.

He slapped his arm and now wore a splat of blood. Always the debate—long sleeves to protect bare skin, or rolled sleeves to enjoy any bit of cool air drifting by?

He hefted himself to his feet and kneaded his lower back with his fists. Surely his body would adjust to swinging an axe all day. Unless they were using the long crosscut saw to fell the trees. Both tasks worked his shoulders—no wonder lumberjacks were such hefty men. At least they were in the pictures he'd seen. Never had he dreamed he'd be a logger one day. Farming had always been his dream. A herd of dairy cows, knee-deep in green grass, and Signe churning butter and making cheese. He stared across the field that had been wrenched one tree at a time from the giants awaiting his axe.

"With all your work, we can now see the garden," he said, looking down at his middle son as they walked back to the house.

"We'll finish it tomorrow, I hope. I'd rather weed the garden than help wash the walls. Although Mor said we'd help with the wash tomorrow. Leif is going to churn the butter." He heaved a sigh. "Bjorn says we're doing women's work."

"Perhaps I better have a talk with Bjorn. We all do whatever needs to be done. And there is plenty to be done here, that's for sure." Rune stopped walking. "Listen."

The owl hooted again.

"Sounds like it's coming from the barn. Have you looked in the haymow to see if one is nesting up in the rafters?" Rune asked.

"No, but Onkel said that bats roost up there. They come out about now too. I want to go watch them. How come people are afraid of bats?"

"That's a good question. I've heard all kinds of stories, but they eat mosquitos, so I am all in favor of having bats roost nearby."

Onkel Einar was sitting at the table, the kerosene lamp set so he could read the newspaper he had spread before him. "Did you get the snares set?"

"We did, and Knute will take care of them." Rune looked around the room. "Where is Bjorn?"

"Bed already. Signe said she needs more firewood split for the morning." Einar closed his paper and pushed back from the table. "Let's get that tree up on the sawhorses so the boys can cut it tomorrow. I got two of the axes sharpened. Seems like Bjorn could learn to do that."

"He learns fast. I'll teach him tomorrow." Rune followed Einar out the door, Knute right behind him. Good thing dusk lasted a long time here. By the time they hefted the dried tree trunk up on wooden sawhorses, they were both sweating again.

"Bjorn should have been out here. He sick or something?"

"No, just not used to such heavy labor. He'll toughen up." *Like we all will.* It was all Rune could do to keep from staggering.

Back in the kitchen, Signe held up the coffeepot. Rune shook his head. "No, thanks. I'm going to bed." He paused to sniff the air. "Something sure smells good."

"The sourdough is working. That's yeast you smell."

"Sourdough pancakes for breakfast?"

"Nei, it won't be ready yet." She turned to Knute, who had just come through the back door. "Where were you?"

"Down at the barn. One of the kittens will come to me now. Well, sort of. I thought maybe you would like him for the house, to get rid of the mice."

Einar turned from the doorway to the bedroom. "No cats in the house."

"Do you have mousetraps?" Signe asked.

"No, don't think so. Gerd killed 'em with a broom."

"Well, they have about taken over the kitchen and the pantry. And there are rat droppings in the cellar." She stared at him.

"Put mousetraps on the list for town. No cat in here."

Rune watched his wife. He knew how much she hated mice—and now rats? That was beyond description. He wouldn't be a bit surprised to find that kitten here at the house soon in spite of Einar.

Once in bed, their pallet on the floor in the parlor, he tried to get comfortable, but tired as he was, his shoulders burned like fire. When Signe slipped in beside him, he flopped on his back. "Did you bring any of that liniment with us?"

"Nei, nor the featherbed. How I wish we had brought that. I assumed there would be beds for us at least."

"I'll make us a rope bed as soon as I can find the time. Need to tell Einar that we need some lumber and rope." He patted her swelling middle. "How are you and the little one doing? Knute said Tante screams at you all the time."

"Tomorrow I am going to rip that room apart and wash the bedding. No telling when that happened last. She screamed when I opened the windows to let the stink out, accused me of trying to kill her."

"Uff da. Wonder why she is so unhappy."

"Doesn't like being sick, I imagine. I sure wouldn't."

Rune was glad he wasn't working in the house. Einar expected a lot from his untrained workers, but at least he didn't yell.

⁕

In the morning when Signe got up to start breakfast, Rune nudged Bjorn, and the two of them went out to the woodpile and started splitting wood. Knute and Leif headed for the barn and their morning chores.

"You ever sharpen axes on the grinding wheel at home?" Rune asked his son.

Bjorn grimaced. "Once, but Farfar took over. He said I was doing it wrong."

"But he didn't teach you to do it right?"

"Nei. He didn't have a lot of patience. I did all right with a file."

"The grinder is faster, you get a better edge. Let's go give you a lesson on axe sharpening."

Down at the barn, they could hear Knute talking to the cow as he milked her. Leif had opened the hen door and was scattering oats for the chickens. The rooster flew up on the roof and crowed to wake any late sleepers.

The grinder was under the machine shed roof, a big gray wheel of stone on a heavy wood frame. A foot pedal made it turn.

"You want to make sure there is nothing to catch fire from the sparks when you are pumping the grinding wheel." Rune sat on the seat, put his feet on the pedals, and started pumping. "You want to keep a steady pace. It'll slow down when you put the axe head to it." He picked up one of the axes and held the cutting edge to the grinder. "About this angle. Then hold it on the spinning wheel." When he touched the metal to the stone, the shriek could be heard clear to the house. Or the next farm. Sparks flew in all directions. "You slowly move the head from side to side, then turn it and do the same on the other side." He lifted the axe and studied the shiny edge, running his thumb over it. "Feels about right." He handed the axe to his son. "We could put a finer edge on it with a file, but this will be good." He stood. "Now you try."

Bjorn sat down and copied all his far had done. He held the axe to the stone, and it bounced back at him.

"You have to hold it square. Bouncing like that can cause a nick and an accidental cut."

"Sorry." Bjorn sucked in a breath and started again.

"Steady, good, good. Keep it going at the same speed. Good." Leif came running up to the shed. "Far, Mor rang for breakfast. I'm getting the cream." He charged off again.

Bjorn checked the edge with his thumb, then compared it to the first axe. "Needs a bit more."

"Go ahead. We'll have two done before breakfast this way."

Bjorn finished the edge to his far's satisfaction, and the two of them headed back to the house.

"Up to you, son, to keep the axes sharpened. Either when we get back in the evening or in the morning. Keep in mind we need to keep that woodbox full."

"It'd help if we could get a bit ahead."

Rune smiled. What a fine son! "We will over the next few days. Keeping that boiler bubbling today is going to need a lot of wood. Both boys are helping with the wash. Oh, and if you make snide remarks about women's work to your brothers again, they'll come out to the woods with me and you'll be helping here. Understand?"

Bjorn nodded and motioned for his far to go into the house before him.

"Wash." Signe pointed to the sink and carried a stack of pancakes to the table. Einar loaded his plate as if he hadn't eaten for a week. She set a platter of fried eggs in front of him, and he slid three onto his plate.

Rune glanced at his wife, who was shaking her head. By the time the pancakes made it around the table, Leif only got one, and the eggs were gone.

"I'll make more," Signe said softly as she picked up the plates to refill.

Setting another stack on the table a few minutes later, she said, "I only have cold beans and whatever is left of the pancakes to send along for your dinner."

"That will be good." Einar motioned around the table. "I never took meals with me before. Count yourself lucky."

"Hard to work on an empty belly," Rune commented. "And logging is hard work. I had no idea."

"What did you do in Norway?"

"Worked on a dairy mostly. Anything I could find. Jobs are scarce there."

Einar pushed back his chair. "You ready?"

Rune glanced at Bjorn, who was shoveling the last of his breakfast in his mouth. "I guess we are."

"How many axes to grind yet?"

"Two."

"I'll go do that, you two split wood." Einar turned to Signe. "Dinner be ready in about fifteen minutes?"

"Ja, it will be. Knute, you fill the water jug for them."

"But I'm not done eating," the ten-year-old protested.

"Do this first," Signe replied.

Rune ruffled Knute's hair as he went by and winked at him. When Onkel said it was time to go, it was time to go. At least they'd gotten two axes sharpened beforehand.

When Onkel drove the team and wagon up to the house to load, they knew it was time to leave. Rune tossed the last sticks of kindling onto the pile and slammed the axe into the chopping block. Signe met him at the door with a covered basket and the water jug.

"Sure wouldn't mind another cup of coffee," he said as he took them from her.

"You be careful out there."

"We will. Takk." Rune rotated his shoulders as he sat on

the wagon seat. How he was going to swing an axe all day was beyond him. Einar managed to keep a steady pace, but his body was used to wielding an axe.

"Shoulders hurt?" Einar asked.

"Ja." Hurt was far too small a word for the burning across his shoulders and down his back.

"Take it easier today. Be extra careful. Accidents happen when you're too tired."

Rune hoped he kept the surprise off his face. "Takk. Splitting wood at home wasn't much preparation for work like this."

"True. We're ready to fell those next two trees. Limbing is easier than felling." He raised his voice. "Bjorn, you all right?"

"Ja," Bjorn answered from the tailgate of the wagon.

Einar turned back to Rune. "Your Signe, she scared of mice?"

"Nei. Outside is fine, but she can't abide mice in the house."

Einar shrugged, his eyebrows drawing together. He muttered something that sounded like *silly women.*

"She hates them with a passion because they leave dirt," Rune explained. "Doesn't like dirt in her house, of any kind. A house needs to be clean."

"She has her work cut out for her here. Gerd used to keep a clean house, but one day I came back and found her on the floor. Thought for sure she was dead. Doctor said it's her heart. She hates being laid up."

That answered Knute's question. But still, screaming at Signe wasn't necessary. No one could get more done in a day than Signe. And the boys were good workers too, all three of them.

Rune took off his glasses and rubbed his eyes, then cleaned the lenses with his shirttail. Some days his eyes were worse than others.

Einar waved a hand. "Hey, Bjorn, see that buck off to the left? What kind of shot are you?"

"He's a fair shot, Knute not as good." Rune stared toward the edge of the woods, but he couldn't see a deer.

"Plenty of meat around here for someone who likes to hunt."

"Is that venison we've been eating?"

"Ja. Also got a smoked hindquarter of a hog hanging in the cellar. Last of the pork. Need to stretch the meat out. Glad to hear you set some snares. Rabbit'll fill in just fine, but that buck would take us right through the summer. That and the chickens. Signe know about raising chicks?"

"Oh, ja. We had chickens in Norway."

Einar halted the team in the shade and stepped down from the wagon. "You ever dragged a tree with a team?"

"Ja, up in the mountains."

"While Bjorn finishes limbing that last tree, we'll drag the other two over to the pile to be shipped. Shame we don't live on a river. We could just stack 'em on the bank to wait for spring, then float 'em down to the mill. Don't cost nothing like the shipping does. For now, that will have to do." He pointed to the logs laid out side by side. "Bjorn, unhitch the team and bring 'em over to that near tree." He reached in the wagon bed and hauled out the chains. "You get the rest."

Rune dragged the other chain out of the wagon and followed Einar to the two downed and stripped trees. How were they going to get the chains wrapped around that giant log?

Einar knelt down beside the log about four feet from the end and studied the ground. "Get that adze. We'll dig it out here."

Rune headed for the wagon again. At least he was walking, not swinging an axe. Between the two of them, they got a trench dug out for the chain, and after feeding it through the shallow ditch, looped the chain around the log a couple of times and anchored the hook over the chain.

Einar beckoned to Bjorn. "Back the team in here."

Bjorn leaned over and picked up the doubletree, the lines in his other hand. Rune watched him struggle, then went to his aid, lifting the doubletree. Bjorn grinned his thanks and backed the team close enough to hitch the chain to the doubletree. Einar nodded his approval. "We'll take it from here." He inspected the hookup, nodded again, and picked up the lines.

"These two can move that log?" Rune asked.

"You watch. Hep, Nellie, Flossy. Let's go." He slapped the lines. Both horses leaned into their collars, their necks arched, dug in their hooves, and slowly, inch by inch, the log began to move. Once it was moving, they dragged it over to lie parallel with the others. Einar backed them a couple of steps to take the tension off the chain, then tied up the lines. He patted both horses, who stood in place, blowing hard, sweat darkening their shoulders and flanks.

"Get them unhitched and take them back to the wagon, Bjorn, then take them to the creek for a drink when they cool down."

"That creek cuts through your land?" Rune asked.

"Ja. Wanted to build the house nearer the creek, but once we had the well drilled, decided where it is now is really the best place. Nearer the road is good, especially in the winter. Besides, those acres were cleared when we bought this."

Rune unhooked the chain from the log and led the team over to the wagon in the shade. "You two sure are a lot more powerful than you look. Someday perhaps I'll have a team like you."

Bjorn's eyes were still round. "They moved that log, all one hundred or more feet of it." He shook his head and returned to severing branches from the tree they had felled the day before with his axe.

"Use the saw on those nearer the bottom. It'll go faster."

"Einar's notching that next one."

"You watch, he'll put that tree down right where he wants. It's all in the notching, unless there's a heavy wind that throws it off."

Bjorn returned to the wagon bed for the bow saw and started on the lower limbs of the tree.

Rune watched his son. He knew Bjorn must be as sore as himself, but today he swung the axe with more precision and fewer pauses. Knute could probably help out here too, but right now Signe needed him a lot more. Rune lifted the seven-foot saw from the back of the wagon and hauled it over to where Einar was leaning on his axe handle, looking up the tree trunk.

"Almost seems sinful to bring such majesty down, don't it?"

Rune stared at him in surprise. So the trees weren't just a means to an end for him.

"You know how to tell the age of these giants?" When Rune shook his head, the older man continued. "See that stump? You count the rings. Bigger space between rings means plenty of water and growing weather. You bring your boys out here and let them see that. You can get enough lumber from these to build a house. Whole country is in a building frenzy. Once these here trees are gone, they'll go searching for another area to strip."

"How'd you get the stumps out?"

"Dynamite the biggest, Flossy and Nellie pulled out most of the rest. We need to be digging them out too." He lifted off his felt hat and wiped his forehead with the back of his arm. "Let's get this one down, and we can have dinner."

Pulling that saw back was right up there with swinging the axe, though it used a few different muscles. Rune recognized where each of his back and torso muscles lay. But they limbered up after a few minutes and let him do the job. Had he known what the work would be like, perhaps he'd not have been quite so enthusiastic about coming.

"Get over by the wagon, boy!" Einar hollered. They made three more passes with the saw and stepped back.

The tree shuddered, picking up speed as it tipped and came crashing down, broken branches big enough to kill a man flying in all directions. The ground shook when it hit. Then silence, as if honoring a fallen hero, the whole world holding its breath. One of the horses snorted. A bird chirped and sang a farewell. Einar bobbed his head. "Let's go eat."

Rune realized he'd taken his hat off as if he were in church. He settled it back on his head.

Chapter 8

The first load of sheets had boiled long enough.

"You fill the rinse tub with cold water." Signe motioned to Knute. "And Leif, you churn the butter; I filled the churn already. You can do it out on the back porch if you like." As both boys started on their tasks, she stirred the boiling sheets one more time with the sturdy stick, well bleached by years of soap and boiling water. "You can take turns turning the crank on the washing machine."

"Signe!" Tante screeched from her bed.

Signe caught the look that passed between her sons. The screeching seemed to bother them more than her. "Coming."

Tante Gerd lay wheezing in her bed. "Pot." She pointed toward the floor. "Under the bed."

"Ja, I know." Signe knelt and pulled it out, then set the stool, which was more like a bench, over it. She'd already dumped and scrubbed the pot this morning so it wasn't smelly—the only thing in the room that wasn't. She pulled back the covers and helped Gerd sit up. Perhaps this evening she could give Gerd a bath. So many things demanding to be done immediately. "On three. One, two, three." She lifted, and Gerd used what meager strength she had in her legs to stand. "Wait, don't try to move too fast. Are you dizzy?"

"Some, but I have to go."

They got her situated, and Signe sucked in a deep breath. For someone who ate so little, the older woman weighed enough that lifting her took all of Signe's strength. She glanced at the chair in the corner. "If I bring that over here, will you sit in it to eat?"

Gerd shook her head, as if even that took more energy than she could afford.

We have to get her moving. If not, she'll be stuck in that bed forever. But how to get Gerd to agree?

"Ready."

They shifted her back to the bed, and Signe stacked the pillows and swung the wizened feet up under the covers. "I'll bring your coffee."

"Is that all?"

"No, I have pancakes to heat up for you, unless you want them cold."

A sigh and a shake of the head as Gerd's eyes drifted closed, but no answer.

Signe returned in a few minutes with cold pancakes, sour cream and jam, and the coffee. "Tante. Tante Gerd. You must eat now."

"Ja."

The growl made Signe's teeth clench. She sucked in a calming breath and set the tray on the bed so she could get Gerd straightened up again. Probably she'd have slept another hour, but then would scream that Signe was not taking care of her.

With Tante sipping her coffee and looking alert enough, Signe returned to the kitchen.

"The rinse tub is full, but what about the machine?" Knute asked.

"We'll dump the boiler into it and fill the rest from the reservoir. You can dip that out into a bucket, and then into the tub."

In spite of the heat of the day, the washing machine steamed like a caldron. Signe dipped the sheets out and into another bucket, then hauled the boiler out and dumped it. Right now, boiling the wash over an outdoor fire sounded better and better. With the sheets in the washer too, she leaned over and grabbed the crank handle. When she turned that, the agitator in the tub of the washing machine started turning the sheets.

"I can do that, Mor." Knute waited beside her.

"Ja, you can." She stepped back, picked up the boiler, and returned to the kitchen to refill it at the pump in the sink. Next would be the unmentionables and long underwear used throughout the winter. No, next would be Gerd's nightdresses so Signe could get both the bed and the woman cleaned up. The *thunk-a-thunk* of the churn said Leif was hard at work too.

Keeping one ear out for Gerd, Signe went to the screen door. "Leif, I need you to pump water for me. Give you a break."

Leif grinned at her as he climbed up on the low bench stool and started pumping. "I think the cream is turning, the churn sounds different."

"Okay, you fill that, and we'll check the churn. Today you get to learn to wash butter."

"Wash butter? With soap?" His eyes rounded.

"No, clear water after we drain the whey off." She could tell he wasn't too sure of this by the questions all over his face.

"Can we drink the buttermilk?"

"Some."

"My chickens would like the buttermilk too."

"I know. So would the hogs."

Signe set the boiler back on the stove and added more wood to the voracious maw quickly emptying the woodbox. After shaving small bits of the quickly dwindling bar of soap into the heating water, she returned to the bedroom. Gerd jerked upright, tipping her coffee cup. At least it was on the tray and the tray had a towel on it.

"See what you made me do?" Gerd brushed drops off her grimy nightdress that, so far, she'd worn 'round the clock. "What are you doing out there? Smells like soap."

"We're doing the wash."

"You'll use up all the soap."

"Someone is going to the store on Saturday."

"Who? *He* won't quit work for a day to do that, and you can't leave me alone. I need you." Gerd's voice rose to a screech.

"We have some fat saved. Maybe I'll make soap here too." How would she ever get to the store if she couldn't leave Gerd?

"Soap has to season."

"We'll see." While they were talking, she'd gathered the pile of clothes from the corner of the room. "I'll be right back for your tray."

Tante shook her head. "Too much."

Signe ignored her. Back in the kitchen, she sorted the clothes and poked what she could into the warming boiler.

"Come see, Mor. I can hear the butter."

Knute straightened from cranking the washing machine. "You think this load is done?"

"Ja. Bring in more wood while I show Leif how to wash butter." Picking up the churn, she carried it inside and set it in the sink. Was there such a thing as a strainer here? "You look for a strainer." She set the largest crockery bowl in the sink and gently poured the buttermilk into the bowl, using her hand to hold back the butter bits.

"A mouse! It just ran out of the cupboard." Leif pointed to the corner where the mouse hid behind the broom.

Signe debated for only a moment, then set the churn down, wiped her hands on her apron, and grabbed for the broom. "Open the door in case I miss it."

The mouse scurried along the wall as soon as she jerked back the broom. Her first slam missed, and at the second slam of the broom, the mouse darted into the bedroom.

"There he goes."

Signe muttered words she knew her mother would have scolded her for. "We are getting traps and a cat."

Knute appeared in the doorway, trying hard not to laugh. "You want me to chase it?"

"Nei—ja! I want you to kill the filthy thing." She slapped the broom back in the corner and set the strainer Leif had found over the bowl before pouring out the remainder of the butter and buttermilk. "And all the others."

She heard what sounded like choking behind her. The boys were trying not to laugh. The whole family thought her rage at mice was funny, and Rune even teased her about it. She set the churn back in the sink and propped her arms on the edge, reminding herself to calm down and breathe.

She knew why she hated mice so severely, besides the fact that they left filth everywhere they went. When she was a girl, she tried to save a mouse trapped in the oats bin. She got it by the tail, but the stupid beast swung around and bit her on the little finger. When she screamed and shook her hand, that mouse didn't even have the sense to run somewhere else. It fell back into the oats bin. She was so furious, she grabbed one of the barn cats, dumped it in the oats bin, and shut the lid.

She listened to the scramble, and when it was quiet, peeked inside. The cat jumped out, mouse dangling from its mouth, and headed up the ladder to the haymow where it had a batch of kittens. Within days, Signe's finger had been infected.

She handed Knute the churn. "Pour some hot water in this and take it out on the porch. Leif can scrub it." She stared at her youngest son. "And it has to be clean! So clean it cannot sour and spoil the next batch of butter! You hear me?"

He nodded and glared at his brother, who was still fighting the snickers. The boys did as she said, leaving her shaking her head.

She poured the buttermilk into a crock from the pantry and covered it with a dish towel. Then, with the butter back in the crockery bowl, she rinsed the golden mound in cold water, dumped that in a pail for the pigs, and repeated until the water stayed clear, no matter how much she worked it through the butter. She salted the golden ball, tasted it, and added more. Surely Tante had butter molds, but she'd not seen any in the pantry or cupboards when she scrubbed them down. Instead she patted the round into a couple of smaller bowls and set them in the icebox.

At least they would have fresh butter for the biscuits or corn bread she made for supper. If only they had bread, they could have sliced bread with butter and sugar on it. What a treat that would be. Tomorrow they would have bread again. She checked the sourdough growing in the crock on the warming shelf and inhaled the yeasty fragrance.

Out on the porch, she ran the sheets one by one into the rinse water. She should have set up two tubs for rinsing, but there had only been one.

"You stir those around, shake them out, and rinse them well." She lifted and dunked one to show him how. "I'll get the next load out here."

After filling the firebox again, she pulled the next load out of the boiler and carried the hot, dripping clothes out to the washing machine. "Keep rinsing." With the next wash in the boiler, she took over rinsing and set Knute to cranking the wringer. She fed the sheets into the wringer and from that into a basket on the floor.

Now for her favorite part of doing the wash. She carried the basket out into the yard along with a bag of clothespins and hung the sheets on the clothesline. She could hear her mor. *"Peg the corners securely. Overlap the sheets to save on clothespins."* Between the sun and the wind, the sheets would be nearly dry before she brought out the next load. Clean—something in this house would be clean again.

Oh, Mor, who ever thought I would be hanging wash in Minnesota in Amerika? She heaved a sigh. At least Mor had said goodbye and that she would write soon. Perhaps someday she would forgive Signe for leaving.

"I'm hungry, Mor," Leif said, rubbing his belly. "I scrubbed the churn with a brush even."

"Good. Set it out in the sun, and let's go fix something to eat. Knute, keep that crank turning, and we'll run that load into the rinse before we eat." Inside, she set a skillet on the stove and poured the remainder of the beans into it. She should have made more pancakes. "Here, Leif, stir this while we get this load into the rinse water. Don't let them burn."

"I won't."

Before she stopped for dinner, they had a load in the rinse, one in the washer, and another in the boiler on the stove. "Let's eat outside in the shade."

She dished up three bowls of beans, had Leif grab spoons, and out they went to sit on the cellar door. A breeze played with the wisps of hair that refused to stay tucked into her braids. She fluttered the front of her shift and apron so the coolness could touch her skin. The boys dug into the beans as if they'd not eaten for days rather than hours.

"Did you check your snares?" she asked Knute.

"Far said to do it tonight."

"It would be a shame for a dead rabbit to lay out there in this heat."

"I'll go see. Do you know how to skin a rabbit?"

"Ja, I will teach you." She'd just finished her beans when the screech came. Pushing herself to her feet, she patted her sons' shoulders and stepped back into the steam bath that was the house. "Coming."

With Gerd settled again and sipping her coffee, Signe asked if she wanted beans for dinner.

"Is that all?" At Signe's nod, she shook her head. "We have eggs, don't we?"

"Ja. I could fry or scramble you a couple."

A jerk of the head was her answer.

"Would you like some buttermilk too?"

Tante Gerd nodded. "You got the butter churned?"

"Leif did."

Should I warn her I am going to change her bed or just do it? The thought nagged at Signe while she fixed the eggs and carried the tray back into the dim room. Setting the tray on Gerd's legs, Signe crossed the room to throw open the windows and, ignoring the screeching, returned to her wash. *There, I did that.* Sometimes one just had to take charge.

Once the second load hung on the clothesline, she checked the first sheets, gathering them to her face to inhale the clean scent of the sun and wind. Dry, as she had suspected. She folded the sheets as she took them off the line.

Knute came running through the garden. "Mor, we got a rabbit! Can we have it for supper?"

"We sure can."

After they had another load of wash in the boiler and the rinsed load hanging on the line, she had Knute tie the rabbit's two back legs together with a piece of twine and hung it from a nail in the porch post.

"First, you need a very sharp knife." She found the whetstone in a drawer and handed it to him.

After a few moments of concentration and careful wielding of the whetstone, Knute handed her the knife. "This sharp enough?"

Checking the edge, she nodded. "Good job. Now, first you cut off the head, and just like skinning a deer, cut around the legs and peel the skin off. Then gut it." With quick motions, she did as she instructed, then handed the hide to Knute. "You nail that on the barn wall to dry, and we'll soak the carcass in salt water and fry it for supper." Knute pumped water into a large bowl and watched Signe swish the meat around to rinse it.

"One less rabbit to graze in the garden," he said.

"This is the last load of wood," Leif announced as he dumped the split wood into the box.

"We'll get through another load of wash, and then Knute can split wood so we have enough to make supper." She knew she was putting off the next big job. "You go turn the crank on the washer. I'll be out in a few minutes."

She sucked in a deep breath, then took the stack of folded linens into the bedroom, set them on the chest of drawers, and pulled the chair over to the side of the bed.

"Tante. Tante Gerd." She gently shook the woman's shoulder.

"Wh-what? Is it suppertime?"

"Nei, but once I get the bed changed, I will bring you a cup of coffee."

Gerd shook her head. "Nei!"

"Ja, think how much you will enjoy clean sheets right off the line. I brought the chair over."

"I can't."

"Ja, you can." She kept her voice soft and firm. She pulled the covers right off the bed and started a pile by the wall. "I am going to hang your blanket over the line so the wind can freshen that too."

"No, I can't!"

When Signe took her hands and helped her sit up, Gerd stubbornly refused to swing her legs over the side of the bed. Sighing silently, Signe simply swept the woman's legs to the floor.

"Now, it will only take two steps. Stand, take two steps, turn, and we'll sit you down." She paused when she had pulled Gerd to her feet, pretending not to notice the fiery glare the other woman pinned her with. "Careful, so you don't get dizzy."

"I can't! I'll fall," Gerd repeated.

Signe began to turn her. "Now take a small step. Lift your feet."

Grumbling, Gerd began to shuffle her feet. Without warning, her left foot caught on the rug, and she began to fall. Signe tried to catch her but only succeeded in being pulled down with her. Both women sat tangled in a heap for a moment before Gerd let out an ear-splitting screech.

"I told you!"

"Are you hurt?" Signe gasped, moving slowly to stand.

"I fell!"

"Ja, but are you hurt?"

After a sullen moment, Gerd shook her head. "How will I get up? Einar is in the woods. You can't pick me up."

"We'll get you up together. Let me help you sit up. Good. Now push with your legs." Moving behind her, Signe pulled with all her might and managed to get Gerd back on her feet. "Good, now turn just a little and sit."

It was more of a controlled fall, but she got Gerd into the chair.

Muttering all kinds of imprecations, Gerd watched as Signe stripped the rest of the bed and tossed the sheets and pillow-cases onto the pile. "We could bathe you before you get a fresh dress," Signe suggested.

"Too tired."

"Then we'll just change your nightdress." Which she did in spite of Gerd's anger.

Figuring she'd scored all the victory she could for the moment, Signe remade the bed and helped Gerd back onto it, which went far easier. With Tante settled, covered only by a sheet—but a clean sheet—Signe stepped back. "Doesn't that feel better?"

A glare was the only answer she received.

"I'll bring your coffee now."

Tante shook her head. "Too tired."

"All right, but I have good news." She paused but got no response. "Knute caught a rabbit in his snare, so we'll have fresh rabbit for supper."

She watched Gerd's eyes drift shut. Surely her hand wasn't stroking the clean sheet?

Bundling up the dirty bedding, Signe took it all out to the porch, where she shook out the blanket and hung it over the line for the sun and wind to work their magic. It needed washing too, but there were only so many hours in the day, and this one was galloping by.

For supper, besides fried rabbit, she would make fried corn-meal cakes. Plenty of them, so they'd have them for dinner tomorrow too. With Knute splitting wood and Leif cranking the washing machine, Signe paused at the clothesline to lift her face to the sun. Nothing smelled as fine as clothes off the line. She smiled at her fancy. Was it her mor who had coined that? She needed to write a letter home. Would she hear from someone from Norway soon?

Chapter 9

JULY 1909

The yeasty perfume of sourdough tickled her nose awake. The thought of fresh bread seemed a small miracle to her. Signe stretched as she started to rise. Three days later, and Signe could still feel the bruises from the fall she'd taken with Gerd.

Rune stretched beside her and groaned.

"I put liniment on the list for tomorrow."

"Good thing. Who would have thought to bring liniment from Norway?"

"But you are getting stronger?"

"I will by next week—perhaps." He rolled to his knees and pushed himself upright, then extended a hand to help her up.

"I should be helping you." She leaned into his chest as his arms came around her. "I think we both need the liniment." She stepped back. "I better hurry."

Rune nudged the three sleeping boys. "Come on, get up." Ignoring their groans, he dressed in all but his boots, which he carried to the back porch. Like Signe, he enjoyed walking barefoot to the privy through the morning dew.

On her way back to the house, Signe shuddered. "I sure will be glad to get the lime. Sometimes the wind blows the stench to the house." As she set about starting the stove in the kitchen, she deliberately inhaled the yeasty fragrance, which her nose needed after the other. Sourdough was good for raising more than just dough.

<hr />

Bjorn grinned at his mor that evening. "Bread, real bread."

"I know." Signe looked at the loaves cooling on the counter. She didn't mention that she and the younger boys had fried bread that afternoon. Even Tante, while she'd not had something nice to say about the treat, had not found something to gripe about either. Signe had baked the two rabbits snared the night before, so supper smelled really good too.

Tomorrow she and Leif would drive to Blackduck. Onkel Einar had assured her she would not get lost. Knute was not happy about staying home to assist Tante Gerd in and out of bed, but Leif was too small to be much help.

Since the loggers had come in early to sharpen the axes and split wood, supper was not ready when they drove in. When she stepped outside, Signe could hear the whine of the axe head on the grindstone. After fanning herself with her apron, she brought out buttermilk for everyone to drink. "To tide you over until supper."

"Takk." Rune lifted his glass in a salute to his wife.

"You're welcome," Signe returned. What a pleasure it was to hear some gratitude. Today she had finished up the wash, so they all had clean clothes too. And she could look around the kitchen and not be overwhelmed by the dirt.

When she had supper on the table, she called the others inside. Fresh bread and fresh golden butter. That was enough for a meal by itself.

"What do you need from the store?" she asked Einar when he slowed down shoveling food into his mouth.

"I wrote a list." He dug a paper out of his shirt pocket. "Oats for animal feed and a bag for seed. That field should have already been seeded." He looked at Rune. "You ever seeded a field?"

"Ja, but by hand, not with a machine like the one you have."

Einar rolled his eyes and huffed. "Never enough daylight to get it all done." He reached for another slice of bread and slathered butter on it. He chewed for a moment, then said, seemingly reluctantly, "They carry seed at Benson's Corner. You better go there instead. Not so far."

Signe looked at him in surprise. He had been so adamant about her going to Blackduck. She glanced at Rune, who shook his head slightly.

"How far is it to Benson Corner?" she asked.

"About three miles. You could walk if we didn't need such heavy supplies."

"Can I mail letters from there?"

"Ja, they have a mailbag. Comes in on the logging train. Tell her who you are. They know you were coming."

This was far better. She wouldn't be gone from Gerd so long, and she would be able to get more done here.

When Einar finished his bread, he stood. "Saw blades to sharpen." He paused. "Rune, you ever sharpened saw blades?"

"Nei."

"Time for you to learn. Leave the woodcutting to the boys and come with me."

Rune glanced down at his plate. "I'll be there as soon as I finish."

At the frown on Einar's face, he shoveled in the last few bites and got to his feet.

"You boys finish your supper," he said softly, earning another frown from the impatient man.

Signe kept from shaking her head but looked toward the bedroom when Gerd screamed her name. How could she scream like that when she was so out of breath most of the time? Signe had barely started on her supper.

"I'll be right there." She pushed her chair back but motioned for the boys to finish their meal. Just because Onkel ate first and so fast, all the others were supposed to jump up when he did. Another small stick of frustration adding to the load she was collecting. She made herself breathe before she entered the bedroom and stopped beside the bed. "Pot first or supper?"

"Pot."

Once Gerd was finished, Signe motioned to the chair. "I'm going to bring that over here by the bed again, and you will sit there to eat." That afternoon she'd decided she would no longer ask. Gritting her teeth and carrying on was not working. True, she'd not been here very long, but she already felt that Norway was another life and that she'd been here forever.

She brought the chair to the side of the bed. "Here we go."

"No!" Gerd tried to pull away, but the effort started her puffing again, and when she relaxed, Signe took both her hands and pulled her to her feet.

"Good, good. Just two steps. I'll help you turn."

"I'm falling!"

"No, I won't let you fall." Gerd shouting right in Signe's ear made her head ring. "Put your hands on my shoulders."

Gerd didn't, but Signe put her hands on Gerd's waist and supported her with all her strength. She turned and swung Gerd toward the chair all in one motion. Ignoring the malevolent glare, she settled a shawl around Gerd's shoulders and straightened her legs and feet.

She paused to inhale a deep breath. "I'm going to get your supper."

How to keep the tray from sliding down onto the floor? She had a feeling Gerd would just let it fall and blame her.

While Bjorn and Knute had gone outside, Leif was clearing the table. He'd left her unfinished supper on the table.

"Did you get enough to eat?" she asked him.

"Can I have another piece of bread and butter?"

"With sugar on it?"

His eyes lit up. "Really?"

"Unless you'd rather have jam." While she talked, she dished up a plateful of food and buttered another piece of bread for Tante Gerd. She set the supper things on the tray. If only she could get Gerd strong enough to come to the table. How to hold up the tray? The ironing board. That could lie across the arms of the chair. Fetching the board from where it hung on the pantry wall, she carried it into the bedroom.

Gerd glared at her. "Now what are you doing?"

"Fixing you a table."

"I'm tired. I need to go back to bed."

Signe laid the board across the arms of the chair and brought the tray from the kitchen. "Here you go. Enjoy your supper." It was a good thing dirty looks did not cut, because Signe would be a mass of bleeding if they did. "I'll bring you more coffee later, if you like." She left the room before she had to listen to another diatribe.

Leif set the dishes in the pan of soapy water steaming on the stove. "Mor, we are out of soap."

"I know. We'll get some tomorrow at the store." She sank down on her chair as a wave of weariness nearly swamped her. "Where's my plate?"

"I put it in the warming oven." Leif picked up the plate with a dish towel and brought it to her.

"Takk." She nodded at her youngest son and forced herself to smile. "That was very kind and thoughtful of you." There were two slices of bread on the plate. She took one and offered him the other.

"I already had another piece."

"Well, if you are too full . . ."

He grinned at her as he grabbed the bread and a knife to butter it with. "Sugar too?"

"Ja, sugar too."

She ate her supper in the quiet of the kitchen and was sipping her coffee when the order came from the bedroom. Sucking in a deep breath, she went to fetch the tray and put Gerd to bed. She'd planned to give her a bath tonight but decided one change was enough. The bath could wait. It had probably been months since she'd had a bath or even washed. One more day couldn't make it any worse.

That night after the others had all gone to bed, Signe poured herself another cup of coffee and sat down at the table to finish a letter to her mor. They had been gone only two weeks or so, even though it felt like forever. She picked up where she had left off, having started the letter on the train in between trying to watch the scenery.

> *We are doing well here. Tante Gerd is bedridden and has been for some time. Onkel Einar was trying to do it all, so this house was filthy. We have scrubbed the kitchen and the pantry and took two days to do the wash. Now we all have clean clothes again. Gerd has a washing machine with a crank handle, which is far better than using a scrub board. She also has a sewing machine, which I will learn to use this winter.*

Lifting the coffee to her lips with both hands, she let her eyes drift closed and took a sip. How often did she drink cold coffee? *Just get up and pour a refill.* The order failed to force her muscles to obey. Instead she returned to her writing.

The boys have weeded the garden and are taking care of feeding the animals and milking the cow. Einar and Rune go out to cut down trees so tall they block the sun. Then Bjorn cuts all the limbs off, which is called limbing, with an axe or a saw, depending on the size. Some limbs are the size of a small tree. Rune taught Bjorn to sharpen the axes and Knute to set snares for rabbits. So far he has brought in four. They stretched the hides on the barn wall. There are plenty of rabbits here, enough to mow a garden to the dirt.

We are still sleeping on pallets on the parlor floor because I have not had time to clean the upstairs. Rune promised to make us a rope bed, but I am sure that won't happen until winter. But then, logging goes on the whole year here. The logs slide more easily over the snow. Einar talks of pulling stumps to clear another field, but I have no idea when. He has big ideas, but he needs more help to do it all. I don't know how he has managed to clear as much as he has.

I'm doing well. I tire more easily than I ever have, but that is to be expected. They say fall comes early here, so the weather will cool down. I will can beans and whatever else I can find, or rather what we can keep the rabbits from eating. Tante had canned beans, peas, pickles, beets. There are still a few jars left. We will need many jars to keep us all through the winter. Onkel Einar says he has a smokehouse for when they butcher pigs in the fall. Or a deer. There are moose here too, and plenty of ducks and geese on the lakes. Rune would like to hunt, but I fear for his eyes. I believe Bjorn will become a good hunter, though, as soon as he gets more practice shooting a rifle.

When you see her, tell Nilda to start saving money for a ticket. There are an abundance of men looking for wives around here.

I must go to bed. We miss you all and pray you are well. Thank you for sharing this with Rune's family also.

Your daughter, Signe

She heaved a sigh. *Surely she has forgiven me by now for following my husband to Amerika.* Rereading what she had written brought on the bitter sting of tears that caused her throat to clog. One tear opened a deluge, no matter how she fought to keep quiet and not wake anyone. Fisted hands propped her forehead off the table until she dug for her apron to stem the flow. *How can I bear this? I am so tired.* The thoughts only fed more tears. *Will this never stop?*

When the tears finally faded, she pushed herself to her feet and refilled her coffee cup. Hot coffee might help more than cold, at least.

Signe knew that the closer to the baby's arrival she came, the less she would be able to lift and support Gerd. What to do? What was the best way to help Tante? Or was helping her get stronger even a possibility? When no answers were forthcoming, she folded the pages of the letter and tucked them into an envelope. After addressing it, she blew out the kerosene lamp and made her way to her pallet.

"Are you all right?" Rune mumbled when she lay down with a sigh.

"Ja." At least her voice sounded like usual. "Tomorrow I can mail a letter home. Did you write one for your family?"

He snorted. "When?"

"I reminded Mor to share the letter with your family and everyone else who wants to know how we are."

"Ja, good thing."

In the morning, after feeding everyone and getting the men out the door with food for dinner, she showed Knute the plates she had fixed for him and Tante Gerd, ignored the sullen looks he sent her, and made sure her list was complete.

"Harness the other horse to the small wagon. Good thing we can do without the draft team."

Onkel had told them that this mare was too old to pull logs anymore, but Gerd used her to plow the garden and pull the wagon. Perhaps she would be used to take the boys to school come fall. So many questions Signe had. She needed to write them down.

"A mouse!" She'd seen it out of the corner of her eye. Grabbing the broom, she slammed it into the corner and either stunned the mouse or killed it.

Leif picked up the mouse. "You got it." He headed for the door but stopped. "Mor, this is a mother mouse. Look." He held it out on his palm.

"Throw it out."

"But she must have a nest. She's nursing."

Signe stared at her son. If he had his way, he would catch the mice and make them into pets.

"We have to find the nest," Leif insisted.

"I agree, or we will have stinky dead bodies. Or more mice running around." But where to look? "Pull all the drawers out, it must be behind them." She had washed the drawers but not pulled them all the way out.

He removed the drawers and then crawled inside the cupboards to look. "In here. Give me the dust pan." He waved his arm, and Signe handed him the pan. "There goes another one! To the right!"

Signe whapped the mouse when it tried to run along the baseboard. She missed and slammed the broom down again. "You got it."

Leif backed out of the cabinet. The dustpan held a nest of chewed cloth and paper with three pink baby mice in the middle.

"Uff da! Take them all down to the barn cats."

Both boys gave her matching wounded stares but did as they were told.

"Signe!" came the call from the bedroom.

"Coming." And here she thought she would be on the road long before now. She took care of Gerd, Knute shoved the drawers back in place, and both boys went to get the horse and cart. When they came to the house, she reminded Gerd that she was leaving and that Knute would be there to help her.

"Do not stop to visit! Come right back! That Mrs. Benson will talk your arm and leg off."

The thought of talking with another woman sounded just fine to Signe. Perhaps Mrs. Benson would answer some of her questions. She climbed up on the seat and waited for Leif to join her, then flicked the reins and clucked the mare forward. Ears swiveling, the old girl trotted out of the yard and headed for the road.

Leif grinned up at her. "Rosie is a nice horse, isn't she?"

"She is."

"She likes oats. When I call her and she comes, I give her a handful." A frown scrunched his forehead. "Would Onkel get mad at me for that?"

"I don't know." They turned right onto the road.

"I don't want him to get mad at me. Knute said he was going to ride Rosie."

"He better ask permission first." She could hear Onkel's voice in her head: *If that boy has time to play with the horse, he is being lazy, and lazy people do not eat at this table.*

"Bjorn said there is a nice creek back in the woods and a lake not too far away. He takes the team to the creek to drink. He rode them back yesterday. I want to ride."

"We'll see. Perhaps when you have all your work done and Onkel says it is fine with him." Would he ever allow the boys to do anything that might be thought of as play? She offered Leif the reins. "Here, how would you like to drive?"

"Really?"

"Take one line in each hand and keep them even."

Leif did as she instructed, watching ahead very carefully. "Takk, Mor."

Signe raised her face to the sun. A breeze tickled the strands of hair that refused to stay in the braid she had wrapped around her head. She should probably be wearing a wide-brimmed straw hat, but since she didn't have one and wasn't going to ask to borrow Gerd's . . . She shrugged. That was just the way it was. And right now, she did not have to think about Gerd and life on their farm.

When they could see several buildings up ahead, she took the reins back. "You did just fine." She pulled off to the shady side of the weathered, silver building where a hitching rail waited. "You tie her up. Use the knot Far taught you, the one you pull loose with a jerk."

"I know. So if something happens, the animal can get free."

Rune had taught the boys the slipknot for tying up cows, but here it would work just the same.

She made sure her list was in her reticule, climbed down from the wagon, and stepped onto the wooden porch that extended the length of the building. The sign hanging from the roof said

Benson's General Store. A bell jangled over the door when she pushed it open.

"Good morning and welcome. How can I help you?"

Signe paused and looked around. *General store* was certainly an appropriate name. Shelves upon shelves of household necessities, tools and farming equipment, leather boots, logging supplies, and food too, evidenced by the barrels in front of the counter that had seen better days. Jars of candy took up one end of the battle-scarred counter, and the cash register sat in the middle.

A round-cheeked woman with graying hair fighting to escape a loose knot on top of her head nodded and smiled. "I'm Elmira Benson. And who might you be?"

Oh dear. English. How could she manage this? "Uh, hello. My name is Signe Carlson. Uh . . ."

And Mrs. Benson, bless her, said in Norwegian, "Oh! You are the people who came over to help the Strands on their farm." She had a strong accent and obviously was not quite comfortable with the language.

Much relieved, Signe replied, "Oh, yes!"

"The mister said you were coming. I know they were in dire need of help. He said you had three big boys who would be able to log and pull out stumps." Mrs. Benson smiled at Leif, who stood beside Signe. "And who is this young man?"

"My youngest son, Leif. The youngest of the three strapping sons."

Mrs. Benson's eyes danced, and she leaned slightly forward. "And how big are the other two?"

"Bjorn is fifteen and helping the men with the logging."

"And your middle boy?"

"Ten and at home tante-watching."

"And you've been here how long?"

"About ten days, but I cannot wait any longer to buy soap and lime. Do you have them?"

"Ah, I'm not sure." Mrs. Benson shook her head. "My Norwegian is not very good. Do you know the English words for what you need?"

"Uh . . ." Signe pantomimed working a bar of soap between her hands, then rinsing and drying them.

"Oh, of course!"

Lime? Signe was going to have to be more coarse and uncultured than her mor would ever have allowed. Pretending to hike her skirt, she pretended to sit, stood up, looked behind her, and pinched her nose. "Phew!" Then she said, "Lime!" in Norwegian and tossed pretend lime down a hole.

Mrs. Benson was laughing heartily. "Oh, I love it! Quicklime! Yes, I have that."

"Quicklime," Signe repeated. "Takk." She handed Mrs. Benson the list. "Onkel wondered if you have oats."

"We do. How much do you want?"

He'd not told her how much to buy. She straightened her spine. "Four sacks for feed and seed." That should last awhile.

Mrs. Benson looked down the rest of the list. In Norwegian, she asked, "You will put this on Mr. Strand's tab, ja? How would you like a cup of coffee while I fill this? It will take a few minutes; the oats are out in the back shed where Mr. Benson is working. You can sit on the back porch in the shade. And perhaps Leif would like some lemonade."

He looked up at Signe, his big eyes asking, *What is lemonade?* Her eyes said, *Be polite.* "Ja, please."

"Come with me."

They walked through a storage area and out a door to another porch running the length of the building, but this one had a small table and cushioned chairs and was shaded not only by the porch roof but by a big maple tree with a wood swing hanging from the bottom branch by two thick ropes.

"My grandchildren play out here," Mrs. Benson said. "You can swing if you want."

Eyes round, Leif looked up at his mor, who nodded.

"Thank you," Signe responded in English. At least she knew those words.

"My grandson Willem is about that age, but they live in Blackduck, so he don't get out here much. You sit down there and be comfortable. Would you like lemonade too?" At Signe's shrug, Mrs. Benson nodded. "You can try it."

Signe sat in one of the chairs with a sigh. She needed to find out where they could water the horse. Leaning back against the cushion, she sighed again. Such a generous soul this woman had. Tante Gerd had said to come right back, but Signe didn't feel like hurrying. Did Gerd ever sit out here and let a breeze cool her head and neck? Or was she rude to everyone, and being sick only made it worse?

Chapter 10

I warned you!"

The screech met Signe at the door. She looked to Knute, who shook his head as he ducked out the back door. Deciding to ignore the accusation, Signe stopped at the bedroom door. "What do you need, Tante Gerd?"

On the way home, with Leif handling the reins, she had decided she could ignore the nastiness and treat Gerd the way she herself would like to be treated if she were ill. Though she wondered if Gerd was so weak because she lay in bed all the time. Wouldn't moving more make her stronger?

Gerd shook her head. "Your son is worthless."

"What did he do that was so terrible?" From the look on her son's face as he escaped out the door, Signe knew it had been hard. Someone attacking her she could handle—attacking her boys, now that was another matter.

"He took forever to come when I needed help, and I almost wet the bed." She motioned to the floor, where a puddle gave mute testimony to her need. "And he brought lukewarm coffee with dinner!"

Signe had to concentrate on keeping a straight face. She'd had too nice a day to let this barrage bother her.

"I will talk to him about that and mop up the floor. Now, do you need help with the pot?"

"A bit late but nei, not now."

"Good. Then I am going to put things away and make sure supper will be ready on time."

She turned back to the kitchen and lifted her apron on over her head. She needed a new apron; this one was about shredded. The urge to either laugh or cry made her want to scream, but she'd need to be way out in the field where no one would hear her, and she dared not get that far from the house again.

Both boys brought the supplies in from the cart and set the bags and paper-wrapped parcels on the table.

"As soon as you put the horse away, I need wood in the woodbox."

"I told Knute about the swing," Leif said. "Wouldn't it be nice if we had a big tree near the house where we could hang a swing?"

"Ja, it would be. You and Knute go unharness Rosie so she can eat."

"What about the sacks of oats?"

"Leave those in the wagon for the men to carry."

Knute brought in an armload of wood and dropped it in the woodbox. "I kept the fire going like you said and stirred the baked beans in the oven. But Far told me to split wood, and every time I got going, she'd scream at me. Couldn't she hear I was splitting wood? I mean, before we came, she was here by herself most of the day, wasn't she?" He shook his head. "And she called me 'hey, you!' or 'boy.'" He turned and went outside, shaking his head. "I'll be down at the barn," he called over his shoulder.

Since she refused to raise her voice at Tante Gerd, Signe stopped at the bedroom door. Gerd was sound asleep, her mouth open, and snoring. She'd probably not slept earlier, too worried about Knute not being there to help her.

After opening the windows again, she checked on the beans and paused to admire the rich brown of beans baked all day in the oven. She had another dressed rabbit out in the well house, keeping cool, to fry for supper. Catching herself humming one of the hymns from back home reminded her to ask if there was a church here. She'd seen the school at Benson's Corner but no sign of a church. Not that they'd been very faithful church attenders back home, something that grieved Gunlaug, Rune's mor.

After filling one bucket with hot water from the reservoir and scraping soap into it, she scooped lime from the bag the boys had set on the back porch into another bucket. Carrying both buckets along with rags and a brush, she headed for the outhouse. After throwing the lime down the hole, she fetched the broom and swept out all the cobwebs, then scrubbed the whole inner building, especially the seat and the floor. By tomorrow they might not have to hold their breath to use it.

On the way back to the house, she noted the weeds along the path. Surely Knute knew how to use a scythe well enough to cut down weeds. She could if he couldn't. She set the buckets on the porch and walked over to the garden. About a third of it, what looked like the potato patch, still lay hidden beneath weeds. Which was more important for the boys to do, pull weeds or split wood? If there wasn't still so much scrubbing to do inside . . . She leaned over and pulled a handful of weeds. Everything was important. According to the sun, it was about four o'clock. If she pulled weeds for an hour or so, she'd still have time to scrub a couple of walls, or go upstairs and sweep and mop the floor so that tonight they could move their pallets out of the parlor.

She bent to pull weeds, tossing them in a pile for the boys to haul to the hogs. With the windows open, she'd hear if Tante screeched for her.

Knute joined her. "Mor, how come you're out here?"

"Because you did such a fine job in the house while I was gone that now I can help you." She watched his tiny grin turn into full bloom. Come to think of it, she'd not seen or heard Knute laugh much at all since they came here. Other than with Rosie. This place and her boys needed a dog, the house needed a cat, and if they were going to eat this winter, this garden needed a whole lot of work.

She could scrub after the mosquitoes came out.

Leif joined them as well, and the three of them pulled weeds, leaving her mind free to think about all the other work that needed to be done. And relive her visit with Elmira Benson at the store. The lemonade was a special treat. Sitting in the shade, listening to the birds chatter in the shade trees, watching Leif swinging and laughing, then jumping off and flying through the air to land with a thump.

"My pile is higher than your pile," Knute said to Leif.

She had finished one row and turned back on the next. Kneading her lower back with her fists, she stretched her neck from side to side. Perspiration dripped off her nose and ran down the sides of her face. She'd not even been aware of it.

"Mor, your face is all red." Leif held up a handful of foot-long weeds. "How come they call these pigweed?"

"Why do you think?"

"'Cause the pigs like them and they grow fast and all over the place?"

Knute added, "That old sow should have her babies any day

now. Onkel Einar told me this morning. He said we need to keep an eye on her so she doesn't lie on her babies when they're born and smother them." He tossed a handful of weeds onto the pile. "Pa said our sow at home was too smart and careful of her babies to do that. He said he thought sure she looked around and counted them before she lay down." He wiped sweat from his forehead with the back of his arm, looking so much like his far that it caught Signe by surprise.

"Your far has always been good with animals," she said as she bent back to pulling weeds. Hopefully Rune could pass that on to his boys, not that there was much time now, with the men out cutting down trees until dusk. When she got to the end of that row, she straightened again. "I need to get back to the house. How much wood is in the box?"

"Enough to make supper. I need to split more." Knute blew out a cheek-puffing breath. "I'll do that when we get the potatoes done. The corn is next."

"You'll need to start chores in an hour or so."

"I know."

Signe returned to the house, stooping to pick up an armload of wood on her way in. The thumps of wood falling into the woodbox brought a screech from the bedroom.

"Signe!"

"I'm right here. Let me wash my hands first and I'll be in to help you."

At least the kitchen smelled rich with the fragrance of baking beans and not the stink of mice and dirt. Out the kitchen window, she could see the boys continuing to weed. How good it had felt to be out there. How Einar had gotten the garden worked up and planted amazed her. He must have been a machine to do it all alone. Of course, he'd not been felling trees, since he needed to be near the house to help Gerd. No wonder he was so desperate for them to get here. Could that be what made him so grumpy?

In Gerd's room, she pulled the chair over by the bed.

"Nei!"

"Ja, you will sit up for a while and then for supper too." She helped the woman stand up, use the pot, and then instead of going back to bed, Signe grasped Gerd around the waist and turned her to sit in the chair. For the effort she got a clout on the shoulder and a string of muttering. "Would you like something to drink? The coffee is not hot right now, but I can bring you water or buttermilk or milk. And, if you like, a slice of buttered bread." Signe paused and watched Gerd's face.

The older woman's eyes narrowed. "Coffee."

"Nei. Milk, water, or buttermilk."

"Coffee!"

"Nei. I'll be back later to help you to bed." Signe left the sputtering woman to think this through.

Deciding to make corn bread for supper, she stepped outside and inhaled the scents of summer. Turned earth, growing grass, and—she wrinkled her nose. Something was missing. Ah, the overlay of the outhouse. The lime was already doing its work. Signe stepped into the well house and stood still for a moment, letting the coolness sink in after the heat of the outdoors. There were four flat pans with the cream risen to the top that she needed to skim. Now or later? Later. With the jug of buttermilk in one hand, she tucked a couple of eggs into her apron pockets and closed the door behind her. The heat smote her, but with the sun falling toward the horizon, the air would cool soon.

Back in the house, she set down her things and checked on Tante. Chin on her chest, Gerd was sound asleep. Leave her there or put her back to bed so she didn't end up with a crick in her neck? Leave her be.

Back at the stove, since she needed to get the oven hot enough for corn bread, Signe set the pan of baked beans on the reservoir and shoved more wood into the firebox. The steam rising from around the pan lid made her mouth water for baked beans. Supper seemed like a long time away. If the boys were as hungry as she was . . . ach, silly! They were always hungry.

She sliced three pieces of bread, buttered them and spread jam, then went to the door and called the boys.

"Sit here on the steps." She brought out glasses of buttermilk and a plate with the slices of bread.

"Is this supper?" Knute asked.

She shook her head. "Because you worked so hard."

"Takk." They spoke in unison with matching grins.

"We never had this back home," Knute said.

"I know. Things are different here." She sat beside them and leaned against the porch post.

A bit later, the boys grinned at each other when the cow bellowed that it was time for milking. They handed Signe their empty glasses and headed to the barn for their chores.

Once she had the corn bread out of the oven and the rabbit all cut up and floured, she returned to the well house to skim the pans, pouring some of the milk into a jug for the house and the rest into buckets for the boys to feed to the hogs. The cream all went into a covered crock for churning butter. One of these days, as soon as she had some rennet, she'd set some whole milk for cheese. Of course, she could set some now and make cottage cheese, then drain that for soft cheese. One of these days. So many things to do.

Back in the house, she put the big skillet on the hot part of the stove and added bacon grease to fry the rabbit. Once it was browning, she returned to the bedroom and laid a gentle hand on Tante's shoulder.

"Tante, wake up, and I'll help you back to bed."

Gerd raised her head. "I was not sleeping. You left me here all afternoon."

"Only for a little while." She took both of Tante's hands. "Stand up now and turn."

Back in bed, the old woman sighed. "I told you I do not want to sit in the chair."

"I'll bring your supper later. I need to go turn the rabbit."

"Did you bake beans?"

"Ja."

"I thought so. Baked beans always make the house smell good."

Signe waited, in case Gerd wanted to say more. But no matter, that was almost a compliment. Might things get better?

⁂

"Benson had oats, eh?" Onkel Einar commented after he devoured his supper. "And lime."

"Along with soap and mousetraps. The three most important things." Signe sat down at the table and dished up her plate. There was one piece of rabbit left. When she put it on her plate, she glanced up to see Rune smile at her. He'd made sure there was a piece left for her. She nodded her thanks. She should have fried two rabbits, but one was all she had.

"Anything in your snares today?" she asked Knute.

"Nei." He nodded toward the remaining piece of corn bread.

Rune shook his head. "Nei, that is for your mor. She has to eat too, you know."

"There is more in the pan. I'll cut some." She glanced around the table. "Anyone else?"

Bjorn nodded and reached for the plate of corn bread.

Einar stopped him. "We need to sharpen the axes. You had

enough." He pushed his chair back. "Rune, you'll work on the saw blades. I saw the house is about out of wood too. I thought you two younger ones could keep up with that woodbox."

Signe stared at Rune, willing him to stand up for his boys. Einar obviously did not remember that one had gone with her to the store and the other took care of Einar's wife. When Rune refused to either speak or meet her gaze, she snapped her jaw shut. While Tante Gerd screeched at her, Onkel Einar expected these boys to carry on a man's jobs. And not eat as much as he did and in shorter time.

And they were all still growing. Growing boys needed a lot of food and time to eat it.

"You've been here almost two weeks now," Einar said as he pushed his chair back from the table, "and we have felled only eight trees. I figured two a day with three of us. We got to do more."

Again she waited for Rune to answer. Sucking in a deep breath and making sure her anger did not glint through, she said, "You've taught them a lot in the time we've been here. Seasoned loggers would do more, but Rune and Bjorn will get stronger and better with time."

As soon as she said the words, she knew she should have kept her mouth shut. But someone had to make Einar see reason.

A glare narrowed his eyes. He grumbled his way to the door. "You two coming?" He stopped. "Knute, that sow look or act any different today? Like making a nest?" He sent a glare Signe's way that brought up her back.

She looked to Rune, but he only shook his head.

Knute thought a moment before answering. "She didn't eat as much."

"That young gilt, she should have hers in another month or so. You need to watch her too. She don't know what she's doing." He looked to Rune. "You ever built a farrowing stall?"

"If you mean nailing some boards at an angle across one corner so the piglets can go under there to get away, ja." His jaw tightened in a way only Signe might recognize. "I can do that, *or* I can sharpen the saws."

Einar did not look pleased. "You better get that corner in place. That old girl is going to drop them any day now. Can't afford to lose those babies. Got three people wanting to buy weaner pigs. Hogs is in demand up here. Bjorn can sharpen the axes, and I'll take the file to the saw blade." He shook his head with its perpetual scowl and stomped away down the porch steps.

Uff da, that man.

Chapter 11

Y ou finish your supper, boys. Bjorn, get down to the grinder quick as you can. Knute and Leif, meet me at the barn."

Out on the back porch, Rune settled his hat firmly on his head. His boys needed to eat. They worked hard all day too. Having never had children, Einar just didn't know. Rune wondered what his onkel's life had been like growing up, but since it was in Norway, there was no one here he could ask. And Einar never mentioned his life in Norway.

Rune found the handsaw, some boards, and a hammer and nails, and went into the dark barn. He'd need a kerosene lantern. Were there any hanging in the milking side of the barn? He couldn't remember. Einar had one in the machine shed, where he was sharpening the saw blade.

"You have another lantern?" Rune asked after walking over. Shouting would have been easier, but they did enough shouting out in the woods.

"Hanging inside the door where the stanchions are." Einar never looked up from his filing. "That boy getting out here before morning?"

"I'm right here, Onkel Einar." Bjorn stepped into the circle of light. "I'll drag the grinding stone over to the light."

"Make sure no dried grass is near."

"I know."

Einar looked up. "If you know so much, why'd you ask?"

Bjorn started to say something, but at the shake of Rune's head, he stopped. "Yes, sir."

Rune helped his son drag the heavy grindstone over to the light, then returned to the barn for the other lantern. This job would have been so much easier during daylight.

Knute and Leif slid to a stop after racing to the barn. Their laughter over who won made Einar look up and glare.

"What do you want me to do, Far?" Knute asked.

"Go light that lantern by the stanchions so we can measure the stall."

Wisely, Einar had built a big box stall in one corner of the barn, across from the horse stalls. He'd done a better job on the barn than the house, but that wasn't surprising. Rune and Leif moved the boards and tools inside, and when Knute brought the lighted lantern, Rune hung it on a nail in a post.

"Now we measure that corner." He motioned to the inside wall. "We'll nail two boards on the stall walls so we don't need to miter the corners. Then we'll nail the two boards we'll cut to the uprights, six to eight inches above the floor. You'll need to get some bedding in here. Cut some grass, or the sweepings from the haymow would work too."

He showed the boys where to nail the uprights and drew a line there with the sharp end of a nail. "Now, Knute, nail those two short pieces up there. Leif, you hold them in place." He watched the boys do as he said. He could do it faster himself, but the boys needed to learn to do everything on a farm, just like he had. Besides, his eyes were not good enough anymore to cut and mark lumber in this dim light. His far had already gone blind by the time Rune was old enough to work in the barn.

With the uprights nailed in place, he unfolded the wooden measuring rule, and they measured the length from one upright to the other. "Now we'll cut two boards that length and nail them across the corner. The baby pigs can hide under here when their mother lies down. Some sows are careless and can lie on their babies or step on them, while others are very careful and check to see where the babies are before they lie down."

"Pigs can't count, can they, Far?" Leif, always the questioner, asked.

"Not in our terms, but they know. God gave animals good thinking brains too. You pay attention, and you'll see that."

"Like the cows knowing which is their stanchion?"

"Ja, that is true. Now, measure that board this length." He held his thumb on the number on the measuring rule.

"And draw a line with a nail again?"

"Right. Then cut on that line. And do it again with the other board."

Knute cut both pieces, and then he and Leif nailed them to the uprights.

"Good job. Tomorrow you get some bedding in here, and we'll move that sow into her new home. Now, you two put the tools away and put the lantern back."

Rune rubbed his eyes. Good thing he'd let the boys do the measuring. He'd not been sure of the numbers. The lines all ran together. At the grinding wheel, he tapped Bjorn on the shoulder. "How are you doing?"

"Two done, two to go."

"Give me the goggles. I'll do those. You boys get on up to bed."

Bjorn handed his far the goggles and Rune settled himself on the grinder's seat. Snapping the goggles over his glasses and picking up the axe, he set his feet on the pedals and pumped the wheel up to a speed sufficient for sharpening. If he didn't keep moving, he'd fall asleep right here.

By the time he finished both axe heads, he realized Onkel had gone up to the house. Rune checked the saw blade. It was finished. He blew out the lantern and waited for his eyes to adjust. The moon lit the path to the back porch. In the parlor, he shucked his clothes and slid under the sheet without waking Signe. She needed the sleep more than or at least as badly as he did.

Tomorrow was Sunday, but it looked like it would be just like any other day for felling trees. Not a day of rest by any means. He'd heard there was a church at Benson's Corner, but no mention had been made of attending. Not that they'd been that strict in church attendance at home either.

Sleep buried the thought so deeply that he didn't even hear Signe get up to start breakfast in the morning. When he finally heard the rooster crowing, the fragrance of coffee dragged him from bed. He shook his boys' shoulders when whispering their names didn't make them stir. Rune did not want Onkel Einar yelling at them for being lazy. They were doing the work of men, and they were not lazy but growing boys.

The wind came up midmorning with the sky overhead turning darker by the moment. They stopped for dinner at midday, although not being able to see the sun made it harder to tell the actual time. Signe had packed them a sandwich of rabbit and cheese. The three of them had sat on a log to eat when light raindrops began to cool the air. They moved under a tree for protection and finished eating. One of Bjorn's tasks was to lead the horses to the creek to drink and to refill the water jug, so he hauled himself over to the horses, raising his face to feel the mist.

"So do we wait it out, keep working, or go home?" Rune asked.

"We wait to see if there is thunder and lightning. Once that passes, we can go back to work. A little rain never hurt anyone. Good for the hayfield and the garden."

"Sure cooled off fast." A blast of wind made Rune shiver. "Just sitting here is chilly."

"Where's that boy of yours?"

"His name is Bjorn, and he just left to water the horses." Rune looked over at Einar. "You ever catch any fish in the creek?"

"No time to fish. But in a mile or so, the creek runs into a lake. Not fished there neither."

"Knute is a good fisherman. Do you have any gear so he could catch fish?" Rune heaved a sigh. "Fried fish sounds mighty good."

"No, but he could hike to Benson's and buy some hooks and line. Any branch will do for a pole."

"I'll mention that to him tonight. What kind of fish might he catch?"

"I've heard perch and sunfish, maybe bass. They catch walleye from boats or long docks. No dock there, have to fish from the bank."

"Trout in the creek?"

"Maybe." It was Einar's turn to shiver at a blast of wind. Thunder rolled toward the west. "Shoulda brought a file to sharpen the saw blade while we wait." A bolt of lightning lit the nearly black sky. "That boy of yours got the sense to bring the team back? We might as well head to the house."

"He'd let the horses get their fill first. He's careful about animals."

Rain dripped down Rune's back from the brim of his felt hat. Another bolt of lightning raced through the sky, and this time the thunder crashed within seconds. Rune heaved himself to his feet and headed toward the path to the creek. The sky lit. Thunder crashed simultaneously. An explosion rocked the ground. One of the horses screamed, and the team came galloping down the path, crashing through the trees.

"Lightning struck!" Einar reached for the flapping tie rope, but the horses flew past.

Where was Bjorn? Rune tore down the path. *Lord God, let him be alive.* Ahead he could see a shattered tree, flames devouring the branches. "Bjorn!" Up ahead, the creek shimmered gold, reflecting the burning tree. Sparks sizzled when they hit the water. "Bjorn!"

He saw a boot off to the right in the brush. *Oh, dear Lord.* Not far from the boot, his son was trying to push himself up but collapsed with a scream.

"Stay where you are. Let me help you."

Bjorn kicked his legs and tried to roll over, but cried out again.

Rune knelt beside him and laid a hand on his back. "I'm here, son. You're going to be all right."

Einar knelt on the other side. "What's wrong?"

"I-I am not sure, but I don't think he can hear me. See, he shakes so. Perhaps something is broken too." Rune leaned close and spoke directly into Bjorn's ear. "Take it easy, we are here to help."

Bjorn grabbed his hand and clung to it as if he were terrified.

Rune looked at Einar. "Let's turn him over carefully, I will hold his shoulders, you take his feet. Turn him your way." He grasped Bjorn's shoulder, and Einar took his legs. "On three." He lifted the shoulder. Bjorn went rigid and then slack.

"He passed out."

"Good."

They straightened his body, and Rune saw that his right arm lay at an unusual angle.

"His arm is broken." Einar sounded disgusted.

"Ja, I see." Rune ripped his shirt open and tore it off. "I am going to tie it to him so I can carry him back to the house." He smoothed wet hair back from Bjorn's pale face. A bump was already swelling on his forehead.

"He's too heavy for you to carry," Einar said. "I'll get the team. They'll have stopped at the barn."

Rune looked up at the tree, still burning. "Lift him so I can get this shirt under him." Together they wrestled the shirt in place and tied the sleeves and front hems together to hold Bjorn's arm snug against his body. *Lord, give me strength.*

Bjorn shook and his eyes fluttered open.

"Easy now."

Terror filled his son's eyes. "Far? Far? I cannot hear." His voice rose to a scream.

That answered one question. Rune nodded and patted Bjorn's good arm. He looked to Einar. "How about if we both carry him?"

Einar shook his head. "Might break that arm worse. You stay here, and I will get the horses."

He took off running before Rune could even answer him. Bjorn was shaking so much that Rune lay down beside him to try to warm him. Under the wagon might be better than here in the rain, with big drops falling from the tree branches.

"C-c-cold."

"I know."

"M-my arm."

Rune raised up on one elbow so Bjorn could see his face. "Broken."

"I-I c-an n-not h-hear you." Tears leaked from his eyes, running into his ears.

Rune nodded. *Oh, Lord, send Signe out here. What can I do? Please let my son have his hearing back.* For a man who so rarely prayed, he sure was assaulting the gates of heaven now. Had the terrified horses really stopped at the barn like Einar thought? He'd sounded so sure. How long had he and his son been lying here, both of them shivering now? Had Einar made it back to the barn?

"Far, Far, where are you?"

Knute was coming. He could help warm his brother.

"Over here, by the creek."

Panting, Knute ran along the trail. The rain had turned into a steady drizzle, which might be good for the crops but wasn't helping Bjorn's rapid loss of body heat.

"Mor is coming, but I ran faster. We started out when we saw the horses at the barn. I will show her the way." He stared at his trembling brother.

"Is Mor bringing blankets?" Rune asked.

"Ja, one."

"Did you see Einar?"

"Ja, he was almost to the barn."

Relief was so warming, Rune almost stopped shivering. "Go show your mor where we are." Knute was off and running before Rune finished his instructions. He looked down at his shaking son. He couldn't even ask if there were other injuries. "Mor is coming and she has a blanket, so we can carry you out of here." They had to carry him at least as far as the wagon.

Each minute seemed more like ten or twenty. How could time move so slowly? The fear and his constant, heavy weariness began to take their toll. *Hurry, Signe.*

He heard her huffing and puffing before he opened his eyes.

Hearing her before seeing her bathed him in relief. "Thank God you are here."

She dropped to her knees beside him.

"Mor, Mor, you're here." Bjorn tried to reach for her and then realized both his arms were restricted. He sniffed back the tears but then gave up and sobbed. "I cannot hear."

She patted his face and nodded, brushing away her own tears. She spread the quilt over both of them. "We will get you home as fast as we can." Her nodding and tremulous smile spread comfort even when her son couldn't hear her words. She looked to Rune. "A lightning strike?"

"Ja, right across the creek. I think the force of the blast is what did it. The horses panicked and tore for the barn, and they must have knocked him into the tree, where he broke his arm and hit his head. I have heard of this before, and the hearing usually comes back after a while. We can pray for that."

"I wish I had brought you a jacket." While she talked, she gently felt Bjorn's arm, nodding and smiling at her son as she moved her fingers, searching out injuries through the shirt tied around him. "We can slip the quilt under him, and the three of us can carry him to the wagon. Difficult but possible, right?"

"Ja, that is what I thought." Rune smiled up at her. "You left Leif to watch Tante?"

She nodded and pushed herself upright, her thickening waist more visible as she arched her back to stretch. Should she be running and carrying a heavy load like this? He was so accustomed to her taking care of things without even a whimper that concern felt like a load dropped on his shoulders. *Please, God . . .* He knelt beside their wounded son. "I will lift him, and you and Knute slide the quilt under him."

It worked; the quilt was crooked, but it was under him.

Signe patted Bjorn's cheek, a mother's touch. "Now we will

carry you. Knute, you take that corner and Rune, this one, and I will carry both corners at his feet." She looked to Rune, who nodded, fighting to get his breath back. They all leaned over, took their quilt corners, and lifted.

"Shame a road was not cleared to the creek. This trail . . ." Rune shook his head.

He hated himself just now! Signe working so hard and long while in the family way. His boys, working like men with no time to even go fishing. And he, struggling to keep up with muscles that had never worked so hard. His eyes seemed to be getting worse, but there was no clear way to tell how much, if any. Why, oh why, had he gotten them into this?

"I need to stop," Signe huffed a few minutes later. "How much farther?"

"Lay him down very gently. One, two, three."

They all gasped for breath, Rune and Knute leaning over. Rune turned to listen. Surely that was the jingle of the harness. "I think Einar is here with the horses. Let us go again, on three."

They hoisted Bjorn off the ground and carried him step by painful step up the last of the trail to where the team waited.

Rune glanced at the horses as he passed. Ears swiveling, swishing tails, the team was obviously restless or fearful after their wild rout. "Go talk to the team," he told Knute. "They need some gentling."

"Rune, climb up in the wagon bed, and we will hand him over the wagon gate," Einar ordered.

Bjorn looked wildly around. Then he took a deep breath and almost shouted, "Far, I think I can help if you keep me from falling. My legs are not broken."

"We can try. Good thing you are not any bigger."

By the time they had him sitting then lying on the makeshift bed in the wagon, they were all puffing and panting. Bjorn's lip was bleeding again from his impact with the tree, so Signe took a handkerchief from her apron pocket and folded it, pantomimed putting it in her mouth and clamping down on it, then held it out to Bjorn. He clamped down on it.

"Should have done that before," she muttered as she climbed up into the wagon beside him. "Rune, you sit on the other side, and we'll cushion him as we can."

As sharply as he felt the jolts of the wagon wheels over the rough trail, Rune was not surprised when Bjorn slumped against him.

"Better this than awake," Signe whispered, then shook her head and spoke in a normal tone. "Why am I whispering? He cannot hear me anyway."

When Einar stopped the team by the house, after an eternity of jolting, Rune reached for her hand and squeezed it.

She squeezed back and raised her voice. "Is there a doctor near Benson's Corner?"

"No, the closest is in Blackduck. You want I should ride to get him, if he's available?"

"Or we take him there in the wagon," Signe suggested.

"Or we can set the arm here. Cheaper that way."

Rune closed his eyes. Set his son's arm here to save a dollar? What was Einar thinking? Did he want to risk the arm not healing properly?

Chapter 12

*T*hey should not have been out there working like that on
the Lord's Day.

The thought kept nagging at Signe. While back home they'd
not attended church every Sunday, they did often, and she always
thought of the day as taking time for the rest the Bible spoke of.
But here there had been no mention of the day being Sunday,
and work went on as usual. And look what had happened. Her
mor would have said it was their own fault.

But it was her son who was paying the price. An innocent!

Einar entered the parlor, where Bjorn lay sleeping on his
pallet.

Signe asked, "Do you have some spirits here? I can make a
medicine that—"

"No!" Einar roared. "There will be no spirits in this house,
on this land, ever! No alcohol! Do you understand?"

"Not to drink. Given with honey as a dose, it helps pain."

Einar's face grew red. "I said no!"

Rune's voice rumbled as evenly as ever. "We must get him
to a doctor."

Einar seemed to settle down a bit. "I say we should set his arm here. Not that difficult, I should think."

Of course he would think that. It was cheaper, and it wouldn't keep him or Rune from his precious logging. And quite possibly poor Bjorn, bearing the brunt of all this, would have a crippled arm for the rest of his life, or worse.

Signe looked to Rune, who looked as puzzled as she felt. His shrug told her the decision was hers to make. She was urging Gerd to step forward, to be strong; in her own way, she too would now step forward.

"No." She said it firmly. "We will bind the arm tight so it cannot move, and Rune can take him to the doctor on Rosie. She does ride double, doesn't she?"

Einar scowled. "Ja, she rides double. But I will take him, because I know the doctor and where he lives. I can go directly there. At least it will cost less than his coming out here. Faster too."

She heaved a sigh. Was that a victory to celebrate? Most important, was she doing what was best for her boy? "We will splint it and bind it to his chest. The ride should be easier on him than the wagon. The wagon springs are practically gone." There, the decision was made. She looked at Einar. "Do you have any smooth flat pieces of lumber out there, the length from his shoulder to elbow?"

"I know where some are. The kindling box. I split some." Leif scrambled to his feet and ran out of the room.

Rune called, "Bring several so we can choose. Knute, help Onkel Einar saddle up."

The door slammed behind them.

Bjorn blinked and opened his eyes. "Hurts."

"I know," Signe said only to herself. She pushed herself to her feet and paused a moment. Sucking in a deep breath, she headed for the shelf where she had gathered up any medical supplies she'd found, including the strips of sheeting she had torn and rolled in case someone was injured. At least they had that.

Leif ran back into the house with an armload of kindling, the door slamming behind him. She paused for a moment to listen for Gerd's normal shriek, but it didn't come. She chose two pieces of wood that matched and wrapped towels around them to pad them well. She gestured what she needed to Rune. "You hold his arm right here, with one hand under his shoulder, and use the other to lift his elbow, here."

"I need a third hand."

"I know. I will place one splint on the top and the other underneath. You ready? You'll have to hold the splints too so I can wrap."

"Ja."

She glanced at Bjorn's face. His eyes told his fear. "We will work fast." She paused a moment. "Now."

Rune slid his hands where she told him, and she laid the splints in place, making sure she had room to bend Bjorn's arm. Her son cried out. Chewing her lip, she wrapped the strips snugly around his arm. After tying off the ends, she positioned the bent arm over his chest.

"Now for the sling." She folded a pillowcase into a triangle and slid the triangle under his arm. "Bjorn, sit up." But of course he couldn't hear her; she kept forgetting.

She and Rune lifted him into a sitting position. He moaned. The bulging lump on his head would make an egg look small. She wrapped torn strips of sheeting around Bjorn's middle and around the sling, binding it all snugly in place.

"Do you think he can walk out the door?" she asked.

"Let's see."

Rune slipped a hand under Bjorn's good arm and tried to

lift him up. Signe grabbed the boy's waistband in both hands and pulled. Apparently Bjorn was alert enough to know what was happening, for he took slow unsteady steps, his parents keeping him erect. Leif held the door for them, then followed them over to the horse waiting just beyond the porch.

Bjorn whimpered, then groaned. "Nei, hurts." Signe kissed his forehead.

Knute stood at Rosie's head, holding her firmly.

Einar positioned himself on the far side. "In case he slides clear over the top."

Bjorn was trying to assist—feebly, but trying. Rune slipped Bjorn's left foot into the stirrup. Together he and Signe boosted him up; Bjorn cried out again in pain, but he got his right leg swung across the saddle. He was on!

Einar came around to their side. "Tie him on."

Signe hurried into the house and got another roll of bandaging. Gerd screeched from her bedroom.

"I can't right now," Signe called and ran back outside.

Einar had swung himself up behind Bjorn. His legs both dangled free behind the stirrups. He looked absolutely, thoroughly displeased.

Signe and Rune slipped Bjorn's feet into the stirrups and tied his legs to the stirrup leathers with the bandaging. Now Bjorn would stay on until someone untied him, even if he fainted or fell asleep.

"He might need to stay there overnight or something." Einar stared down at Signe. "But I'm not going to. We go back into the woods tomorrow like usual." He turned Rosie's head, and they were on their way. The horse's *splack-splack-splack* in the mud grew fainter.

Signe's heart ached as they rode away. *I should be the one going with him.*

When Rune said they must pray for their son, it was all she could do not to shake her head. Why bother now? Where was God when He sent that lightning bolt? If He could see all and know all, why would He injure her son like this? If that arm didn't heal correctly, Bjorn would suffer all of his life. This wouldn't have happened if they had not left Norway and come here.

"Signe!"

She turned and forced herself up the porch steps. They needed a railing on the steps if they were ever going to get Gerd outside again. What an impossible idea—Gerd couldn't even stand up by herself let alone walk up or down steps.

When Gerd screeched again, Signe told her she'd be there in a minute. *Now's the time*, she promised herself. *Tante Gerd, if there is any way possible, you are going to get stronger, starting right now.*

In the bedroom, she folded back the blanket and sheet, then extended a hand. "Come, take my hand, and I'll help you sit up." There would be no more spending all day in bed. And no more meals in bed.

"I-I can't."

"Ja, you must. Take my hand."

The glare Gerd shot at her would have stopped a charging moose. Signe waited, hand out.

"I cannot do that."

Signe steeled herself. Just assisting as usual would be far easier. "Ja, you can. Take my hand."

Still glaring, Gerd reached for the offered hand. Signe barely pulled, but it was enough to get the woman started moving, and she sat up.

"Just like when you need to use the pot, you stand up, and then turn to sit in the chair."

"I'm hungry."

"Ja, I'm sure you are. We will sit you on the commode, then move to the chair, and I will bring you some bread and jam. The coffee is probably cold by now. I have been taking care of my Bjorn, and I let the fire die down. It will be a while before the stove is hot again."

"What happened to him?"

"Lightning struck a tree near him when he was watering the horses. They panicked and knocked him into the brush. He broke his arm and cannot hear anymore."

"Why didn't anyone come tell me?"

"We were busy caring for him. Plus, you were asleep, and we didn't want to wake you." Signe returned to the kitchen and rattled the grate to liven the coals, then added kindling and smaller hunks of wood. After adjusting the damper, she returned to the bedroom to help Gerd up from the commode.

"Back to bed."

"Nei. You can eat more easily in the chair."

"I want to go back to bed."

Signe ignored her and together they shuffled two steps to the chair. One day soon, Signe planned to move the chair to the window so Tante Gerd could look out over the garden. Someday she wanted to plant trees out in the yard, especially fast-growing ones to shade the house. But right now, she wanted to be with Bjorn, who would soon see the doctor.

Gerd sat glaring at her.

"You want a glass of buttermilk while we wait for the coffee to heat?" When Gerd didn't respond, Signe shrugged at her glare. "Suit yourself."

Shaking her head, she returned to the kitchen, where she looked up at the clock on the wall. Five o'clock. She should be making supper. The rabbit and dumplings she had planned never got started. At least the rabbit was waiting out in the well house. Fried it would be.

Where were Rune and the boys? That thought jerked her back to Bjorn. Were they there yet? How was he? Did the doctor have some of the newer pain medicines she'd heard of?

She served Gerd her bread and jam and returned to the kitchen to feed the fire again. On a whim, she poured two cups of coffee when it was hot and returned to the bedroom.

"I had a broken arm once," Gerd said.

Signe nearly dropped the coffee cups. "When?"

"Back in Norway. Mor set it, and it healed up."

"How old were you?" Signe sat on the edge of the bed and sipped her coffee. How tempting it was to lie back on a real bed for a change.

Gerd shrugged. "A child." She propped her elbows on the arms of the chair and sipped her coffee. "Supper?"

"Fried rabbit."

Gerd nodded and drank her coffee.

When Signe finished her coffee, she picked up the empty plate and cups to return to the kitchen. "I'm going to the barn to see what Rune and the boys are doing. You want to stay up or go back to bed first?"

"Bed."

Signe helped her back into bed. Gerd had actually sounded— what? Almost pleasant. Would wonders never cease?

Rune and Knute were in the machine shed, sharpening the axes and the saw. Rune had taught Knute to use the grinding wheel, so he was filing the saw teeth. Leif had let the cow and heifer into the barn for milking. The heifer didn't like to be left in the pasture alone, so she was getting trained to use her own stanchion. A scoop of grain was a good reward.

"We need wood split," Signe said, wishing she could stay

here where no one screamed at her. The whine of the sandstone sounded pleasant compared with Gerd.

"Figured. I'll be up to the house to do that," her husband answered. Was that a smile or a grimace?

"Knute can manage the grinder?"

Rune nodded. "Ja, he is capable." He raised his voice to be heard over the scream of axe on stone.

Peaceful. That was what she felt down here at the barn and machine shed. Like working in the garden. That was peaceful too. She watched Rune deftly file the teeth on the seven-foot crosscut saw. "Has Leif fed the chickens yet?"

"Nei, nor gathered the eggs. He was cleaning up around here, but the cow told him it was time to milk. Since the rain has stopped, I thought after supper we could all work in the garden. You want to?"

She'd planned on going after the dust in the attic so they could move out of the parlor and up to sleep where there would eventually be beds. A sturdy set of stairs would make access easier, but the ladder was better than nothing. "Ja, I do." Keeping busy was the only way to keep her mind off Bjorn. What if the jolting of the ride made his arm worse? Surely the doctor would not keep him there. When might he and Einar possibly be home again?

"I need to go make biscuits."

"Good, you make the best biscuits."

She turned back and smiled at Rune. Compliments as rare as his demanded to be savored like a treasure. "Takk."

She was just sliding the pan of biscuits into the oven when she heard Leif laugh. No one laughed much around here. Then came the slam of axe heads and the thunk of split wood being tossed in a pile. Within minutes Leif brought in his first armload and dumped it in the woodbox. "Smells good in here. Knute and Far said the sow might farrow anytime. I want to watch."

"She will probably wait until late at night."

"Far said that too. Maybe me and Knute could sleep at the barn."

"Maybe." She watched him run out the back door, the screen slamming behind him. She needed to remind him that Tante Gerd did not like the screen door banging like that.

Setting the table, her mind leaped back to the man carrying her eldest son to the doctor. Were they there by now? How long would it take to ride five miles? He wouldn't lope that horse all the way, would he? Oh, so many questions.

She lifted the pieces of rabbit from the frying pan onto a platter to set in the warming oven and checked the biscuits. Almost done. She sprinkled flour into the drippings and stirred to smooth it out for gravy, then stirred milk into the sizzling pan. She had made enough biscuits for both buttering and smothering in milk gravy.

When Leif dumped another load into the woodbox, she told him to call the others in for supper.

"One more load."

"All right, but I am dishing up now." Buttermilk to drink, biscuits still hot, and she had poured the gravy into a pitcher. With the food all on the table, she stood back and nodded. "Oh, jam."

Knute brought in an armload of wood too, and they lined up at the sink to wash. Leif splashed water at his brother, giggling when Knute splashed back.

"Enough." Their far's voice held laughter too.

"Come and eat." Signe could feel a smile twitching to be let loose.

"Mor, if we carried Tante Gerd in her chair to the table, could she have supper with us?"

Signe stared at her youngest son. The woman had done nothing but holler at them, and here Leif wanted her to join them. Only Leif. She looked at Rune, who was nodding, his face smiling without moving his lips.

"Not tonight, but we will ask her and help her get strong enough to join us. That is very kind of you."

They all sat down at the table.

"I think we should say grace and pray for Bjorn and Onkel Einar to come back safe and soon." Rune bowed his head, so the others did too.

Signe swallowed the words that lurked at the back of her tongue. If Rune wanted to pray, so be it, but if left to her preference, she would not. Why bother?

"Our Father in heaven, please bless this food and all of this house. Takk for Signe making us such good meals, and we ask you to bring Onkel Einar and Bjorn back safe. Takk there is a doctor to help Bjorn's arm. Make it heal properly. Amen."

After supper, Signe joined the others out in the garden to hoe and pull weeds.

"The chickens and the pigs sure like the weeds." Knute loaded their pile into a wheelbarrow.

"Can we sleep down at the barn tonight?" Leif tossed his pile on top of the others. "To see if Daisy has her babies. I want to watch." The boys had named the sow after her favorite flowering weeds.

Rune shrugged, then shook his head. "Perhaps tomorrow night. So much going on tonight."

The boys frowned, but that was all.

When the long dusk had nearly slipped into dark, the boys took a lantern down to the barn so they could see the sow.

"She was up eating the weeds," Leif announced when they returned to the house.

"Then she won't be farrowing tonight," Rune told them.

Knute stared at his far. "How do you know that?"

"She will stop eating and get restless, even build a nest of sorts. When she is ready, she'll lie down."

"Really?"

Rune smiled. "We'll keep checking on her. But right now, it's time for bed."

After the boys left the kitchen, Signe looked at the clock for the millionth time. She knew she'd never be able to sleep until horse and riders arrived home. She went into the parlor, where the boys were sound asleep. Rune looked to be joining them soon.

"Come to bed. Remember they might not return until morning."

She shook her head. "Einar will not miss a day out in the woods. Horses can see in the dark, you know."

He patted the pallet beside him. "Just lie down and rest, then."

She folded back the sheet on Bjorn's pallet so it would be ready for him. What if he was deaf or crippled for life? Or both?

Chapter 13

"Help!"

Signe heard it again. "Help us now!"

Onkel Einar! It wasn't a dream. She shook Rune and staggered to her feet. "Coming!" she called.

She headed for the door, glancing back to see Rune shoving his feet into his boots. The clouds had long since moved on, and brilliant moonlight made it possible to see Knute getting up too.

Einar sat behind the saddle as before, holding a sleeping Bjorn, who was slumped back against his chest. The moonlight painted his face in shadows.

Signe shook her son's knee. "Wake up, Bjorn. Wake up." She'd forgotten again that he could not hear.

"The doc gave him a sedative, so he slept much of the way home." Einar shook his charge carefully. "Come on, Bjorn. We're home."

Bjorn muttered and blinked. "M-mor."

Rune went around the horse and shook Bjorn's leg. "Swing your leg over the saddle, and you can slide down. Come on, wake up so we can get you to bed."

"You got him?" Einar asked. "I'll get down and help. Better if he stays asleep."

Between them, they dragged Bjorn off the horse and half carried him up the steps and into the house, where they laid him on his pallet.

"I'll take care of your horse." Knute left before Einar could answer.

Bjorn's whole arm, from his shoulder nearly to his wrist, was encased in a thick white cast. Signe paused only a moment to admire it—it looked very neat and professional—before she knelt and untied her son's boots so she could pull them off. "Takk, tusen takk. What did the doctor say?"

"He said you did a good job splinting and stabilizing that arm. Made his job easier. Bjorn is not to use the arm for six weeks." Einar shook his head. "That's a long time. Too long."

Signe nodded. "Ja, but he will be able to use his arm again. That is the important thing."

"Mor, thirsty." Bjorn's voice was oddly loud. Signe realized anew that he could not hear himself speak.

Rune dashed to the kitchen and returned with a cup of water. "Anything else?"

"Nei, takk." She helped Bjorn sit up so he could drink and then laid him back down.

Einar handed her a few paper packets. "Doctor said to give him this for pain. He figured we'd need some on the way home, so I used one of the packets already. Figured the ride would be easier if he slept. Long ride in the dark, even with the moon."

"Did you eat?"

"Could use something."

"I will fix you something." In the kitchen she lit a kerosene lamp so she could see to slice bread and spread butter and jam. She handed it to Einar, who had followed her. "I could go out to the well house and bring in buttermilk." She glanced at the stove. "Or heat the coffee."

"Neither. I'm going to bed." He blew out a breath. "Sun will be up before we know it."

She watched him shuffle to the bedroom. "Takk."

Gratitude swelled her heart. He had brought her son back with no other accidents. She blew out the lamp and returned to the parlor, where Rune sat beside his son, arms around his bent legs and resting his chin on his knees. He looked up at her. "Thank God for bringing them home safe. So many things could have happened."

"You shouldn't have been out there working on Sunday." She knelt to feel Bjorn's forehead. Cool, no fever, not that she expected one. Just a reflex action.

She should not have said that. It was not Rune's fault they had been working on a Sunday. Was God vengeful and punishing them? If that were so, why punish an innocent boy instead of the man who decreed they would work until they dropped?

She removed her shoes and lay down. Dawn would be here too soon to bother undressing.

Knute was nearly asleep when he muttered, "Did you check on Daisy?"

"Ja, I did. No babies yet." Rune removed his boots and lay down again. "We must be thankful."

True, but . . . it should not have happened in the first place. Signe rolled onto her side only to feel the baby moving around. Could babies get uncomfortable? This one certainly was letting her know. A wave of weariness washed over her, leaving her drowning in the need to sleep, to rest. She would think about all this tomorrow. Not that sunrise was very far away.

She groaned at the rooster's crow. It seemed she'd just fallen asleep, but an urgent need for the outhouse brought her to her feet. Barefoot she hurried out the back door. Back outside, she paused to breathe the fragrances of a summer morning. Green growing things, pine trees, split wood, blooming wild flowers—both daisies and sun-gold dandelions—all overlaid with a touch of both cows and pigs.

The rooster crowed again. The cow bellowed that it was milking time.

Past time to get going.

"Morning, Mor." Knute came out the door as she stopped at the bottom step.

"The cow said she's waiting."

"Then I'm late."

Leif came out behind him. "Bjorn is waking up."

"Good." She heard the grate rattling. "Far?"

"Ja, he said he'd start the stove. What is for breakfast?"

"Fried cornmeal mush and eggs."

"From the well house?" At her nod, he grinned. "I'll get them."

"Takk." She watched him scamper off toward the barn.

Rune was adding more wood to the fire and had already pulled the coffeepot over to heat. He smiled at her, but weariness still sagged his eyes. "Leif went to check on Daisy?"

"Ja. How is Bjorn?"

"Probably needs the outhouse. You start breakfast, and I'll go help him."

"Takk." She reached for two frying pans and scooped lard from the crock where she kept the bacon drippings. Leaving the pan to heat, she hurried to open the back door for Leif, who had his hands full.

"I'll be right back with the cream. Do you want milk or buttermilk too?" he asked.

"No porridge this morning, so the cream will be enough." Out of the corner of her eye, she saw him turn and grab the screen door before it slammed. While her smile didn't quite reach her face, she could feel it. She sliced the cornmeal brick she had set in bread pans and laid the slices in the sizzling grease. Eggs would go in the other pan.

Was Onkel Einar up and out already? He didn't usually sleep in, but then, he wasn't usually up until just before dawn.

"Morning, Mor." Bjorn sounded so strange and distant. His far stood right beside him, ready to catch him if he started to collapse.

She turned to smile at her son and watched them go outside. Breakfast would be easy for Bjorn to eat, no meat to cut.

Still no noise from the bedroom. Was Onkel Einar that weary, or was he sick? Should she knock on the door? Surely Tante Gerd would be demanding help any moment.

Leif and Knute came in together, both looking confused. "Can't Bjorn hear us?"

"Nei." Signe pointed to the sink. "Did you strain the milk?"

"Ja, but the pans need to be skimmed so we can pour the milk into them. We got enough cream to churn butter again," Knute announced. "You think Bjorn is always going to be deaf?"

"I wish I knew. Only time will tell."

"Onkel Einar said to call him when breakfast is ready. He's down sharpening another saw." Leif scrubbed his hands. "Daisy is still eating. I think she likes being by herself. She doesn't have to fight for food."

Signe slid a plate of fried mush in the warming oven and cracked eggs into the pan of fat. "Knute, pour the milk."

Bjorn and Rune made their way back into the house, Bjorn with his jaw clenched against the pain. He took his regular seat at the table.

"Leif, run and get Onkel Einar." Signe motioned out the door. He took off, shoving open the screen door, but with a slick turn caught it before it slammed shut. He grinned at her and jumped to the ground, ignoring the steps.

Uff da, to have such energy.

When Einar came through the door, he nodded at seeing Bjorn at the table. He dropped his voice and looked at Signe. "Can he hear at all yet?"

"Nei." She slid the fried eggs onto a platter and set it on the table, along with the platter of fried mush. "There is syrup or jam for the mush, so help yourselves." The look on her boys' faces at the mention of syrup made Signe glad she'd traded some of the butter for it at Benson's store.

As usual Einar filled his plate full before passing it on to Rune, who took far less and slid mush and eggs onto Bjorn's plate, giving him a smile of encouragement.

"He can't use his right arm at all, huh?" Leif asked.

"Not for several weeks. And then it will be weak." Signe cracked more eggs into the pan, thankful she had made plenty of fried mush.

Einar glared at Leif. No talking at the table.

Signe filled the men's coffee cups and set the pot back on the stove. She'd just slid the next batch of eggs onto the platter when the summons came from the bedroom.

"I'll be there in a minute."

"I need you now!"

"Coming." Sliding the pans to the cooler part of the stove and wiping her hands on her apron, she hurried to the bedroom. They had closed the windows again, so the room smelled bad and was stuffy. "Good morning."

Gerd shook her head. "Help me."

Signe flipped back the covers and held out her hand, delib-

erately making Gerd reach for it, earning herself another glare.
"Come on, sit up."

She waited until Gerd reached for her hand and used it to
help pull herself up.

"I will help you." *But I will not do it for you anymore.* "Good,
good." She nodded as Gerd inched her feet to the side. Signe
helped her twist and scoot toward the edge. When her feet hit
the floor, Gerd panted, hanging her head.

"You are trying to kill me!"

"Just trying to help you get stronger. Leif suggested the
men carry you in your chair to the table so you can eat with
all of us."

"Nei, I cannot do that."

"We will see."

When Gerd finished her business, Signe helped her stand and
moved her to the chair.

"Bed!"

"Breakfast is ready. We are having fried mush and eggs. How
many eggs do you want? And syrup or jam on the mush?"

"Two. Syrup. No syrup for a long time."

By the time Signe had served Gerd, the others had finished
eating. "More coffee?"

"Ja." Einar held up his cup. "Soon as we finish here, Rune,
you and me will go out and start limbing those trees that are
down. Saws are all sharp for tomorrow." He narrowed his eyes
and looked at Knute. "You think he can handle an axe for the
limbing?"

"Ja, I can do that." Knute nearly bounced in his chair.

Rune looked at Signe. "The garden is clean, so we can keep
it up."

He is too young for this, she thought. *He can split wood, but
that is different. Rune, why do you put me on the spot like this?*

She gave Einar a stolid look. "He is not a man yet. Who will do his chores here?"

"I can milk the cow," Leif offered.

"And I expect Bjorn out there again." Einar sipped his hot coffee. "He still has one good arm. He can drag limbs to the pile one-handed."

Signe's doubt and concern fell aside as fury slammed into her. "Absolutely not! He remains here at home."

Einar's voice rose. "I give the orders here. You seem to forget that."

"And I am responsible for my son's welfare. When he is alert and well enough to move freely, we will consider it. Today he remains home to rest."

Einar's glare burned into her.

Her glare burned just as hotly back at him.

He leapt to his feet, his coffee not quite finished, and stormed out.

Rune stared at the door. "I'm not sure you should have done that. He paid our way."

"He did not buy slaves. If you will not stand firm for your son, I guess I will have to."

Rune did not reply. He stood up and silently plopped his hat on his head on his way out the door.

What a mess, and it was all Signe's fault. She should never have said that. She had thought it a hundred times, but she never should have said it.

She glanced at Bjorn, who looked about to fall off his chair. "Come, I will fix your medicine, and you can go back to bed."

Of course he could not hear her. Why did she keep forgetting? Gerd would just have to wait.

Signe poured the doctor's powder into a glass of water, stirred it vigorously, and handed it to Bjorn. He looked at her, then at the medicine, and wrinkled his nose, but he gulped it down.

Leif looked at Bjorn. "Should I help him back to bed?"

"That would be good, ja. Takk."

She watched while Leif took Bjorn's good hand and pointed toward the parlor, then mimed sleeping. They both stood and walked to the parlor. Signe followed a few feet behind and watched as the younger brother laid back the sheet and motioned for Bjorn to lie down. A bed would be so much easier for him to get in and out of. Bjorn grimaced and grunted as he dropped to his knees and propped himself up with his left hand. Surely a bench or a chair could help him.

Signe went to Gerd's room.

"What took you so long?" Gerd grumbled.

"I had to give Bjorn his pain medicine."

Gerd shook her head. "Must hurt a lot."

Signe removed the tray and set it on the chest of drawers so she could help Gerd back to bed. The older woman was asleep before Signe made it to the kitchen. Leif was putting the dishes in the dishpan on the stove.

"Takk," she said.

He smiled at her and handed her a plate of breakfast that had been in the warming oven.

"Tusen takk." She sat down at the table and poured syrup on the mush. The egg yolks were hard, but she ignored that and finished her meal in peace. Leif even poured her a cup of coffee. She smiled at him. "You are a good helper. Takk again. I think there might be bread you can eat with butter and jam."

With another grin, he fixed his treat and sat down with her. "If it looks like Daisy might farrow tonight, can Knute and I sleep in the barn?"

"If you want." She propped her elbows on the table and sipped her coffee. "Knute might be too tired, you know."

He shrugged and finished off his bread. "Good thing it rained. The garden liked it."

"Ja, the weeds will really grow too. We need to hill up the potatoes and the pumpkins. Do you know how?"

"Ja. I will. How long will Bjorn sleep?"

"The longer the better." She picked up her plate and put her dishes in the dishpan. The two of them finished clearing the table.

"He will be able to hear again, won't he?"

"I hope so. Oh, I hope so."

Chapter 14

Rune strode along with an axe on his shoulder, sometimes glancing down at Knute, who held a lighter axe. The thought of his younger son on the way to a man's work set his insides to grinding. Not that he wasn't already doing a man's work with sawing and splitting wood and all the other chores he did around the farm. He learned quickly. But—Rune still shuddered. The accident with Bjorn was too new, and the uncertain outcome made it hard for him to sleep.

Knute could haul branches to the burning piles, so he needn't use that axe. After all, Bjorn spent a lot of his time out here doing just that.

A crow greeted them when they reached the cleared land. Einar led the way to the felled trees that awaited limbing. He looked down at Knute. "You start cutting off the limbs about a third of the way down from the top, going upward, then you can drag the limbs over to those piles. We'll burn the brush piles when winter comes. Chop from the underside and close to the trunk."

Knute nodded and made his way to the fallen trees. Rune

started limbing the lowest branches and worked toward his son.

"They look even bigger on the ground." Knute turned to Rune. "Some of these branches are bigger around than other trees. Shame to waste all that stove wood. Leif and me could cut these up with the saw."

"Good idea, but I think Onkel Einar figures that takes too long."

Knute shrugged and headed for the upper part of the fallen giant. "Far, how will we ever roll the log over to do the branches underneath?"

"You'll see."

They both started chopping. Every once in a while, Rune would look up to see how Knute was doing. Once the boy was stretching his arms over his head, another time he was wiping sweat from his face. Einar worked on another tree, the steady ring of their axes against green wood now a familiar beat after these weeks in the woods.

"How your hands doing, boy?" Einar asked when they were nearly done with the first tree.

Knute wiped the sweat from his forehead with the back of his gloved hand. "Not so bad."

Rune stopped swinging his axe and went to his son. "Pull off those gloves and let me see." He knew his son well enough to know he would keep going until he dropped.

Knute flinched when he pulled off the leather gloves and held out both hands. Several blisters rose on each palm.

"I think you've done enough chopping for today. Go back to the house and have Mor take care of those."

"But what about dragging branches over to the pile?"

"Ja, good idea." Einar nodded as he spoke. "We got plenty to drag now."

Knute looked at Rune. "What will Mor do to my hands?"

"Drain the blisters, soak them for a while, and then she'll bandage your hands. Can't afford infection." He glanced over at Einar, who shrugged and turned away.

"I can work another couple hours anyway," Knute suggested. "See how low the sun is?"

Einar wiped his forehead and reset his hat. He raised his axe and buried it in the next branch. "You can start a new pile closer by. Over there." He waved an arm.

Knute gingerly pulled his gloves back on and leaned over to grab a branch with each hand.

Rune looked off to the west, where the sun had started its evening plunge to the horizon. Trees blocked their view, so the light was already dimming. He watched his tired son for a moment. He should have insisted Knute head for the house immediately. Instead he was letting a woman do what he as a father should be doing: standing up for his boys. His cowardice—that was what it was, cowardice—made him angry with himself.

"That's a good place for the next pile," Einar called.

Knute dropped his load and headed back for more.

The next time Rune looked up, his son was staring at the growing pile, his chest heaving, head drooping. "That's enough, Knute. Go on back to the house. Tell your mor we'll be there in an hour or so."

Knute nodded and trudged toward the road.

"Did you check your snares this morning?" Rune called after him.

Knute waved his hand and nodded but kept on walking.

Einar called a halt some time later. The shadows were long in the woods as they walked back to the house, but dusk had yet to appear between the trees. Evening birdsong heralded the closing of the day. When they cleared the woods, the cow stood outside the barn door. They set the axes in the machine shed and headed to the house for a drink. They met Leif on the back porch.

"Any change in the sow?" Onkel Einar asked.

Leif shrugged. "Not that I could see. The hen that was setting now has three chicks. There are three more to hatch."

"What are you doing next?"

"Milking. Mor said to give Knute time off. She wrapped his hands all up."

Einar shook his head. "Needs to toughen up."

He and Rune pulled the screen door open and stopped at the sink. Rune took the pump handle, and after a few pumps, water gushed into the glass he held. He handed that one to Einar and filled his own. They both drank, turning to lean against the sink.

Signe paused in the far doorway. "You're back."

"How is Bjorn?"

"Sleeping again. I gave him more of the laudanum." She shook her head. "He can't hear yet." She looked to Einar, who had refilled his glass. "Did you ask the doctor about the hearing?"

"He said it can take a couple days or longer, or sometimes not at all."

Signe wiped her face with the edge of her apron. "Uff da." She closed her eyes for an instant. "Supper is not ready. Not for an hour or so."

"I'm going down to put a better edge on the axes." Einar left, carrying another glass of water.

Rune set his glass down. "I better get to splitting wood."

"Ja, Leif just isn't strong enough to do much splitting."

"He can cut kindling when he gets done milking." Rune

stretched his shoulders and neck. "Shame we can't get enough split ahead. What is Knute doing?"

"The rest of the chores. There's a bucket of skim milk to haul to the barn for the pigs. We're having ham for supper. I cut into the last smoked haunch. Knute ran his snares, and there are two rabbits to dress out. He hung them in the well house."

Rune looked in the woodbox. "Enough to finish making supper?"

"Maybe."

So what to do first? Dress the rabbits so the meat did not go bad. With one boy sleeping and one with blistered hands . . . He took the knives out of the drawer and ran his thumb across the blades. They needed sharpening.

"Is there a whetstone here?"

"Signe!" The screech came from the bedroom.

He looked at his wife. "Does she always scream like that?"

Signe nodded as she dug the whetstone out of a drawer and handed it to him, then headed for the bedroom.

He would much rather work in the woods.

The breeze in the shade out on the back porch lifted his spirits as he sat down. What a shame they could not bring Tante Gerd out here. He spit on the whetstone and began rubbing a knife edge against it in a circular motion.

He studied the blade on the stone. What was he seeing, really? Not enough. He was sharpening this knife expertly because he had been doing it all his life. His hands knew exactly what to do. He could sharpen a blade with his eyes closed, literally. But if he had never done it before, could he see well enough to do so simple a task?

Probably not.

He looked up to see Leif carrying the milk bucket to the well house. Leif wasn't tall enough to hoist the bucket up onto the bench and pour the milk in the flat pans. Rune laid the knife and stone down and hastened to catch up to his son.

He stepped inside the well house. "You need some help?"

Leif turned to grin at his far. "Takk, I just can't reach."

"The counters are high. Nice and cool in here, isn't it?" Rune set the bucket on the bench that lined one wall and held the flat pans, still full, and the strainer.

"Can you carry that bucket of skim milk to the pigs?"

"Who usually does that?" Rune asked.

"Knute. I cleaned the manure out of Daisy's pen. If you don't fill the wheelbarrow so full, it doesn't tip over."

"Good lesson, ja?"

Rune poured the milk through the strainer and into the crock to set in the cold water. "Can you skim the cream?" He nodded toward the pans on the counter.

"If you show me how."

Rune set the cream crock on the counter. "Run up to the house and get that bench I made for you to stand on. I'll carry the skim milk to the barn." Leif scampered off, and Rune picked up the bucket. At five gallons, it was indeed heavy.

Knute came out of the chicken house with a basket of eggs as Rune exited the barn. "The chicks are so cute, but that mama. Good thing I had the bandage on. She would have got me good. I just wanted to see how many more she had."

"Perhaps when they're all hatched we should move her into the other stall so the chicks don't get trampled by the others."

Knute nodded. "Leif and me are going to sleep out here tonight. Daisy wasn't interested in her supper." He walked with Rune up to the well house. "Leif did good milking. If I keep helping in the woods, he'll take good care of the cow. She needs a name." He set the basket of eggs on the bench. "Feels good in here."

Leif set his step stool on the packed earth floor. "Ready, Far."

Rune took a shallow ladle and skimmed the thick cream, pouring it into a crock. He handed the ladle to Leif. "Now you do it."

Knute propped his elbows on the counter and his chin on his closed fists. "Can I go pull branches tomorrow?"

"I think so, as long as you wear your leather gloves and don't use the axe. A day or two, and you should be good. Go ask your mor if she wants anything from the well house for supper besides the milk."

"I got it all." Leif pointed at the flat pans. "Now we wash them good, huh?"

"Along with the milk pail. Take them up to the house. This job needs hot water and soap."

They picked up the rabbits and walked up to the house.

Rune looked out over the hayfield, which seemed to be growing so fast you could see it. Even dusk seemed hesitant tonight, as the golden light bathed the land. In Norway, few people owned this much land, and the mature trees were only in the mountains. By now, the older girls and young women would be up at the seders, the mountain summer farms, with all the cattle, goats, and sheep. Signe had done that when she was younger, before she married. After her first husband died, she had been left to raise their son, Bjorn, alone.

Here, they could have a whole new start. He sat down on the porch to finish sharpening the knives, dreaming of a place of their own. But first they had to work off their tickets from Norway that Einar had paid for.

Knute hung the hind legs of the rabbits over the nails in the post on the porch. "I can do the rabbits."

Rune shook his head. "I'll do it. Your mor will skin *me* if she has to rewrap your hands."

Leif pushed open the screen door. "Mor said to move the hen and her chicks to the stall in the barn, so we need to find a waterer and feeder. She said to ask Onkel Einar where they might be."

"Check down in the cellar first."

Both boys headed for the cellar door on the south side of the house. Rune could hear them laughing. What a good sound. He dressed out the rabbits, then got the cleaver out of the kitchen to cut them up. "You want me to put salt in the soaking water?" he asked Signe.

"Ja. Supper is almost ready."

"I'll tell the boys and Einar."

When all the tasks were complete, Rune ushered the boys inside to wash and joined Bjorn at the table.

"You're looking better," Rune said, knowing Bjorn would not hear. "Sleepy, but better."

"Both tired and from the laudanum." Signe set a platter of fried ham on the table. "Pain makes you tired."

Einar stopped at the sink to wash and took his place at the table. "Ham. Must be the last haunch."

She set beans and gravy on the table, along with a plate of corn bread. "You want milk or coffee?"

"Coffee."

"Milk would be good." Rune nodded. "Is there buttermilk?"

"We're out. Bjorn can churn tomorrow. It's something he can do with one hand." She watched Bjorn trying to cut his ham with a fork. When the ham almost slid off his plate, she looked at Rune and nodded toward Bjorn.

"Here, let me help you with that." Rune leaned closer and cut his son's meat. "I should have thought about that."

"Takk." Bjorn had yet to learn not to shout, since he could not hear his own voice.

"I sure hope his hearing comes back soon." Einar nodded toward Bjorn. "He can't work out in the woods if he can't hear."

Rune nodded. *Ah, but Einar, what about someone whose vision seems to be failing?*

Chapter 15

"Today you are moving to the window." Signe spoke in her no-arguments voice.

"Nei! I cannot walk that far." Gerd scowled at her.

"Ja, we will do it together."

"Then I must walk back."

"One thing at a time." She needed to bathe Gerd again too. And do the wash. So much to do, but the only way to get it done was one step at a time. She would change the bed while Gerd was up. The breeze blowing in the window helped freshen the room.

"Mor!" Leif yelled as he charged into the kitchen and on to the bedroom. "Daisy is having her babies!"

"Where is Bjorn?" One more thing to add to the list.

"Down at the barn, watching her."

"Are the babies all right?"

"She only had one so far. She doesn't mind me coming into the stall. Far said sows are real protective of their babies and don't want anyone near."

Gerd nodded. "But not for a couple of days."

Leif stared at Gerd, his mouth hanging open.

Signe tipped her head to the side. "You used to take care of the pigs and chickens?"

"Who else would have? Einar is always out in the woods or building."

Signe smiled at her son. "You go watch and come get me if she is straining and nothing is happening." She turned back to the woman in the bed. "I'll get your breakfast."

Wonder of wonders, Gerd had not screeched at Leif for being too noisy. Could she be getting better? She'd never strung this many words together.

Signe dished up pancakes with sour cream and chokecherry jelly, poured the coffee, and taking the tray into the bedroom, set it on the boards she had laid across the arms of the chair.

If she moved Gerd to the window, she would not be able to leave her. Better wait and see how the sow's birthing progressed. Bjorn had been more like himself this morning, even though he was living in his silent world. He had gone down to the barn with Leif. She would have to write to communicate with him if sign language did not work. Much could be said with pointing and hand motions.

She set the boiler on the stove and filled it with water from the pump. Today was a good day to sweep and wash the attic floor.

Laying a hand on her abdomen, she paused. "What, you do not like me raising the bucket?" Whatever caused it, the baby was moving more often. At first it had been tiny flutterings but now . . . She murmured, "Lord, takk" and caught herself. She used to pray but no more. No more.

"I'm done," Gerd called.

That too was new. Signe returned to the bedroom. "Can I get you anything else?" She set the tray on the dresser.

"The pot."

"All right." She helped Gerd to her feet but made her do

163

more to get herself up from the chair. Her steps were firmer, and by the time she was seated, Gerd was puffing some but not gasping for breath.

"Next I will bathe you, then you can sleep."

"Nei, tired."

"I know, but tomorrow I'm doing the wash, and you need a clean nightdress." Without waiting for an answer, she took the tray back to the kitchen and filled the dishpan with water from the reservoir. Armed with a bar of soap, washcloth, and towel, she returned to her charge. "How long since you washed your hair?"

Gerd shrugged. "Too hard."

"I know. Not today but soon." She studied Gerd on the pot stool and nodded. "I am going to wash you while you sit there." Without waiting for an answer, she pulled the nightdress over Gerd's head and threw it in the corner with the other dirty clothes. By the time Signe had washed her, Gerd could hardly hold her head up. Some lotion would be good. Signe thought of the soaps and lotions she had made from goat's milk in Norway. Where might she find goat's milk here? Perhaps she'd ask Mrs. Benson.

Once she had dried Gerd's feet, she fetched a clean gown from the dresser and pulled it over Gerd's head. With Gerd back in bed, Signe took the pot out to dump and scrub. "I'm going down to the barn," she said from the doorway, but Gerd was already sound asleep. On her way to the barn, Signe dumped the contents of the pot down the hole in the outhouse. That needed lime again too.

Raising her face to the sun, she stopped for a moment to let the breeze kiss her skin and lift the tendrils of hair that escaped from her crown of braids. The chickens were scratching and pecking around the chicken house, and the rooster raised his head to watch her approach. She should have brought the scraps she'd saved for them. A crow scolded her from the top of the barn. The barn swallows dipped and dove, returning to their nests under the barn eaves to feed their young. She paused in the door of the barn, letting her eyes adjust from the bright sun.

Neither of the boys could be seen, but then she heard Leif talking to the sow in a gentle voice. This youngest son had a way with animals. His far did too. Farming was indeed where Rune belonged. How long would it be before he could think of land of his own? Would they homestead, and if so, where?

She crossed to the stall and leaned against the half wall. "How many?" she asked softly.

Leif looked up from the corner, closest to the sow's head, where he sat, stroking her ears. Bjorn sat cross-legged in another corner, leaning against the wall.

"Three up and nursing. I helped one find a teat," Leif said.

Bjorn smiled up at her. The bruise over his right eye showed even in the dimness, but his egg-sized bump had gone down. The sling tied to his chest stood out with almost a white glow. She nodded and smiled at him.

"I asked him not to talk 'cause he talks too loud and might shock her," Leif explained.

"I see." Of the three piglets, one was nursing and two were sleeping. "She has not gotten up since they started coming?"

"Nei." He watched her carefully. "I think another is coming."

Signe watched the sow and sure enough, another piglet slid out onto the sawdust bedding the boys had spread for her. The baby wiggled out of the sack and another followed it. "Two in one sack. Sometimes I've seen four come right after each other." Within minutes, the babies were trying to stand up, rocking back and forth and plowing into the sawdust again. Bjorn moved in reach of them, in case one needed help. His smile matched Leif's. He looked up at his mor and nodded.

"I'm going back to the house to clean the attic, so if you need me, that is where I am. Do not holler and wake Tante Gerd."

Leif nodded. "How many more do you think she'll have?"

"Didn't Einar say she usually has eight to ten? Her mor had more, but she lost a lot of them. Daisy is more careful."

"Good, I don't want any to die."

Back at the house, Signe tied a bandana around her head and took her broom and dustpan along with some rags in a bucket to the parlor and pulled on the rope that brought the ladder down. Maybe this winter they could build real stairs to the attic. The larger she grew, the more difficult the climb up the ladder would be.

Once in the attic, panting a bit from the climb and the heat, she shook her head. The dust seemed inches deep, and cobwebs draped from floor to ceiling—not that the ceiling was far above, other than in the middle of the room. Rune would have to be careful not to hit his head on the rafters. The windows were open and screened, one of the many right things Einar had done when he built this house. Screens on the windows to keep the army of mosquitoes at bay.

First she swept down all the cobwebs, then the floor, dumping all the dust into the bucket. Back downstairs to dump the bucket and fill it with hot water from the boiler.

"Signe!" A summons from the bedroom.

Heaving a sigh, Signe paused at the sink and pumped water over her hands, filled a glass, drank it down, and filled one for Gerd. She found Gerd sitting up in bed and inching her heels to the edge of the mattress. Progress.

"I'm cleaning the attic."

"Dirty?"

"Ja, very dirty." With Gerd on the pot, Signe handed her the glass of water. "You need to drink."

"Coffee."

"I will make a pot for dinner."

"How many babies?"

"Five when I was out there."

"Takes a while."

They got her back to bed, and Signe hauled her bucket of soap and water up the ladder, one rung at a time. It almost tipped one time, but she caught it and then wrapped one arm around the side of the ladder, breathing hard. That was a close call. She could have fallen. She rested for a moment, then hoisted the bucket up a couple more rungs. With her head and shoulders above the attic floor, she lifted the bucket one more time. Water sloshed on the floor, but the bucket did not tip over. Crawling up into the attic, she sat down and dropped her chin on her chest. What if she had fallen? She wrapped her arms around her ever-extending belly and rocked back and forth on her haunches. "I could have lost my baby."

They had been so pleased when she became pregnant after so many barren years where she thought there would be no more children. She was hoping for a daughter. She heaved a sigh and rolled over on her knees so she could stand. No more just pushing herself upright with both legs at one time. Already it was the cumbersome way, but at least she could still do that.

She carried the bucket and a large rag to one end of the room, and after folding a couple other rags together for a kneeler, set to washing and rinsing the floor. At this rate she'd need to go down for more water. And haul it up again. Just not as full a bucket. She wasn't even half done.

"Mor?"

"Ja, I am just coming down." Going down was easier than

going up, and this time she clung to the ladder with her free hand. With her feet on solid floor again, she puffed out a breath and turned to her youngest son. "How are the babies?"

"Eight of them. All alive. I showed the older ones how to find their little safe house. Daisy has not tried to get up yet, so there must be more." Leif took the handle of the bucket with both hands. "I will dump this." He grinned up at her. "While you make dinner?"

She ruffled his hair. "Is it that time already?" Her stomach grumbled, making him laugh. Leif laughed easily, a gift for the whole sober family. "Dump it by the back porch."

"I will take it to the garden."

She watched him go, unconsciously kneading her back with her fists. He could slice the bread when he came back. Maybe she would add a fried egg to each of the ham sandwiches. And they could eat outside in the shade of the house. After working in the hot attic, a breeze sounded like the best part of dinner.

How dark it would be upstairs come winter. And how cold. Although the stovepipe from the kitchen went up through the attic. If Einar would purchase a vent, the attic would be warmer.

While she was thinking, she sliced the ham she'd brought in earlier from the well house, set a frying pan on the hottest part of the stove, and spooned in enough fat from the drippings crock to fry the eggs.

"Could you please go out and bring in some eggs?" she asked Leif.

"Then can I go check on my babies?"

"Bjorn will come get you if there is a problem."

"I know, but I like to see them born and learn to stand and find a teat to nurse."

"Eggs first. Now hurry, the pan is almost ready." Instead of waiting for him, she sliced the bread and laid ham on one side.

A couple minutes later, he set a basket of eggs on the counter. "Here. Ham and fried egg sandwiches? I'll go get Bjorn."

With the pan beginning to sizzle, she broke the eggs in and cooked them hard, then slid each on top of one of the ham sandwiches. They were definitely eating better here, even if Einar thought everyone should be finished when he was. She set the sandwiches on a platter, putting one aside for Tante Gerd, and met the boys at the door.

"We are eating outside. Leif, bring the glasses of milk. We'll sit in the shade."

When they were all seated, her on the chair off the back porch, she held out the platter. Bjorn fumbled, trying to pick up his sandwich, so when Leif handed it to him, he smiled and nodded. She smiled and nodded at Leif. "Takk."

"Is there more?" Leif asked when he finished his.

"Do you want a slice of bread with butter and sugar?"

Leif leaped to his feet and disappeared around the corner and into the house. Bjorn looked his question at her, then, frustrated, jabbed a stick in the ground.

She nodded and mouthed, *wait*, then held up a hand. She must remember to carry a pencil and paper in her apron pocket. When Leif returned with two slices of bread folded over and handed one to Bjorn, his eyes lit up. The two boys headed for the barn, eating their sandwiches as they went.

A wave of weariness broke over Signe, nearly sending her to the ground. Instead, she got up and took the dishes back into the kitchen. Eating outside had been a good idea. She fed Gerd, told her what she was doing, and headed for the barn rather than filling the scrub bucket.

The boys were back in their places with the sow sleeping between them.

"Ten babies, Mor. Two born while we had dinner." Leif

pointed to the baby corner. "They come out when they're hungry. Pigs learn fast, don't they?"

"They're smart, especially at finding ways to get out of their pens."

"What are we having for supper?"

"Fried rabbit. I sure will be glad when we have potatoes out of the garden. How are the peas doing?"

"About ready to pick."

"Maybe enough ready for supper?"

He shrugged.

Signe returned to the house by way of the garden. When she found several pods full enough, she brought out a basket and called for Leif to help her pick peas. There weren't a lot, but they would each get some—if Einar didn't eat them all first. When she caught Leif popping peas into his mouth rather than her basket, she shook it at him. "In here, so we can all have some."

Sitting out on the back step, shelling peas, reminded her of home. All the children and younger women would shell peas, snap beans, or scrub cucumbers out on the porch, the children begging for stories of what life was like in the earlier years. Her children would never hear their grandparents' stories. The thought sent an arrow through her heart.

"We have fresh peas from the garden," she announced at suppertime when she set the bowl on the table. "Not very many yet, but enough for everyone to have a taste." She stared at Einar, hoping he would get the hint.

"Creamed peas and new potatoes. That will be a fine meal." Einar spooned peas onto his plate, started to take a second scoop, then stopped and passed the bowl to Rune instead.

Signe made sure her surprise and pleasure did not show on her face. "Along with biscuits and ham. I will dig under the potato plants and see if any are big enough." As always, she had kept some back for Gerd. Maybe that was one reason Tante was getting stronger—she was eating better. Signe sat down at the table and helped herself.

"How many baby pigs so far?" Einar asked Leif.

"Ten. She's still lying down."

Einar nodded. "The more the better. I see you moved that hen and chicks to the other stall."

Leif flashed his mor a questioning look.

Einar concluded, "Good."

She could see Leif relax. She glanced over at Knute, who was almost asleep in his chair. "How are your hands, Knute?"

He startled and shook his head.

"Maybe tomorrow he can use the axe again," Einar growled.

"We'll see how his hands look in the morning." Signe stared right back at Einar, refusing to give in.

He slapped his hands on the table, muttered something about coddling, and left the kitchen, the screen door slamming behind him. Leif flinched as they all paused in case Gerd yelled about the noise.

Bjorn picked up a pencil and scrawled, "I could drag branches with one hand." Bjorn looked to his far.

Rune shook his head. "Not until you can hear again." He grimaced and wrote it below Bjorn's message.

Signe wrote, "Tomorrow you can weed the garden." The look on his face told her what he thought of that idea.

The next morning, Leif brought a dead piglet into the house. "We had twelve, but now eleven."

"I'm sorry," Signe said, smoothing his hair. "You did your best."

Einar waved a hand dismissively. "Throw it on the manure pile. Happens all the time."

Leif nodded. On his way out the door, he dashed tears away with the back of his hand.

Did Einar have to be so cruel?

Chapter 16

N eed anything else?" Rune asked.

Einar shook his head and climbed up on the wagon seat. He waited until Rune sat down, glanced over his shoulder to check on Knute, and clucked the horses forward. Always a taciturn man, today his jaw was set and he stared straight ahead.

Rune thought back to Signe confronting Einar. Even Einar had to realize that she was a mother bear protecting her cubs. And she made Rune realize that he must protect his cubs as well.

He looked at the stumps that dotted the field they crossed to get to the big trees. "Did you clear all the land you are farming?"

Einar glanced at him. "No, a homesteader cleared part of it but gave up, and I bought his half section. He lived in a tar-paper shack that burned down, so when we came, we had what logs I felled milled and built the barn and the house." He added, "They had traveling lumber mills back then. Might still have them. I worked in a logging camp for our first two winters, and Gerd worked in the kitchen. In the summer we lived in a tent here, working on our place."

"No wonder you know so much about logging. How will we get those stumps out?"

"I plan on dynamiting them this fall after the fire danger passes."

Rune nodded. That made sense.

"We'll cut hay in a couple days. Need to sharpen the blades on the mower. You ever done that?"

"Nei, we used a scythe at home."

"Found a used mower cheap and bought it last year. Needs cleaning up." He shook his head. "Too much to do. Was counting on your boys being bigger."

"They work hard."

Einar halted the team in their usual spot and climbed down. "We'll start with those two trees I marked yesterday." He grabbed the handle of the crosscut saw and pulled it out of the wagon.

Rune took the other end and looked at Knute. "You take care of the horses."

"Ja, I know what to do. Then limb or drag branches?"

"See how your hands do with the axe. If they start to blister again, drag branches."

"I will."

He and Einar each took a side of the chosen tree and started chopping out the notch that would keep the saw from binding up and guide the tree which way to fall, the song of their axes in perfect rhythm. As he swung each beat, the shock of it reverberated up his arms and into his shoulders, which had grown far more than he dreamed possible. He didn't need fine eyesight to dance the duet of axes. When they switched to the crosscut saw, the tone changed, but the beat remained the same: pull, release, pull. Sweat poured down his face and neck, soaking his shirt. When they stopped for a breather, he stripped his shirt off, mopped it over his face, and slung it over a nearby bush. Hats back on, they kept on sawing until the tree quivered.

"It's going to fall, Knute. Get by the horses." Rune made sure his son did what he was told, then looked upward. The giant pine trembled, and with a groan and a shudder, breaking the branches of a nearby tree, it crashed to the ground with a mighty roar. Other branches crashed down around it, and the forest fell silent, as if honoring the death of a patriarch. Each time a tree fell, Rune stood silent like the forest around him. Death was never easy.

Rune wiped his face with his shirt again. "I am going for a drink." Both men walked over to the wagon bed, sat in the shade, and drank, water running down their chins. Cool water felt like the kiss of an angel.

"We'll eat now before we start the next one." Einar turned to Knute, who had joined them. "Did you water the horses?"

"Ja. That creek is a pretty place."

"Give 'em some grain after a while."

"How are your hands?" Rune asked.

"I cut a lot of limbs."

"I see that. And hauled some too."

"You want me to fill the jug at the creek?"

Einar jerked a nod.

They felled another tree after dinner and started limbing them both. Rune stopped to wipe his face and looked around. These trees were far too big for building a log house, but what would it be like to live in a clearing in the middle of this?

Signe wished she could walk to Benson's Corner and see if there was any mail. But she needed to remain here and get the jars ready for canning the peas the boys were picking. Perhaps Leif could go on the horse. Or Bjorn could walk there and back before dark. At least they'd finally been able to move their pallets up into the attic and had their own space.

After kneading more flour into the leftover pancake batter to make sourdough rolls for supper, she joined the boys out in the garden. They already had nearly half a basket of peas and had more than two rows to go.

"Mor, you need to see the baby pigs. They're running all over and so funny." Leif dropped a handful of pea pods into the basket.

"I will after we finish picking." She watched Bjorn, who was keeping up easily, getting very adept at picking with one hand.

Leif stopped picking to split a pod open and pop the peas into his mouth. "These are the best before they're canned."

"I agree." Signe copied her son. It was a shame the pea season was so short. But considering how late the garden was planted and then finally weeded, having a crop like this was almost a miracle. She watched Bjorn try to split a pod open with one hand. Frustrated, he bit the end and pulled the string down. He squeezed the pod, and the peas popped out. Two fell on the ground, and he bent over to pick them up and wipe them on his pants. Clearly it had to be Bjorn who went to the store. The need to mail her newly written letter and read one from home was like an animal gnawing on her insides. If there was one from home. What if her Mor stayed so angry that she did not write? It wasn't Signe's fault her husband chose to emigrate.

"You two try to finish these rows before dinner."

She walked back into the house, sat down, and wrote a note to Mrs. Benson. Could she sell any eggs or butter? When did school start, and must she register her boys? Might Mrs. Benson also have any mail for the Strands? She added, "Bjorn cannot hear." She put the note with her letter for home.

After scrubbing the jars she'd found in the cellar, she set them boiling on the stove and helped Gerd again. While waiting for Gerd, she moved the chair to the window.

"Nei!"

"Ja, you have to walk some every day, and one of these days you will be able to walk to the table to eat."

Gerd shuffled more than walked, but she made it to the window and sank down in the chair. "Coffee."

"I will bring it." Signe stopped at the door. "Did you used to knit or crochet?"

Gerd nodded. "Long time ago."

"I would knit in the winter. Do we buy yarn in Blackduck?"

"I have a sewing machine."

"Ja. I have nothing for the baby, so I need to sew come fall." She had not given that much thought, but she had better start soon. First all the canning and drying food for the winter. "Do you like fresh raw peas?"

Gerd nodded. "And coffee."

When Signe returned to the kitchen, she heaved a deep breath. They had almost had a real conversation. And no shrieking.

"We finished, Mor," Leif called from the porch.

Three full baskets waited beside the door.

Leif's eyes shone. "Daisy will like the pea pods. Will the chickens too?"

"Ja. How are our hen and babies?"

"All fine. When will we put her back with the others?"

"When they're ready. Wash your hands. Dinner is ready."

She ladled ham and bean soup into bowls and set sliced bread on the table. Tomorrow she would have to bake bread again. "Has anyone checked Knute's snares?"

"He did this morning. No rabbits. He says he better move them to a different spot."

When they finished eating, she wrote her instructions to Bjorn and sent him on his way.

She and Leif sat down to shell peas. At home, all the women would be sitting outside in the shade, shelling peas, talking, laughing, almost like a party. A longing for home made her sniff and blink. She'd never known being homesick could hurt so bad, like a band tightening around her heart. It seemed to be getting worse, not easier.

"Mor, are you all right?"

"Ja, just missing home."

"Me too. We would be up at the seder with Tante Gretta now. We had to shear the sheep and milk both the goats and the cows. Are they haying yet, do you think? Remember when the lynx attacked the sheep and our big old cattle dog chased after it, and we all ran out and chased it away? It was not my turn that day to be herding the sheep. I had the cows, so I missed it all."

"That was a frightening time."

"Knute was so mad they didn't kill it. This year I might have been big enough to shear a sheep. Bjorn was good at that. He never missed when he grabbed a sheep and flipped it over to shear. I carded a lot of wool. Do you miss the mountains?"

Signe sighed again. "Ja, I do, but mostly I miss Mor and all our families there." *Maybe someday we will be able to bring some family over.* There was no sense dreaming of returning to Norway. It would never happen—she knew that when they left.

"Are you going to make cheese here?"

"We will see."

When Gerd called, Signe went in to see to her and help her back to bed. "See, you are stronger today."

Gerd sank back against her pillows, breathing hard. "Tired."

In the kitchen, Signe punched down the dough and rolled it out to cut into squares for supper. Creamed ham and peas over raised rolls this time. On a whim, she cut part of the dough into small pieces, let them rise, and fried them. When they were finished, she set them on a plate with a bowl of syrup and called Leif inside. His eyes lit up and a grin nearly split his face.

"Takk, Mor. Oh, yummy." He dipped one of the pieces of fried dough in the syrup and ate it in one bite. "We haven't had this since Grandma made them."

Signe ate one, then poured a cup of coffee and dipped several in syrup to take to Gerd. "Coffee and sweets." She waited for Gerd to get herself sat up and set the tray in her lap.

Gerd ate one and almost smiled. At least Signe chose to believe that was what the change in her face meant. Back in the kitchen, she sat down and ate a couple more pieces with Leif. "We need to put the rest away for Bjorn. He should be back soon. Time to get back to the peas."

"Can we take the pods to Daisy? You can see the babies."

The need to work argued with her love for her son, but for a change the love won out. "We must hurry. Did you feed her the butter washings yet?"

"Part of them." He picked up the baskets of pods, and together they walked to the barn. He let himself into the stall, and Daisy scrambled to her feet to join him at the trough, grabbing for the pods before they hit the wood.

"Throw some in her water. She'll like that."

"Look." Leif pointed down. One of the piglets had picked up a pod and was trying to chew it. The others all gathered around the sow and started nursing, tails wagging in delight.

"You need to watch her. Soon she might turn on you if you pick up one of her babies. Sows are like that."

"Far warned me too. I wish she could go out in the mud with

the others. I pour water over her sometimes when it's hot. I wet the sawdust too. She likes that."

"Good." Signe crossed the aisle to where the hen and her six chicks were busily scratching away. "They need to go outside to scratch for their food."

"I throw it on the floor for them." He tossed some pea pods in their pen too. The hen clucked to her brood and started pecking at the pods, so they did too. "I bring weeds from the garden sometimes. She likes green stuff."

"You're doing good. You are a farmer like your far."

Leif turned and looked at her, his eyes shining. "And you are too."

Back at the house, they settled in to finish shelling the peas. When only a few were left, she went inside to where the jars waited for her. She glared at the woodbox—they would need more wood before she put the jars in the hot water. She pushed in what chunks she had. Hopefully there was more already split. After filling the jars with peas, she added a teaspoon of salt to each jar and poured boiling water up to the lower edge of the neck.

Leif brought in the last of the peas.

"We're having those for supper. I need wood right away."

Leif stared down into the woodbox. "I thought we had plenty."

"Canning takes a lot of wood. Is there some split?"

"I hope so." He trudged out the door. The thud of axe on wood started up.

Signe set the warmed rubber rings on each rim of the six quarts she had ready and fit the glass tops in place. Using a folded dishtowel to protect her hands, she carefully placed each jar in the steaming water. After pouring in enough hot water to cover the jars, she set the boiler lid in place.

Leif dropped an armload of wood in the box. "More soon."

"Takk." Signe blew out a breath. There was no feeling like that of putting up food to feed her family when the north wind was howling around the eaves and trying to blow the house down. Granted, they needed a whole lot more, but this was a start.

With the boiler bubbling gently and Gerd assisted again, Signe glanced at the clock. Soon it would be time for chores. Bjorn should be back anytime.

Leif charged in with another armload of wood. "Bjorn is almost here."

Please let there be a letter. She stepped out onto the front porch. When Bjorn saw her, he waved something above his head. A letter, surely it was a letter.

"Two letters, Mor!" Bjorn shouted.

Signe flew down the three steps, no longer able to wait. Surely, a letter from home.

He handed them to her. "From Norway."

Signe clutched them to her breast. Both with Mor's handwriting.

He shouted, "I tried to hurry, but I tripped and almost fell so I walked slower. When I got there, there was a sign on the door that said, *Back in two hours*, so I sat down and waited. Mrs. Benson apologized. She said to greet you and after she read your note, she wrote you back. And guess what? She gave me three peppermint sticks, one for each of us."

Signe nodded vigorously, carefully mouthing, "She is a very nice lady."

Mrs. Benson's note told Signe that school did not start until after mid-September because of harvest, and the schoolteacher would call on her.

She tore one letter open with her thumb. Three whole pages

of news from home! She opened the other one too and started to read the earliest.

My dear daughter . . .

Her eyes welled with tears until she could not see a word on the page.

Chapter 17

Signe adjusted the wick in the oil lamp to burn a little brighter. The others had all gone to bed, and she and Rune were sitting at the kitchen table, something they tried to do once in a while. Most nights they were far too weary, but otherwise when could they talk?

"Read the letters to me again, ja?" Rune asked.

Signe nodded and took the letters from her apron pocket. Perhaps now she could read without dissolving into tears.

"Dear Daughter Signe and all the family,

"You have only been gone ten days, and yet it feels like months."

She paused. "This one was written not long after we left home." *And here I was afraid she had not forgiven me.*

"Ja. Did you read this to Gerd?"

"She did not show any interest." She looked at Rune. "You think I should?"

He nodded again. "She is part of the family."

She studied the page without really seeing it. "Sometimes I wonder. . . ."

He waited patiently for her answer. He was not one to jump right in; quiet did not unsettle him like it did some people. Like it used to bother her.

Part of the family. Ja, Gerd was a relative, but part of the family? Was Einar part of the family? He at least ate meals with them, provided a house and work and food. But as hard as they all worked, they earned every bite. Signe huffed out a breath. She would think about that later.

"You better read fast, or I will be sound asleep, right here at the table," Rune said with a smile.

"I trust you are all well and pray that the voyage was not hard on you. I am sure your pregnancy did not make it any easier. I look every day for a letter, knowing full well that you cannot write until you land in New York. But then you are boarding another ship, oh my. So I will give you the news from here.

"Your far is recovering from his broken toes where he dropped a maul on his foot. He has been hobbling around, but it is no longer so black and blue, and the swelling is going down, so he can put his boot back on.

"Gretta and the younger children are all up at the seter. They just went up so we have not heard from them yet. Elmer drove a wagon. You remember Elmer from around the hill. And your brother drove the other. Far and Onkel Rafe rode on ahead to make sure no animals larger than rats and mice inhabit the house. Remember the year a wolverine took up living in the house? What a stinking mess!

"The gardens are growing well, and the crops appear to be a good harvest. And we will have that, God willing.

Will you be able to put up vegetables for the winter? Will Tante Gerd and you do that together? Or is she still too ill to help much? I pray for you every day, for your baby to be born healthy, and that God will keep you all safe.

"Nilda Carlson says she is coming to help you as soon as she earns passage money. She is saving every penny. The boys want to come to Amerika to be lumberjacks. They are envying your boys.

"Please write soon.

"Your Mor"

Signe folded the letter and put it back in its envelope to be read and reread later. She looked up, but Rune had fallen asleep, head back against the chair. She shook his shoulder and motioned toward the attic, where the boys had gone long before. "Come to bed. We will read the other tomorrow night."

Mor had said she would pray for them. One side of Signe's mind said, *Bosh, a waste of time.* But the other side, the one that grew up praying and believing that God was indeed real and in His heaven, that He cared about His people here on earth and listened to their cries—that part fought to break free from the chest where she had banished it.

Her mor still believed and prayed for her children. Would that Signe could sit at her mor's knee and ask the questions that fought to regain a place in her mind and heart.

Fighting to banish those thoughts, planted in her heart since she was at her mor's breast, drained her strength. *Just give up,* whispered another, more tender voice. *Let me help you.* Signe dropped into the well of oblivion before she could answer.

"Mor? Mor."

Someone poked her arm. She opened her eyes. Bjorn knelt

beside her. "I went to the outhouse, and I could hear the outhouse door slam! I could hear it!"

Signe sat bolt upright, and Rune turned toward them, sleepy. She gripped her son's shoulders. "Can you hear my voice?"

He frowned. "Almost."

She hugged him. He hopped up and returned to his pallet. Sleep returned and smothered her joy.

Putting breakfast on the table, she sensed that Onkel Einar had not changed his mind or feelings about her. How an already silent man could be more so, she didn't know, but this time his silence screamed his anger at her. When he finished, he pushed his chair back, barked, "You boys come," and stomped out the door, letting the screen door bang behind him.

Leif stared at her, his eyes round in horror.

Sure enough, as if someone had flipped a switch, Gerd screamed, "Will you ever learn not to slam the screen door?"

Knute stared at his far and started to push his chair back, stuffing the rest of his pancake in his mouth at the same time.

"Sit and finish eating," Rune said, looking at each of his sons.

"Takk." Signe's one word referred to far more than the boys would understand. Rune was standing up for her. The song in her heart was enough to lighten the load of a morning that hung heavy with a portent of rain. They could use rain for the garden, but it would not be good for the hay.

And Bjorn was recovering his hearing!

"When will you start haying?" she asked Rune.

"He said two more days, but we will see what today brings."

"Will you go back in the woods if we have thunder and lightning?"

"I am sure. That was a freak accident. Einar has cut and

limbed many trees in spite of rainstorms. At least that is what he said."

Signe packed their dinner, wishing she had more to send out with them. She stopped Knute at the door. "Did you check your trapline?"

He nodded. "Nothing. Tonight I will move it farther out."

Bjorn stood up. "A yearling buck comes in to graze east of the barn. Can we go hunting?"

Signe jotted on the back of a torn envelope, "I will ask Tante," and showed it to him.

"Is our basket ready?" Knute asked. "Onkel has the team all hitched up."

Signe handed him the basket and the jug of water.

"I wish Bjorn could go with the men," he muttered.

"I know you would rather stay here, but that is not possible right now. Just do your best. Does he yell at you?"

Knute shrugged. "Nei, but I am not as good with an axe as Bjorn. I can drag branches just fine." He leaned closer. "I miss Daisy and her babies, and I like to work in the garden."

"I know you do."

"I need you!" The call came from the bedroom, but at least it was one level down from a screech.

Signe got Gerd settled in her chair and brought in her tray. "Would you not rather come to the table to eat?"

Shaking her head, Gerd reached for her coffee cup.

"I have a question for you. Does Onkel Einar ever go deer hunting?"

Gerd looked up. "He used to, but now all he thinks about is cutting trees. Why does Rune not go?"

Because he couldn't see. Did she dare admit this weakness so soon into their new life? "He cannot see distance so much."

Gerd stared at her. "Is this new?"

"No, it's been with him a long time. A young buck grazes near the hayfield every morning and evening."

"Tell Einar tonight."

"Ah, he is not happy with me right now."

Gerd stared at her, eyes narrowing.

I should not have mentioned that, Signe scolded herself. *We need the meat.*

"Can you shoot a rifle?" Gerd asked.

Signe shook her head. "Bjorn can, once he's healed, and Knute could learn if Rune had time to teach him."

"I will tell Einar he needs to go hunting. Do you know how to smoke meat?"

Signe nodded.

"We have another broody hen," Leif announced when he returned from finishing the chores. "That one who is molting?"

"If you and Bjorn can catch her, we will dress her out and have chicken and dumplings for supper," Signe told him.

"We'll catch her." Leif looked a bit sad. "Poor Bjorn. He can't even chop her head off."

"Never mind, I'll handle that part."

Leif brightened. "But he just figured out a way to chop wood. Slow, but he gets it done. Come watch."

Signe stepped out on the back porch as Bjorn set a small spool up on the block, picked up the axe with his left hand, and, grasping the handle halfway up, raised it and slammed it down into the chunk of wood. It did not even split halfway, so he wiggled the axe free and slammed it down again.

Signe ached for her son. What if this slight return of his hearing was all there would be? "Are there any splitting wedges?"

"Maybe around the grinding wheel somewhere. I'll go look.

Oh, and I think some of the beans are ready. Enough for supper." Leif ran off to the shed.

"Takk," Signe called after him. She returned to the kitchen to find the sourdough starter bubbling over the edge of the bowl. "Uff da!" And the dishes were not washed yet either. She started stirring in the flour and kneading the dough. This should have been done an hour ago.

How many batches of bread had she kneaded in her lifetime? As a young child, a young woman, a young wife, a young mother. How time flew. And how she wished her mor was standing beside her, kneading dough right along with her.

"Mor, we caught the hen." Leif bounded into the kitchen but spun and caught the door before it slammed. He grinned at her. "Close."

She nodded and smiled back at him. "What is Bjorn doing?"

"Holding the chicken."

"Put her under the box on the porch and start picking peas."

"Canning peas today?"

"Ja, they are ready again."

He sighed, nodded, and closed the screen door carefully behind him.

She set the dough on the warming shelf to rise, not that it really needed that extra heat today, and pumped water into the boiler to boil the jars in preparation for the peas. With the water heating, she looked in the woodbox. Half full. Good for a while. With more water heating to dunk the chicken in prior to plucking its feathers, she fetched the hen from under the box.

She lopped off the chicken's head and looked over the garden toward the dark clouds moving in from the west while the blood drained. After dunking the hen in the pail of hot water a few times, she was easily able to pull out all the feathers.

A few minutes later, after gutting the naked chicken, she

singed the hairs off over the open firebox and set the bird in a pan of cold water in the sink to cool.

Instead of asking one of the boys, she headed for the garden to dig a couple of onions. Thunderheads were building in the west, and while the air hung heavy, a breeze tickled the escaped hairs around her face.

"When is dinner, Mor?" asked Leif. "We're hungry."

"You have not been eating peas?" The onions came easily from the ground. She brushed off the dirt and looked at her sons.

"Well, some, but we're still hungry." Leif tossed another handful of pea pods in the basket. "We have one full basket and this one almost."

"Hurry to get done before it rains. I will pick the beans."

Signe clamped her jaw at the screech from the house. How to get that woman strong enough to help herself? Surely it was possible. Stomping did not help with Gerd, but it made Signe feel a bit better. She eased up her footfalls when she entered Gerd's room. "I'm trying to get the beans picked before the rain comes."

"I fell asleep, and my coffee spilled. I need to use the pot." Her eyes slitted. "Now."

New nightdress or let it dry? Signe picked up the empty coffee cup. "You can stand up."

Gerd sent her a look that shredded Signe's determination. But instead of letting her feelings be known, she waited.

"Help me up!" A queen could not be more imperious.

Fight this out or get it over with so she could pick the beans? Thunder rumbled in the distance. It was coming closer. Expelling a sigh that said more than words, Signe took Gerd's hands and pulled her upright with more force than necessary.

Gerd swayed. "Careful!" She clamped her claw-like fingers around Signe's hands.

Turning her around, Signe set her on the pot and then fluffed the bed pillows. She stripped off Gerd's nightdress and grabbed a clean one off the dresser.

Gerd snarled, "Would not have happened if you had been here."

Signe slid the woman's garment over her head and held the sleeves for her. "Help me here, please."

"Too tired." She was white around the mouth. Signe helped her sit on the bed.

"Do you want the sheet?"

"Ja." Gerd waited for her slave to flip the light covering into place. "Looks like rain, all right."

"Ja, it does."

Attacked by doubts and recriminations for her own behavior, Signe headed back to the garden. Yesterday she'd thought they were making progress, but today she wondered.

"Get me another basket," she told Leif as she made her way to the bean rows. She should have gotten one herself. So much for good intentions. The slow burn in her belly had flared into real flames that burned both her throat and her stomach. When she got back to the kitchen, she'd drink some buttermilk. That always helped.

Getting Gerd to help herself might take a quart or two of buttermilk—daily.

The rising breeze brought a chill with it. Once the rain hit, she would no longer be able to pick beans without causing the leaves to turn brown. But the black clouds held more than a sprinkle. Lightning forked to the west. The thunder answered, but slowly.

"Mor, put the chickens in?"

"Ja, we better." She straightened. "Set your baskets on the porch first." She broke off another handful of beans. Her bulging belly was beginning to make bending over more difficult, the baby pushing up into her rib cage and making her puff. She'd just have to make do with what she'd picked.

Lightning and thunder, closer together. Would Einar stop or keep going? Was that thunder from the woods? No, a giant tree had just crashed to the ground. Einar would keep going. She watched her two boys shooing the chickens back to their house. The wind blew their feathers up along their backs. She'd better get the house windows closed, or she would be mopping floors. To the west, the falling rain made a silvery curtain from the clouds to the ground, drawing ever nearer.

The curtains on the west side of the house were not fluttering but blowing straight out. She slammed the windows down. The attic. She hadn't closed the two windows up there.

In the parlor, she reached up to pull down the ladder to the attic. Once secure, she placed one foot on the bottom rung. The wind whistled through the attic. The house grew darker with every passing moment.

Gripping the side rails, she heaved herself up to the second rung and planted both feet on it. The attic opening seemed farther away, not closer.

"Mor!" Leif's voice demanded her attention.

"In the parlor."

Both boys stopped in the doorway. "What are you doing?" Leif asked.

"Going up to close the windows." She clung to the ladder and reminded herself to breathe.

"We will do that." Bjorn sounded just like his far. A boy stood on each side of the ladder, their eyes round. "Far said to watch out for you. Please come back down."

"I can go up faster," Leif added, nodding as he talked. "Please, Mor."

The roar of the rain on the roof hit like a freight train.

Signe looked up, then nodded and stepped down, careful to do one rung at a time. Leif scurried up the ladder. She hurried to the kitchen to get something to mop up the water.

She heard a window slam shut. Thunder crashed right on the heels of the flash that lit the room. Another slam, and Leif grinned down at her. Bjorn climbed the first three rungs and handed up the rag she had fetched.

While the boys attended to the blown-in rain, Signe returned to the kitchen, pausing to check on Gerd. *Sound asleep with all this noise, how can that be?* Head wagging, she pulled the copper boiler off the heat so she could put the chicken on to stew. Rain sluiced down the windows, and gusts of wind almost shook the house. Surely Einar and Rune would come home early with wind and rain like this.

But they did not.

The storm dragged dusk in behind it as it moved on.

Signe watched out the window. Shouldn't the men be back by now? Not that supper was ready, but dumplings did not take long. Between the rising bread fragrance and that of chicken stew, the kitchen smelled so good she could not keep from smiling. The jars of peas bubbling on the stove added another ingredient to her feeling of satisfaction.

Her grinning sons came in with Leif carefully keeping the screen door from banging. "We strained the milk. There is enough cream for butter again. Far and Onkel Einar are back."

"We need more wood," she told them, and they headed back outside. The bread had risen enough, and she slid the pans into the oven.

Dumplings finally rising in the stew, she flew around the kitchen, setting the table. With the table ready, she went outside to bring in an armload of wood. The boys had gone to the barn to do their chores. She should have insisted on wood first.

"What are you doing out here?" Rune asked as he leaned over to load his arms too.

"The boys ran off to the barn when they heard you drive in."

"That is one determined man, that Einar. He absolutely refused to quit, no matter the rain and wind."

"He did not learn a lesson from the lightning strike before?"

"Does not seem that way. I felt sorry for Knute, but we felled another tree and got most of the limbing done. He plans to take down another one first thing in the morning." They walked into the house and dumped their armloads into the box. "I'll go split more."

When the men came in, Einar announced, "The wind and rain flattened the hayfield. Cutting that with the mower is going to be impossible."

"So we'll have to scythe it then?" Rune asked.

"Give it a couple of days to see if some stands back up, then you'll have to do that." Einar looked at Knute. "You know how to use a scythe?"

"Some."

"Thing is almost as big as you are."

Einar stomped through the kitchen to the parlor and pulled down the attic ladder. Signe heard thumping and rustling in the half of the attic she had not swept or dusted.

She checked on the bread, tapping gently on the loaves. Almost.

"Can we have some for supper?" asked Knute.

"If it's done in time. The dumplings are about cooked."

Leif inhaled. "Smells so good."

Einar came back into the kitchen with a large, heavy rifle and a handful of shells. "Bjorn!" he roared.

Bjorn went to him. Signe rejoiced—Bjorn had heard him! The rejoicing ground to a halt. Einar was handing Bjorn the rifle and shells.

"Careful where you shoot, understand?"

"Ja!" Bjorn glowed. Lovingly, he ran his hand along the barrel. Clouds of dust fell to the floor.

"Come to dinner," Signe announced.

Bjorn laid the gun aside and sat down.

What did Rune think of this? Signe looked at him. He was his usual stoic self, with no particular expression on his face. She served up the chicken and dumplings and checked the bread once more, thumping the loaves to make sure they were done. After tipping each loaf out of the pan, she spread butter on the tops with her fingertips.

Her little boy with a deer rifle. Her heart pounded. Bjorn did a man's work in the woods, and now he had a man's weapon. But he was fifteen.

She sat down at her place and filled her bowl with the stew. "Onkel Einar, are you sure he's old enough for that?"

Einar scowled at her. "Boys eight years old go hunting around here."

No more was said.

Later, when the others were asleep, replete with fresh bread and jam, Signe stood at the window and looked out at the moon and stars flitting in and out of the racing clouds. What time was it in Norway? Another wave of homesickness threatened to drown her. At home they would have stayed around the table and talked over the day. Her younger sister, Gretta, might tell a funny story. She had such a gift for turning daily events into funny stories. Far would bring out his carving or something to repair.

"I miss you all so," she whispered to the evening breeze.

"How can I be so lonesome when the boys are around me all day and the others in the evening? I always have more work I can do." She rubbed her rounded belly and tipped her head from side to side. The longing felt like a ten-pound weight sitting on her chest.

Soon school would start. Could Leif and Knute even wear their same boots from last year? Tomorrow she would make butter, and the next day she would take eggs and butter to trade at the store. She would not ask Onkel Einar for money to clothe her children, that was for sure. She lay down on her pallet.

A gunshot! Signe sat straight up. Rune sat up beside her. Bjorn's pallet was empty.

Another shot! The sky was gray in first light. Signe stumbled to her feet and ran into the kitchen barefoot.

Rune ran past her toward the barn. She wanted to go too, but she needed the outhouse first. She knew that was the way with pregnancy, but she regretted having to take the time.

Rune and Bjorn came toward the house. Einar stepped out on the porch. Rune and Bjorn were jubilant.

"He got it!" Rune exclaimed. "His first buck!"

"I didn't quite kill it with the first shot," Bjorn said, "so I had to shoot it again. And yes, I slit the throat to bleed it out."

Einar jerked his head in what might have been a nod. He looked at Rune. "Get the wagon."

Chapter 18

Signe was late getting up the morning after Bjorn shot his buck. Rune and Einar had gutted and hung the buck in the barn the day before, and the men and Knute went out as always to cut trees. At the end of the day, they had skinned the carcass and quartered it. It took a good while, and all were late going to bed.

Signe came out of the house with her trade goods, butter and eggs, and watched Knute finish hitching Rosie into the little coalbox cart. He had grown so much in the month since they arrived, in confidence as well as size.

She had pressed the butter into squares and wrapped them separately. Several dozen eggs, nestled into a large tin and padded with towels, would be her trade, hopefully for boots for Knute. Leif could wear Knute's old ones.

Saying nothing, Einar handed her a list and walked off toward the barn.

"Bjorn," she said, "take good care of Tante Gerd. You can hear her call, right?"

"The way she shrieks? It's louder than the doors slamming."

"I realize you think that, but you should not say it out loud."

"Sorry, Mor."

Einar returned with the buck hide rolled tightly under his arm. He stuffed it in the wagon box. "Get a good price for it, you hear?"

"I will try." It was the most he'd said to her for a while. Signe felt like shaking him. How could he still be cross with her? She had heard about people holding a grudge, but this was going too far. What would he say when she insisted they build stairs up to the attic so she could take a baby up and down after it was born? If only they could have a home of their own. Someday, somehow. Surely they would not all live in this house forever. Not if more children were born to them.

Rune gave her a hand up into the box, and Leif scrambled up beside her. She flipped the reins, and the horse broke into a trot, making the cart bounce in the ruts. In her reticule she carried a drawing of the outline of Knute's foot. Bjorn's boots were shabby, but he did not complain they were too small. She also had letters to mail, and perhaps there would be something from home.

She knew her smile had not left since they turned onto the lane. Perhaps Mrs. Benson might invite her to coffee again. She kept the horse to a trot so they would get home sooner.

Leif sat beside her, gripping the seat edge for dear life. "Just think, pretty soon Knute and me will be going to school every day."

"You will have to read English, you know."

He stared at her. "But I do not know how to read English."

"You will learn quickly, I'm sure. You can talk English much better now, and you know the alphabet."

"Mostly. I hope the teacher speaks Norwegian." He slumped against the back of the seat. "Does Tante Gerd know how to read and write English?"

"I don't know. We could ask her when she feels better."

He sat up straight and pointed off to their left. "Look at the herd of cows over there."

"A fine herd. I think Onkel Einar wants to have a herd of milk cows."

"Why is he always so mean?"

Signe heaved a sigh. "I wish I knew. Perhaps he is happier out in the woods. I guess some people are just more pleasant than others."

She stared longingly at the farm houses they passed. Why did no one ever come to welcome them? After all, neighbors in Norway did that. Perhaps she would ask Mrs. Benson. Perhaps if they joined the church, they would get to know some other people. Did the women get together for quilting? Mrs. Benson had given her the name of a midwife, but she had no idea how to find the woman or talk to her. She needed to learn how to sew on Gerd's sewing machine to make diapers and clothes for the baby, as soon as the boys went to school and the canning was finished. Today she would buy some flannel for the diapers and begin to hem them by hand.

"There is someone else there." Leif smiled up at her when they saw the store ahead. A wagon and team were waiting at the hitching rail along with a saddled horse.

Signe smiled back at him. "We will speak English."

"Ja, I know." Leif jumped to the ground as soon as she halted Rosie, and tied her to the rail, while Signe turned around and stepped down backwards. It might not look graceful this way, but it was safer. Leif opened the screen door to the store for her as a bell tinkled above them.

"Why, good morning, Mrs. Carlson, how wonderful to see you." Mrs. Benson waved to her from behind the counter, where she was waiting on another woman. "Come and meet Mrs. Solum. She lives in the next lane beyond yours."

Signe ignored the butterflies leaping in her middle and returned the smile. "Takk."

Leif glanced up at her, eyebrows raised.

"Ja, thank you," Signe corrected.

Mrs. Benson introduced them, then added, "Mrs. Carlson and her family came from Norway to help Mr. Strand."

"I am glad to meet you," Signe said carefully.

"Welcome to America. I hope you like living here." Mrs. Solum turned back to Mrs. Benson. "Thank you. I hope you will have the corduroy in soon. I need to get to sewing for the girls. My land, they have outgrown nearly everything this summer." She turned back to Signe. "Nice to meet you."

She gathered up her parcels and headed out the door, leaving Signe wishing she had been friendlier and stayed a bit longer.

Mrs. Benson shifted into her funny-sounding Norwegian. "Now, Mrs. Carlson, how can I help you today?"

"I have a list. I brought butter and eggs to trade, if we can. I need to buy boots for one of my boys." She pulled the paper from her bag. "Here is the size and the list." She laid the other paper on the counter. "And I need to know what we do about school."

"Let's see. The boots are over there." She leaned over the counter to address Leif. "You want to go tell the men in back what feeds you need?"

He grinned. "Ja. Can I pet the cat?"

"Of course, and her kittens are out and about now too." She looked at Signe. "Might you be interested in a kitten? You can have your pick."

"We have barn cats but no house cat. The mice seem to know this. Is the mother a good hunter?"

"She keeps the mice out of the store and the feedstore too, and that is a big job."

Leif looked absolutely piteous, his eyes riveting hers. "Please, Mor, can we have one?"

"Are they old enough to leave the mother?"

"They are, but if you leave it here for a few weeks, she will have taught them how to hunt. The boys could bring it home with them after they start school."

The thought of having a growing cat in the house made Signe smile. But what about Einar and Gerd? After all, it was their house.

Leif could hardly stand still. "You would not have mice in the house again, like we did." He looked at Mrs. Benson. "You should have seen the mouse nest we found in the kitchen. Mor didn't think we would ever get them all."

Signe laid a hand on his shoulder. "You go see about the feed."

"But can I choose one?"

"Usually a female is a better mouser, isn't it?"

"We have found that to be true. The yellow tabby and the gray one are both girls. You go through this way." She pointed to a doorway closed off by a curtain.

Flashing her a grin, Leif skipped out the door.

Mrs. Benson smiled at Signe. "He is a fine young man."

"Takk. Tusen takk. I have some questions. How do I find the midwife? I've not talked to her yet."

"Ah. She lives . . ." Mrs. Benson jotted a note to herself on a small pad by the register. "I will have her come out and talk to you next time she comes in. Easier to find the Strand farm than for you to find her little house. I know she will want to meet with you in those final months."

Signe smiled her gratitude. One concern off her mind. "I need flannel for diapers and other baby things, and yarn for soakers."

Mrs. Benson walked to the dry goods in the corner. "I just

got a shipment in. Some of this print flannel for gowns might be nice, and this heavier outing flannel for blankets."

Signe nodded and decided to be honest. "Ja, but I cannot afford all that right now."

"Surely you can put these on Mr. Strand's account."

Signe shook her head. "I would much rather not."

Mrs. Benson paused and said softly, "I understand. In that case, we will start an account for you, and you send me butter and eggs when you can. We'll let the boys do the carrying on their way to school."

"Mrs. Benson, could you please answer a question for me?"

"I'll try."

"Why has no one come by to welcome us? In Norway, we always did that."

Mrs. Benson smoothed her hand down the bolt of flannel. After a sigh, she looked at Signe. "I'm not sure how to . . . Uh, no one goes there because the Strands do not like visitors. At all. They ordered several neighbors off their land, drove them off, and said they were not to come back." She flinched as she spoke. "I'm sorry. They have a very bad reputation here."

Signe sucked in a deep breath and straightened her shoulders. No wonder no one came to help Gerd when she fell sick. Surely there must be something she could do—but what?

Chapter 19

Signe was sweeping off the back steps as Einar and Bjorn dragged two great limbs into the yard. She announced, "Supper is ready."

Bjorn jogged right into the house. "Those hickory limbs are to smoke the venison. Onkel Einar knew exactly where a hickory tree was."

"That is going to be mighty tasty." Signe followed Einar into the house.

Once they were seated at the table and the food was dished up, Leif asked, "Mor, what grade will I be in?"

Signe smiled at her youngest. "I'm not sure. I was not able to talk with your teacher. Mrs. Benson said—"

"There will be no school. You have work to do here." Einar continued shoveling in his food.

Eyes wide, Leif looked from the stern man to Signe. "But—"

"No buts. You heard me."

Signe looked at Rune, who shrugged and kept eating.

She felt anger boiling up, but she kept her voice even. "Our agreement was that the boys would go to school. Knute and

Leif are too young to quit school. Bjorn is old enough to stay here and work."

"If he ever gets that cast off. Can't even wield an axe yet."

"True, but he still managed to bring down a deer so we have meat to eat." Rune spoke as if there were no tension at the table.

Signe stilled the words that threatened to erupt, about where and how Bjorn broke his arm, but instead she glared at her husband. *My boys will go to school.* Her chin rose to a dangerous angle. She said softly, "We will discuss this later."

"There is no discussion. I paid your fare for you all to work here." Einar shoved his chair back. "I'll be in the machine shed." He stared at Rune. "I'll light the lantern so we can get all the tools sharpened tonight."

Rune nodded. "I'll be out shortly."

Einar stomped out and let the screen door slam behind him.

Signe waited for Rune to say something, but he calmly finished his supper. He looked at the boys. "Do you have more chores to do?"

All three shook their heads.

"Then finish eating. Bjorn, you come with me." He looked at Signe. "Is there more for the boys to do in the garden?"

She nodded. "And Knute needs to run his trapline."

"Then we will all finish eating." The look he gave her let her know they would discuss the school issue later. He was not ignoring the situation.

She collapsed against the back of her chair. "Would you like more coffee?"

"I would."

Bjorn heaved a sigh. "I want to be back out in the woods, Mor." He raised his now filthy cast. "When can I get this off?"

"You have two weeks yet."

"I've been careful." He flexed his fingers, first on the weak hand, then the other. "When I fired the rifle, I pulled the trigger with my good hand and steadied the gun on my cast. It worked fine."

Leif finished his meal. "Why doesn't he want us to go to school?"

"He's worried there aren't enough trees ready to ship to the mills. He wants a lot more logs than what we've cut so far." Rune cleaned the rest of his plate with another slice of bread. "That is what brings in money for us all to live here."

"How will he get the trees to the railroad?" Knute reached for more bread. "Mor, do we have jam? I need to move my trapline. Guess we got all the rabbits close by."

"Signe." The call from the bedroom was growing stronger.

"Coming." She poured Rune's coffee and stopped at the doorway. "I'll bring your supper now."

"Good."

Signe returned to the stove and started dishing up another plate. "Rune, I think we need two canes for Gerd. She's getting stronger, and I want her walking."

"I could get two sticks at least."

Bjorn frowned at his mor. "Onkel Einar should do that."

"Ja, well." She shook her head and set the plate on a tray, along with a full coffee cup. "At least she is eating and beginning to feel better."

Her mind kept churning as she got Gerd propped up and the tray on her lap. Never a *please* or *thank-you*, not even a friendly greeting. All orders and commands. Was he that bad out in the woods too? If Rune had to put up with that out there, how could he stand it? Right now she felt like storming down to the machine shed and—and . . .

As if her mor were standing right beside her, Signe heard

her say, "*Remember, Signe, a soft answer always turneth away wrath. If you remember nothing else that I have taught you, remember this verse above all else.*"

But, Mor, yelling at him would be so much more satisfying. Signe felt the sting of tears behind her eyes. There was no way to describe how desperately she needed to see her mor, to talk these things over with someone. She could try with Rune, but why lay more on him? He was already carrying enough. The baby gave her a good kick in the ribs, as if telling her to calm down.

At that, she smiled and shook her head. She returned to the table. "Do any of you need anything else?"

"You never make cookies anymore," Leif said hopefully.

"You're right. Perhaps one of these days. How about another piece of bread with jam instead?" She fetched the jam from the pantry and set it on the table, then sliced more bread.

"A cookie with my coffee would certainly be good. As you say, one of these days." Rune pushed back his chair but paused. "You did not finish your supper, and now it's cold."

The kindness in his voice almost did her in. "Thank you. It will be fine."

"What do you want the boys to do in the garden?"

"The beans need to be picked again. And we need to clean out the cellar to be ready to bring in the potatoes and other things."

"Ja, so much to do, I know." He and Bjorn put on their hats and headed for the machine shed.

Leif and Knute finished their bread and followed the men out the door, Leif as always making sure the screen door did not slam.

Signe knew why she had not baked cookies. She never had a moment to roll them out, and she was too conscious of using up the precious sugar. Surely Einar would appreciate cookies sometimes, and she knew Gerd would. If only she could talk over some of these things with Gerd.

That night after all the others had gone to bed, she motioned for Rune to sit with her in the parlor. Just in case Einar was still awake, she did not want to talk in the kitchen.

He waved her into the armchair, then perched on the horsehair sofa. She glanced around the parlor. What should she bring up first?

Rune began, "You know I believe the boys going to school is necessary as much as you do."

"Takk. I thought so, but I wondered when you did not say anything."

"I've learned that it does no good to argue with him when he's in that demanding mood."

"He's not like that all the time?"

"Nei. When we're in the woods, he's almost pleasant."

She shook her head. "That does not make sense. At least not to me."

"It doesn't need to make sense. That's just the way he is."

Signe swallowed the questions pushing to be asked. "Maybe he should stay out in the woods all the time."

"He is there all he can be."

Signe shrugged. She should know better by now than to waste sarcasm on her husband. "I know. But what do we do about school?"

"We follow our original agreement with him. Bjorn will work in the woods with us, and the other two will go to school. I mean, what can he do but bluster and yell and be angry? They *will* get all the school they can. I would prefer that Bjorn go too, but he doesn't want to. He has said so—repeatedly. So it is not to be. Right?"

"But what if he yells again? Leif is trying so hard to do what they say. You watch—he makes sure the screen door never slams because Gerd screeched about it." She nodded thoughtfully. "I—I thought life could be so good here. Hard work, I know, but we are not afraid of hard work." She rubbed her teeth over her bottom lip, then looked at Rune. "Why are they so mean? Do you suppose they were always like this, or that something happened here to turn them that way?"

Rune shrugged and shook his head at the same time. "Who knows." He blew out a cheek-puffing breath. "I just know that we are all working as hard as we can to fulfill our part of the agreement. When I think this is too much, I think about a house of our own on our own land. We agreed to work for them to earn back the money he spent to bring us from Norway. After that?" He raised his hands. "Only God knows."

Signe stared at him, willing herself to ask her next question. Hands twisting in her lap and her breath catching in her throat, she swallowed. She started to ask, stopped, then took a deep breath and looked into his dear face.

"D-do you still . . . still really believe that?"

Confusion chased itself across his face from ear to ear. "Believe what?"

"That God really exists and knows and cares about us?" The words rushed out.

"Signe, of course I believe. How can I look at those giant trees every day, and the animals here, and you and our boys . . ." His head wagged as he spoke softly yet firmly. "The sun coming up in the morning and going down at night. Of course I believe. I cannot *not* believe in Him. Why do you ask?"

Signe heaved a sigh—of what? Frustration? Fear? No, mostly confusion.

He turned his head slightly to study her. "Do you doubt?"

She nodded without looking at him.

He reached over and, with a gentle finger, turned her face back to him. "Why?"

"We—we never talk about God or go to church anymore. And—and when I prayed, He didn't answer—not like He used to."

"Do you pray for us and our boys and—" He stopped as she shook her head. "I see." The silence deepened along with the fading lamplight. "You no longer do?"

"Nei. But . . ." She struggled with the proper words and clenched his hand in hers. "I-I think—I . . . I want to." There, it was out. She nodded. "Ja, I want to."

A pause stretched. Was he angry at her? Disappointed? She was afraid to search his face.

"Then do so."

The words fell gently into the pool of her mind, sending out ripples. This time the silence seemed full of life, no matter how quietly the ripples splashed upon the shore. *Then do so.* Of course. After all, what could it hurt? Rune held her hand, gently now, peacefully. And waited.

"Are you there, Lord? If you are listening, I-I'm sorry." Tears gushed from her eyes, a spring freshet dancing down the rocks at home, singing and sparkling in the sunshine. Peace washed over her, the likes of which she had never felt. It bathed her heart, her mind, and deep inside it washed away the doubts like bits of bark or grass caught in the mountain spring cleansing. *He restoreth my soul.* The verse followed, only instead of dancing onward, it rested upon her.

"Ah, my Signe, your face shines, so I know you are back where you belong. In Him and in me."

"Ja." She wiped away her tears and squeezed his hand.

"Takk." Together they rose, and she stepped into his embrace. His arms around her—she realized she needed that right now even more than someone to talk to. "Tomorrow?"

"Now is where we are."

"I did not bank the stove."

"I will."

"I need to go outside first."

She left him quietly banking the fire and hurried to the outhouse. Lately the pressure to go had not allowed her as much time as usual. Another sign the baby was growing, as if the occasional kick in the ribs was not a sufficient reminder. She stopped and stared up at the stars flung so brilliantly against the cobalt, distant lights to remind that her someone was indeed home, like putting a lamp in a window to keep travelers from being lost in the wilderness of life.

She met Rune as she entered the house. "The outhouse needs lime again."

"I will take care of that first thing in the morning."

"Takk."

She could soon hear Rune's gentle puffing that said he had fallen asleep immediately, as usual. She tried one side, then the other. In spite of the cushioning of the pallet, getting comfortable was becoming more difficult all the time. Remembering her other pregnancies, she knew this was not unusual. But at home she'd had a feather bed rather than a hay pallet, and ropes that held up the mattress, not an unforgiving floor. She hated to add another thing to the list of tasks that needed to be done; the stairs were far more important than a rope-strung bed. However, the bed would take far less time. Strange—Einar had known they were coming, but had he made any preparations for five more people to live in this house? None at all.

Do not think about that! Do not think about him at all! She rolled onto her back, knowing that she would have a backache in the morning from sleeping this way. But in spite of the discomfort, she fell asleep halfway through the Lord's Prayer.

Chapter 20

AUGUST 1909

How to ask him about building some stairs?

"Far?" Knute tweaked Rune's shirt from where he sat in the back of the wagon.

Rune turned to his son, ignoring the man driving the team. Not a word had been said since they left the barnyard.

"Can I ask about fishing?" He spoke softly so Einar would not hear him.

"Go ahead." *My boys should not be afraid to talk about life here.* Rune heaved a sigh. This was not the life he had envisioned when he agreed to emigrate.

"Onkel Einar, do you ever go fishing?"

"I used to, but it takes too much time."

"Where did you go?"

"A little lake a couple miles away."

"Did you catch a lot of fish?"

"Sometimes. I went ice fishing a couple times, but I need to fell trees more than fish."

"Could I go fishing sometime? I really like to fish."

Einar snorted. "Not worth it."

"Oh."

Rune could tell how disappointed his son was. But what to do? Right now, school was more important. And getting a stairway built, which meant buying lumber. Perhaps while they ate dinner, he would bring it up.

Knute leaped out of the wagon as soon as it stopped, to take care of the horses, and the men took axes and saws out of the back. Einar always paused for a moment at the growing collection of felled trees. They had three or four more to be dragged over.

Knute asked, "How will you get them to the railroad?"

"The lumber company comes with a steam engine to load them on sledges. Then they load the train cars with cranes. If we were close to a river, we would skid them there on the snow and float the logs to St. Paul in the spring."

"Far says you built the house with lumber from trees right here. How did you cut the boards?"

"I dragged them to a portable sawmill. It was set up not far from here." He pointed to the trees he had marked and signaled for Rune to follow him. They notched the tree, each of them wielding an axe from either side. Rune liked the rhythm they had grown into. They leaned their axes against a stump, took either end of the seven-foot saw, and set it into the notch, slipping with ease back into the pull motion. He'd learned the first day that one never pushed, always pulled. The fear of snapping the blade was a good motivation to learn. That was why two men were needed.

When they paused for a breather, he looked over to see Knute dragging branches. He was growing a good-sized pile. His boys were such hard workers, even Bjorn, who was itching to get back out here in the woods. Einar might make a lumberjack out of him.

"Ready?"

"Ja." A short time later, the telltale creak of a tree in the final throes of life told them to pull out the saw—now. They did, and both men automatically checked to see where Knute was. The tree was not cut to fall toward him, but they were taking no chances. "Get back!" Rune yelled and waved his arm. Knute waved back and scurried off to the side.

The tree groaned and shuddered. Rune stared up at the shaking branches. An instant of slowness, and then the tree stormed through the surrounding trees and with a mighty roar crashed to the ground, sending limbs and bark and clumps of needles flying. Rune felt like praying, as if the tree's soul had died. The forest stood silent.

Rune and Einar both wiped the sweat from their brows with their sleeves, Einar nodding. "Knute, bring the jug!"

But Knute was already halfway there, anticipating the order. After several long swallows, Rune handed the jug back to Knute. "Go ahead and take the team over for a drink."

Knute grinned and nodded. "This is the part of the day I like best."

"Start a new pile when you get back, closer to that tree."

"Yes, sir."

Einar and Rune set to limbing the tree, Rune with an axe and Einar using the bow saw on the lower branches, which were as big around as small trees. By the time the sun was directly overhead, they were more than half done. They leaned their tools against the trunk and headed over to the wagon.

"I don't like to see the trees fall," Knute said around bites of his sandwich.

"Can't farm the land with these trees in the way, and besides, they bring in good money." Einar glugged the coffee Signe sent in a quart jar, one for each of the men.

Dusk came early in the shadows of the giant pines, so when it became harder to see the branches they were lopping off the second tree, Einar called it a day, and they returned to set their tools in the back of the wagon. Knute had the team all hitched up again and impatient to head for the barn.

Rune was no closer to asking about the stairs, but now he would wait until dinner time tomorrow, so Einar could work off his anger and not take it out on Signe. It took a while sometimes, but Rune was learning.

As soon as the team stopped at the barn, Knute jumped out and went to check on the pigs and chickens. The chickens were wandering back to their pen, so Knute fetched a can of oats from the grain bin and scattered them in the yard to encourage any laggers. He scratched the two sows and studied the two butcher hogs, which were rooting all around the edge of the pen, trying to get to the bits of grass growing outside the fence.

Rune leaned against the pen with him.

"Hank and Henry are big enough to butcher, aren't they?"

"They are. You've done a fine job feeding them."

"When I pulled the suckers on the corn stalks for them, they really liked that."

"They would love corn too, but then, pigs will eat about anything. At home we let them loose in the gardens after everything was harvested. They turn the soil over real good."

"And fertilized it too."

Rune ruffled his son's hair. "You are most certainly a farmer at heart."

Knute rested his chin on the hog fence. "I like the animals the best. I wish we had sheep. I miss Grandma's sheep. And the geese." He turned to Rune. "Will we go hunting when the ducks and geese fly south?"

"Doesn't look that way. No time." Rune slapped his hand on the fence rail. "Lock up the chickens, and let's go see if supper is ready."

"Onkel Einar was nicer today."

"Ja, he was."

"Why?"

"I have no idea."

That night they had the first of the corn on the cob for supper.

Einar wagged a hand. "Get me a sharp knife."

Rune saw Signe's slight hesitation before she did his bidding. Could the man not say *please* or *thank you*? Had he never learned, or did he just not care? Rune realized this was the way he always was, not something new since he had met Signe's resistance to obeying his every command.

She laid the knife on the table beside Einar and returned to the stove to dish up a plate for Gerd. Rune knew she was working to get Gerd strong enough to join them at the table for meals. Did Einar even understand how hard Signe was working here? Rune mentally shook his head. All this introspection was certainly not like him.

While Einar carefully cut his corn off the cob, Rune and the boys attacked the platter of corn with delight. They slathered on butter and made their way through the stack, almost ignoring the meatballs Signe had made from ground venison. Add gravy over just-dug potatoes, and none of them took time to talk, just the way Einar liked it.

The older man cleared his plate with a slice of bread, pushed back his chair, and with a belch that said plenty, left the table and then the house. The pall over the table left with him.

"When will you take this cast off?" Bjorn asked after a brief silence.

"Saturday will be six weeks," Signe said, "but you have to promise not to overuse it. Those muscles are weak, and you could strain one easily."

"I have been using it some, you know."

"I know, like splitting wood and the other chores you have figured how to do mostly with your left hand."

"I shucked the corn using these fingers." He wiggled the ones sticking out of his cast.

"This supper was one of the best since we came here." Rune raised his cup in the way of one who hoped for a refill.

Signe smiled at him. "You could just ask."

"I know. One should not waste words."

Signe filled his cup. "You boys want coffee too? There is cream and sugar for it."

"Really?" Leif grinned at her. "Almost like dessert."

"Gingerbread would be good one of these days, don't you think?" Rune said.

"Ja, it would. We have molasses even. I thought of making an äggakaka. I have extra butter and eggs I could take to the store. Once you boys start school, you can deliver that for me."

"How many days to school?" Leif asked, then glanced at Rune. "We are going to school, right?"

"You are," Rune said.

"And I can go out in the woods with you and Onkel Einar?" Bjorn made certain.

"Ja."

"And I can go out and drag branches as soon as I get home," Knute threw in.

"Ja, that too."

Leif stared hopefully at Rune. "I could drag branches."

"Ja, you could, but then who would milk the cow and feed the animals?"

"I could milk later."

"And all of us could do the rest of the chores then too," Bjorn added.

Rune looked at each of his boys. All he saw was an eagerness to help that threatened to overwhelm him. "Soon it will be too dark to work in the woods, so this will not be a problem any longer. And you can do chores by lantern light. You will soon anyway." He nodded, carefully rubbing his eyes. "Uff da," he muttered under his breath.

"Your eyes are bothering you?" Signe said.

"Ja, some." He pushed back his chair. "We better get down there. Bjorn, have you tried using the grinding wheel yet?"

"Ja, I sharpened the hoe. It works better now."

"Good. Try one of the axes tonight."

Signe reached out. "Pass me your plates."

Down at the machine shed, while he and Einar started filing the teeth on the saw, Rune sucked in a deep breath. Now—now was the time.

"Einar, with Signe in her condition, it is getting dangerous for her to be going up and down the ladder to our beds." He almost mentioned building a bed but thought better of it. One thing at a time.

"So she can sleep downstairs again. She was the one who insisted on going up there."

Rune decided to ignore that idea. "I want to build stairs. It would be safer for all of us, but especially her and the baby."

"She can sleep in the parlor again."

Rune exhaled and inhaled, his mind darting here, there, and

everywhere to find the best way to deal with Einar. "Have you ever constructed stairs?"

"Ja, but we do not need stairs."

"Can we get lumber down at Benson's or do we have to go into Blackduck?"

"I said we are not building stairs."

"I'm thinking we need to cut a vent over the kitchen stove to get heat up into the attic this winter."

Einar waved the file in the air. "The house is fine just the way it is."

"The house was fine for two people, but we are now seven with another on the way. Some things have to change. Benson's or Blackduck?"

"Blackduck! And I do not want to hear any more about stairs and a hole in the ceiling."

"I was thinking about putting the stairs in the parlor, but on that wall in the kitchen would be better. Then the entry would be in the center of the attic."

"Are you deaf? I said no stairs."

"Einar, I understand what you are saying, but along with working for you, I need to take care of my family. If Signe falls and gets hurt, who will take care of Gerd?"

Einar started to say something, then growled instead. His hand clenched the file so hard that his knuckles turned white, and the fury shooting from his eyes made Rune's stomach clench. He kept right on filing. At least he had opened the subject, giving Einar something to think about.

Later, when Rune and Signe were talking in the parlor as had become their habit, Rune told her what had happened. "He was so furious I thought he was going to attack me."

"Because you told him about the need for stairs?"

Nodding, Rune studied the calluses that had built up on his

hands. His head was getting too heavy to hold up. "I do not know, Signe. I just do not know."

"Just let him chew on it for a while."

"I guess." *If only we lived in our own house.*

Chapter 21

Leif burst through the back door. "Mor, a hawk got one of the young chickens!"

"Did the rooster try to save it?"

"No, and we were too far away." He brushed at his eyes. "The red one."

She knew that had been his favorite. "Oh, Leif, I am so sorry."

"We need a guard dog. Something to protect the chickens and the pigs and everything."

"You did the best you could."

"Bjorn said he needs a shotgun. Blast that hawk out of the air."

"Signe." The call came from the bedroom.

"Be right there."

"Bring Leif with you."

Signe and Leif stared at each other, shrugged, and went to see Gerd, who was sitting by the window.

"I saw the hawk too. Happens every once in a while." She pointed to the closet. "Look on the top shelf."

Signe reached as high as she could but felt nothing. "Get me the stool," she said to her son. When Leif set it down for her, she climbed up, hanging on to the doorframe. Clear on the back of the shelf, she felt it. She looked over her shoulder. "A gun?"

"Ja, a shotgun. The rifle Bjorn used is over the door in the kitchen where it used to be, but we keep the shotgun up there."

Signe handed the gun to her son and stepped down, dusting her hands on her apron. "Are there shells for it?"

"Maybe not. But we can buy some. If one of your boys likes to hunt . . ."

"Bjorn does. He got the deer."

"Then he can hunt ducks and geese when they fly over. Sometimes they land in our pond."

Signe had never heard Gerd say this much in one day, let alone in one conversation. "Will Onkel Einar mind?"

"He doesn't like to hunt, but he does like to eat." She nodded at Leif. "You boys should all know how to shoot a rifle and a shotgun." She heaved a breath. "I'm ready to go back to bed."

"Takk! Tusen takk." Leif took the gun out to the kitchen table while Signe helped Gerd back to bed.

Gerd nodded. Her eyelids closed, and she heaved a deep breath. Walking that far exhausted her, but she was doing better. Signe let the hope bloom in her chest.

"Today is the day!" Bjorn waved his cast at her a couple of days later.

"After chores and breakfast." She slid a pan of corn bread into the oven.

"Two more weeks until school starts," Knute whispered in her ear as he headed for the barn.

To Signe that meant that sometime in the coming days, there

would be a violent war of words with Onkel Einar. Trepidation sent tentacles of fear from her heart to her middle. What was the best way to make him agree that the boys needed to be in school? Or probably not agree, but at least give his permission to attend. And if he did not give permission, at least not try to stop them. She and Rune were in agreement that the boys would go. Rune said to just pack the boys' dinner pails and send them off. Not to make a secret out of it, but go ahead as though it were perfectly normal.

She heaved a sigh. What was the matter with Einar?

After breakfast, with Gerd fed and the men on their way to fell trees, she sat Bjorn down out on the porch and laid his cast-encased arm on the table. She brought out a hammer and the meat cleaver. Bjorn's eyes went wide, and he gulped.

"Hold your arm very still. Very, very still."

Carefully she placed the cleaver just so, its nose pressed against Bjorn's arm and its blade poised on the upper rim of the cast by his elbow. She began to tap it with the hammer.

Nothing. She tapped harder. The cleaver blade bit into the plaster-and-rags cast. Slowly, a tiny bit at a time, the cleaver cut through the cast, down his arm and to the wrist. She brought the bone shears out from the kitchen and cut through the last shreds, pulling it apart.

"It stinks!" Bjorn cried. "Ach, do I stink! And look at that rash. No wonder it itched so bad."

"We will wash it, of course, and put salve on the rash."

"It sure is white . . . and skinny." Bjorn held his two arms side by side. "Looks like a stick."

"That is why you still have to be very careful. It takes time to rebuild those muscles." She rubbed his arm, pressing to the bone, but it had no telltale bump. She watched his face, and he never flinched. "Does it hurt at all?"

"Nei." He shook his head, clenching and releasing his fist. "I can use the axe right now." He stood and leaped off the porch, pulled the axe free of the block, and split a spool of wood in half. He grinned at her.

"How does your arm feel?"

"Like it has been lazy for too long." He grabbed another spool and repeated his actions, then looked around. "Looks like Leif and I better get a log up on the sawhorses and get some sawing done."

"We need to pick the last of the beans too. So do that first. No, wait. Do that after you wash that stinky arm."

Cackling with joy, Bjorn headed for the washbasin.

Once the boys returned to the garden, she answered Gerd's call. "Today is a good day to walk to the window again."

Gerd shook her head, but she didn't grumble. "You took his cast off?"

"I did, but he is not going to the woods tomorrow. He can go out on Monday. Would you like a cup of coffee and a bit of corn bread?"

"Ja. With jam?"

Signe nodded. "You could snap beans while you sit here. The boys are picking the last of them."

"Ja, I will."

Signe nearly floated out to the kitchen.

When she returned with a bowl of beans, Gerd was dozing but she jerked upright when Signe set the bowl on a stool beside her, with another bowl for her lap.

"I always cut the beans."

"Ja, just snap the ends off. I will cut them."

Hands shaking, Gerd picked up a handful and began the job. "Have some for supper?"

"If you like."

That night at the table, Einar studied Bjorn. "The cast is off. You will go with us in the morning."

"I cannot wield an axe much yet."

"It's time you went back to work. Past time."

Bjorn looked to Signe, who shrugged. She would remind him to be careful in the morning. She looked to Rune, who answered with a slight nod.

"He will not use an axe yet." Rune spoke firmly but softly. Einar shot him a glare, but Rune nodded and kept on eating. "Knute is doing well with the axe lately."

She could see Knute's chest swell with the praise. It took so little to encourage the boys. Why could Einar not see that? But then, she should not be surprised. He never even said *takk*. Perhaps he did not know how? The thought made her almost smile.

After supper the boys set to sawing into stove lengths the last of the limbs and logs set aside for firewood. When it was too dark to see, they came inside.

"Can we have bread and sugar?" Leif asked.

Signe was just finishing the dishes. "One of you get the pitcher of milk from the well house, and I will heat up the coffee. We'll have a celebration."

"For what?"

"Bjorn is no longer wearing a cast."

"And school is going to start," Knute added.

"And I get to go back to the woods," Bjorn hollered over his shoulder as he charged out the door.

Signe threw Leif the dish towel. "You finish drying these while I slice the bread. Then go ask Tante Gerd if she wants to join the party. Knute, you go tell the men. If Onkel Einar does not want to come, Far can anyway. Tell him Mor said." Signe started slicing the bread. She would have to set the sourdough starter for the bread tomorrow, but so what?

She had the bread sliced and buttered when Knute came back in. "Far is coming. Onkel Einar just glared at me and said he had to finish."

"So be it." Signe set a plate on a tray with a full cup of coffee, sprinkled the sugar over the butter, and carried it to Gerd. "Here you are, Tante Gerd. A party treat." She set the tray on Gerd's lap and smiled at the nod she received. That was far better than a mean scowl.

When Rune came into the kitchen, they were all sitting around the table, waiting for him. "What are we celebrating?"

"My cast is gone." Bjorn raised his arm. "And I get to go back in the woods. Finally."

"And school starts soon," Knute said.

"And we have not celebrated anything since we got here," Signe finished. "It is about time. Tante Gerd has hers in her room." *And that is another thing to celebrate.* But Signe didn't say that aloud. She closed her eyes for just a moment, whispering, "Thank you, Lord." Like her mor used to do and most likely still did. It was time someone around here was thankful.

<hr />

For the next two weeks, both Bjorn and Knute worked out in the woods with the men. They were both nearly staggering by the time they sat down at the table for supper. They ate, washed up, and climbed the ladder to their beds in the attic.

"Maybe tomorrow we can fell another tree just before dusk and get in an extra two a week, maybe even three." Einar finished his coffee and started to push back his chair.

"School starts tomorrow. Knute and Leif will be going," Signe said.

Einar slammed his fist on the table. "I told you they're going to work here. We agreed on that." His angry glare could have nailed her to the wall.

"No, our agreement when we said we would come was that the boys would go to school. Bjorn has chosen not to, as he would rather work in the woods." Rune kept his voice even and reasonable.

"Last week I told you—"

"The boys are going to school, and Knute will come help in the woods as soon as he gets home."

Signe kept her mouth closed, but her mind kept repeating, *Please, God. Please, God.*

"You, you . . ." Einar stared from Rune to Signe and back. "This is my house, and you will do what I say."

"Bjorn and I will work with you. The other two will go to school and do the regular farm chores when they get home. If they take the horse, they will get home more quickly."

"No school!" Einar stormed out the door, the screen door slamming behind him. They heard him stomp back up the porch steps and holler, "Are you coming?"

"I will be right there." Rune drained his coffee cup and nodded at Signe. "It will be all right."

Signe nodded. Rune had dealt with Einar and not left it up to her, as he did so often. She knew how much he hated arguing. But this time—this time . . . Tears burned behind her eyes, but she had no time for weeping.

Getting back on her feet took an extra boost of will. She had to set the starter. They would need more bread now that she had to pack two separate dinners. She had found two lard pails in the cellar for the boys to take their dinners to school in. Her feet ached, her back ached, and all she wanted to do was go to bed. She left two starters on the warming shelf and banked the fire. She was just getting ready to go up the ladder when she heard the men on the porch. Go back to the kitchen or on up the ladder?

She chose the ladder. She could not stand to look at that man again tonight.

In the morning, she rose early to get everything done, but Rune was up before her. She could hear him setting the lids back on the stove. From her hands and knees, she pushed herself upright. Getting up off the pallet was growing more difficult day by day. Stairs or a real bed—which did she need most? Once she was dressed, she inched her way down the ladder. Her foot slipped on the final rung, and she landed on the floor with a jerk. She leaned against the ladder for a few moments to let her heart settle down.

"Did you roust the boys?" Rune asked.

"Nei, not yet. They can sleep for a few more minutes."

Rune held out his arms, and surprised, she walked into them. Heat was already coming from the stove. The comfort of his arms made her sigh. "Takk." She rested her cheek against his chest. "I'm dreading these next hours."

"Sometimes when you let Einar think on things, he changes his mind. He will not tell you so, but I've seen it happen."

"He has such a temper."

"Ja, but he works harder than anyone I know."

"Ja." *Tell him I slipped on the ladder or no?* But somehow

228

the words bypassed her resolve. "I slipped on the bottom rung of the ladder. I have to be more careful than I thought."

"Oh, Signe." Rune heaved a sigh that shook them both. "One thing at a time. Get the boys off to school, and then I will bring up the stairs again. Perhaps you and I should move our pallets back down to the parlor."

"I hate to do that." She stepped out of his arms and reached up to pat his cheek. "You are a good man, Rune. I thank God for you."

"I'll go call the boys so they can get down to the barn."

Signe fixed the coffeepot, did the same with the cornmeal for mush, then stirred more flour into the starter and kneaded the dough for the first time. Wishing she had three hands, she inhaled the fragrance of yeast rising from the dough. There was something special about kneading bread dough as the daylight was just breaking. The rooster announced the rising sun, and one of the horses whinnied.

Would he be angry if the boys rode off to school? Rune was right—they would get home more quickly if they rode.

She sliced the last loaf of bread and made sandwiches for both men and the boys. Butter and jam for the younger boys and thinly sliced smoked venison for the three woodsmen. If only she had cheese. Today she would set the older milk for cheese rather than skimming off the cream. She had enough to churn butter already. One more thing to do today.

Once everyone was at the table, she dished up the mush, and Einar, as always, reached for the cream pitcher first.

She glanced at Leif, who was looking from Einar to her, questions all over his face. Shrugging, she set the jam and the butter on the table, along with the biscuits she'd reheated from the night before and a bowl of scrambled eggs.

Rune nodded to her and passed the biscuits to Einar.

Einar never looked at her, never said a word until he pushed his chair back.

She watched him leave the room, her head wagging slowly.

"Can I have the rest of the eggs?" Knute asked.

"Ja, go ahead. Bjorn, take the basket with you when you go."

He nodded and grinned at her. "I like being back in the woods. No school. Ja!"

"I will bring the water jug." Rune patted her shoulder as he went by and leaned over to whisper, "See, I told you all would be well." He looked at the two boys still at the table. "You boys do your best now. And hurry home."

"Should we gallop all the way?"

"No, but an easy lope might be a good idea."

The boys went down to get the horse ready, and Signe scrambled a couple more eggs for Gerd, who was sitting up in bed, waiting for her.

"Perhaps you could come out to the kitchen for dinner today."

"Perhaps."

Signe knew her face must show surprise. She returned to the kitchen and set the dishes in the dishpan on the stove. When the boys called from outside, she took their dinner pails out to them, all the while wishing she had something more to put in them.

"You two be careful, and make sure you water Rosie when you have dinner. On your way home, stop at the store and see if there is any mail."

"Ja, we will." Knute reined old Rosie around and started down the lane. Leif waved to her, hanging on to the pails with one hand.

Lord, keep them safe. Keep everyone safe, and thank you.

She should have had them bring the churn up from the well

house. Having help around here all summer had made life a lot easier, but she was on her own now.

Carrying the churn to the porch gave her a backache. Churning, making bread—everything seemed to do that lately. She sat down on the steps and promptly burst into tears, the soul-wracking kind that wrung one out.

Chapter 22

"Mor, you have a letter from Norway!"

Signe ran to the door and saw Leif sliding off the horse's back.

"A letter from home! Oh, oh thank you, Lord." Leif met her at the steps and handed her both the letter and their dinner pails.

"I'll put Rosie away."

Knute charged up the steps. "Mor, I'm so hungry. And I have to get to the woods."

"Ja, I will slice some bread for you." She set the dinner pails in the sink and cut two slices of fresh bread, slathered butter and jam on them, and out the door he went. "How was school?" she called after him.

"Leif can tell you."

Signe tucked the letter in her apron pocket and sliced bread for a sandwich for Leif. After pulling the coffeepot forward to the hot spot, she checked the beans baking, stirred them, and shut the oven door. The letter crinkled in her pocket.

From Gerd's room came "Signe, is that coffee heating?"

"Ja. You want bread with jam? The bread is still warm."

"Oh, ja. That would be good."

Signe strode to the doorway. "I'll serve our bread and coffee at the table. Come, we will walk."

Since they had walked around the bed and back and forth to the chair by the window, she knew Gerd could do this. It was the perfect time. With only a small huff, Gerd swung her feet over the edge of the bed and stood. Clinging to Signe's arm, she made her slow, halting way to the kitchen. They paused once for Gerd to catch her breath, then shuffled the last steps and sank down on a chair at the table.

"You made it." Signe wanted to hug her, but she settled for a pat on the shoulder. "Very good."

Gerd looked around the kitchen, from the stove, where the canner was processing quart jars of carrots, to the sink. "The boys are home from school?"

"Ja. Leif is taking care of Rosie, and Knute ran to the woods to work out there until dark."

"What is for supper?"

"Baked beans with smoked venison." She poured them each a cup of coffee and handed Gerd a plate of bread spread with butter and jam. Sinking into a chair, she tried to catch back a groan but missed. She had sat down for dinner, hadn't she? Or had she eaten dinner? She could not remember for sure.

She smiled. "There is nothing like fresh baked bread."

"Ja, very good."

"I'm glad you're strong enough to come to the kitchen."

"Ja."

To Signe, this felt like more than a simple thing. She had been afraid Gerd would be bedridden for the rest of her life, but she was getting stronger. Even if they moved forward only a little at a time, they were making progress.

"When is the baby due?" Gerd asked.

"Late November."

"Did you hem the diapers?"

"I figured I could do that when the garden is in."

"So, no diapers yet."

Signe heaved herself to her feet to fetch the coffeepot. She did not remember getting clumsy this soon before. After all, the baby was not due for two months.

"Nei. Not yet." The silence stretched while they sipped their coffee. "Did you ever make cheese?"

Gerd shook her head. "You?"

"Back home I did. Soft cheese."

"I have not had cheese like that since we came to Amerika."

"Did you buy cheese at Benson's?"

"Einar does not like Benson's."

"Oh." Questions that she dared not ask welled up. *Why?*

"More coffee?" Gerd raised her cup.

After helping Gerd back to bed, Signe took the canner off the stove and set the jars on the counter. They could eat carrots saved in sand in the cellar for several months, but canning would feed them for the rest of the year. Dusk was already creeping among the trees, so she mixed up corn bread, then added wood to the fire and set the kettle of beans on the cooler end of the stove.

Leif pulled open the screen door, a jug in one hand and a basket of eggs in the other. "I strained the milk, but there are no pans free to pour it into."

"Uff da. I was going to skim the cream."

"The churn is full too."

"And churn today. Bring the churn up to the porch, and we will churn it there." She brushed her hair back and wiped her brow with the back of her hand. "I will churn, you go skim the cream."

"I need a lantern in the well house."

"Use the barn one."

With the corn bread in the oven and the table set, she sat down at the churn and let the evening breeze cool her face and neck. The rhythmic thunk and swish of the churn danced with the peeper frogs and the evening insects. A thrush sang farewell to the dying sun. The nip of autumn floated in on the breeze. Knowing Einar, it would be full dark before he gave up in the woods.

By the time her arms were too tired to raise the handle again, she finally heard the change in tone that signaled the cream had given up and turned into butter. She gave it a few more plunges and rested her forehead on top of the churn dash. She blew out a breath and felt her shoulders and upper back relax. Her eyes closed in spite of herself.

"I'm done, Mor."

Signe jumped at the sound of Leif's voice. She caught her breath and blinked several times to clear her head.

"Were you sleeping?"

"I—I guess I was." She patted her chest to help settle her heart back to normal. "So all the chores are done?"

"Everyone is fed, and the chickens are back in their house. The cow is out in the pasture, the milk strained and put in the pans. I rinsed them out."

"Good for you." She heaved herself to her feet. "Get me a bucket to pour the whey into, and I will get the butter washed." How could she possibly have fallen asleep leaning on the butter churn?

She had already dished a plate for Gerd when she heard the tramp of boots on the steps. She told Gerd, "I'll come back for your tray. Tomorrow night, perhaps you will come to the kitchen for supper."

As always, Einar refused to look at her, even when she greeted him. Rune rolled his eyes, but rather than saying anything, herded the boys to the sink to wash. Einar sat down in his chair without stopping at the sink.

"How did it go?" she asked Knute.

He shrugged and took his chair next to Bjorn, who was rubbing his arm.

She wanted to ask if he had used the axe too much, but instead she dug the ladle into the pot of beans and venison and passed full plates around the table. Corn bread squares and a bowl of cooked carrots filled out the meal.

"Can I get you anything else?" She picked up the pitcher and passed the buttermilk around to fill the glasses, then poured the coffee. By the time she sat down, Einar pushed back his chair and headed for the door.

As soon as the screen door closed behind him, it was like everyone could breathe again.

"So how did you do out there?" she asked Bjorn.

"Pretty sore."

"Did he use the axe all day?" she asked Rune.

He shook his head. "But probably more than he should have. Knute dragged a lot of branches when he got there too." He passed his plate over for more beans. "We're doing the best we can, and that is all we can do." He looked at Knute and Leif. "Do you have any lessons you have to do?"

They both shook their heads. "The teacher said we have to take some tests since this is our first year in an American school."

"Did he say what subjects?" Rune asked, dipping his corn bread in the bean juices on his plate.

"Arithmetic and spelling. But we do not know many English words."

"And reading and American history. We can read fine in

Norwegian, so he's finding someone to teach us English for a couple hours each day."

"He does not speak Norwegian?"

"Ja, some, but not real good."

"When he talks fast, I can't understand him." Leif wiped his mouth with the back of his hand.

"Are you the only ones who need help speaking English?"

"I don't think so, but the other teacher teaches the little kids." Rune pushed back his chair. "I better get to the machine shed." He looked back at his sons. "Are the chores finished, Leif?" Leif nodded. "You boys get on up to bed. Bjorn, how is your arm?"

"Sore."

"How bad?"

Bjorn shrugged.

"Sore when you move it or pounding pain?"

"Hurts but not pounding, like in the beginning."

"I will rub it," Signe said. "There's liniment under the sink."

"You will not use that axe tomorrow, no matter what Einar says." Rune stared at his son until Bjorn nodded, then he patted Signe's shoulder as he went out the door.

"Do we have to go to bed now?" Leif asked.

"Clear the table and start the dishes." She wagged her head when he rolled his eyes, making Knute send his little brother a knowing big-brother look. Signe nodded to Bjorn. "You come sit here." She pointed at her chair. After fetching the liniment from the cupboard, she poured some in her palm and rubbed it into his arm, lightly at first, then deepening as she worked the muscles. When he flinched, she softened her touch.

"Please get Tante Gerd's tray from her bedroom too," she told Leif.

A wave of weariness nearly swamped her. She blew out a breath and forced herself to keep working on Bjorn's arm. "How long did you use the axe?" When he shrugged, she pressed, "All morning?" He shook his head. "At all in the morning?" Another half shrug. "Look, tell me what you did."

"If I do, you'll get mad at me."

"I'm already getting angry at you for not facing up to the questions."

"I dragged branches until they felled the next tree. Then Onkel Einar said to start where I used to, and Mor, I did not want him to be angry at me too."

"What do you mean, *me too*? Who else is he angry at?"

"Well, he is really mad at you and sometimes at Far and . . ." His voice slid into a whisper.

Why did Rune not stop him? "Look at me."

He was not in any hurry to meet her stern gaze.

"We—your far and I—agreed to let you work in the woods again, but you knew what the restrictions were." Onkel Einar did too, but nothing she said mattered to him.

Bjorn nodded while she debated. Let him go back out, or make him stay home? "Are there enough branches to pull to keep you working all day?"

"Ja, because I cannot haul as many at a time as before."

"Or throw them as high on the stacks?"

He nodded again.

"What if you made several smaller piles, closer to where the trees fall?"

"I do what he tells me."

She heaved a sigh. "Ja, I know. But I cannot let you reinjure your arm." She thought a moment. "You will pull branches tomorrow until Knute comes to do that, and then you may use

238

the axe until dark. And if your arm hurts too much, you will not use it." She stared into his eyes. "You understand me?"

"Ja, but . . ."

"Your far and I will deal with Onkel Einar." She waited. "Do you hear me? Bjorn?"

"Ja. I hear you."

She watched him rub his arm. *I know I'm right. That man will not destroy my son.*

When Rune and Einar came in, she had the coffee hot and cinnamon cake just out of the oven.

Rune smiled at her. "Smells good in here."

"I thought you might like something to go to sleep on."

Einar sat down at the table, still without looking at her. Even when she set a cup and a plate of cake in front of him. He picked up his fork and ate it in four bites. Downed the coffee, pushed his chair back, and headed for the bedroom.

Rune and Signe stared at each other. Signe started to fume but instead clapped her hands over her mouth to keep her laughter from breaking out. Rune shook his head, his eyes laughing even if his mouth didn't.

"Would you like some cream in your coffee?" she asked.

"Nei. Sit down, and we will eat together. Knute said he brought a letter from home."

"Oh my goodness. I forgot all about it." She drew the bent envelope from her apron pocket and slit it open. "From Mor." She looked at him. "How come we have not had a letter from your family?"

"Guess they do not write letters much."

Shaking her head, she started to read.

"Dear Signe and family,

"We are still missing you so. Tante Elvira said that

would go away, but I think, for a change, my big sister is wrong. I still find myself looking for you to come in the door.

"I am sure the boys are growing like the beans up the poles in the garden this summer. I know you have been working so hard to lay all the food by that you can. To think that Bjorn brought down a buck even with his arm in a cast is rather amazing. He was getting to be quite a shot, and this proves it. It might behoove you to let him go hunting more often. When will the cast come off his arm?

"Rune's sister Nilda is saving every penny for her ticket to go to Amerika. If I had extra money to give her, I would help, but you know how scarce money is here. But at least we have a house to live in and food enough on the table.

"I have been knitting sweaters for the boys and will send them to you as soon as they are finished. They must be in school now. How hard that would be if one did not speak the language! I think that is why so many adults do not go to school there. What are you doing to learn to speak English?

"I have included the recipes that you requested. Greet Gerd and Einar from all of us. Please write soon, as I check daily for your letters.

"Love from

"Your Mor"

"She does not mention the others."
"I know. Strange. I told Bjorn that you and I would keep Einar from making him overuse that arm. He does not want Einar angry at him."

Rune nodded. "I will stand by that. Einar and I had a talk down at the shed. He just wants as many trees ready to skid to the train this winter as he can."

"I know that, but he will not abuse my boys to get his way with the trees. We have to agree on this, or . . ."

The *or what* she was not sure of.

Chapter 23

B jorn will not be using the axe today until late afternoon."
Einar stared at Rune, his brow tightening as his glare
deepened.

Rune waited, without moving and with no change of expression.

Einar started to say something, then spun and resumed harnessing the team.

"I will get our dinner basket." Rune turned and strode back to the house, bidding his heart to settle down as he sucked in several deep breaths. *Takk, Lord God, we got through that one.*

Bjorn and Signe met him on the porch. She handed him the water jug, and Bjorn carried the basket of food. While her eyes sparked with questions, he just nodded. He could feel her gaze on his back all the way to the wagon, where he turned and waved to her. He wanted to tell her not to worry, but not with Bjorn right beside him.

When they drove into the cleared area, Einar and Rune unloaded their saws and axes, and Bjorn took care of the horses, unhitching them, taking their bridles off, and tying them to a tree, where they rested in the shade. He patted both the horses and talked to them, then hustled over to the men.

"Start a new pile over there." Einar pointed at a spot much closer than usual.

"Yes, sir." Bjorn grabbed a couple branches small enough to drag and started out.

Einar had marked the next two trees, and the men settled into their normal routine. By dinnertime, Bjorn had taken the horses for a drink and fed them their measure of oats. He had the dinner basket set out, and as usual they fell to without much conversation.

"How is your arm?" Rune asked after Einar went out to mark two more trees.

"Hurts some, but not like yesterday."

"Good. But if wielding that axe starts it up again, you stop." While his son nodded, Rune added, "I mean that, Bjorn. You do as I say, not Einar. You understand?"

"Ja." Bjorn started to say something else but apparently thought better of it.

"Good." Rune clapped his hand on his son's shoulder.

"Far, I was thinking maybe I could use the bow saw and cut up some of those bigger branches into stove lengths."

"I'll see what he plans to do."

By the time Knute came jogging out to join them, Rune and Einar were sawing on their third tree of the day. After the third tree fell, Bjorn set to cutting limbs and Knute to dragging. Einar had said nothing about sawing the bigger branches.

The next time Rune looked over, both boys were dragging branches, and he saw Knute was throwing all the branches up on the pile. Rune wiped the sweat from his face with the back of his arm and returned to swinging his axe.

That night on the wagon ride back to the barn, Einar broke

the silence. "One day we will cut all the big branches into lengths to dry and cut for the stove. There is a stack of those to haul back later."

"Do you have another tree dried for the house? We cut up the second to the last one already," Knute asked.

Einar grumbled under his breath. "Ja, there is another dead tree down by the hayfield, back in the woods. Never gone through so much stove wood before."

Rune ignored him. He knew that would be another thing held against Signe. Would the day ever come when this man appreciated what Signe was doing for him?

Probably not. He did not seem to understand anything but felling trees. What had Gerd put up with all these years? Had he always been this way?

"Looks like it might freeze tonight," Einar announced after supper as he left the kitchen.

"We're running low on wood," Signe called after him. She heard a snort behind her and turned to find Rune staring at her, mouth slightly open. Bjorn rolled his lips together to lock his laughter in, but his eyes gave him away. Knute's eyes were too wide to blink, and Leif was choking on his laughter.

"Anyone for äggakaka?" Signe asked as if nothing were amiss. "Milk?" She dished up the last of the äggakaka from the night before and served it to her family, keeping back a piece for Gerd. "So, Bjorn, how is your arm tonight?"

"Sore, but not as bad as last night."

"And how long did you swing an axe?"

"We dragged branches mostly," Knute offered.

"Good. Then tomorrow, do the same. Perhaps you will be able to swing that axe a little longer, build the strength back.

You will heal faster that way." She looked around at her family. They were most certainly fulfilling their part of the agreement with Onkel Einar and Gerd, no matter what Einar said.

"Is there anything else in the garden that might freeze tonight?" Rune asked.

"Nei. Mostly root crops still out there. We'll dig them when we can. The potatoes are all in, and the squash. Mostly I need wood. Tomorrow I must do the wash again."

"How will you manage that washing machine by yourself?"

That was not what concerned her. Carrying all the water did. She'd just have to only fill the buckets partway. She shrugged.

"You boys get to bed. I'm going down to the machine shed."

Rune picked up his plate and cup to set in the dishwater, so the boys did the same.

"Do you need anything?" Signe asked him.

"Ja, I need you to get up to bed."

"I wanted to get a letter ready for the boys to take in the morning."

"That can wait another day or two."

"If we had stairs . . ."

"I know, I know. I will talk to him again."

⁂

Crossing the yard to the outhouse in the morning made Signe grateful she had grabbed her shawl and put on her shoes. The world wore a mantle of brittle shine that crunched beneath her feet. The stars still hung in the west while a band of dawn pink widened in the east. The breeze made her shiver. Doing the wash today would not be so miserable as weeks earlier in the heat. Smoke from the chimney bent toward the west, growing visible as the world lightened. The rooster crowed, then cleared his throat and announced the dawn.

"A bit early, Mister R. Your flock is not ready to wake yet."
Any more than we humans. How she would have loved to stay
in her warm bed for even another few minutes. But while Rune
had gone down to start the stove for her and said she should
sleep a bit longer, the rest of her body had rebelled. So she
started her day.

The heat of the stove felt like the kiss of a friend. Holding her
hands in the heat seemed to warm her entire body. She'd just set
the coffeepot on the hot part of the stove when her sleepy-eyed
sons trooped past on their way out to do the chores.

"You better check your snares, Knute. We'd all appreciate
some fresh meat."

"Is the venison gone?" Bjorn asked.

"Nei. We have another smoked haunch. And some that I
canned."

"I could go hunting again. I read once about so many ducks
and geese flying south, they darkened the sky sometimes. You
think that was true?"

"Perhaps Onkel Einar would know."

Bjorn rolled his eyes. "Good thing we're raising pigs."

Each of the boys carried buckets of water to fill the reservoir
and the boiler on the stove before they sat down to eat. Knute
had laid a skinned and gutted rabbit in the sink.

Once the others were all out the door and she'd taken care of
Gerd, Signe sorted the clothes and stirred the first of the sheets
in the boiler on the stove. She filled the washing machine and
wisely sat down to crank the handle. By the time she hung out
the first sheets, the sun had driven the morning nip away and
felt comforting on her back. The sheets would be dry in no time
with the wind making them dance.

"Can we have coffee?" Gerd called sometime later when Signe
had just added more wood to the stove.

"If you come out here." Signe stopped in the doorway. Gerd had gotten up and was sitting in the chair by her bed, knitting soakers for the baby. "Let me pull the pot up, and I will be right in." No matter how tired she felt, between fresh-smelling sheets on the clothesline and now this, her day had donned a fresh dress.

Gerd laid her knitting aside and used both hands on the arms of the chair to help her stand. She picked up the yarn again and, using the cane Rune had made her, started toward the kitchen. One step at a time with Signe beside her, more for confidence than assistance, they progressed to the kitchen table.

"Does Onkel Einar know how well you're doing?"

Gerd shrugged. "He never even mentioned the cane leaning against the nightstand."

"Perhaps he did not see it?"

Gerd sat down at the table, taking a deep breath and slowly letting it out as Signe had taught her. "Toast to go with the coffee?"

"That sounds good." Signe sliced the bread, slid the long toasting fork into it, and removed the front lid on the stove. After holding one side of the bread over the flame until golden, she turned it over and repeated. "Here, you butter this one while I toast the next." When she sat down, she breathed a sigh of accomplishment. With her elbows propped on the table, she nursed her cup of coffee and thought. "It seems to me that you could eat at the table with us all tonight."

Gerd shook her head. "Dinner, yes, but not supper yet."

"All right. But how about sitting in the sun for a while? You and I will have dinner on the front porch." It meant extra work for Signe, but it would be good for both of them. "I'll move the little table between the chairs, and we can eat there."

Gerd nodded slowly. "I think I would like that."

"The more you walk, the more you will be able to walk."

After dinner, when she helped Gerd back to bed after putting fresh sheets on it, Signe felt like she had climbed a mountain. Until she saw a mouse run from behind the stove to the pantry. Time to set the traps again. With fall settling in, the mice were seeking shelter too. But not in this house.

"Gerd, have you ever had a cat here?"

"Nei, Einar does not like cats."

"What about you?"

"I don't mind cats a bit. They're useful."

Signe smiled. "I am sure, too, he would not like mouse droppings in his oatmeal. Mrs. Benson said we could have two of her kittens when they were older. The barn cats are too wild to bring up to the house. Kittens would be perfect. I just saw a mouse in the kitchen."

"Traps?"

"I already set them. They can't keep up when the mice are breeding new litters all the time. We need cats around here." She looked at Gerd.

"Ja, I always wanted one, but . . ." Gerd shrugged.

But it was not worth the fight. Signe could understand that. Einar on a rampage was not a pleasant sight.

Two days later, when the boys returned from school, Leif slid off the horse with a gunnysack in his hand. "Come see what we have." A grin nearly split his face. He set the sack on the back porch and opened it. A plaintive *meow* announced the occupants. "Mrs. Benson said to keep them enclosed until they got used to us. They cried a lot on the ride home." He reached in the sack and lifted out a fluffy gray half-grown cat with white paws. Signe gathered the frightened kitten close, gently murmuring and soothing it.

"What does the other one look like?"

"Mrs. Benson says she's a yellow tabby, but she looks more gold or orange to me." Leif lifted the other cat from the sack and the animal clamped both front feet around his arm. "Where will we keep them?"

"Gerd says Einar does not like cats, so where might he not look?"

Knute said, "They can climb out of a stall in the barn. They were real tame before we stuck them in the sack. Mrs. Benson said their mother trained them to hunt already. Maybe we should put them in the grain bin. There are always mice in there."

"But Einar might look in there," Leif argued. "How about the harness room?"

Knute turned toward the house. "I am starved."

"Your sandwich is on the counter." Signe peeled the cat loose from her apron and handed it to Leif. "Let's put them in the pantry for now and fill a saucer with milk. Food works for everybody."

Knute ran out the door to go help in the woods.

"Leif, bring in more wood, please."

He stood tall and straight in front of her. "My name is not Leif. My name is Bring in Wood because that's what you always call me." He scampered off.

Signe laughed and sat down at her churn. The firm, rhythmic *sloosh sloosh sloosh* comforted her. Where to put the kittens when Einar was home?

If she were to ask Einar why he always had to have his way, of course he would reply, *"It's my house and I paid your way here."* But he was also blood kin and, in a large way, a host rather than a master. Give and take? They only gave, he only took. Always. The boys enjoyed the kittens, and so did Signe and, she'd bet, Gerd.

Signe made a decision. Einar could give this time. They would not hide the kittens. The kittens were here because they were trained to do an important task—catch mice—and if they happened to be warm, cuddly, and cute, so be it.

That night when the men came in from the woods, Gerd was sitting at the table. Leif smiled at her and nodded. "Glad you are here."

Gerd nodded, but her smile did not quite make itself visible. Signe could tell their tante was pleased, though. She set the pot of beans and rabbit on the table, returning from the oven with a pan of corn bread. All the while she watched Einar. All he did was nod to Gerd. He showed no care, no affection. A slow burn started in Signe's middle.

Rune smiled across the table at Gerd. "We are all glad you're strong enough to join us."

Signe ladled supper onto plates and passed them around. As always, Einar fell to eating without waiting for any of the others to receive their food. He broke one piece of corn bread over the top of the beans and sliced another to butter.

Signe shot a glare at him that would have curled anyone else's hair, but as always, he shoveled in the food, ignoring everyone else. Catching Rune's slight shake of the head, she made herself take a deep breath. Each of her family said thank you, as did Gerd. Signe kept her face from registering shock—at least she hoped she did. That alone was enough to make her sit down to eat with a lighter heart.

Do not serve him anything until he asks politely. The thought made her smile to herself. That was the way she had trained her boys, but this was a grown man, grown mean.

"Tante Gerd," Leif asked, "can you read in English?"

She shook her head. "But I can talk more in English."

"Could you maybe help us learn English?"

Gerd stared at him, her brow wrinkling.

Signe wanted to say something, but she kept quiet.

Gerd nodded. "Maybe I can." She looked at her husband. "Einar speaks better English than I do."

Einar finished his second helping, stuffed the last of his corn bread in his mouth, and pushed back from the table. Without a word, as usual, he headed out the door, letting it slam behind him.

So much for that. Signe swallowed a sharp comment and said, "Would anyone like more beans? We have spice cake for dessert." *And perhaps we will eat it all up and not leave Onkel a single bite.*

Two days later, out in the woods, Rune again reminded Bjorn, "Stop chopping when your arm begins to get stiff or hurt. There are plenty of branches to pile."

Einar huffed and shot Rune a dirty look but headed for the last felled tree to cut off the branches. "Bjorn can finish the upper branches on this tree, and we will drag these last four trees over to the logs after dinner."

"Yes, sir." Bjorn did not look at his far but began chopping immediately.

Rune wagged his head. What was the Scripture verse? The spirit is willing, but the flesh is weak. Still, he was proud of his son's enthusiasm and strong work ethic. He hefted his axe to his shoulder and strode over to the last downed tree. Once into the rhythm, he worked his way up the trunk until Einar, who had already moved on, called him to the other end of the long saw at the next tree to be felled. He glanced over and saw Bjorn still swinging his axe. Step in and stop him, or let him learn from experience? Rune took up his end of the crosscut saw. A sore arm was a better lesson than a father's constant reminders.

Einar called for them all to step back as the tree trembled and crashed to its death. "We'll eat dinner now."

Rune glanced up to see clouds hiding the face of the sun. It did not feel quite like noon yet, but this was as good a time to stop as any.

"You water those horses yet?" Einar grunted at Bjorn, who was setting out the dinner basket.

"No, sir, I was—"

"You know those horses come first. Get that done before you eat."

"Yes, sir." Bjorn stopped putting out the dinner and untied the horses instead.

As they ate, Rune contemplated explaining to Einar the value of a little patience and thought better of it. Some days Einar was harder to please than others. It was just part of life.

Einar stood. "We'll drop that next tree and then drag the others. Bjorn, you get that tree done."

"Yes, sir." Bjorn glanced at Rune with a slight headshake and went to do Einar's bidding.

"I told him to drag limbs when his arm started to hurt," Rune said.

"Lazy. He's just getting out of work."

"Nei. He works as hard as a grown man. We want that arm to finish healing, not be re-injured."

Einar hefted his axe and headed for the next marked tree. Rune picked up the saw and followed him. The man changed his mind like a weather vane.

When the tree was notched, they set to sawing. When they paused for a breather, Rune saw that Bjorn was dragging branches. Good.

After the tree fell, Einar hollered to Bjorn, "Get those horses over here and bring the chain so we can drag trees."

Bjorn dropped what he was doing and trotted over to the horses.

Einar looked at the felled trees and screamed, "Boy! You lazy lout, you didn't finish the limbs on this tree. Now we can't drag it over. Lazy! Can't even follow directions." He ranted and yelled until Bjorn stumbled over the whiffletree dragging behind the horses. A tear trickled down his cheek.

Rune laid his axe in the back of the wagon, then picked up Bjorn's axe and did the same. He stepped to Bjorn's side, spoke softly to him, and the two of them walked off, heading for the road to the barn.

"Where do you think you're going?" Einar screamed after them.

Rune kept on walking. "Come along, Bjorn."

"But . . . but what are we going to do?"

"Start packing, if we must, but he will not treat you—or any of us—like dirt."

Chapter 24

"Perhaps you did too much yesterday."

"Tired."

"I can tell." Signe studied her patient. "Would you like a cup of coffee?"

"Nei, just sleep."

"I will bring you some soup later."

Gerd nodded without opening her eyes.

Signe returned to the kitchen, where she had sourdough bread started, dishes to finish, a floor to scrub, and chicken stewing on the stove. When she finished the dishes, she used the same water to scrub the floor. As she scrubbed herself out onto the porch, she tossed the water along the porch and swept it down and off the steps. Back in the kitchen, she caught a flash of brown along the baseboard. Another mouse.

Suddenly a gray bullet flashed by. The kitten slammed down upon the luckless mouse. Signe almost shouted for joy.

She kneaded the dough that was now at the top of the bowl, soon to slip over the sides. The rich yeast fragrance filled the kitchen and, as always, enriched her soul as well. There was just something about making bread that always made her feel good.

If she was angry at something, she pummeled and pushed the fragrant dough even longer, making the bread even lighter. So something good came of her frustration. The first slice of fresh-baked bread became either a gift to someone else or a reward for her. A clean floor, bread rising, and still she was missing even the small conversations she had with Gerd. She thought of sitting down and writing a letter to her family, but instead she opened the pantry door to find the gray cat growling over her nearly finished catch. "Good Gra." She picked up the other, Gul, and stood at the window, petting the cat and still feeling gray like the sky. She felt the purr before she heard it. The cat snuggled under her chin and rumbled in pleasure.

"At least someone is here talking with me." She let the tears overflow from her eyes and trickle down to her chin. "Stop it!" she ordered herself. "You have no reason to cry."

Ah, but she did. Everyone said homesickness faded after a while. Homesickness might perhaps, but not isolation. The constant loneliness ate at her. Gerd slept most of the time. Einar? Hardly a conversationalist. Rune and the boys were always somewhere else, it seemed.

How good it would be to sit with her mor to catch up on the news, share a new recipe, talk about the coming baby, perhaps invite someone else to join them for coffee. What a sad, sad situation, that callers were not welcome in this house. So unlike Norway.

"And I have only a cat to comfort me, and she would rather be eating a mouse."

Right at that moment, Gul leaped from her arms and dashed across the kitchen, too late to catch a fleeing mouse. How many had managed to move in? Or was there a new nest, and if so, where? Signe opened all the cupboard doors, including those in the pantry, to let the cats sniff anywhere they desired.

Signe pulled the chicken kettle to the side and lifted the chicken out onto a plate to debone it. The jingling of a harness came from the front of the house. Who could that be? She headed for the front door.

A woman was climbing down from a buggy.

"Mrs. Benson, what a surprise. You can tie your horse there to the post."

"Good morning. I was returning from delivering an order, and my horse just turned into your lane. How are you?" The storekeeper smiled as she snapped the tie rope on the post to her horse's halter. "I can't stay long, but I had to see how you are faring." She fetched a basket from her buggy, pausing at the steps. "I can come in?"

"Ja, of course you can come in. Why do you ask?"

"Well, you see, Mr. Strand made it quite clear that no one is to visit here."

"Onkel Einar is back in the woods with my husband and our eldest son. They do not return until nearly nightfall."

"And Mrs. Strand?"

"She is feeling poorly again today, but overall she is improving." Signe ushered her guest into the parlor. "I hope you can stay for coffee, at least. And perhaps Tante Gerd will join us."

Mrs. Benson sniffed the air. "You are baking bread?"

"I am. Sourdough." Signe motioned to the shawl draped around her visitor's shoulders. "May I hang that up for you?" She hooked the shawl over the coat-tree and ushered Mrs. Benson into the fragrant kitchen. "I—I am so happy to see you." She sniffed and took a handkerchief from her apron pocket. Company, she finally had some company. She could have danced around the kitchen. "Here, sit and make yourself comfortable." She pulled the coffeepot to the hotter part of the stove.

"You are making chicken soup?"

"I thought chicken and dumplings. Rune really likes dumplings."

"So your son who had the broken arm is back to work?"

Signe paused before answering. "Ja, but not full-time with the axe." She had better not mention her ongoing battle with Einar. That would not be polite.

"I see your two younger boys every morning on their way to school. They are fortunate to have a horse to ride. Oh my, I forgot. I brought a letter for you." She pulled it out of the basket at her feet, along with a jar of honey. "We just finished bottling the last of the honeycomb. I thought you might like some."

"Oh, what a treat. Takk, tusen takk. And a letter from home. And here I was about to write to them."

"You said Mrs. Strand is doing better? That is good news." Mrs. Benson lifted a round tin from her basket. "I brought some cookies too."

Signe covered her cheeks with her hands. "I was just wishing I had cookies or something baked to offer you."

"Applesauce. One of Mr. Benson's favorites. Our tree had plenty of fruit this year. By the way, if you would like some apples, I could send a bag home with your boys." She glanced down at one of the cats, which had come to see her. "Oh, look. You have them in the house?"

"And already earning their keep. They have caught several mice."

"I know the boys were a bit hesitant about taking them. I say every house needs a good cat, as do the barns."

"Signe?" Gerd called.

"I will be right back," Signe told Mrs. Benson. At least Gerd had not shrieked this time. Signe pushed open the bedroom door. "I am right here."

Gerd had been getting up to use the pot on her own. "Did I hear another voice?"

"Ja, Mrs. Benson came calling."

Gerd shook her head. "Einar forbids visitors."

"Why?" Signe clamped down on the anger that flamed inside her.

Gerd shrugged. "He said . . ." She shook her head again. "He . . . he does not like the people around here."

"But why?" Signe knew her voice was sharp, but the man made no sense. Living out here like this made having neighbors even more important.

Gerd shook her head slowly, then sank back into her pillows. "I do not need to use the pot after all. If Einar sees her . . ."

"Einar will not know she has been here. Besides, I live here too. She is visiting *me*." Signe knew she was drawing a battle line, but she did not care. If Einar wanted them to stay here, he might have to do some bending too. *Lord, how can I live like this?* "I have the coffee hot. Would you like some?" She watched Gerd carefully. From the looks of her, she was not the one to banish the neighbors, but she went along with his edict. Understanding why no one called on them cleared up a lot of questions. How on earth had Einar forced himself to write to Norway to ask for help? It also explained why he did almost all his shopping in Blackduck rather than Benson's. Hers and Rune's insistence on their sons going to school—no wonder he was so adamantly against it.

Finally Gerd nodded. "Ja. Coffee would be good."

Signe paused to drum up her courage. "Would you like to come to the table for coffee and cookies?"

"Did you bake cookies?"

"Nei, Mrs. Benson brought us some applesauce cookies, and she will send apples home with the boys if we want." *What he does not know cannot hurt him—or us.*

Gerd heaved a sigh. "Bring my coffee here."

"I will." Signe felt a surge of pity for the woman married to a man like Einar. And here she had thought Tante Gerd was the wicked one. "And cookies?"

Again Gerd hesitated. When she nodded, she did not look at Signe but at the floor.

"I wish you would join us." Signe spoke softly, and instead of turning to the kitchen, she reached out and patted Gerd's shoulder. "Takk." Back in the kitchen, she asked her guest, "Do you take cream with your coffee?"

Mrs. Benson shook her head with a gentle smile. "You serve her first, please."

Signe poured three cups of coffee, then set one on a plate, added two cookies, and served Gerd. *I do believe she would really like to join us.* The thought invited more thoughts in, questions about Gerd that Signe had not bothered to consider before. Why she had married Einar being one of them, but then, perhaps Einar had not always been like this. Although he had not had a charming reputation at home either.

Uff da. Life was not easy to understand, especially not other people.

Signe joined Mrs. Benson at the table. "I'm sorry for the delay."

"Don't be, my dear. You are doing your best, I'm sure. And life here is not easy." The storekeeper picked up her coffee cup. "Nothing tastes better than a cup of coffee with friends."

Signe blinked back the burning behind her eyes. "Takk." She inhaled a deep breath and nodded. "Ja, with friends."

"So how have you been feeling? And when is this baby due? You told me, but I confess I forgot. By the looks of you, the time is coming near."

"Not until late November. But I seem to be bigger sooner this time."

"Are you sure of the timing? It is hard to tell sometimes. Has Mrs. Jungkavn been by yet?"

"She is the midwife you mentioned, right? No, she has not. How many children do you have?"

"Four, and we lost two. Our older son works for one of the timber companies. Our oldest daughter was married last winter, and they farm on the other side of Blackduck. The other two are attending high school in Blackduck. During the winter, they live with my sister in Blackduck." She glanced up at the clock. "Oh my goodness, I told Mr. Benson I would be home by dinnertime." She finished her coffee. "I must be leaving, but I will return, and you are invited to come visit me—and not just when you need supplies from the store. I'll send a box of apples home with you." She pushed back her chair. "If you feel like driving the wagon, that is."

"I will bring the boys to school next week and deliver my butter and eggs, if that's all right."

"That will be fine. I'll leave this basket for you. Use it for sending eggs." Mrs. Benson flipped her shawl around her shoulders. "Takk."

Her smile made Signe feel warm from the inside out. She watched as the buggy kicked up dust on the way down the lane.

Now to fix dinner for herself and Gerd. She put the honey on a shelf in the pantry and the cookies in a tin. Shame that she could not serve them for supper, but just in case Einar realized they were applesauce cookies and they had no apples, she'd keep them put away. Did he really keep track of things like that? All he seemed to think about was felling trees and taking care of his tools.

"Do you feel up to coming to the table for dinner?" she asked Gerd when the beans and venison had been reheated. She had sent the same out with the men, but at least she and Gerd could have a hot meal. Beans always tasted better hot.

Gerd was sitting in her chair by the bed, knitting a larger soaker for the baby. "In here. We must talk about the sewing machine so you can hem diapers."

"What if I moved the machine in here or the kitchen?" Signe surprised herself with the question.

Gerd nodded. "Over by the window would work best. But it is ungainly to move."

"And I am ungainly too." Was that a smile lurking on Gerd's face? "I will fix us a tray."

Later, after the bread was rising in the pans and the carrots were dug and scrubbed for supper, Signe cleared away the wooden bowls and utensils and other random things that had accumulated on top of the sewing machine cabinet. She pulled and pushed it into the bedroom, grunting at the effort. The baby started kicking. She stood at the window to catch her breath, both hands massaging her growing abdomen.

"Are you all right?" Gerd asked.

"I will be. Scrubbing the floor this morning caused the same reaction, but she will settle down again."

"You say 'she' now?"

"Did I? I didn't realize that. Wishful thinking, I guess." Signe kneaded her lower back with her fists. "Uff da. This baby is getting more active all the time." Had Gerd ever had a baby? Did she dare ask?

"Have you washed the flannel?" Gerd asked.

"Ja. It is in our trunk in the parlor."

"Do you have scissors?"

Signe shook her head. "I thought to rip it for the diapers. That is what Mor did for baby diapers."

"Look in the upper left sewing machine drawer. There should be scissors, along with needles and thread. Pins too."

It was hard to believe this was the same woman Signe had been caring for. There was even a change from this morning. What brought it about? Gerd had been so weak again, and now she seemed stronger. Signe left off trying to figure it out. Instead she went for the flannel, grateful she had washed it.

Back in the bedroom, a movement outside caught her attention. "Oh, no!"

"What?"

But Signe was already lumbering to the back door. "Rune and Bjorn are here," she called over her shoulder.

"Something happened."

But Signe was out the door without answering. "Are you all right?" she called.

Rune nodded and kept on walking, Bjorn by his side. "We are not injured, nor is Einar, so you can stop worrying." He mounted the steps. "Bjorn, bring your mor a chair. We will talk about this out here on the porch."

Signe stared at her husband. Resolute was the only word she could think to describe him. She looked at Bjorn, who shook his head as he strode into the kitchen.

"What is going on? Rune, this makes no sense."

"It will. Sit down, and we will talk."

"No one is hurt?" Questions rampaged through her head like a swarm of bees on the move. Never had she seen Rune like this. She nodded as Bjorn set a chair down for her. "Takk." She looked at his arm, just in case, but he was using both arms with the chair.

Rune pulled a wooden box in front of her and sat down, motioning for Bjorn to do the same. Bjorn sat on the top step.

"Einar lit into Bjorn unjustly; Bjorn was doing his best. I

will not tolerate him abusing our boys. We will move away if we need to."

Signe felt her jaw drop. She stared at her husband, who remained as calm as if he had just announced a plan for the day. "But . . . but . . ."

"I know. If need be, we will sleep in the barn tonight, but we will move if we need to."

"To where?"

"I do not know, but we are good workers, and someone will hire Bjorn and me. I have been thinking that—"

"I—I cannot leave Gerd. She needs me."

"I know, but I can go work for someone else. Bjorn too."

"What about Knute and Leif?"

"They would stay with you and continue to do their chores here."

"Do we tell Gerd before Einar comes to the house?"

"If you want. The boys will be home any time. Bjorn and I will start the chores."

Lord God, what will happen now?

Chapter 25

Y ou will not be leaving." Gerd stared at Signe from her
chair by the window.

"You heard?"

"Enough to know that Rune has drawn a line."

Signe nodded. This was a Rune she did not know. "They
went to start the chores."

The sound of laughter almost made her smile as Leif slid off
the horse by the back porch and pulled Knute off with him. They
all needed more laughter here. Leif waved at the two women in
the window as he led the horse to the pasture.

Knute whirled his way into the kitchen. "Can I eat quick,
Mor? I got to get to work."

"You will not be going to work in the woods today. Far and
Bjorn are down doing chores."

Knute's jaw dropped. "But—but Onkel Einar, is he all right?
What happened?"

"Ask your far." She fetched the tin of cookies and handed
him two. "To hold you until the bread is finished. It should be
out any minute."

"But Onkel Einar will yell at me."

"I do not think so." How much should she tell him? She took out another cookie and ate half of it. "Talk with your far. He can explain better than I can." Hopefully the times of Einar yelling at the boys—or anyone, for that matter—might be over. She knew that was probably wishful thinking.

"Signe."

"Coming." On her way to the bedroom, she pulled the coffeepot forward to heat. "What is it?"

"Is there coffee?"

"Ja, shortly, and the cookies Mrs. Benson brought us."

"Why would she bring us cookies?"

Signe shrugged. "To be neighborly, I guess."

Gerd made a face. "She must have a reason. There is always a reason."

For a change, Signe did not just ignore such a comment. "She's been very nice to me every time I went to her store for supplies. Friendly."

"Good for business."

"Was she ever rude to you?"

Gerd shook her head. "But Einar said we would never go there again."

"Oh." She'd not ask any more questions. She really did not want to know what had gone on, if Gerd had been mean or if Einar bore all the blame. Signe resolved not to mention Mrs. Benson around him.

It was nearly nightfall when Einar finally came banging in the kitchen door. Signe expected him to be furious, but instead he was almost pleasant. No, not pleasant. Smug.

He looked around the room. "I just drove into Blackduck and talked to the sheriff. I told him how you are all lazy and refuse to work, even though the letter of agreement says you must. He thanked me for bringing it to his attention, and he is going to investigate. Your insolence is coming to an end. I'll be surprised if he doesn't arrest you." He sat down. "Bring me my supper."

Something rattled in the cabinet beside the stove. Signe opened the cabinet door, and a mouse leapt out, startling her.

"Haven't you trapped those pesky mice y—" Einar gasped as the yellow tabby flew across the room from the open pantry door. It pounced and missed. The mouse and kitten ran behind the coatrack, and the kitten pounced again. Victorious, she crossed the room with the mouse in her mouth, headed back to the pantry.

"I told you there would be no cats here!" Einar yelled. "Get rid of it now! Do you hear me?"

"Ja, I hear you." *And the cat will stay.*

"Take it out and drown it. I don't want to see it again!"

"Onkel Einar!" Leif stared at him in shock.

Signe felt horrible; not because Einar was yelling at her, but because her youngest son had just seen his uncle for what he was. She had not thought ahead far enough to realize what might happen.

But the next morning it was as if there had never been any friction at all. Einar ate breakfast and stomped out the door as he always did.

"Try not to worry," Rune said. "We will take the days as they come." Rune and Bjorn took the basket and jugs and headed for the wagon. But Signe could not stop worrying, and the boys were so somber and quiet that she knew they could not stop worrying either.

Several days passed. Dark was coming more quickly day by day. October, and the shadows were already long by the time the horse brought her boys home from school. And even longer when the workers came in from the woods.

Gerd was growing stronger and Signe growing bigger. She and Signe had dinner together at the table every day now, and Gerd was knitting a baby sweater. While she still slept in the afternoon, this day she had helped Signe bake cookies for the first time, so her nap was later. Signe started making supper after she fed the boys their afternoon snack.

When Gerd called for Signe as the others were coming in from the day's work, she found her gathering her knitting together. She announced that she would eat supper at the table that night.

Signe nodded but could not keep from smiling. "It is warmer in the kitchen, and the light is better."

"I can knit without much light." But she stood and, taking Signe's arm, walked to the kitchen. When they reached the table, she asked, "Is there room enough for me?"

Signe and Rune swapped amazed looks. Gerd had made a joke. Could that be possible?

Leif grinned. "You can sit by me, Tante Gerd. Knute and I can move our chairs closer together."

"Should we go ahead or wait for Einar?" Signe whispered to Rune.

"Wait a bit. He should be here before dark." He turned to Knute. "You and Bjorn go wait by the barn so you can unharness the horses."

Minutes after the boys left, Einar came inside and stopped at the sink to wash his hands. He did not say a word when he saw his wife at the table. Gerd glared at her husband, gave a slight shake of her head, and when she caught Signe's glance, rolled her eyes. Without looking at anyone, Einar took his place and waited to be served.

To Signe, the temperature of the room seemed to drop fifteen degrees. All talking stopped. Bjorn and Knute came in, washed, and took their places.

Signe brought bowls of chicken and dumplings to the table, along with one of carrots and a plate of sliced bread. They passed the food around, and as always, Einar started shoveling his in, still without looking at anyone. Her boys exchanged looks with each other and Signe.

"Mrs. Benson sent apples home with us. We left the sack on the porch," Leif said as he buttered his bread. "This sure smells good."

Signe glanced at Einar, but while he did not look up, his jaw tightened.

"We planted two apple trees, but the deer ate them before they could produce apples." Gerd buttered her bread and dipped the crust in the chicken and dumplings. "I will need more yarn when you go to the store next, Signe. We need to make a list."

Signe almost fell off her chair. Gerd had just tacitly approved Signe's friendship with Mrs. Benson despite Einar's wishes. What had the Carlson rebellion come to?

"We could bring some things home after school." Leif smiled at Gerd. "If you give us a list."

Rune nodded to his son. "Good idea."

"I'm going to the store one day next week, so you will have to walk home after school, since I will have the horse and cart," Signe said. What she should have said was *ancient coalbox buggy,* for it was practically falling apart. She looked at Einar. His stare impaled her to the back of her chair. She nodded. So this was the way it would continue. So be it.

At least the cats had not been an issue again. They spent most of their time in the pantry or the attic, two places Einar never went. And Signe had not seen a mouse for days.

Einar pushed back his chair. "Tools to sharpen." And out the door he stomped.

Rune nodded. "You boys get your schoolwork done. Bjorn,

you can split wood. Have you cut up that dried tree you dragged in?"

"Mostly. There's another down where we got that one."

"Dry?"

"Ja. Needs limbing, then we can drag it up. Perhaps tomorrow?"

"We'll see. Gets any colder, and we'll be butchering hogs. Einar mentioned that the other day."

Signe shook her head. Here she had been prepared to be sent away or even get arrested, but things had simply gone back to normal.

"I will get the coffee." She paused. "And the cookies." Einar had left; he could just do without. Tomorrow she would make an apple cake with the gifted apples and hope to buy another box when she went to the store. Apples could last a good while in the cellar.

After the coffee and cookies, she helped Gerd back to bed.

"I'm glad you had supper at the table. I know you are tired."

"Ja, but . . ." Gerd paused. "In the chest in the parlor, I have flannel nightgowns. Could you fetch one for me?"

"I could air it on the line tomorrow."

"Nei. I will wear it tonight."

Back in the kitchen, the boys had cleared the table and she could hear wood being split outside. Leif had started washing the dishes.

She stepped in beside him. "I will wash and you dry."

"Teacher said I have to read aloud in English."

"Do you understand what you're reading?"

"Pretty much, and arithmetic is the same as at home. The history is very strange. We played baseball at recess. Knute really smacked that ball! He got a home run."

That night after all the others had gone to bed, Signe and

Rune sat down with their coffee at the table, as had become their habit. "So, has he said anything?" she asked.

"Not really, he just grumbled about having to take time off to butcher the pigs. He said we needed to bring in a maple tree to use in the smokehouse, and he would show Bjorn and Knute where it is. I think he knows how much he needs us and that I will no longer tolerate his cruelty toward the boys."

"I'm finding it easier to ignore him."

"I never dreamed Gerd would get strong enough to come to supper. Your hard work is reaping benefits."

"Ja. She has knit soakers in two sizes for our baby and will teach me how to hem diapers on the sewing machine. Perhaps she'll even do some herself." Signe shook her head. "So many surprises."

"Einar explained what all we have to do to get the hogs butchered, since I've not done it before. I think he wishes you would just handle it all so he could continue working in the woods."

"No apology or mention of the sheriff?"

Rune shook his head. "Apology? Einar? Surely you are joking." He drained his coffee cup. "I think I will sleep downstairs with you from now on."

"You tired of climbing the ladder too?"

He gently shook his head. "I was so hoping he would agree to building the stairs. I will talk to him again when things settle down."

Rune took her hand and helped her to her feet.

⸎

The next morning when Rune rose to start the stove, he could see his breath as he headed for the outhouse. He hurried, since he'd not donned a jacket. Working in the woods today would be cold too. According to Einar, they needed a week of freezing weather for hanging the hogs to age after they were slaughtered. They would hang them in the machine shed, like they had the deer.

With the stove fire crackling and popping, he climbed up the ladder to call his boys. Signe groaned as she used a chair to help pull herself to her feet. They needed a bed along with the stairway. Perhaps he would be able to build a bed now that they came in from the woods earlier. But there wasn't room in the parlor for a bed unless they moved the furniture out. Uff da. The *someday* when they would have a house of their own seemed farther off than ever.

On the fourth day of the cold snap, the weather steadily grew colder. Einar announced they would butcher the next morning, so the boys were not to feed the butcher hogs that night.

"Can we stay home and help?" Knute asked the next morning.

"Nei, go to school; you can help when you come home." Rune looked at Einar, who had gone back to eating his breakfast. Knute groaned, but Leif looked relieved.

"Just the two that we penned up, right?" Leif asked.

Rune nodded. He knew how Leif felt about the pigs he'd been feeding. One of those to be slaughtered was his favorite. "You go on and head for school." He shot Einar a warning look. There would be no making fun of his tenderhearted son. He asked, "We'll send the rest of the gilts and barrows to market on the hoof?"

Einar nodded.

"Come on, Leif, you'll make us late." Knute grabbed their dinner pails. "You want to ride in front today?"

Rune nodded and smiled at Knute. He knew Knute did not want to be there when Einar killed the hogs either, but he had grown tougher since they came to Amerika.

By the time they had the hogs winched up and dressed out,

they were all sweating in spite of the cold. Dressing a hog was not that different from dressing a deer, so Bjorn took his turn stripping the guts out into a bucket.

"Take the heart and liver up to the house," Rune told Bjorn, "and ask Mor if she plans to make headcheese. Tell her these two hogs are plenty fat, so she'll have lots of lard to render."

After they scraped the bristles off the hides, they wrapped the carcasses in sheeting and hung them up. Einar sharpened the knives and saw he would use to cut up the meat while Rune and Bjorn cleaned up the mess.

When the boys got home, Knute said, "You're all done?"

Einar did not reply. He simply said, "We'll go for that maple tree now."

Rune nodded. His idea of resting after their labor obviously was not going to happen. "You want Bjorn too?"

"Ja."

His tone reprimanded Rune for not figuring that out, but instead of commenting, Rune went to harness the team. One thing to say for Einar, he was not afraid of hard work. Not that any of Rune's family was either, but more and more he was realizing the importance of gratitude. It was a shame he had to learn that through someone else's cruelty.

Thanks to a nearly full moon, they did not have to drag the tree up in the pitch dark.

"Do sugar maples grow here?" Rune asked.

Einar grunted, leaving Rune to assume the answer was yes. The thought of making maple syrup in the spring made his mouth water.

They dragged the tree near the sawbucks, where the boys could cut the trunk into smokehouse lengths.

"The boys will bring up the bigger branches tomorrow." Einar did not say "after school." He never mentioned school.

When they finally stepped up onto the porch, the fragrance of liver and onions greeted them. Rune walked into the kitchen and kissed Signe's cheek. "Thank you for the wonderful food you prepared."

Gratitude was valuable. He would not forget that.

⁂

The weather stayed below freezing for the rest of the week, giving Signe time to grind and render out the lard before she had to start canning meat. She had bought two pounds of pepper at Benson's. She would work that into the ground pork to make sausage, which would be made into patties and stored in crocks in the cellar with a layer of lard on top to seal them.

Without asking permission, the day she decided to go to the store she had the boys put a small crock of lard into the wagon so she could sell that to Mrs. Benson too, if she desired. If not, Signe would bring it home again. Surely not everyone around here raised hogs.

She motioned for Knute to drive. His grin made her smile. Most of the leaves were dancing across the road rather than hanging on the trees. She sucked in a deep breath. "Do you smell that?"

Both boys nodded. "Fall smells as good here as in Norway." Knute clucked for the horse to pick up her feet a bit faster.

When they reached the store, Mrs. Benson invited her in for a cup of coffee while Mr. Benson loaded all the supplies from her long list. Signe leaned back against the chair, twisting her body to be more comfortable.

"Are you sure you're not due earlier than late November?" Mrs. Benson asked as she set the coffee and a plate of apple pie in front of Signe. "Unless you are carrying twins." She eyed Signe's girth. "I don't know how you got up in that wagon."

273

"I've only felt one kicking and bucking around." She laid her hand on the mound that now took up all of her lap. "I do not remember anyone in my family having twins. But this is sure an active baby."

"Are you sleeping well?"

"Other than needing to get up for the outhouse more often." Signe inhaled the cinnamon perfume of warm apple pie. "Takk for the box of apples. I wish you would let me pay you though. I thought the lard . . ."

"I am happy you brought the lard. I'll get the crock back to you as soon as it is empty. If you wanted to sell half, or even a whole pig, we would be happy to buy it."

Signe stared at her. She'd not thought of selling, only of smoking and canning. "I will ask and send a note with the boys. Takk—er, thank you. Knute insists I learn to speak English better."

"Oh, by the way, there is mail. I will make sure it goes home with you. I wish you could join our ladies at church so you could get to know some of the people around here. We have a relief society that meets once a month when the weather is agreeable."

The thought made Signe sigh. "Perhaps after the baby comes." What if she could get Gerd to come with her? She forced a smile. "We shall see."

How marvelous it felt to be sitting in someone else's warm kitchen, sun shining through gingham-curtained windows and apple butter cooking in the oven, enticing her to accept another offer of pie.

"Thank you, but no, I had best be on my way." Hard words to say, but there was no one at the house if Gerd needed help.

"Then let me get a box of apples for you into the wagon." Mrs. Benson patted Signe's hand. "Several of the women brought some baby things for you to use. How are you coming on hemming diapers?"

"Gerd has been hemming some on her sewing machine. I have been so busy with putting up the pork that I haven't had time to learn yet. Someday. She even made a baby blanket."

"Your coming has indeed saved her life. I hope that husband of hers realizes how fortunate he is to have you all here to help them."

Signe kept the truth from bursting forth by a strength she did not know she had. How she would love to tell how things really were, but what good would that do? She had been careful in writing home, only hinting at what she thought of Einar Strand. After all, the sheriff had never shown up. It could be a lot worse.

"Thank you for the coffee and pie."

"Of course."

After the goodbyes and Mr. Benson had helped her up in the wagon, Signe patted her bag, which contained two letters. What if someday Nilda could indeed come?

Chapter 26

MID-OCTOBER 1909

Signe heaved a sigh. Gerd was finally asleep.

She sat down at the table. She still thought about how warm and inviting Mrs. Benson's kitchen was. Perhaps she could put gingham curtains in this kitchen. It would help. Maybe after the baby came. She would not mention them, just make them and hang them. Einar probably would not even notice.

Leif burst into the kitchen with Knute right behind. Knute caught the door just in time to keep it from slamming. "Mor, you got a letter. It looks important. It's from a steamship company." Leif hesitated. "We're not going back to Norway, are we?"

"Nei." Signe ripped open the envelope and studied the letter. Then she got out the piece of paper she had been calculating on, and her heart sang. She was right! "Knute, thank you for keeping the door quiet. There is still enough daylight to spread the manure from the pile by the barn onto the garden. Make sure we have gotten all the carrots and rutabagas dug out first."

The boys hurried out. She spent a long time studying the letter and her calculations, deciding how she would bring up this subject. She laid her hands on the papers. "God, help me with my words and thoughts. I am so frightened. Help me do this right."

One thing was certain—she had to be bold so she could keep her nerve when Einar started yelling.

The boys came in with a bucket of root vegetables just as Signe heard the wagon rattling into the yard. "Takk, now go get your chores done. You are late." These boys. They were so ready to work. What fine sons they were. They deserved the best, and she was going to do everything she could to get them the best.

She watched Einar all through the meal. His scowl relaxed as he put away a second helping of pork chops with creamed gravy. Eventually he sat back, rubbed his belly, belched, and for a change did not glare at her. Then he surged to his feet as he always did after he finished eating, even though the others were not done.

"Sit down, Onkel Einar," Signe said. "We're not finished here."

He stared at her. "You forget who gives the orders. I'm going to sharpen the axes. You boys come along and help."

"I received a letter from the steamship company today. Sit down, please."

Rune's mouth dropped open.

"The what?" Einar's face showed a whole series of emotions all at once. He sat down carefully, as if the chair might explode.

"This is more important than sharpening axes. You are a fine teacher, Einar, and Bjorn is learning to be very good in the woods. He loves logging, and he thinks he doesn't need more schooling. I am about to demonstrate to Bjorn why he does need to learn more." She pulled her papers out of her apron pocket, plopped them in front of Einar, and smoothed them open.

He gaped at the letter from the steamship company.

She stabbed with a finger. "This is the fare for an adult's passage from Norway to America. The boys' fares were even less. Adding them all up, this is what you paid for us to come here." She circled the sum with her pencil.

Fury painted itself over Einar's face.

Rather than running, as her body urged, Signe pointed to the paper covered with her calculations. "On average, we each work a twelve-hour day. More in the summer, less in the winter. Average. Take an hour off for meals, and we each work eleven hours. That is a full day's work in service to you, boys as well as grown-ups. And we all work seven days. Five laborers times seven days is thirty-five workdays per week. I've accounted for the time the younger boys have spent in school as well.

"This"—she circled a number—"is a fair day's wage. I asked Mrs. Benson what was usual around here. Multiplying thirty-five by that number gives this figure. This next number is the number of weeks we've worked for you. Multiplying this and this"—she pointed with the pencil—"gives the total value to you of our labor since we came. You can see that this value is over three times the cost to you of our passage."

Einar sputtered, "Yes, but . . . I feed you! And house you! You didn't add that in."

"That is this sum down here. You see I subtracted it from the value of our labor, even though we raised or hunted the food ourselves—most of it. You did not."

"But Bjorn didn't work all that time his arm was in the cast! You have to subtract that."

"He worked just as hard, but it was around the farm here and not in the woods. His labor counts." Signe stood up and looked at Bjorn. "You see, son, that you must have skill with arithmetic as well as skill with an axe. If you don't, others will take unfair advantage of you."

Einar leapt to his feet. "You're accusing me of cheating you?" She kept her voice steady; inside she was nearly paralyzed with fear. "We have more than fulfilled the terms of our contract, Einar."

"That does it! I'm going to the sheriff right now. He'll take care of your insolence!"

"If you force us to leave, then who will take care of Gerd? The farm chores? The garden? And the cooking and canning? And who will help you in the woods? I doubt any judge, seeing these figures, will side with you in this argument."

"You can't do this! You—"

"We can, but we will not. We will not abandon you." She turned and looked toward the bedroom, where Gerd had chosen to go to bed early. "We will continue to work with you in the woods, take care of the house, help Gerd. All that we are already doing. You need us desperately. But we no longer need you. And so, Einar, I tell you this. We will remain here, and our boys will continue to go to school, all three of them. Bjorn starts tomorrow."

"No!" Einar roared. "I need him!"

"Not as much as he needs school. When it's light enough, he can help you after school. But he will go. He'll learn English. He'll learn everything an educated man must know."

"But, Mor, I don't want to go back to school." Bjorn shook his head and kept on shaking it. "I want to work in the woods."

"Could you have done all that arithmetic?"

"I think so. You could teach me in the evenings during the winter. I can study anything else I need too. And I will, I promise."

"And speaking English?"

He stared at Einar, who was glaring at Signe with a fury that rocked the room.

Einar wheeled toward Rune. "Don't just sit there! Put this—this *woman* in her place!" *Woman* sounded like an expletive.

Rune's voice purred, low and even. "No, I will not put her in her place. She tells the truth. We have completed our obligation." He tapped the paper. "The figures don't lie. She is also correct that from now on, we will work for you as we have been, but it will be as blood relatives helping relatives who desperately need us. You know what it was like before we came, trying to log single-handed and take care of Gerd. We will not abandon you. But my boys, at least two of them, will go to school. We will talk about Bjorn later."

Inside, Signe's heart rejoiced. Rune stood with her! Well, mostly. They would have to talk about Bjorn's desire later.

She watched Einar nail Rune with the same fury he threw at her, then stomp out of the room, slamming both the wooden door and the screen door on his way out.

Everyone else sat as if frozen.

"Signe! Signe!" Gerd called from her bed.

"Excuse me." Signe hurried to her, hoping this was not something grave, like a bout of fever or diarrhea.

Gerd looked terrified.

"What is it?" Signe paused at her bedside.

"Don't leave me, Signe! Please don't leave me. I'll die if you leave me!"

The battle was won! Signe had won! She smiled and clasped her tante's cold hands in hers. "I will never leave you, Gerd. You are safe." And then she said something she had not even realized until the words came out of her mouth. "I love you, Tante Gerd."

Gerd slowly moved her head from side to side, still clutching Signe's hand. "Nei, you cannot, not the way I—we have treated you. Love is impossible."

"Love is never impossible. You sleep now, and you will feel better in the morning. I will be here." *As long as God wills,* she finished in her mind.

"Einar—he . . . he . . ." Gerd heaved a sigh.

Signe watched the older woman carefully. Was she strong enough to endure more? She had already come a long way.

"Tomorrow we will sew diapers." Gerd collapsed back against the pillows, her gaze never leaving Signe's face, as if searching for any hesitation.

"Ja."

Back in the kitchen, Signe saw that Rune and Bjorn had gone outside. She could hear them sawing, working by the light of the moon. Knute and Leif were clearing the table as quietly as they could.

"Is she all right?" Leif whispered.

Signe nodded. "She will be, just like we all will. I made pudding for dessert. We can have it now."

"I should go split wood," Knute answered. "Can we eat it later?"

"Ja, we can. Let us hurry with the dishes, Leif."

"What will Onkel Einar do?" he asked, staring up at her, his blue eyes troubled.

"I do not know. But I know we will keep on doing what we always do and wait to see." She paused. "We must trust that God will take care of this—this mess." She could not come up with a better word.

"Will we ever go to church again?"

His question caught her by surprise. She looked into his eyes. "Ja. We will. We will go to church again. But in the meantime, we will read God's Word here, in the evenings."

"But—but what if it makes Onkel Einar mad again?"

Oh, child, such hard questions. Lord, what do I say? She

handed him a dish to dry. "Then I guess he will just have to be mad."

Leif stared at his hands. "I don't like when he yells, Mor. He scares me."

She wanted to say, "Me too," but instead she put her arms around her son. "Things will get better." *Please, Lord, let that be true.* "Let us hurry and finish the dishes, and we will make some whipped cream to go with the pudding."

"Can Tante Gerd have some too?"

"Ja, for sure."

Einar had not come back into the house yet when they gathered at the table, but Gerd decided to join them. She sat next to Leif and ate her pudding along with the others.

"I have not had pudding since we moved here from Norway," she said.

Knute stared at her. "When did you come?"

"Fifteen years ago. We were so young, but strong."

Later, Rune and Signe skipped their nightly coffee at the table and crawled onto their pallet. Einar had still not come back to the house, although they could see a light in the machine shed. They clasped hands, and Rune raised them to kiss the back of her fingers.

"I am glad that is over."

"I hope it is," she answered. What if . . . ?

Sleep banished that thought.

<hr />

In the morning, Einar showed up at the table as usual. While he wore a scowl fit to scare demons, he did not say a word until he finished eating and pushed back his chair. "Let's go."

Rune nodded. "When will we cut the hogs for brining?"

"Tonight." Out the door he went.

Rune went back to eating his breakfast, as did the others.

"Will we have biscuits in our dinner pails?" Knute asked before stuffing the last of his in his mouth.

"I made you sandwiches, but I will add a biscuit with jam." He grinned at her. "And an apple?"

Signe finished packing the basket for the men and poured coffee in the jars. "Apples?" she asked Rune.

"Ja, that will be good." He patted her shoulder as he went out the door.

I must get the winter things out of the trunk upstairs, Signe reminded herself as she brought a tray in to Gerd, who was dressed and sitting by the window with a shawl over her shoulders, knitting away.

"Did you look in the box of baby things Mrs. Benson gave you?" Gerd asked.

Signe could feel her mouth drop open. Had she not had the tray in her hands she would have put her hands up to her cheeks. "Uff da. Nei, I forgot all about it."

"Where is the box?"

"Out on the porch, I suppose. The boys unloaded the wagon when they came home from school that day."

"I thought we better look in it before we sew more than diapers."

Signe set down the tray. "Here, and I brought my coffee in too. However, it would be warmer in the kitchen."

"True." Setting her knitting aside, Gerd used the arms of the chair to help her stand. "You better take the tray first. I need you to walk by me."

Signe did as ordered, but with a small smile. When she had Gerd settled at the table, she fetched the box from the porch and set it on the chair beside her. Piece by piece, she put the gowns, shirts, and even a baby-sized quilt on the table. At the bottom was a tiny sweater with matching booties. "My land, and no diapers or soakers, the only things we already have."

Gerd studied the booties. "I will make more of these. And I have a larger sweater half done." She turned and dug into her oatmeal. "And you made biscuits. Do you ever sleep?"

"Ja, I did. Until she decided to get moving." As always when talking of the baby, Signe laid her hand on the mound of her stomach.

"Have you thought of names?"

She shook her head. "Not much." How she wanted to ask about Einar, but she refrained—barely. The set of his jaw told her he was still angry, but he'd said nothing about the arithmetic lesson, as she had taken to referring to it in her mind.

"More coffee?" Gerd tapped her cup.

"I saved his pudding."

"He don't deserve pudding."

Signe stared at her, again her mouth agape. Gerd shrugged. After refilling the coffee cups and the stove, Signe sat down again, only to get up and stir the lard rendering in the oven. Once enough had melted in the flat pans, she poured the lard into a crock that stood waiting on the counter.

"Did you ever think of selling butchered hogs?" she asked. "Mrs. Benson was pleased that I took her a small crock of lard. She asked about buying pork."

"We never had any to sell before. We almost didn't get the sow, but I insisted that I would take care of her. Same with the cow. All he thinks about is timber. He said he'll trade for a boar now that we have the gilts."

"You took care of the pigs and cow?" Signe closed the oven door.

"Chickens too. Until I could not walk that far. But we had to

284

have food to eat, so he kept them." She placed the baby things back in the box. "I should have had you get more yarn."

"I got all she had. I want to knit scarves for the men and boys for Christmas. I will pay for the yarn."

"You will not. Nor any clothes nor boots."

Signe shrugged. "Einar said to put the supplies on his account, but these are not really supplies for everyone. I trade eggs and butter for what I can."

Pushing herself to her feet, she cleared the table again and hung the dish towel on the rod behind the stove.

"If you have time now," Gerd said, "I will teach you how to use the sewing machine."

"Will Einar take care of smoking the hogs?" Signe looked at the jars of chopped pork she had canned. Since it wasn't cold enough to freeze, the remainder would have to be smoked. Without thinking about it, she used both hands to rub her lower back.

Gerd shrugged. "He will expect you to do the smoking."

"But I have not done that before."

"Has Rune?"

"Ja, I think so."

"Then he will have to take care of it. Come sit with me at the machine so there will be diapers for this baby."

For the next hour, Gerd showed Signe how to thread the machine, work the treadle, and feed the material under the foot. Getting the rhythm of the treadle made Signe groan. "I do not—my feet—this looks so simple."

"It is. Remember, push with your toes and rock back with your heels. Keep the beat, like dancing. Again. Push, rock, push, rock. Better—that is right. Good, now you will thread the needle and sew on this scrap."

She rethreaded the needle, lowered the foot and started the

treadle again. The stitches walked across the fabric and she let out the breath she didn't know she'd been holding. "I did it."

Gerd took over and showed her how to fold the hem in place and stitch it down.

When Signe returned from a rush trip to the outhouse, Gerd had the machine rocking and one side of the flannel already hemmed. By dinner time, Gerd had hemmed six diapers, all folded and stacked on the table. She had a system. Hem one side, back stitch, pull on the thread, and set another square in place to start again. She set Signe to snipping the threads of the diaper train, then she would hem another side, and the trains continued.

"How did you ever figure out something like this?" Signe asked, admiration shading her voice and widening her eyes. What other wisdom lived in the brain of this woman who barely even talked when Signe took over her care?

Gerd shrugged. "Made sense, is all. Dish towels, anything you need a lot of."

After they finished their soup and biscuits, Signe helped a weary Gerd back to bed.

"Takk, tusen takk." Signe adjusted a pillow.

"You are welcome." Gerd nodded. "There is a burlap sack in the attic, in the corner."

"Ja, I saw it. I don't know what's in it."

"Heavy outing flannel. I was going to make Einar a shirt someday, but we will make blankets for the baby. Bring it down."

"Ja, I will." Signe started to back up quietly.

Gerd opened her eyes again. "Could you please make corn bread with cracklings in it for supper?"

"Ja, I will do that."

It was the first time Gerd had ever asked for something special. Might she indeed become a friend, someone to talk with?

Like real family. Might they become a family? Probably not like her family in Norway, but at least talking and doing things together. Signe sniffed back her liquid joy and drained the lard pan again, this time keeping out enough cracklings to make the corn bread.

Now to get the sack of outing flannel. Going up the ladder left her huffing and puffing as she lifted her bulk up each rung. Once through the large opening, she clung to the ladder posts and stepped carefully onto the attic floor. Dust motes danced in the sunlight shining through the little window at the far end, showing a layer on the floor again. She should have brought up the broom and mop. The boys' pallets lay over by the window, where they had moved them to get some breeze during the heat. They needed hay-filled ticking to help keep them warm now that winter was coming. A grate cut into the floor above the kitchen would be best, but at least the metal chimney would help warm the room during the winter.

She found three burlap bags in the corner. One was dark cotton duck, probably for making trousers for Einar. The second one she opened was the flannel. It smelled musty. No matter. She'd wash and air it before they sewed it.

She returned to the ladder and threw the bundle down ahead of her. How much easier it would be had Einar been willing to build a stairway. Sometimes her resentment burst into a flame at the way he acted. But as her mor had always said, a soft answer turned away wrath. Signe would add "sometimes" to that.

Step by step, she cautiously climbed back down the ladder. Nearly down, she glanced to the side to see where the burlap bundle had gone, and her foot slipped off a rung. The floor came up to meet her. The impact cut off her scream.

Chapter 27

Signe clutched her belly with both hands. Pain, pain. Had she broken anything?

How could she get up? Her head, she'd hit her head on something. The floor? A knife stabbed her in the back, and pain tore around her middle. *Lord, please, my baby. Take care of the baby.* More pain, enough to cause her gaze to dim. Someone was sobbing. It had to be her.

A gush of heat poured from her. Water, blood? *Lord, help me!*

But there was no one to help. She had to get up, get off the floor. Could she crawl to her pallet? When she tried to roll over, the pain blinded her again.

Her vision dimmed and darkened. *Give in to the darkness, rest.* She needed rest.

Roll on your side. I—I cannot. What could she grab to help her turn? *Lord, I cannot.*

"Signe!"

She heard the voice. *Mor. Help me!* The darkness sucked at her, ravenous, like Jonah's whale.

"Signe! I'm coming."

Who? Who was coming? She tried inhaling a deep breath,

but that too only caused more pain. Too early. If the baby was coming, how would she live? Too small. More hot liquid flowed out of her.

"Signe, oh my—"

Signe forced her eyes to open. "Gerd?"

"What happened?"

"The ladder. I—I slipped."

"What were you doing on the ladder? Oh, never mind, I remember. Oh, Signe, there is blood. We have to get you to the bed."

"Nei." She clenched back another scream.

"The baby? The baby is coming?"

"Ja, I think so." The blackness sucked at her again.

"Nei," Gerd ordered. "Do not faint on me now. Signe!"

Surely she was far away. A long distance. *Listen to her!* That voice was within her. Signe tried to focus.

"Can you roll over?"

"I—I tried, but . . ." Had she tried? How long had she been lying here? It felt like hours. She clamped her teeth together as another wave of pain rolled over her.

"I will be right back."

Do not leave me. Had she screamed that aloud or only in her mind? Panting, she stared up at the ceiling. *I have to get up. Get up, Signe—now.*

Something was scraping against the floor.

"I brought you a chair." Gerd set it beside her. "Grab hold with your left hand so you can pull yourself over onto your right side."

Signe reached for the chair leg. Gerd sat on the chair. "Now pull."

Lying on her side seemed to take some pressure off her back.

"Now! Signe, listen to me. Do not faint. We have to get you up."

"Ja, ja. I—I am."

"I'll put the chair against your back to brace you. Bend your knees. On three, you will roll." Gerd barked the orders. "Now, one—two—three. Roll!"

In spite of herself, Signe did it. She was up on her hands and knees. Head hanging, she panted.

Gerd patted her shoulder. "If only I were strong again."

Signe clenched her teeth against another searing pain. She panted past it and nodded. "I can stand up."

"Use the chair." Gerd shoved the chair next to her shoulder and sat on it again.

By some miracle, Signe grabbed the back of the chair, and with a strength beyond strength, got her feet flat on the floor and stood up with a shriek. "I did it." Warmth trickled down her leg. Her belly convulsed. "The baby, she's coming."

"I know. We're going to walk to the bedroom now. Lean on me."

Signe wagged her heavy head. *Lean on me,* what she used to say to Gerd. "Your cane?"

"Right here." Gerd thrust it into her hand. "Now walk. One step at a time."

"I cannot." The doorway looked forever away.

"Ja, you can and you will. Now walk!"

Together they staggered to the kitchen, where Signe clung to the doorway to inhale a couple of breaths. To the table, where she leaned on one chair after another. Now toward the bedroom. Her eyes demanded to be shut.

She looked down. "There is blood on the floor."

"I know. Walk! Help this baby come."

"It's too early. She will not live."

"Nei, I think you are further along than you figured."

"She will die."

"This baby is going to live. Now walk."

Anger surged up, snarling at the back of Signe's throat. "Leave me!"

"Nei! Walk!" Gerd tugged on her hand.

One step after another. Signe leaned, puffing, against the doorframe.

"Yoo-hoo, is anyone home?"

Was she hearing things? Signe slowly looked toward the back door. "Is someone out there?"

"Ja! Now walk!"

"But—"

"Walk. I will go see." Gerd yelled over her shoulder, "Come in. We are in the kitchen." She turned back to Signe. "Now get to the bed."

"Take the sheets off." Signe panted between words.

"Nei. They can be washed."

Signe took three steps, paused, then three steps more. Another pain was building. She literally threw herself in the direction of the bed and braced her arms against the mattress as the contraction rolled over her. The bed, she had made it to the bed.

"Turn and sit," Gerd ordered.

"Oh, no."

Signe heard the voice from the doorway. She looked up to see Mrs. Benson charging across the room. With one hand, the storekeeper threw back the covers, then grabbed Signe's hand with the other. "Here, lean on me, and we will get you situated."

Gerd leaned against her chair, puffing like Signe. "We did it."

"From where?"

"The parlor. She fell off the ladder."

"Oh, Lord above . . ." Mrs. Benson turned back to Signe. "Can you stand there while we remove your skirt and petticoats?"

"Ja, maybe."

"Do not faint on us!" Gerd switched back to giving orders, even though her voice was weaker.

They finally got Signe in the bed with another sheet under her. A wave of pain tried to drag her under.

"How often are the pains coming?"

"Too often. She has lost a lot of blood."

Signe heard them talking, but her mouth wouldn't cooperate, nor would her eyes stay open. She felt herself drifting. This pain seemed even stronger, rolling her over like a wave on the shore. A wave nearly got her when she was little. Or had that happened to someone else? She heard Gerd calling her name. *Too tired, too tired.*

Mrs. Benson shook her shoulder as another wave crescendoed and crashed upon her. Moving, she needed to push.

"You have to start pushing now."

As if she had a choice. She clamped her teeth hard. And felt limp and tossed back on the sand.

A soft voice said, "Here, a soft rag to bite."

She did just that as her body prepared to push again. *Tired, too tired. Push.* The rag dimmed the scream that ripped through her, forcing itself until no breath propelled it.

"One more, come on, Signe, one more. We can see the crown. When it comes again, push with all you have."

Signe threw her head from side to side. "No." But it came again, and she pushed, and her body kept on, and she could feel the release when the baby slipped into Mrs. Benson's waiting hands.

"You have a baby girl."

A stutter that built to a yell announced that this new baby girl was not happy with the situation.

"She has a good pair of lungs," Gerd said with a snort.

"Too soon," Signe murmured, "too soon."

Mrs. Benson laid the baby on Signe's chest. "Baby girl, meet your mor."

"There is an awful lot of blood," Gerd muttered.

Signe raised her head enough to see her daughter. "Oh, oh my." She looked at Gerd, who was grinning like a cat with canary whiskers sticking out of its mouth. "Is she all right?"

"Seems to be. She wasn't hurt in the fall, if that is what you mean. But rest easy, Signe. She might be a few days early or perhaps a couple of weeks, but not a whole month." Gerd laid one of the diapers over the baby. "To keep her from getting a chill."

Mrs. Benson tied off and cut the cord, then wrapped the baby in a bigger blanket. "Glad I gave you that box earlier. I see we're putting it to good use." She smiled down at Signe. "You are still bleeding too much, so we need to get that afterbirth delivered. That is why I am kneading your belly. Gerd has gone to make some tea."

Signe gritted her teeth against another wave of pain. "Is she really all right?" She unclamped her fingers from the sheet under her and touched her daughter's cheek.

Mrs. Benson returned to her doctoring duties and left Signe and her baby to study each other. "I will wash her as soon as I'm finished here."

"Gerd is all right?"

"Oh, ja. Weak, but she saved your life. You have lost a lot of blood already—please, God, get it to stop. We might have to send for a doctor." Mrs. Benson looked toward the window. "I hear the boys returning from school. Let me close the door."

Signe heard Leif greet Gerd in the kitchen.

"Can I see her? Is Mor really all right?"

Gerd said, "Go tell Knute to ride out to the woods and tell your far that he needs to come home right now."

Leif charged out the door, not bothering to close either one. Gerd returned to the bedroom. "Do we need to send for the doctor?"

"Maybe." Mrs. Benson picked up the baby. "Is the pan set with warm water?"

"Ja."

"Can you clean up some in here? I will wash the baby. Do you know if she has a clean gown?"

"Ja, it is folded on the shelf in the parlor." Signe did not bother to open her eyes. "How bad is the bleeding?"

"I pray it will let up soon. Did you have bleeding problems with your other birthings?" Mrs. Benson rocked the baby in her arms.

"Not that I remember. I think the fall is causing the problem." Answering the questions took every bit of strength she had. *Please, Lord, stop the bleeding.*

They heard the back door open again. "Tante Gerd?" Leif called.

"In here. I will be right out."

"Tell him he can come see me in a bit," Signe whispered. The place on her chest where the baby had lain seemed cold without her. How bad was the bleeding? How often had they changed the packing? "Takk, Tante Gerd. Tusen takk."

"You gave me the scare of my life." Gerd sank down on the chair by the bed. "But the little one doesn't seem any worse for it. Have you thought of a name for her?"

"I want to name her Inga, but Rune wants to name her after his mor, Gunlaug." She fought to keep her eyes from staying closed. But she wanted to put her daughter to the breast to get her a good start—not that Signe had milk yet, but she had always had plenty before.

I have a baby daughter. After three boys, I have a girl who is healthy. They had lost a baby girl within an hour after she was born several years earlier. Signe had not gotten pregnant for several years after that. *Please, Lord, let this one live and thrive like our boys have.*

By the time they heard a horse galloping toward the house, the women had cleaned up Signe and the room and set the baby to her breast. The baby rooted around, then with a bit of help, began nursing.

Rune hit the porch running and burst into the bedroom, dropping to his knees beside the bed. "Are you all right? What happened? You weren't in labor this morning."

"I slipped off the ladder, and the fall sent me into labor."

She saw the horror in his eyes. "But what were you doing on the ladder? I thought . . ."

"I needed some things from the attic." She shook her head. "I know, but I . . ."

"You could have been killed, or the baby killed. Signe, how could you do such a thing?"

She ignored his question and folded back the diaper thrown over her shoulder as she nursed. "See, Rune. Meet your daughter."

He reached out and touched her bald little head with a reverent finger. "Oh, she is strong. I thought not until November."

"So did I, but she seems to be near term, so . . ." She trapped a yawn with her other hand.

"You are all right?"

"Pray the bleeding stops."

He turned to look at Mrs. Benson standing at the end of the bed. "How bad?"

"Steady, but if it doesn't let up, I think you should send for the doctor."

"What will he do?"

"I don't know. I am not a midwife or a doctor. But I have had six and helped with several others."

"How did you know she needed help?"

"I didn't. I came to visit with Signe and arrived just after her fall."

"Tante Gerd helped me get up and walk in here." Signe nodded to the older woman.

Rune turned to her. "You did?"

"Ja, desperation can give one strength when needed. I was sleeping when I heard a scream. I found her on the floor at the bottom of the ladder."

"The ladder." He shook his head slowly. "I should have built the stairs in spite of Einar."

"Far, can we come in?" Knute asked from outside the bedroom door.

"Ja, let them." Signe knew she needed to sleep, but her boys needed her more. When they tiptoed over to the side of the bed, she showed them their baby sister.

"She's so little." Leif stared at the bundle in his mor's arm. "How come she's all red?"

"Babies are like this. Getting born is hard work."

When both boys had touched her, Mrs. Benson shooed all the males out of the room. "You can come back in a few minutes, and then your mor needs to sleep. See, the baby is already sleeping." When the boys were gone, she pulled back the covers and checked the packing. "Soaked again." She changed it. "We better send for the doctor, and if he can't come, Mrs. Jongkavn, the midwife. She knows as much as a doctor anyway."

Rune leaned over the bed. "I will be back as soon as I can. You sleep and get some strength back."

"I could go, Far," Knute offered from the kitchen.

"I better. But takk. You go get started with the chores."

With addresses in his pocket, he kissed his wife on the forehead, shrugged into his warmer coat, and rode out of the yard at a gallop.

Mrs. Benson came back to look down at Signe. "Tell me what you planned to make for supper, and I will do that." She nodded toward Gerd, who was sound asleep in the chair. "She is worn out too."

"Does your family need you?"

"Not as much as you do. But while you are telling me, I will massage your belly again. We have to get this to stop."

Signe nodded, told her what she had started, and in spite of her wish, drifted to sleep. *Please hear and take care of me—of all of us—Lord.*

Chapter 28

A slow lope was easier on the horse, but not on Rune's mind.

Fears bombarded him for Signe, their baby daughter, himself, the boys, even Einar and Gerd. He tried blinking them away, reminding himself to pay attention to the horse and the road and getting the doctor.

"Please, Lord, let him be home and able to come take care of Signe—now."

The horse flicked her ears back and forth, as if trying to gauge what he was doing.

Rune blew out a breath and settled deeper in the saddle. Riding was not one of his joys in life. *Stop the bleeding, stop the bleeding.* He caught himself chanting in rhythm with the horse's hooves.

By the time he reached Blackduck, dusk had succumbed to dark, but he managed to find the doctor's office. He flipped the horse's reins over a hitching post and hustled up the walk to pound on the door.

"Come on in." A woman's voice. Not the doctor. She smiled at him. "How can I help you?"

"My w-wife had a baby and now the b-bleeding won't stop," he stammered in his consternation. He watched her face, trying to understand her words. "What do you mean he's out of town? He can't be. We need him now!"

"I am so sorry. But he will not be back for two more days, on the afternoon train. Where do you live?"

"A couple miles from Benson's Corner."

"Then I suggest you go to Mrs. Jongkavn, the midwife. She is closer to you, and perhaps she can help. I am so sorry."

"Do you have any kind of medicine that might help?"

She went to a cabinet, pulled out a container, and measured some powder into a packet. "Try this. Mix with water, warm but not hot."

"Takk—er, thank you."

"You know the way?"

"I hope."

"One mile straight past Benson's Corner. On the right."

Rune let himself out and stared at his tired horse. No loping or galloping now. He mounted and reined her around to head back the way they had come. The thought smacked him. *Why did I not go to the midwife first, since she is closer?* He tried to settle against the cantle of the saddle. If only the moon would come up. *Lord, help me.*

It seemed like hours before he saw a lighted house on the right a mile past the store. Crossing a creek had been one of the landmarks Mrs. Benson had told him. He hoped Mrs. Jongkavn had a horse, since his was so tired he should lead her home.

A woman answered his knock.

"Are you Mrs. Jongkavn?"

"Yes, and by the look of you, you need the midwife. Where do you live?"

"Two miles west of Benson's Corner. I tried the doctor, but he is out of town."

She called over her shoulder, "Harness up, please," then turned back to Rune. "Ah, you are the people staying with the Strands. Never mind, I will come anyway. You can ride with me, since your horse must be exhausted if you've been to Blackduck and back." She gathered up her bag and shrugged into a wool coat. "Brisk out there, eh?"

"Ja, I guess so. I'll carry that for you. My wife has been bleeding since the baby was born."

"How long ago?"

"This afternoon." He followed her out the door. "She fell off a ladder and . . ."

"And that sent her into labor."

The trap stopped by his horse, and a big man stepped out. "Drive carefully."

"Yes, dear." She handed him her bag, and he helped her into the buggy. "Thank you."

Rune tied his horse to the back of the trap and swung up onto the seat. "Can we hurry?"

"As fast as is safe, so we get there." She flicked the reins, and the horse obediently picked up the pace. "Now, tell me all that you know. Were you with her at the time?"

"Nei, I was out in the woods, cutting trees with Onkel Einar."

"Einar Strand."

"Ja, do you know him?"

"I know of him."

Rune stared straight ahead. *Of* him. So he had a reputation, and not a good one, from the tone of things. He chose not to ask for more information.

"And your wife?"

"Signe. Oh, sorry, my name is Rune Carlson."

"I see. How many babies has your wife had?"

"We have three boys." He gave her their history, the miscarriages and long barren years. "So we now have a baby girl and . . . and you have to keep Signe alive. This baby needs her. . . ." He choked back tears. "I—we all need her. She has made Tante Gerd regain her strength and . . . and . . ."

"I understand, Mr. Carlson, we will do the best we can, but the most important thing is prayer."

"I-I have been praying all the way and . . . and we did not pray much for a while, but we are doing so again."

"I am glad to hear that."

They had turned at Benson's Corner and were well on the way to the Strands' lane.

Finally, finally, he could say, "Turn here." Lights from the windows beckoned them in. "You go right in, and I will take care of your horse."

"Of course."

Rune was out of the trap before the wheels stopped turning. "She's here!" he shouted when the back door opened.

Mrs. Benson came to the edge of the porch. "Good evening, Velma. I'm so glad you could make it." She took the midwife's bag. "Come this way."

Rune returned to the house to the sound of a baby crying. Was that good or bad? Good that she was strong enough to cry, bad that her mor might not be able to feed her.

The boys met him at the door, Leif dashing away tears, the other two wide-eyed and terrified. The bedroom door was closed, and he gripped each one on the shoulder. Leif attached himself to his far's side.

"Any word?"

All three shook their heads. "Mrs. Benson made supper, and

Onkel Einar went back to the machine shop. He was not very nice," Knute reported, looking to Bjorn, who nodded.

"He did not say anything," Bjorn added, "just ate and left. Tante Gerd ate with us too."

"We got to see Mor and the baby, but not for long. Far, what is happening?"

What to say? How to explain? "Your mor is having complications from the baby coming so soon and so fast."

"Is she going to die?" Leif's blue eyes were puddles of tears.

Not if I can help it. But that was the agony. He couldn't do anything. Could any of them help? Really, this was in God's hands. *Mercy, oh Lord God, I plead your mercy upon us. Only you can make the bleeding stop. Please, use the others to keep Signe here for all of us. Lord, you know how we need her. Mercy, please, mercy.* He hugged his boys close. Bjorn stood back just a bit and when Rune looked at his face, all he could see was agony. No matter that Bjorn was trying to be strong, he was close to crying.

Mrs. Benson came out of the bedroom, and the four of them moved toward her as one. "Keep praying," she said softly. "Your mor is strong, and we are doing all we can."

"How is the baby?" Rune asked.

"She nursed again, so she is content. We have her sleeping in a drawer for now."

"I did not get the cradle finished."

"She does not need that yet. She'll be swaddled next to Signe most of the time."

"What can I—we do?" Bjorn asked.

"You can fill the woodbox so we can keep the fire going. The dishes are in the dishpan. . . ."

"I can do the dishes." Leif broke away, as did the others, Bjorn and Knute headed for the door.

"Take a lantern." Rune fetched one out of the pantry and lit it for them. At least keeping his hands busy would make the time go by. He joined Leif at the dishpan. "I will wash, you dry." Leif stared at him, round-eyed.

"It's all right. I do know how to wash dishes." He washed a plate, dunked it in the rinse water, and handed it to him. "See?"

One by one, Mrs. Benson let each of them in to say good night to Signe. She reached up and patted cheeks and managed some sort of smile. "I will be better by tomorrow. Now, you pray for us and sleep."

"If—when there is a change, I will tell you," Rune told the boys.

"Promise?"

"Ja, I promise." He watched them climb the ladder that had brought all of this on. Whatever had possessed her to go up in the attic? But more important, how soon could they get the stairs made? But why bother if she . . .

Rune stepped out onto the back porch. *I cannot allow myself to think such thoughts. Lord God, help me. What do I do? Why oh why did I not go ahead and build the stairs? I knew they were needed.* The other side of his mind answered his question. *Because this is Einar's house. And he said no.* He felt like banging his head against a porch post.

He reached back in the house for his coat and shrugged into it. "I am going for a walk," he said softly to Mrs. Benson.

"Don't be gone long."

"I won't."

He stepped off the porch and headed to the machinery shed, where a lantern still shone. Where would Einar sleep tonight? In the parlor on the floor? Stepping into the light, he saw a quilt folded on the seat of the side bench. Einar stood at the workbench, the lantern on the shelf in front of him.

"Are the tools all sharpened?" Rune asked.

Einar spun around, dropping whatever was in his hand. "Can't you let a body know you're coming?" His growl sounded the same as ever.

"Sorry. I need something to do." What he felt like doing involved fists, but violence would not help either of them.

"I got it all sharpened."

Rune nodded to the quilt. "You going to sleep in the hay-mow?"

"Better'n a floor. Got no bed."

If he says one thing about Signe, I will no longer be responsible for my actions.

"Any change?" Einar asked.

Rune gaped. "Nei."

"Then it looks like I'll be sleeping out here in the cold for a while. You better get some sleep, or you won't be worth anything tomorrow."

"I won't leave her."

Einar glowered at him. "Did I say that?"

"Nei." *Apologize.* "Sorry."

Einar shook his head. "Put out the lantern when you leave." He grabbed his quilt and strode off to the barn.

Rune reached for the lantern and stared down at the board Einar had dropped. Lines had been drawn into it with a nail. It was a diagram for building stairs. Rune propped his arms on the workbench and hung his head. Surely this was an act of God. He blew out the lantern and returned to the house.

Mrs. Jongkavn nodded from a chair at the table, where she sat drinking a cup of coffee. "I think it is slowing. It could change again, but for right now . . ."

"Can I see her?"

"Of course. Mrs. Benson is sleeping on the davenport, Gerd

on a pallet in the bedroom." She shook her head. "That is the only bed in this house?"

"Pallets make do."

She rolled her eyes. "Signe is sleeping now. It might be better not to wake her."

"I won't. I just want to sit with her a bit."

"And pray?"

"Ja. Never prayed so much in my life."

She nodded. "Possible death brings that on. But I got a feeling the grim reaper is not going to take her. We will know more in the next couple of hours." She swigged the last of her coffee. "Get some sleep."

He slipped into the bedroom and took the chair beside the bed. As if she sensed his presence, Signe's eyelashes fluttered open. A slight smile touched her mouth as she raised her fingers off the blanket. He took her hand and blew out a breath. Ever so gently, he bent over and raised her hand to his face. The kiss was lighter than feathers, but her smile widened, and she nodded slightly before drifting back to sleep.

"I love you, heart of my heart," he whispered so softly the angels barely heard it. Laying her hand back down by her side, he watched her breathe. A tiny whimper came from the drawer at the foot of the bed. He rose and looked down at the baby whose entry had caused such problems. So tiny. He had forgotten how small babies were. He and Signe thought they would never have more children, and now look. Born in Amerika, a new life in a new land. He wanted to touch her, hold her, but he refrained. Anything to let Signe sleep and recover. *We need a name for you. Gunlaug for my mor, or maybe Christina from Signe's family. We are in a new land—how about a new kind of name? What could that be?*

He left the room without a sound and spread his pallet on

the floor in the parlor as always. Fully clothed, since morning would be coming so soon, he feared he would not sleep. They had promised to wake him if there was any change.

He heard the clatter of stove lids. Had he been asleep? It was still dark. Who was in the kitchen? Was it time to get up? He folded back his cover and reached for his boots. Perhaps he should check on Signe and the time.

"Good morning, Mr. Carlson, looks to be a fine day." Mrs. Jongkavn was just coming through the back door. "I hope I did not wake you feeding the fire."

"I wasn't sure if I slept or not, but it looks like I have."

"The bleeding has slowed to near normal, if I may be so frank."

Rune felt a monstrous weight fly off his shoulders. "I-I was so afraid—for her. We have lost babies before, but I could not bear losing Signe." He heard himself saying the words, but had he ever told her how he felt? They had married almost as a favor to each other. She already had a son who needed a far. He knew he wanted a family, but circumstances had prevented that.

In these years since, why had he never spoken? *Because I am a man of few words. And Signe loved to talk with her friends and relatives. What if I said the wrong words?*

"Has Mrs. Benson gone home already?" he asked.

"No, she is outside. She plans to make breakfast before she leaves. I will go home as soon as it is light enough to drive safely."

"I will harness your horse. We put her in a stall in the barn for the night."

"Thank you. I get so involved with my patients, I forget all about my horse."

"We can never say thank you enough. I-I . . . ah, what is your fee?" he blurted.

"I am grateful for anything you can offer."

"Would a dollar and a ham do?" That was all the cash he had. "The hams are nearly done smoking, so we could bring that to you in a day or two." How humiliating.

"That would be just fine. We don't raise hogs, so ham is a rare treat. Thank you."

And if Einar yells about the ham gone, that is just too bad. One of these days he is going to be forced to pay us something. He rubbed his eyes.

"I will go get your horse." He nodded to the midwife and grabbed his coat off the tree by the door. The narrow strip of light in the east promised that the sun would return. He hunched down in his jacket. This morning was not chilly, it was downright cold. After lighting a lantern, he murmured softly to the midwife's horse as he entered her stall, patting her on the rump as he passed. He lifted the harness that had been draped over the stall wall, settled it in place, and slid the bit in her mouth.

Once outside, she tossed her head and pricked her ears at the sound of the rooster crowing. Dawn came swiftly once it started. Harnessed to the trap, she quietly followed him to the house, where he tied her to the hitching post.

Mrs. Jongkavn met him at the door. "Thank you. I look forward to the ham."

He dug in his pocket and brought out his remaining dollar. "I wish it could be more. Thank you for saving us."

"I just did my job. God does the saving."

He helped her into the trap and waved as she trotted down the lane.

The boys, on their way to chores, met him at the door.

"Mor is better." Leif shrugged into his coat. "We gotta hurry so we aren't late. Mrs. Benson wants eggs—can you get the eggs from the well house and whatever else?" he threw over his shoulder as he jumped the porch steps.

Both Bjorn and Knute grinned at him as they followed Leif. "What fine boys you have," Mrs. Benson said as he set a basket with eggs, cream, butter, and a jug of milk from the well house on the counter. "Thank you. The coffee is nearly ready." She leaned closer. "Does Mrs. Strand eat at the table with all of you?"

"She does now that she is stronger. She could not walk, she was so weak when we arrived. Signe has been helping her."

"Now that is good news. She is still asleep, so I wondered. Will Mr. Strand join us?"

"Ja. At least, I think so. He always does."

"I have to go home right after breakfast. Do you think you can manage until someone else comes to help? I have a friend I will ask. Signe should not get out of bed except to use the commode." She studied him. "Can you manage? She lost a lot of blood and that makes one very weak. It takes time for the body to rebuild blood."

"Ja, we will manage. I'm not going out in the woods today, but Einar and Bjorn will, I am sure."

Despite his words, he felt worry creep back in. How would he manage? He hoped more help would hurry.

Chapter 29

Right now, all Rune could do was think one moment ahead. He helped Mrs. Benson up into her cart and waved good-bye. The boys had gotten off to school with their dinner pails. Einar and Bjorn had left for the woods, even though Bjorn hesitated.

"I could stay here and help."

"I think this is a better idea," Rune told him. *Keep the monster tamed* was not a kind thought, but desperation took precedence here.

"All right."

But Rune could tell his eldest son was less than pleased to be going out with Onkel Einar by himself. He leaned closer and dropped his voice. "But if he gets mean again, you come back to the house. Like we did before."

"Ja." Bjorn hoisted the dinner basket, picked up the coffee jug, and headed down to the barn.

Lord, protect him. Have I made the right decision? What if . . . ?

Rune returned to the house to see Gerd sitting at the table. "Can I get you some coffee?" he asked after a brief hesitation.

"Ja. Signe is sleeping. Did she eat?"

"Nei." He poured her coffee and pulled a skillet forward on the stove. "Eggs and toasted bread?" He had watched Signe toast bread by laying it right on the hot stove. He figured he could do that as well.

"Takk. Is there oatmeal for Signe?"

"Ja, Mrs. Benson saved some." He nodded to a pot by the reservoir.

She sipped her coffee, eyeing him. "Have you ever taken care of a baby?"

He shook his head and cracked the eggs over the potatoes that were already in the pan, accidentally dropping some shell in as well. Stirring the eggs, he finally got the eggshell lifted out. The sliced bread browned more than necessary. Dishing up Gerd's plate, he realized there was enough left in the pan for Signe. If she felt like eating. She *had* to eat, that was all there was to it. If he had to hand-feed her, he would. He slid the frying pan to the cooler part of the stove.

"I'm afraid I am so weak I may drop the baby." Gerd buttered her bread. "But I can change her and help Signe with her. But you must pick her up, I think."

Was this the same Gerd who had shrieked at Signe and ordered her around?

"Ja." He poured himself some coffee and sank down on a chair. Signe always made everything she did look easy, including not burning the toast. At least Gerd had not yelled at him. "The baby is right beside her?"

"Ja, it is easier that way. I will hem more diapers. The ones we have need to be washed."

"Ja." He nodded, and for some strange reason, his head kept going up and down. His mind bounced around inside his head, and he could not think clearly.

"First fill the boiler with water and set it on to heat," Gerd said, her voice almost gentle. "The soap is outside with the washing machine. The boiler, too."

"Ja." He checked the woodbox. The boys had filled it like they always did, but he was using a lot of wood. When would he have time to split wood? He should have allowed Bjorn to stay home and help.

After refilling the stove maw and setting the boiler on the hot part, he shaved some soap into the water.

Gerd stood, taking her cane, and wobbled her way to the bedroom.

The baby whimpered. Rune joined Gerd at the bedside, where Signe was awake but too weak to even set the baby at her breast.

Where did propriety end and need begin? He'd helped calves learn to nurse but never a baby. His daughter's tiny mouth latched on to her mother's breast to nurse but let go after a minute or so. She screwed up her face to cry.

"What's wrong?"

"Signe has no milk."

Rune stared at Gerd. "But how do we feed her, then?"

"We need a baby bottle."

"Where do we find one of those?"

"I hope Mrs. Benson thinks to bring or send one out. In the meantime . . ."

"Soak a clean rag in warm milk." Signe's voice was so weak, he asked her to repeat herself.

Gerd turned to him. "We need milk from the well house. Boil a soft rag and dip it for her to suck."

"Ja. Signe has to eat too."

"I know. Hurry." Gerd started to pick up the crying infant, then looked to Rune.

"You sit down—"

"Nei, pick her up and put her on the table. I will change her."

Rune nodded, picked up his daughter as if she might break, and set her on the table they had padded with a towel at the foot of the bed. He waited until Gerd had a hand on her. Red-faced and waving her fists, the baby paused only an instant. Rune ran all the way to the well house, grabbed a jug of milk from the tank, and ran back to the house. He dug out a small pan, poured milk in it, and set it on the stove.

The boiler steamed and bubbled. The diapers. Where were they? Where was a rag to boil?

"In here," Gerd called.

And Signe had not eaten yet.

"Please, Lord, help me," he muttered as he returned to the bedroom. His daughter had a fine pair of lungs, that was for sure.

Gerd was sitting in the chair, rocking the little one back and forth.

"A rag? The diapers?" he asked.

"In the tall cupboard. Do not burn the milk. And there." She pointed to a bucket of water and dirty diapers. "You have to rinse them outside, then add them to the boiler."

"Ja, the milk!" He dashed back into the kitchen, grabbed the handle of the pan, and pulled it over to the reservoir. The milk was steaming. Had he burned it? A rag. He found one in the cupboard and threw it into the steaming water.

"How is the milk?" Gerd called.

"Hot." He sniffed the steam. "But not burned."

"The rag?"

"In the boiler."

"Rinse it good to get the soap out."

Rune rolled his eyes. He should have thought of that.

The baby kept on fussing, her cries louder.

When he finally brought the pan of milk and boiled rag to the bedroom, he followed Gerd's orders like a confused puppy follows a two-year-old. How would they ever get his daughter to suck on a rag?

"I will hold her, and you dip the rag and hold it to her mouth," Gerd ordered.

"And spill milk all over her."

"We can wash her. I will hold her face—hopefully."

"My baby," Signe murmured.

"We are trying to feed her," Gerd explained. "You have no milk."

"Oh, I—afraid—of that."

Rune dipped the tip of the rag and tried to drip it into his baby's mouth. And again. Each time it hit her cheek or chin, anywhere but her mouth. *Lord, help us.* "Would a spoon work better?"

"Hush, little one, shhhh." Gerd looked up at him. "Keep trying."

This time Rune touched his finger to her mouth. She opened to nurse, and he slipped the rag in place. She quit squalling immediately and sucked. After two or three pulls, he repeated his actions. "How about laying her on your knees? Might be easier."

Gerd shifted the infant to lie in her lap with her head toward Gerd's knees. She kept up her murmur, laying her hands on either side of the child's face. "She learns fast."

"Is she eating?" Signe asked, her voice no more than a whisper.

"Ja, she is."

"Th-thank G-God."

Gerd and Signe shared a look that shouted of their agreement.

When the baby lost interest in the rag, Gerd wrapped her up again, and Rune tucked her in next to her mor.

"Set me up on the porch with the diaper bucket, and I will take care of those while you fix Signe something to eat. Beef broth would be best, but that is impossible. There might be leftover chicken soup in the well house."

Rune almost smiled. Never had he heard her talking like this. How Signe must appreciate the change. *Lord, please give her strength like only you can give.*

Gerd took her cane and tapped her way to the kitchen. "If there's no soup, bread in milk might be easier for her to eat."

Rune carried the diaper bucket out to the porch and set a chair beside it. "I will hurry." He shot the washing machine a stern look. If he needed to use that too, he would.

But first, get some food into Signe.

Feeding her was easier than getting the baby to suck on a rag. He propped a pillow behind her and sat down to spoon chicken soup into her mouth. "You have to eat to get your strength back. Come on, Signe." She nodded, a small nod, but her eyes fluttered open.

"I-I am." She opened her mouth when the spoon touched her lips. "Slowly," she whispered after a couple of bites.

"Gerd said you have to drink too. I will make tea, if you like. Or perhaps warm milk? Gerd said bread in warm milk might go down easily." How strange—here he was the one talking while Signe drifted off. How often had he fallen asleep when she was talking?

A minute shake of her head said she was finished.

"One more." He held the spoon firm.

She raised a finger.

"Ja, only one. But I will be back as soon as I get the diapers in the boiler on the stove."

With the diapers bubbling on the stove, he stirred them with a heavy faded stick that had been used in the wash for years.

His mor had one just like it. How he wished Gunlaug were here with them. He heard the thumping of the sewing machine as Gerd hemmed more diapers. Where was she getting the strength to rinse out diapers and now sit at the sewing machine? Surely this was another miracle. It wasn't that long ago that Signe had forced her to walk.

When the boys got home from school, he would send Knute back to Benson's for a baby bottle. If only he had gone ahead and built the stairs. He clenched his teeth against the anger at Einar that seemed to fester inside.

Was that the baby again? So soon? He returned to the bedroom. Signe lay sleeping, but the baby was squirming. Did all babies eat this often, or was it because she never really got full?

"S-sorry." Signe turned her head just enough to see their daughter.

"I will heat the milk again. Gerd is hemming diapers, so I'll get her."

Gerd returned to the bedroom when he had everything together again. She changed the baby, sat down and held her just so, and he fought to get the milk in her mouth.

"Can we keep her alive this way?" Rune whispered, not sure if he was asking himself or Gerd.

"Ja. We will." Gerd looked toward the bed, where Signe was now awake. "We will bring you something to eat when she is fed."

Signe nodded. "My baby . . ."

Rune glanced at his wife, and milk slid down his daughter's cheek.

"Careful," Gerd said.

"Sorry." He focused back on his daughter, not on his wife. *Lord, please let them both live.*

With the baby fed, diapered, and back with her mor, he

brought in a load of wood, fed the fire, stirred the diapers he'd forgotten on the stove, and pulled the coffeepot to the front to heat. His stomach reminded him to eat. He needed to get the diapers on the clothesline, or they would never dry. How on earth did Signe keep up with all these demands on her time?

The tapping of Gerd's cane made him look toward the sound. She carried a loaf of bread to the table. "Is there sour cream in the well house?"

He shrugged. But more important, what were they going to have for supper? "I will go see. Anything else?"

"Eggs. Did you add wood to the smokehouse fire?"

He heaved a sigh. "Nei. But I will."

"Bring in buttermilk. We'll have eggs and pancakes for supper."

"Ja." He returned with buttermilk, sour cream, and eggs, setting them all in the pantry. Getting a jar of jam from the cupboard, he brought the sour cream and jam to the table, where Gerd had sliced bread for three plates.

"You think Signe can eat this too?" He watched her spread the sour cream on the bread and the jam on top, his mouth watering already.

"You feed Signe and eat with her."

He poured Gerd's coffee first and then a cup for himself. Then, with cup and plate in hand, he returned to the bedroom and sat down by the bed. "Signe, you must eat."

Her eyes blinked open and a smile twitched her mouth. "S-sit up?"

He stuffed a pillow under her head and shoulders. This time, when he held a spoon of food for her, she opened her mouth.

"Good?"

A slight nod, but at least she chewed and swallowed. He ate a bite himself and fixed her another. They finished the first slice and started the second before she turned her head away.

"Coffee?"

She managed three swallows before her eyes drifted closed again.

He finished the bread and his coffee, watching his girls sleep. *Lord, please make them well and strong, and help me to always appreciate what Signe does for us. I never knew, and I will never understand how she does all that is needed. If I don't get the diapers scrubbed and hung, this baby will not have diapers to keep her dry.*

He sighed and heard the thump of the sewing machine again. Gerd did not seem able to stand and work, but she could sit. So very different than the months earlier.

Lugging the full boiler out to the porch, he dumped the diapers and water in the washing machine, then returned with water for the rinse tub. Cranking the machine was simple, adjusting the wringer took some doing, but once he had the diapers wrung through into the rinse water, he felt like he'd won a battle. After hanging them on the clothesline, he returned to the house.

"The baby is fussing again," Gerd said.

Leif and Knute both burst through the door. "Mor?"

Gerd shushed them with a finger held to her mouth and pointed to the bedroom. "She is sleeping."

The boys tiptoed in to see her, then rushed back out.

"One of you has to ride back to Benson's for bottles for the baby," Rune said.

Leif got to the door first.

"Knute, we need more firewood. If we both split . . ."

"Ja, I will."

Gerd stood up. "Eat first."

Leif grabbed his sugared bread and butter, the list his far handed him, and ran back out the door.

"You ever butchered a chicken?" Gerd asked Knute.

He shook his head. "But I know how."

"For supper?" Rune asked.

"Nei, soup for Signe. One of the older hens, not laying."

"I will help you." Rune pumped water into the boiler and set it on the stove.

They lopped the head off the chicken, dunked it in hot water to loosen the feathers, and stripped the old hen clean in a matter of minutes. "Now you gut her, and I'll start splitting wood."

"Gerd is calling you."

Feed the baby again, it must be. *Leif, hurry back with those baby bottles.*

Chapter 30

M rs. Benson beamed at Rune when he answered the door. "I have brought you help."

"Come in." Rune stepped back politely, motioning the two women inside.

"How is Signe? And the baby?"

He shrugged. "They are both sleeping for the moment." He led the way to the kitchen.

"Mr. Carlson, this is Mrs. Engelbrett. She has come to nurse your baby. She can tide us over until Signe's milk comes in. I was pretty sure this would happen, so I went ahead and asked her to come. She can't stay here, but she can come out once a day, nurse your baby, and bring her milk for you to use later. I hope you have given your daughter a name by now. When is feeding time?"

Rune hoped he was smiling as he nodded. "I see." He felt run over by the gush of words.

"I also brought several baby bottles. Good day, Mrs. Strand." She nodded to Gerd, who looked up from her hemming. "And we brought supper, if you would be so kind as to fetch the basket in the buggy, Mr. Carlson. Several of our ladies brought gifts of food for us to bring you." She paused to catch her breath. "We met young Leif on the road. He went on to the store to get the other things on your list."

"Takk, tusen takk." Rune led them into the bedroom. "Signe, we have company." He touched her shoulder and smiled down at her when she forced her eyes open. "A woman has come who can nurse the baby." He turned to Mrs. Benson. "We have not done well having her suck on a bit of cloth dipped in warm milk."

"But you got enough in her that she is not fussing." Mrs. Benson removed her coat and laid it on the foot of the bed.

"Sorry." Rune took the coats and started toward the door. "I will get the basket from the buggy. Do you need anything else?"

"No, we are fine."

As he left, Mrs. Benson was introducing the two women. He brought the basket in, set it on the table, and hustled back to Signe. Both women hovered over the bed. They had just finished changing the baby. The wet diaper lay on the floor.

Mrs. Engelbrett was saying, "Gud, gud. And how long since you fed the baby?" Rune was relieved to hear that she spoke Norwegian.

"About two hours," Gerd announced from the doorway. "So far she wakes up every two hours, so she should be hungry anytime."

As if on cue, the baby whimpered and scrunched her mouth and face, searching for milk.

"May I take her?" Mrs. Engelbrett scooped up the bundle and sat in the chair. With a little assistance, the baby stopped rooting and attached herself to a nipple.

"She is so smart! Look, she took right to this." Mrs. Benson beamed, her smile warming the room. "I see you have diapers on the line and it is nearing dusk. Would you mind if I brought them in?"

Gerd laid two new diapers on the only remaining clean one. "They might not be dry yet." She tapped her way back to the kitchen, where she pulled the coffeepot forward on the stove.

Now what? Rune suggested, "Since we have help in here, I will go out and split wood."

Gerd nodded. "We can string a clothesline in the kitchen if we need to, to dry the baby things."

Stepping outside, Rune took over the splitting, and Knute stacked the wood on his arms to carry in to the woodbox.

"Who is here?" Knute asked.

"Mrs. Benson, and she brought someone to nurse our baby."

"Did she see Leif?"

"Ja, and she brought baby bottles. He went on to the store for the rest. Haul a couple loads in, and then go start chores. I will be down to help you." He glanced up when he heard the screen door slam. Mrs. Benson on her way to the clothesline. He should be doing that, but how could he, when they needed wood for the fire? Working out in the woods was far simpler. You just kept swinging the axe.

He hefted the axe and slammed another quarter round into two pieces that fell to the ground. This axe needed sharpening.

He and Knute filled the woodbox in the kitchen. "Were the diapers dry?" he asked Mrs. Benson.

"Mostly."

"Do you need anything from the well house before we start chores?"

She shut the oven door and smiled at him. "I think we're fine for now." She came closer and dropped her voice. "When do you expect Mr. Strand in from the woods?"

"Anytime now."

"I see. Ah, could you keep him down at the barn until we call that supper is ready?" Her hands fluttered like nervous birds.

"Ja, I suppose so."

"You see, young Mrs. Engelbrett, she is, ah—a bit fearful of him, what with his shouting and all."

Rune heaved a sigh and nodded slowly. "I see. I will do my best. Will you be staying for supper?"

She shook her head quickly. "I—ah—no, we will leave as soon as she has finished her work here."

Questions bombarded him about Einar's previous actions, but instead of commenting, he nodded again. "I will do my best."

"Supper is in the oven, and some other dishes might need to go in the pantry. Is Mrs. Strand able to, ah, put the supper on the table?"

"I will take care of that. Takk for your help."

What in the world had Einar done to terrorize folks in the area?

If only Signe could keep her eyes open, pay attention. The tiny bundle beside her squirmed and started mewling. Like a brand-new kitten or puppy. Perhaps it was a universal language of hungry newborns. If only she had milk for her tiny daughter. Had she the energy, tears might have leaked from her eyes and into her hair.

"There now, hush, you don't want to wake your mor."

The whisper sounded so sweet, no wonder the baby ceased her fussing.

I want to be the one who feeds and comforts her. But her whole self fought to drag Signe back into a dark land where she wandered alone. She forced her eyes open as she felt the baby lifted away.

"Takk." She tried again, and this time the woman paused.

"You are awake. Oh, Mrs. Carlson, how wonderful. You have such a beautiful baby girl. She's smart too, nursing like an older baby. Took her no time at all to figure out what to do." She paused. "I-I hope you don't mind I feed her."

"Takk, tusen takk." Signe hoped the sound carried farther than her mind. Mrs. Benson had introduced this woman, but Signe could not remember her name.

"Ja, you are welcome. You just keep getting better so you can nurse her yourself." She disappeared from Signe's sight.

Mrs. Benson took her place. "I brought you some chicken soup. I mashed the dumplings and vegetables so you can eat more easily."

"Takk." Signe tried to help raise her head but lacked the strength to even do that, let alone feed herself. At least she could swallow, and that she did, forcing herself to swallow a few more spoonsful than she wanted, but Lord willing, she would get better.

Mrs. Benson patted her shoulder. "You ate a good half a cup."

"Where . . . is . . . Gerd?"

"She is rolling out biscuits for supper. I made the dough. She still has more diapers to hem. Babies sure go through the diapers."

"Wash . . . diapers?"

"Mr. Carlson did that. He is a good man."

Signe managed a nod and what she hoped was a smile. Ja, Rune Carlson was a good man. A good man who was doing things for which he had no training. In Norway her mor and sisters had taken over when she had the boys.

In spite of herself, she drifted back to sleep.

She woke to someone shouting. Einar. She had to get out of his bed. But when she tried to move, the baby squeaked. The fright woke her completely. Perhaps it had been a dream.

Gerd leaned over her. "You awake?"

Signe nodded and this time the "ja" came more easily. The room was dark but for the lamp. She could hear the sounds of forks against plates and food being passed.

"Can you eat again?"

"Ja."

"Your soup is hot. I will bring it."

Gerd returned in a short time, her cane tapping the floor. "Good, you are still awake. Ah, the baby settled back to sleep. Mrs. Engelbrett's milk fills her up, so she can sleep longer."

"They are gone?"

"Ja, but will come tomorrow."

Signe swallowed obediently. "Did you eat?"

"Nei, but I will."

When they came from Norway, she had fed Gerd, and now look. *Thank you, God above.* "Do you have a Bible?" Talking took more strength than eating, but she could tell she was stronger. Not a lot, but some.

"Ja, in the trunk." Gerd paused. "You want more soup?"

"A bit."

"Good. I will get it." When Gerd returned, Signe was nearly asleep again but she forced her eyes and mouth open. "I will have Rune get out the Bible."

That was good. A good idea to drift off on. Signe slept again.

Sometime later, she felt the baby squirm and make her searching noises. Before she hit the whimper stage, someone picked her up. Rune murmured to the infant. She heard a sniff and opened her eyes. She could see Leif outlined against the light from the kitchen.

"Mor, you're not going to die—are you?" Leif sniffed between the words.

Her fingers twitched to take his hand. "Nei. I-I am getting better."

She could see his face split by a sun-rising smile. "Mor can talk!"

Rune hushed him. "Go get the baby bottle from the reservoir and bring it here."

"Gerd?" Signe asked.

"Hemming," Rune replied.

So that was the noise she heard. "Sit up?"

Leif returned with the baby bottle.

"You want to feed her?" Rune asked.

"Nei, but . . ." She heaved a sigh as he stuffed a pillow behind her neck and shoulders. "Tomorrow."

She watched as he sat in the chair, the baby in his arm, and took the bottle from Leif. He moved like he had fed babies all his life. He learned quickly, that she knew. Mrs. Benson's words echoed in her mind. *That Mr. Carlson is a good man.*

"The diapers?" she asked.

"Drying on the line Knute and I strung in the kitchen. He's at the table doing his homework. Bjorn took the house axe down to sharpen, and Einar is in the machine shed too. He has been sleeping in the barn."

Leif watched the baby eat. "Mor, we need a name for our baby. What about Kirstin, since we are in a new land?"

His suggestion caught her by surprise. None of their relatives were named such. Kirstin. She nodded. She heard the *tap tap* of Gerd's cane.

"What do you think of Kirstin for our baby's name?" Rune asked Gerd.

She shrugged as she set more hemmed diapers on the pile. "Ja, better than Baby."

"Then Kirstin it is."

Each day when Mrs. Engelbrett and Mrs. Benson arrived, they brought some food and cooked. They did the wash one day and baked bread another.

One day Mrs. Engelbrett brought a shawl. Signe watched as the young mother showed Gerd how to tie it to her with the baby snug inside. "See, she will stay warmer this way, and babies like to be held close."

Gerd wore the shawl over to the bed to show Signe. "When you get strong again, you can carry her this way." Gerd looked down at the baby with the closest thing to a smile Signe had ever seen on her face. Soon Signe would be able to carry her baby next to her heart again, but on the outside now. *Lord, please make me stronger faster.*

That night Rune sat beside her bed. "As long as the women come, I figure I could go back out and work with Einar. I know they do not stay all day, but Gerd is stronger, and I think she can manage for short periods of time. She can lift the baby now, and I saw her tie the baby in the shawl on her own."

"I-I wish I could get up."

"You will soon." He laid his hand on her cheek. "Ah, Signe, I am so grateful you are still here. God was merciful as He promised."

She nodded and leaned her face into the strength of his hand.

Even so, when he left the next morning, she felt her heart pick up speed and her chest tighten. What if the women did not come? The house was silent, as if waiting in either dread or anticipation. When she heard the jingle of the harness and the thud of hooves, she breathed a sigh of relief and instantly fell asleep.

The third day, Mrs. Benson greeted Signe with a letter from home. "I figured this might cheer you up."

Signe took the letter with tears of joy bubbling to the surface. A letter from home. "Oh, I have not even told them the baby came."

"I know. Let me get the ham and beans started, and then I will sit here and write what you tell me. You will have to spell most of the words. And it will probably be a short letter."

"Would you do that—really?"

"Of course. You must eat something first and take a nap, and then we will write the letter. How about boiled eggs and toast?"

Signe nodded. Could she maybe feed herself, if someone helped her sit up against the pillows? How weak she still was—it did not seem possible.

Mrs. Benson helped her sit up, and Gerd, with the baby nestled in the shawl, sat beside the bed, ready to help her. After three bites, Signe dropped the spoon. "Oh," she groaned and shut her eyes. It was too hard.

"No, you managed some on your own. That is good." Gerd scooped the dropped egg off the towel they had draped over Signe and held it to her mouth. "Eat. Remember when you forced me to eat?"

Signe's eyes flew open. She stared into Gerd's. "You were furious with me."

"Ja, I am sorry, but now it is you." Gerd leaned forward with another spoonful. "Eat."

<hr />

The next morning at breakfast, Rune announced that he was going to Blackduck for lumber for building the stairs.

Einar slammed his hand on the table. "For three days you don't work, and now you think to go to Blackduck instead. Nei!"

"I told you we are going to build stairs." He leveled a look at Einar, wondering what had changed since his uncle had drawn that diagram in the machine shed. "I will be back in the woods tomorrow if all is well. Bjorn will be with you today."

"Ja, Bjorn, he—"

"Is a good worker and doing the work as well as a man, even though he is still a boy. He could go with me instead." Rune kept his voice even and finished the food on his plate. "I will drive you out to the woods and then go to Blackduck."

"You—so you have it all decided? This is my house and I—"

"Hush, you will wake the baby." Gerd's voice penetrated her husband's fury.

He stared at her, shoved his chair back, and strode from the room, grabbing his coat on the way past the coat-tree.

The silence was finally broken by a whimper from the sling.

"Finish your breakfast, boys. Bjorn, go help him harness up. You two get your dinner pails. Knute, is your horse ready?"

"Ja. Tied up outside."

"Good. Gerd, do you need help with the baby?"

"Nei. I will warm the last bottle. You go. Do you have a list for the lumber? Add enough to make beds too."

"Takk." Rune pushed back his chair. "Make sure you bundle up, boys, it is cold out there." He stopped in the bedroom to find Signe awake.

"I thought he might hit you," she said.

"Nei. Thank God for Gerd. You should have seen his face." He dropped a kiss on her forehead. "You are not to worry. Just keep getting stronger."

"Ja. Oh, Rune, I want my milk to come in. You think it will?"

"If it does, wonderful. If it doesn't, baby bottles work just fine. Is there something you want from the store in Blackduck? Say, a peppermint drop?"

"Ja, that would be good. But not necessary."

"I am trying to think beyond necessary."

He shrugged into his coat and tucked a scarf around his neck. Food baskets in hand, he went out the door and paused on the porch. The boys on the horse were nearly to the road. The wagon must be about ready. *Lord, keep us all safe today and every day. And keep me from responding to Einar with anger, adding fuel to the fire.*

Chapter 31

"You stacked the lumber in the machine shed," Einar said accusingly the next morning.

Rune nodded. "To keep it dry. I figured we can build the stairs the first day of heavy snow."

"Snow don't stop us cutting trees."

"If all three of us work on the stairs, we should be able to finish in one day." Rune kept eating his breakfast.

"I will not build stairs." Einar's glare could have nailed Rune to the wall.

"Then it will take Bjorn and me an extra day."

"Bjorn works with me."

In the bedroom, Kirstin worked her way into a full-fledged cry.

"Now see what you did." Gerd's glare nearly matched her husband's. She left off packing the dinner basket, took the bottle she had heating on the top of the reservoir, and headed for the bedroom, shaking her head the whole while.

"The dinner basket is not ready. So we do not eat today?" Einar yelled after her. He jerked his hat with earflaps down on his head. Shrugging into his coat, he stormed out the door.

"He sure gets mad." Knute looked at Rune. "Tante Gerd did too." He shuddered. "I don't want him to get mad at me."

"Onkel Einar is mad at everybody." Bjorn picked up his plate and that of Einar and set them in the dishpan on the stove. "Far, you want me to go help harness?"

"Ja, I will take care of the basket. Keep in mind, his bark is worse than his bite." His boys all stared at him, uncertainty chasing doubt across their faces.

"He doesn't like us." Leif finished his cup of coffee that was really mostly milk plus a bit of sugar. He set his dishes in the dishpan too. "Hurry, Knute, or we'll be late."

Gerd returned to the kitchen. "Signe is feeding the baby, and I will finish the dinner basket. You are putting a horse blanket over it so it won't freeze?"

"Takk, Gerd. Ja, we are. The ladies are coming again?"

"Ja. Good thing."

"You are getting stronger every day. Something to be grateful for."

"Ja, I never thought I would." She looked toward the bedroom. "Thanks to Signe." She paused, studying the knife in her hand. "I thought I'd never . . ." A puff of a sigh and a nod. She blew out a breath and went back to cutting the ham and cheese for sandwiches. "Einar . . . uff da, that man."

That afternoon, Mrs. Benson came into the bedroom followed by Mrs. Engelbrett.

"I'm sorry, Signe, but I cannot be here tomorrow. Mrs. Engelbrett can't either."

Signe nodded. "I understand. You both have been such a great help."

"We will manage." Gerd's head bobbed as she spoke. "Thank you."

"If you want, I could take your baby home with me and nurse her there for another week or two," Mrs. Engelbrett offered.

"I would have to talk with Rune, but I do not think so. She can drink cow's milk if she must." *Lord, please, let me nurse my baby.* "You have been a godsend." She reached for the young mother's hand. "Takk, tusen takk. I–I'm sorry, I have nothing to pay you with."

"I couldn't accept payment. Just knowing your baby is getting stronger and doing well is all I need. I love babies." She ducked her head. "You see, I will be having another, and I'm not sure I should keep nursing. I know Kirstin will do well."

"Your supper is in the oven, and I will take the butter we churned and apply it to your account, if you want." Mrs. Benson leaned over to peek at the infant nestled in Signe's arms.

"Ja, that would be good," Gerd answered before Signe managed to.

"We will be off, then. I will return probably two days from now, I think. If you send a list with the boys, I will bring the stores when I come. If not Wednesday, soon after." Mrs. Benson started for the door and turned. "By the way, Mrs. Jongkavn said that sometimes a mother's milk will come in again after a while if the baby tries to nurse often. Let's all pray that this will happen here."

Signe heard the sounds of departure while studying the face of her infant daughter. She remembered when her boys were nursing, the baby would cry, and she would feel a rush of milk. One time they were in church, and someone else's baby cried, and it was a good thing she'd had padding under her camisole. *Please, Lord, bring this about. Her mother's milk is so much better for her.*

Gerd snorted. "Ach, I should have asked her to bring more yarn. I could be knitting mittens for the boys. Easier than using the rabbit skins right now."

Signe hoped she was learning not to show her shock when Gerd said things like that. *Thank you, Lord, for the miracles you have brought to us and Gerd.* If only she could get up.

"From now on, when she starts to fuss, I will do as Mrs. Jongkavn said."

"Ja, and I will go heat a bottle. We have enough milk here for two more feedings. Then cow's milk it is. Do you know if Einar took the milk cow over to a bull?"

"I have no idea."

"He never mentioned it. All he can think of is felling trees."

"Is there a bull nearby?"

"Ja, about a mile away. The heifer will need to be bred too, but not for a couple of months." Gerd paused. "Do your boys know how to watch for the signs?"

Signe shrugged. A yawn threatened to crack her jaw, and her eyelids closed without her volition.

"I will take her." Gerd brought the shawl over, lifted the baby into it, and bent over to loop the tied ends over her head and shoulder. Kirstin made nary a whimper.

At least I get to feed her, even with a bottle. Signe pushed one of the pillows propping her off to the side and lay flat. Ja, she was getting stronger, but so terribly slowly. She should be able to get up and walk, but at least she could sit on the edge of the bed now. And hold her baby. And wear her in the shawl like Gerd was doing.

For the next few days, every time Kirstin started her quest for food, Signe held her to the breast, praying that this time her milk would be there, but the baby would spit out the nipple and root around for one that worked. Gerd would bring a warmed bottle, and Signe would feed her daughter. Gerd would change her, tuck her back in the shawl, and go about the kitchen chores, sitting down often but getting up again and cooking. She had the boys bring food up from the cellar when they came home from school and make sure the woodbox was always full.

Each evening after supper, Rune helped Signe stand and walk around the room. Each time she sank down on the bed and fell back exhausted. "Will I never get better again?"

"Of course you will. You are not hanging on to me so hard anymore. I'm not holding you up."

Since they were nearly out of diapers, Gerd had the boiler on the stove, partly filled with water, when she had to sit down for the second time and catch her breath. They heard Mrs. Benson's horse trotting up the lane. The weather had not gone above freezing for the last two weeks, so while there was still no snow, the ground had frozen deeper daily, and horse hooves and iron wheels made a racket.

"She has perfect timing," Gerd muttered under her breath.

"I told you to wait until the boys came home from school." Signe was sitting in the chair by the bed with Kirstin in the shawl around her shoulders. The chair was turned so she could see into the kitchen.

"I know, but there is never enough time then. Can you see me hanging diapers on the clothesline in the dark?"

"You are not hanging up the diapers outside. Knute and Leif can do that, after they crank the washing machine."

Mrs. Benson knocked on the back door and entered when Gerd yelled, "Come in!"

"My goodness, what do we have here?" Mrs. Benson looked at Gerd. "You were going to wash diapers?" When Gerd nodded, the storekeeper tsked. "More strength to you."

"Bit by bit I can do about anything. Just do not expect me to hurry."

Mrs. Benson hung up her coat and scarf. "I'll finish filling that boiler and add the dirty diapers. I brought you some more flannel for diapers and the yarn you requested. Can't have too many diapers in a Minnesota winter. Have you strung a clothesline on the porch? We did that a long time ago when the snow was too deep to get to the clothesline."

"Not yet. Good idea. We'll see if we have enough rope left after stringing one in here."

"I brought some apple cake. I thought we could have that with coffee. How about I make another one here for the whole family for supper? I know you have smoked pork—did they smoke the loin too?"

"Have canned down in the cellar."

"Good, then I shall make a pork potpie. You have a good supply of vegetables in the cellar."

"Signe did all that."

"Gerd, she's awake," called Signe, sorry to interrupt the conversation.

"Be right there, soon as I put the bottle on."

Gerd kicked the rug back in place when she shut the pantry door, to help keep the draft down. She set the bottle in the bowl to warm. By now they could all hear Kirstin's imperious demand for food.

"She is not a patient baby," Signe said apologetically. "When she wakes up, she wants to eat now, not later."

Mrs. Benson smiled. "Some babies are like that. I will change her while the milk heats. Mrs. Engelbrett sends her greetings. Her milk dried up quickly when she quit coming here." She entered the bedroom. "And how is our Kirstin today?"

"She was good until . . ." Signe sighed. "I did not get her to the breast soon enough, and there was nothing there for her. Do you think babies get angry?"

"I sure do. They are happy or content or restless, and right now she is telling us in no uncertain terms that she is hungry."

Gerd tapped her way in with the warmed bottle in hand. "Here, cranky one."

Signe put the nipple in her daughter's mouth, and Kirstin set to draining her meal as fast as she could suck. After a few swallows, she slowed down, her gaze always on her mor's face. Signe smiled down at her. "See, that was not so bad." She looked up at the two women, both smiling down at the baby.

Gerd was smiling. She was actually smiling. Signe felt warm all over. Tante Gerd had smiled. *And you, little one, brought it on.*

Two days later, Gerd had Kirstin in the shawl sling while she worked in the kitchen when the baby started to fuss and whimper. "You have to wait until I get my hands free," Gerd groused.

Kirstin gained volume.

"Gerd, Gerd, bring her here," Signe called excitedly.

"Coming. Got to get the bottle on."

"Nei, come now. Look. I felt a rush and now I am soaked. Give her to me quick." Signe cuddled her baby against her chest, and within seconds Kirstin located the milk-soaked breast and started sucking. "I really have milk. Thank you, Lord. Gerd, I have been praying and praying my milk would come back for her." She glanced up to see a look of astonishment on Gerd's face.

"I cannot believe this, but I am seeing it with my own eyes. I have to believe."

Signe felt the baby pull away. The grunting and mewing

started again but turned to sucking as soon as she was moved to the other nipple. "Look at her," Signe said a bit later. "She should sleep with a full tummy."

The snow started during the night, and several inches had fallen by morning. By the time the men returned from doing chores, it was piling up. Rune looked thoughtfully out the kitchen window.

After breakfast, Einar reached for his coat. "I will meet you at the barn."

Gerd turned from fixing the dinner basket and pails. "Can you see five feet in front of you out there?"

"Nei, but I know the way."

"My boys are not going to school," Rune said. "They could get lost in this. We are going to build the stairs today."

"No wind, so no blizzard."

"As you have often said, that can change in an instant." Rune buttered another biscuit. "You might as well sit down and have another cup of coffee."

"You do not tell me what to do!"

"Just making a suggestion."

"We are cutting trees like every other day."

"You are. We are not."

Kirstin started to wail.

"There, now look what you did. Scared the baby! Einar Strand . . ." Gerd shook with anger, but she did not raise her voice. "You . . . you go cut trees, and God help you if you get lost." She handed him the dinner basket. "It would serve you right."

Rune pushed back from the table and went into the bedroom to find Signe trying to calm the baby while she struggled to get her nightdress shifted around enough to let Kirstin nurse.

"Here, let me hold her." He took the squalling baby, who had kicked off her blanket, and rocked her in his arms. "There now, little one, Mor is trying to feed you. But you ate not so long ago. Surely you are not hungry again so soon."

"She is always hungry. At least it seems so." Signe held out her arms, and within moments the impatient wailing ceased and the sounds of a nursing baby took over. "She does not like loud, angry noises."

"Who does?"

"Are you really going to start on the stairs?"

"Ja, and even a handrail on the outside. It will be steep."

"Rune Carlson, you are an amazing man."

"I'm sorry it took an accident to stiffen my backbone. We . . . well, I hope the pounding does not disturb her."

Rune smiled down at the baby, trying to remember if he had felt this way about the boys. He didn't think so. Perhaps all those years of losing babies had changed him too.

He heard Einar stomp back in the house. "Rune!"

Rune nodded to Signe and returned to the kitchen. "Ja?"

"You come to the woods with me now, or I will ship you and your family back to Norway."

Rune started to respond but caught the look on Gerd's face out of the corner of his eye.

"Einar Strand," she said, "I will say this only once. If they leave, I will leave with them."

Chapter 32

After a long, tense moment, Einar said, "Put the stairs in the parlor."

Rune stared at him. "If you want." He did not ask why. "Against the kitchen wall?"

"Load the lumber in the wagon and put it on the back porch."

Rune nodded. He'd thought of that, but with the wagon out in the woods . . . He turned to Bjorn. "Go hitch up the wagon, and you boys do as he says."

All three of them headed for the coatrack.

Rune caught the fearful glances the two younger ones sent Einar's way. Bjorn had learned to ignore his cutting remarks, not that there had been that many when they were out in the woods. Einar was a different man out there. What a shame that the younger boys were afraid of him. "So we will use the opening that is already there for the ladder?"

Another curt nod.

Rune nodded, thinking on the changes. He had figured a stairway in the kitchen would allow more heat to rise to the attic. Now they would need a grate. The stovepipe did not heat the attic sufficiently for the winter. The inside of the windows were already painted with ice in the mornings.

In the parlor, they shifted the furniture away from the wall and measured the distances, Rune writing them down.

"Did you get two-by-fours for the wall?" Einar asked.

"Nei. I thought to leave it open with a handrail." *It would have been nice to discuss this before I bought the lumber.* "That will be easier."

Einar's answer this time was only a grunt.

Gerd called them to dinner at noon. The hot ham and beans eaten at the table tasted much better than cold ones out in the woods. Hot coffee also was a treat. The snow was still falling but was no longer a white curtain.

"How deep is it?" Rune asked the boys.

"About six new inches," Bjorn answered.

"We'd better run a rope down to the barn."

"I chopped the ice on the water tank this morning." Knute looked at his far. "What if it freezes clear to the bottom?"

"Never has," Einar grunted.

"The well house does not freeze over either. Sometimes we have had to carry hot water out to melt waterers for the pigs and chickens." Gerd's comment caught them by surprise.

Leif grinned at her. "Maybe we should bring the chicken waterer up to the house at night."

After dinner Knute and Leif picked up the dishes and set them in the dishpan. Gerd nodded her thanks.

"You help with the dishes, Leif," Rune said.

He shrugged. "Knute can dry."

"You boys do the dishes, and I will bake cookies." Gerd did not look at Einar, who snorted but didn't say anything.

"Really? What kind? Mor makes the best sour cream cookies ever." Leif looked toward the bedroom when he heard Kirstin fussing. His wistful face told Rune how much he missed his mor being around.

"Gerd, do you think Signe could make it out here if I help her?" he asked.

Gerd nodded. "I wish we had a rocking chair for her and the baby."

Einar harrumphed.

Leaning on Rune's arm, Signe joined them in the kitchen, sitting on a chair by the stove. "I made it." She smiled at the boys.

"Can I bring Kirstin in?" Leif asked.

Signe nodded. "She is in the sling, so just pick it up and bring her."

Gerd followed him and made sure he was careful.

Leif's grin as he handed the baby to his mor lit up the room. "She sure is little."

Signe unwrapped the baby and held her on her knees. All three boys gathered around her. Kirstin yawned and turned her head, as if she knew she had company.

"She is awake more now," Signe said.

"Mor, how come calves and piglets and even chicks are cuter than babies?" Leif asked.

"And they can eat and do things faster than human babies too," Knute added.

"I wonder if it is because people live longer than animals," Rune said.

"God made it so, and so it is." Gerd nodded to the dishpan.

Leif and Knute took the hint and started on the dishes.

The men and Bjorn set up the sawhorses on the porch, brought up the saws, hammers, and a ladder, and set to building the stairs. With the door opening and closing so often, Rune helped Signe back to the bedroom.

"Takk. It seems I will never be up and moving around again."

She sank against the pillows. "Just that little bit and I-I . . ." She sucked in a deep breath. "But I am stronger. Every day." "Ja, good." Rune patted her shoulder. "Every day."

When the snow finally stopped that afternoon, the sun managed to break through the clouds and turn the outdoors into a glittering world of white. Rune thought briefly of Norway. He did that a lot.

The kitchen was warmer than the parlor, so he took the stair treads to the kitchen table to do the finish woodwork.

Gerd and the boys seemed to be a smooth-running team. Rune was proud of that. Knute took over stirring the cookie dough when Gerd had to sit down to catch her breath.

"You ever rolled out cookies?" she asked.

Both boys shook their heads.

"Then you will start now. Leif, sift flour onto the table, there." She pointed to a spot. "Knute, dump half the dough on the flour and pat it into a circle."

The boys swapped wide-eyed looks but did as they were told.

"Good. The rolling pin is in the first drawer of the pantry." Leif brought it in, and Gerd pushed herself to her feet. "Now I will show you how to roll the dough." She rolled out the dough and showed them how to cut the cookies, then lift them onto the baking sheet. "Now slide that in the oven." She sat down again. "And pull the coffeepot forward."

Smiling to himself at his sons and their baking adventure, Rune finished planing and sanding the stair risers at about the same time the cookies were all baked and the mess cleaned up.

Gerd instructed, "Now go tell Einar that coffee is ready." She motioned for Leif to get cups and a plate for the cookies.

"Mor will want some," Leif reminded her.

"Of course your mor wants some. They smell so good."

Leif grinned at Gerd, who managed a bit of a smile. "I can take her some?"

Gerd turned to Rune. "Would you help her out here again?"

"Cookies, such a waste of time," Einar muttered as he sat down. But when he caught the glare Gerd directed at him, he wisely said no more.

Rune sat Signe down at the table. "This reminds me of a winter day at home," she said.

"Grandma liked to bake cookies, huh, Mor?" Leif said.

"Ja, she did, and I am sure still does." Signe smiled at Gerd. "Takk."

Einar slammed the final nail in the steps just before supper. "Done."

"We still need a handrail on the outside," Rune said.

"I will be out sharpening the saw."

Rune suppressed a sigh. "Bjorn and I will build it. Takk for your help."

Einar glared at him. "Two trees lost," he muttered. "Maybe three."

I will build our bed after supper. Since the evenings were longer now that darkness fell so early, Rune knew he could do that. Perhaps also a cradle for Kirstin, but could he manage a rocking chair?

That night after supper, he sat in the bedroom with Signe while the boys did their homework at the table.

"Would you really leave here, move us somewhere else?" she asked.

"If need be, but it would be easier to stay. Gerd surprised me, though. I think she surprised Einar too."

"She could not bear to be parted from Kirstin. I heard her singing to her the other day. It makes me wonder if she was ever around babies much. She has never mentioned a baby dying or being with child."

"I have a bad feeling that we have not heard the last of this yet. It is getting too cold for Einar to sleep out in the barn."

"Ja. And the boys' pallets need to be filled with hay to keep them warmer."

"Now that the stairs are up, we will do that tomorrow after supper. I'm going to build rope beds after that. Then the pallets can serve as mattresses."

"So much to do." She laid her hand over his. "But see how much better Gerd is?"

"Ja."

Life resumed as usual the next morning, with the men preparing to leave for the woods and the boys to school. As usual, there was no talking at the breakfast table. Rune could tell, though, that Signe was getting stronger. *Thank you, God!* She sipped on a cup of coffee as the others bustled around her.

Einar huffed out the door as usual.

"Mor, what if they had school yesterday but we didn't go?" asked Knute. "We'll get a demerit."

"I'll write you a note."

"Takk." Leif leaned closer. "Today we have cookies in our dinner pails. And we helped make them. Bjorn said that was woman's work, but I don't care. Everyone liked the cookies, even Onkel Einar. How come he never says thank you?"

Signe just shook her head as she carefully wrote a note to the teacher in English and patted each of her boys. "You are doing a fine job. Soon I will be fixing your dinner pails again."

Rune smiled. Signe knew the value of gratitude.

After two days of felling three trees each day, the men were down at the machine shed, Einar sharpening, Rune cutting boards for the bed. "You ever build any furniture, Einar?"

"Some. Why?"

"Do you have a miter saw?"

"Ja, but it got rusty." He pointed to a corner where a couple wooden boxes were stacked. "Maybe in there."

Rune found assorted woodworking tools, some rusty, some missing pieces, and all filthy. "Do you mind if I take these to the house?"

Einar shrugged.

"You ever thought of enclosing this end of the shed and putting a stove in so you could work here on winter nights?"

"Maybe someday."

The next morning, daylight seemed delayed due to the near blizzard conditions outside. As the world lightened slowly, the only thing visible was blowing snow.

Einar stood on the porch. "Shoulda strung a rope to the barn yesterday." He knotted a coil of rope to the porch post and spoke to Rune. "Play this out, but keep it taut. I'll tug on the other end when I reach the barn. If I'm gone too long, follow the rope to come find me."

Bjorn and Knute joined Rune on the porch, and he told them what Einar had said. When he felt the tug on the rope, Rune breathed a sigh of relief. Holding on to the rope, he kicked a path through the snow, the boys behind him doing the same. When they reached the barn, he squeezed in the door and fetched the shovel.

"You boys go ahead with your chores. We'll haul water for the animals after breakfast."

"I will haul water," Einar said. "You fork down hay for the horses and cows."

Inside, the barn felt warm, redolent with the smells of horse

and cow, of hay and manure. The cow mooed from her stanchion, where they had wisely left her and the heifer overnight.

"The pig bucket is frozen," Leif reported.

"We'll bring down hot water to thaw it. What about the
chicken waterer?"

"It's fine. I cleaned the sawdust out of it." They had hauled
sawdust down from where they cut firewood and spread it on
the floor of the chicken house and pigpen.

Leif dug two dried cobs of corn and entered the chicken
house, scraping one cob across the other to break off the kernels,
which set the chickens to fluttering and fighting. The dried cobs
he threw in for the pigs.

As soon as Rune forked down the hay, Leif forked it into the
mangers. Knute finished milking and hung the pail on a nail so
dirt would not fly into the milk.

"Water is here!" bellowed Einar from outside. Rune pushed
open the door and helped him pull the wagon inside. "Need
to get the sledges out. We can do that tonight. If the snow lets
up, we're going to the woods." He glared at Rune to get his
point across.

Rune dipped two five-gallon buckets in the water barrel, and
Einar hauled them into the horse stalls. While the horses drank,
Rune did the same with two smaller pails for the cow and heifer.

"Are we going to school?" Knute asked.

"Not unless it lets up."

The two younger boys grinned at each other as they stepped
outside into the whirling, windy, snowing world.

"Hang on to the rope," Rune warned them.

The snow was up to the boys' knees on the path sides. Rune
followed them to the house, which he couldn't see until they
were a few feet away. Stomping the snow off their boots, they
grabbed the broom and swept each other off.

"Shut the door quick," Gerd ordered from her place in front of the stove. "You can bring in wood after breakfast."

After hanging up their coats and hats, both boys stood as close to the stove as they could without burning their clothes, rubbing their hands to get warm again. Rune peeked into the bedroom to check on Signe. She was sleeping. Good.

He returned to the kitchen. "Bad out there."

"Is winter always like this here?" Knute asked.

Gerd shrugged. "Sometimes, but usually it's sunny, with really cold days."

"Do people go ice fishing here?"

"Ja. Start your oatmeal."

"Before Onkel Einar?" The boys spoke in unison, their voices quivering.

"Here, put this at his place." She handed them a bowl of oatmeal. "Cream, brown sugar, and milk are on the table."

Einar pushed through the door, trailing snow behind him.

Gerd bristled. "Sweep off on the porch! Even the boys know that."

Einar glared at her and went back outside. He returned with most of the snow brushed off, flipped his gloves into the warming box behind the stove, and sat down. When he picked up his spoon to eat, the others did the same.

Leif sent Gerd an apologetic look before spooning in his oatmeal.

After breakfast, as the storm continued to rage, Einar stood at the kitchen window. Rune heard him cursing under his breath. Then he bundled up and left.

Rune motioned the boys to help Gerd with the dishes and told Bjorn to come help him sand down the handrail so there would be no slivers. He sent Bjorn to the top of the stairs, and he started at the bottom.

Gerd came into the parlor. "Rune, we need to wash diapers again. Could you and Bjorn move the washing machine inside?"

"You need more wood too?"

"The boys are doing that, but there's not much to bring in."

"Ja, you are right. Where is Einar?"

She shrugged.

He nodded. "We'll get as much done as possible. Cutting wood is a good chore for when you can't be out in the woods."

"Just don't stay out long. Frostbite is dangerous too, you know?"

"Ja, I know."

They moved the washing machine inside, made sure there was enough water heating, and headed out into the cold, scarves wrapped over their faces.

They had to shovel snow to find the sawhorses and the chopping block. With two blocks and two people swinging axes, the split stack grew quickly. Gerd was right. There should already be a cord of wood or more stacked on the porch for winter. Rune should have realized this, but instead he did what Einar demanded. The boys could not keep up with the wood splitting and all the home chores too.

"Let's stack this on the porch to dry, then we'll split the rest. At least you boys brought another dead tree in."

Bjorn said, "I could have bagged another deer too, and ducks and geese if he would let me."

"I know. Shame."

Bjorn leaned on his axe. "If he says leave again, I think we should."

"But where would we go?"

"I don't know. I like lumbering."

"Your mor will not leave Gerd in the lurch."

Bjorn shrugged. "She can come with us, like she said. Let him learn his lesson."

"I gave my word, son. I will keep my word." *If there is any way I can. I can ignore his yelling, but if he hurts one of us, we will leave.*

Chapter 33

Lord, I have to get stronger faster. This is all too much for Gerd.

Signe stared out the window at the swirling snow. Even in here she could feel Einar's anger at not being in the woods. But Rune and the boys were wonderful. Tonight she would join them for supper if she had to drag herself out there.

Kirstin nuzzled against her breast. At least she had grown a little more patient in regard to eating immediately. "Shush, shush, little one, you can sleep longer. Tante Gerd needs help out there, and here you are about to wake up." The baby quieted as if listening to her voice. Signe hummed a tune her mor used to sing to her. "Your mormor would so love to see you. She would sing to you and rock you in the chair her far built for her. Your aunties would pass you around and tell you how beautiful you are."

Both hands on the chair seat, Signe pushed and wobbled to a standing position. How could something so small seem so big when she was so weak? She sat back down. The next time one of her boys or Rune came in the door, she would call for

LAURAINE SNELLING

them to help her into the kitchen. She could help Gerd if she
didn't have to stand or walk. Or carry the baby.

Gerd came in and sank down on the edge of the bed beside
her. "Would you like some coffee and a cookie?"

"Of course, but let me come out there."

"Nei, I will bring it in here. The diapers are strung all over
the kitchen. I forgot to ask Rune to string a clothesline on the
porch."

"You would freeze hanging them up. This is better. Something
certainly smells good."

"Ham and beans again. Not being able to get down to the
cellar from inside the house is disgusting. I told Einar I wanted
stairs but . . ."

"Like the stairs to the attic?"

"Ja, something like that. Your man and boys are out cutting
up a tree and splitting wood."

"In the snow and blizzard wind."

"They are more protected on that side of the house, but ja.
Getting too dark already, and time to start chores. I heard them
laughing out there." Gerd paused and nodded. "This house
has not heard much laughter." She heaved herself to her feet.
"Maybe two cookies. I might bake again tomorrow."

"Now that the baby has diapers again, eh?"

Gerd returned a few minutes later with a tray. As always,
the first sip of coffee made Signe sigh in delight. Just enjoying
food and drink again, rather than forcing herself to swallow,
was something else to be thankful for.

"Thank you, Gerd." She took a bite of cookie and closed her
eyes. Dipping her cookie in the coffee made her smile again.
"Cookies are such a treat."

"The boys helped me, you know. They are good boys."

"Leif told me how much fun he had. They never helped in

the kitchen before. There were always girls around to do that. Cousins and tantes, everyone pitched in to help."

"So different for you here."

"Ja, but look how much better you are."

Gerd nodded. "That I am, and I have you to thank for that."

"And God. He answered my prayers for you."

Gerd stared at her, her mouth half open. "You prayed for me?"

"Not like I should have, because for a while I decided God was not listening and did not care. But then Rune reminded me of the ways He has taken care of us. He prayed for you more than I did."

"Does Rune pray for Einar?" At Signe's nod, Gerd shook her head. "Waste of time."

Kirstin squirmed and made her waking-up noises.

"You take care of her, and I will go start the corn bread. Need to bake bread again, but the kneading . . ." Gerd shook her head. "Just do everything a little at a time, I tell myself. And you'll get it done."

<hr />

"Re-measure that one, Bjorn. Make sure you are accurate. If the bed is not exactly square, the ropes will pull it apart."

Rune stood in the machine shed with his sons. They had started a fire in a protected corner to keep warm.

"We finished cleaning that up." Knute pointed to the throw-away stack in the corner. "The tools we found are in the first box. Broken metal pieces are in the other. Now what?"

Rune picked up the plane. "See the rust on here? Sit down and scrub it with sand to remove the rust. Wet the sand just enough to make it stick." He demonstrated, using his gloved fingers to scrub. Clapping his hands together to warm them,

Rune returned to drilling four holes in each side of the bed and two in either end.

Einar left off oiling the mower parts and went to stand near the fire, rubbing his hands together.

Bjorn laid the last pine frame board on top of the other one. Rune measured where the slots would be. One of these days, he would cut down an oak or maple to use for furniture for their own house. "My far would find good trees and keep the trunks up in the haymow of the barn to dry out."

"We could do that," Bjorn said.

"Not till all the big trees are cut down." Einar returned to his machinery. "Knute, hand me that oilcan."

"If we had a dead tree in here, we could be splitting firewood."

Einar shook his head. "On the porch. You stacked that on the porch. Besides, keeping that box full is Leif's duty." He glared at Leif. "You, boy, hand me that file."

Leif looked at Rune, who nodded. Leif picked up all three files and held them out for Einar to choose the one he wanted.

"The big one," Einar growled. "Don't you see what I'm doing?"

Leif dropped the other two. "Sorry." He picked them up and dusted them off on his pant leg.

"Put them back in the right place."

"Yes, sir."

Einar jerked his glove off and swore at the same time. "Hand me that wrench." He pointed to one up on the seat of the mower. Leif climbed up on the mower to get the wrench and handed it to Einar. Somehow the wrench dropped down into the mechanism. "Can't you do anything right?" Einar's roar shook the windows.

He reached over to retrieve it, shifting his balance, and

slipped, ramming his hand against one of the newly sharpened blades. Blood spurted onto the floor. Einar swore and grabbed his wounded hand.

Rune leaped to his feet, whipping off his scarf. "Here, we'll wrap it in this until we get you to the house."

"Stupid boy!" Einar held out his hand, blood dripping from the slice across his palm. He pulled his handkerchief out of his pocket with the other hand. "Use this first." All the while he muttered and glared at Leif, who had tears streaming down his face.

"I didn't mean to . . ."

"It was an accident." Rune wrapped the handkerchief around Einar's hand. "Put pressure on that while I get the scarf around it." He glared at Einar. "Enough! Let's get you to the house. Signe is good with wounds."

"Never get that mower done now."

Rune spoke softly. "You boys keep on with what you're doing. I'll be back as soon as I can."

Leif sniffed. "Far, I'm so sorry."

"It was not your fault, accidents just happen." He threw the words over his shoulder as he and Einar walked out into the snow, which seemed to be letting up. Their tracks had not filled all the way with snow in the hours they had been in the machine shed.

Einar staggered, so Rune took his arm.

Einar shrugged him off. "I'm fine." Snow lay several inches deep on the porch steps and had blown into drifts even on the porch. They kicked through it and stomped their boots on the mat as Rune opened the door.

"Sweep off," Gerd ordered.

"No time. You ever sewn up a gash?" Rune asked.

"Nei." She stared at the red seeping through the scarf. "You need a doctor."

"Signe will take care of it."

Einar mumbled more expletives as he sank down on a chair. Leaving him, Rune shrugged out of his coat and strode into the bedroom.

Signe had the baby tucked into the bed and was already standing. "What happened?"

"Einar cut himself on one of the saw teeth. Pretty bad." He helped her into the kitchen.

"I need to wash my hands first." She scrubbed her hands at the sink, and he eased her into the chair by Einar. "We will need strips of cloth, something for disinfectant, and probably a needle and thread, both of which need to be boiled." She unwrapped the scarf and then the blood-soaked handkerchief. "Get me a basin and hot water. We have to stop the bleeding. I need a dish towel. Einar, we have to get your jacket off." She wrapped the towel around his hand. "Rune, help him." All the while she pressed against the blood vessels just above his wrist.

With Einar grunting and cussing, Rune got his coat off his other arm and gripped the cuff above the wound. "Ready?"

"Ja." Signe released his hand, then grabbed it again once the sleeve was gone. She looked Einar in the face. "If you do not stop your vile language, I will walk away."

The fiery glare he sent her could have knocked her off her chair, but he closed his mouth and fell quiet.

"The needle and thread are boiling." Gerd set a bottle of carbolic acid on the table along with strips of an old sheet.

"Takk." Signe pressed against Einar's wrist. "Rune, see where I'm pushing? Please take over. I'm not strong enough."

He pressed against the vessels in Einar's wrist and saw it was working. The flow slowed, nearly stopped.

"I'm going to pour carbolic acid over the cut." Signe looked Einar directly in the eyes. "This will hurt."

A curt nod was his only response.

"Ready?"

"Get it over with. I got work to do."

She looked at Rune and shrugged. She poured, keeping the lips of the cut open with the fingers of her other hand. "It looks clean."

"Bled enough." Sweat beaded on Einar's forehead. He was sure brave; Rune could admire that.

"Needle and thread."

Gerd returned with those. Signe threaded the needle and turned to the hand. She looked up at Einar, who was turning white around the mouth. "You have to hold still. Rune, keep pressing. Do you want to lie down?"

"Nei. Just get it over with."

Signe forced the needle through his tough skin, knotted it, and clipped the thread like she had seen a doctor do.

By the third stitch, Einar groaned. Keeping his eyes clamped shut, he waited. "How many more?"

"Two. I'm sorry. This is a bad one."

Signe put in the final two stitches, and Rune slowly released his pressure on Einar's wrist. No more bleeding. *Thank you, Lord.* Folding a piece of cloth to make a thickly wadded dressing, Signe laid it over the wound. Using the strips, she wrapped his palm and knotted the ends at the back of his hand. Rune considered it quite a professional-looking job.

"You might say thank you." Gerd had her own brand of needling.

Einar grunted and got to his feet. "Put your coat on, Rune. We got to get the wagon bed moved over to the sledge so we can get to the woods tomorrow."

Signe stared at him with her mouth open. "You cannot work in the woods with a cut like that!"

"I am cutting trees tomorrow!" Einar's roar made the house shake. His good arm slid into its sleeve, but the bad one he had to force in. His jaw clamped until his skin turned white. He grabbed his hat and headed for the door. "Rune?"

"In a minute." He helped Signe to her feet. "You sure earned a rest. You and Gerd both." With his arm supporting her, she made it to the bed and sat. He lifted her feet and pulled the quilt over them. "Sleeping is a good idea," he whispered, kissed her on the forehead, and left the room.

Einar and the boys were in the machine shed, where Bjorn had just drilled the last hole in the bed frame.

"All we have left is the mortise and tenons for the legs." Bjorn stared at Einar's wrapped hand, which was too big and sore to pull a mitten over. "Are you sure you should be down here? I mean, what if you hurt that worse?"

Einar raised his hand. "Now a stripling lad is telling me what to do!"

You don't consider him a stripling lad when you expect him to do a man's work. But Rune held his peace.

It took over an hour for them to unbolt the wagon bed and lift it off its axles using the hay pulley, so it was completely dark by the time they got the bed lowered onto the sledge frame and bolted in place.

Einar had to eat supper with his left hand. He looked like he was going to explode any minute. Sweat beaded his forehead every time he touched something with his right hand. He finally finished his bowl of ham and beans, ate his corn bread, and drained his coffee before he rose, pushing his chair back with his legs.

"I am going to bed."

Signe stared right at him, meeting his glare. "I think we should bury your hand in snow, since we do not have ice."

"Nei!"

"You better sleep in the house." Gerd spoke as calmly as Signe had.

"There is no bed." He glared at both women.

"You can sleep on a pallet in the parlor."

"I'll go get your quilts from the barn." Rune stood and headed for the coatrack.

Bjorn asked, "Mor, is there any of the pain stuff that the doctor gave me left?"

"Ja, I think so. The powder packets are gone, but we still have the bottle of laudanum. In the pantry on the second shelf, far right side."

Bjorn went to find the medicine. "Here, Onkel Einar, this can help you sleep tonight. Mor put it in water for me."

Einar started to reach with his right hand but quickly caught himself.

"Two spoonsful to a glass of water," Signe said.

"It tastes vile, but it works." Bjorn made a face.

"Can't I just drink it from the bottle?" Einar asked.

"Two swallows," Signe said, "but . . ."

Einar held the bottle against his chest with his right arm and twisted the cap off with his left. He took two swallows and made a gagging noise.

Gerd handed him a glass of water, shaking her head. "Stubborn fool."

At least he did sleep. His snoring in the parlor testified to that.

<hr />

The next morning, Rune walked out to breakfast with two lovely ladies on his arms: Signe on his right, and Gerd on his left. Einar was already sitting at the table, tapping his fork impatiently as Bjorn turned sausages and fried eggs out onto a plate. He set the plate before Onkel Einar and turned back to the stove to pour coffee.

"Bjorn, I'm amazed!" Signe sat down, and Rune continued to the stove to help Bjorn.

Bjorn grinned wickedly. "You know how long I have waited to be able to say this? Bring in more wood!"

Even Gerd laughed heartily. Rune glanced toward Einar, who had not so much as cracked a smile.

He brought in an armload of wood, and the fierce wind slammed the door behind him. "Sun out there, but bitter cold."

"The wind will die," Gerd assured him, "and the snow in sun is beautiful."

Rune warned, "You boys better leave for school early. Rosie will be slow plowing through the snow. Out on the road, others might have already broken a trail. Get off and walk when she's struggling with drifts. Let her pick her own way."

All bundled up, the schoolboys headed out the door.

"Rosie is saddled, and I harnessed the team after I watered them," Bjorn said. "It sure is cold out there."

"Too cold to work in the woods safely." Rune looked at Einar as he said, "We're not going out there, Bjorn."

Einar looked ready to erupt, but his mouth was full.

"What'll we do instead?" Bjorn asked.

"Cut a hole in the kitchen ceiling right up there." Rune pointed. "Then we'll build a wood—"

"I said no! No hole in the ceiling!"

"—den grate so that no one steps in it and turns an ankle."

Einar slammed his good hand on the table. "That does it! I'm done with you! You *all* are going to jail!"

He snatched his coat off the rack, grabbed his mittens, and stormed out the door.

Rune looked at Gerd. "Would he try to go clear into Blackduck?"

"Who knows what the silly fool might do. But you are wise, Rune. This cold wind will give you bad frostbite out in those woods. Another log or two is not worth the danger."

Bjorn looked up at the ceiling. "I can help you cut the hole."

"I'll go get the brace and bit and keyhole saw. You help with the dishes." Rune grinned. "And then bring in more wood."

Signe pulled Kirstin's soaker up around her diaper and laid her on the heavy baby blanket. She wrapped and tucked until her baby was in a warm, close cocoon. Kirstin drifted instantly to sleep. Signe picked up the papers on the dresser and carried them and the baby to the kitchen. "Where are Rune and Bjorn? I thought they would be back by now, cutting their hole."

Seated at the table, Gerd looked up from peeling potatoes. "Leif found the old potbelly stove out behind the shed. They're setting it up to keep the pigpens warm."

"Ah." Signe sat down and laid the baby on her legs.

Gerd put down the peeler. "How dare you neglect the poor thing so. Give her to me." She held out her arms.

Smiling, Signe handed over her daughter.

Tante Gerd cooed and cuddled Kirstin as she watched Signe lay out the papers and pick up her pencil. "What are you doing?"

"If Einar does go into Blackduck to talk to the sheriff, and should the sheriff actually come out here, I want my calculations to show all the days we've worked since I showed this to Einar. The calculations are months out of date. Also, I have the letter of agreement we all signed, just so Einar cannot make false statements."

Bjorn and Rune came inside with tools and a stepladder.

Rune mounted the drill bit into the brace. "Bjorn, go up into the attic. I'm going to drill a hole straight up. Then you will tie this string to the bit and the other end of the string to a pencil and use it to trace a perfect circle on the attic floor. Like this, see?"

"I see!" Bjorn pulled the pencil out of Signe's hand. "May I borrow this? Takk." He jogged toward the new stairs in the parlor.

"Did you get the stove set up?" Gerd asked.

"Ja. We vented it out the window with a baffle and wired the flue to stay in place. If it does not blow down in this wind, it will never blow down."

Signe copied onto clean paper the figures that stayed the same and figured out how much their labor was worth since they'd arrived. It was now five times what Einar had paid! She put it aside and gave Kirstin her midmorning meal.

At noon Gerd announced, "Time for dinner. Slabs of ham on fresh bread?"

"Perfect. We can eat as soon as Rune and Bjorn come back from the barn." Signe heard sleigh bells jingle out front. "Uh-oh."

Gerd stood up. "That is either Mrs. Benson or the sheriff."

Someone pounded on the front door.

"Mrs. Benson does not knock so loudly." Signe made her way carefully to the door and swung it open. The wind nearly whipped it out of her hands and sent her sprawling. A large man grabbed her arm and steadied her, just in time.

"I'm Sheriff Daniel Gruber," he said. "You are Mrs. Carlson?"

"I am." Signe had better stick to English here. She got her feet back under her and waved a hand toward Gerd, who stood in the kitchen doorway, cradling Kirstin in her arm. "Mrs. Strand."

Gerd called in English, "Do come in, and welcome."

"Thank you. This is Officer McGuthrie. I'm sure you two are aware that I am . . ." Signe could only understand a few of the words.

Gerd gestured. "Yes. Please join us in the kitchen. It is warmer here."

The two men followed Signe into the kitchen. Her English was so woefully deficient! How would she ever know what was going on?

Triumphantly, almost grinning, Einar stomped in the back door, his boots shedding clods of snow. Rune and Bjorn entered behind him. "These are the other Carlsons. The two smaller boys are in school," Einar explained.

Signe asked Gerd in Norwegian, "What is English for *bryte?*"

"Violated."

"Thank you. Sheriff, I think Mr. Strand says we violated our agreement. Broke the law."

"That is correct."

Gerd frowned at Einar. "Please take the men's coats and hang them up. Try to be civilized."

As the officers removed their coats, Signe laid her papers in front of the sheriff. "This is the agreement. And this paper shows how much we worked. The family worked."

Einar lost his smug smile. "Wait! You can't believe that! She made up the figures."

"Mr. Strand, I am doing the investigation."

"Would you two like coffee? We have fresh bread and jam." At least Signe knew those words.

Officer McGuthrie smiled, and Gerd translated his reply. "Yes, ma'am. Gotta keep the furnace stoked in this weather."

The sheriff was reading the letter of agreement, so Signe set out cups and jam. Bjorn was already slicing the bread into generous slabs. Rune poured the coffee.

The sheriff put down the letter and picked up Signe's sheet of calculations. He studied it for a long time, so Signe did not try to explain it. She waited.

Einar warned in English, "Don't trust those figures." At least, that was what Signe thought he said.

The sheriff asked Gerd several questions in rapid-fire English, and she responded. Signe could not keep up. He spoke tersely to Officer McGuthrie, and the young man unfolded a map of some sort. They began to talk to Einar about it. Einar might have walked into the kitchen looking smug, but now he looked worried or frightened.

Then the sheriff sat back and looked at Rune. Gerd translated as he went, so that Rune and Signe would not miss anything. "Mr. and Mrs. Carlson, Mr. Strand wanted me to lock you up and deport you because you would not obey him. In fact, he mentioned a hole in his ceiling, in his personal property." He pointed to the new vent. "Did you cut that?"

Rune nodded. "Ja, I cut it. To get heat into the attic where the boys sleep." Bjorn stood wide-eyed.

The sheriff nodded and just sat there for a few moments, obviously thinking. "What you may not know, Mr. and Mrs. Carlson, is that Mr. Strand got into some legal trouble years ago, in the matter of his purchase of this land." The sheriff waved Signe's piece of paper. "I doubt, Mr. Strand, that you want to bring that old business up again, and that is what may happen. What I see here, Mr. Strand, is de facto slavery, and that is an offense that could land you in jail."

"Wait." Gerd raised a hand. "What is *de facto*? I don't know that word."

She translated his response. "In this case, it means that the action taken is not called slavery—not labeled such—but it is indeed slavery all the same. Mr. Strand, you do not want to go to jail, I'm sure. Do you think it is time—past time—to give the Carlsons the land you promised them?"

Einar sputtered and squirmed. "Ja, I suppose so."

"Good!" The sheriff picked up Signe's pencil and drew some lines on the map. "Perhaps this parcel right here."

Einar bellowed, "But that's cleared land! That's good farmland. And that part there—the timber has not been harvested yet from that area."

"So you were intending to eventually give the blood relatives who have worked for you so faithfully for nearly six months and produced for you a profit of over five times the cost of their passage some uncleared stump fields. I see."

"Well, uh, maybe there would be some stumps on some of it, but—"

"Mr. Strand, shall we look more closely at the ownership of all this property?"

Einar scowled as blackly as Signe had ever seen him scowl. "Nei. I will give him that parcel."

The sheriff nodded. "I will expect you, Mr. Strand, and you, Mr. Carlson, to appear at the courthouse on Monday morning next, to complete the transfer of title. The judge will be waiting. And now, Mrs. Carlson, might I have a slice of that excellent bread before we leave?"

Chapter 34

If Rune were the sort of man who sang when he was happy, he would be warbling like a thrush. He finished his breakfast, shrugged into his coat, and wrapped his scarf around his neck.

"You start a fire out there and keep it burning, you hear?" Gerd told him. "Don't want any frostbitten hands or toes. Keep your face covered too."

Signe finished her coffee. "How he thinks he's going to pull that saw with one hand is beyond me."

"He thinks he will use both," Rune said.

"You remind him. If he pulls out the stitches, he will have to go see the doctor, because I cannot sew that up again. He could lose his hand if infection sets in."

"I will remind him, whatever good it will do." Rune kissed her forehead, scooped up the dinner basket, and went outside. A blast of frigid air hit him.

With no crust yet on the new snow, the sledge broke through instead of running on top of it. They were forced to break trail for the horses, who were dripping with sweat by the time they got into the woods, where the snow was not as deep or drifted.

"Throw blankets over them and in a while, give them some

extra oats." Einar carefully lifted the axes out of the wagon bed. "You bring that saw. Bjorn, finish limbing that last tree. Stay on the path."

Rune lifted out the saw. The sun glinting off the snow made his eyes water, which froze his eyelashes. He pulled his hat down tighter both to warm him and shade his eyes. It didn't work well; he could still barely see.

Ahead of them, Einar tripped on a branch under the snow and went sprawling, slamming his right hand into the ground. His roar was followed by a string of expletives that could have melted a trail all the way to the house. He struggled to get to his feet and fell onto his hand again.

The stupid, stubborn fool. Rune dropped the saw and used the trail Einar had broken to get to him. "I will help you up."

"You will not. Back off. Leave!" Einar waved him away, his good arm swinging wildly and barely missing Rune's jaw.

Rune almost landed in the snow, dodging Einar's flailing hand. He sucked in the bitter cold air, taking a moment to adjust the scarf across his lower face. *Lord, help me. Help him.* What he really wanted to do was knock the fool out and drag him back to the wagon, hopefully knocking some sense into him at the same time.

Einar strangled the axe handle with his left hand, and on the second attempt, finally inched himself to his feet. Like a wounded bear, he swung around as if searching for his attacker.

"We're trying to help you!" Rune yelled at him. Tying him up and throwing him in the back of the wagon was looking better by the moment. He glanced over his shoulder to see Bjorn starting toward them. "Stay back," he told his son, who obeyed. At least he was acting wisely.

"I don't need yours or anyone else's help!" Einar waved his arm again. "Get out of here! You're all useless anyway." Sucking in a freezing breath made him cough and choke. When he caught his breath, he muttered, "I don't know why I ever brought you here. Go on, go! I don't need you!"

Rune watched him stagger back with the force of his rage. He heaved a sigh, then turned and walked toward the wagon. "Come on, Bjorn. You heard the man. We're just following orders."

"But he could freeze to death out here."

"Ja, he could. That's up to him now." Rune threw the saw in the back of the wagon. "Your axe too."

Bjorn shook his head, turning back to look at Einar again. "But Far . . ."

"He said *leave* once too often." Rune strode back up the track through the snow. "Bjorn!"

"Coming."

Together they trudged toward the homestead. Anger still sizzled and snapped in Rune's gut. *He's like a wounded bear. You shouldn't leave him alone out here. I should not have lost my temper like that. He has to learn he cannot treat people like this. But he isn't thinking clearly. What if he hurts himself worse? That is his problem. He told us to leave, and we are.* The thoughts bombarded him like a hailstorm. But like a hailstorm, it blew over as they slogged back through the snow. Hot under the collar would have applied to him, but he knew better than to answer wrath with wrath. *If that fool man dies out here, it will be my fault. How will I live with that?* He stared toward the woods. Go back and get yelled at again, or on to the house? Perhaps this would give Einar's temper time to cool off. The cold should be good for something.

They had walked only a short distance when one of the horses nickered.

Bjorn stopped. "What about the horses?"

"They're blanketed. They'll be okay for a time." Rune paused to catch his breath and stared heavenward before continuing onward.

They reached the barn, and Bjorn asked, "What are we going to do now?"

"We're going to cut up the remainder of that tree, split and stack it so Gerd has plenty of firewood. We'll have dinner, and then if Einar has not come back, I will go looking for him. You can help Gerd."

"I would rather come with you. If he's hurt, you'll need two more strong arms."

"So be it."

"Will we really leave here?"

Rune heaved a sigh, his breath puffing white through his scarf. "I want to, but . . ." He shook his head. "I gave my word to stay. I try to live up to that."

"Tante Gerd does not want us to go."

"I know, and really, I don't either."

"He yells a lot, but he has never hit any of us."

"True." *But he barely missed me out there. And it wasn't on purpose.*

He thought of how Knute and Leif were so frightened of Einar. Even Signe was fearful, although she tried not to let it show. What could he do to make it better for all of them? Move his family out? Bjorn did not want to leave. Neither did Signe. And he knew Einar did not really want them to go either. The bear with the wounded paw tromped through his mind again.

He had two choices: go or stay.

If he chose to go—where to?

However, if he chose to stay—what needed to change? Or did they just go on as if nothing had happened? That was usually what Einar did the next morning. *Lord God, I know you have a plan, but you need to let me know what it is.* In spite of the effort of walking home, the cold was seeping deep into his bones.

"Let's go cut wood."

"What happened out there?" Gerd asked when he and Bjorn both carried armloads of wood inside and dumped them in the woodbox. "Soup will be ready soon."

"I will tell you over dinner."

And so he did, Signe at the table with them as they ate their soup and the bits of raised dough Gerd had fried.

Gerd frowned. "And he has still not come back to the barn?"

Rune and Bjorn both shook their heads.

"Leaving the fool out there is tempting, I know, but . . ."

"But we will go out after dinner to check on him."

"He could be lying in a snowbank."

"More likely he is trying to cut limbs one-handed."

Bjorn shook his head. "I've done that. Hard enough to split wood that way, let alone fight the snow to cut off limbs."

"Ja, you know, eh?" Gerd nodded. She looked from Signe to Rune. "I want you to know that I do not want you to go, not now, not any time. I do believe when Einar gets his wits about him again, he does not want you to go either. He has always had a temper but has never hit anyone that I know of."

She started to stand to get the coffeepot, but Rune beat her to it.

"Takk."

"I think we should bake cookies this afternoon," Signe said, with a slow nod. "And maybe bake a custard. We need to use some of the eggs. That does sound good."

Rune laid his hand on her shoulder as he refilled their coffee cups and squeezed gently. He set the coffeepot back on the stove. Looking around the room, he nodded. This place felt more and more like a home—their home.

When he and Bjorn shrugged into their coats and headed out to the woods again, they found the team and sledge by the barn, but no Einar. They searched the barn, called his name. No Einar.

"Go up to the house and get some quilts," Rune told Bjorn. "Ask Gerd for strong coffee and to put on a boiler of water. Hurry!"

He took the blankets off the horses and folded them into the wagon bed. Turning the team and sledge, he waited for Bjorn to toss the quilts in the back and climb up on the seat with him. All the while, *Dear God, let him live* screamed through Rune's mind.

They found Einar facedown in the snow in the runner tracks, heading toward the homestead. Rune swung the team out to park the sledge right beside him. He and Bjorn leaped out and rolled the fallen man on his back.

"Einar, Einar!" Rune shook him. "Come on, man, open your eyes." He turned to Bjorn. "Grab one of the horse blankets."

"Is he dead?"

"Nei. See, he's breathing. Let's get him up in the wagon." He shook Einar again. "Wake up so we can get you home."

Slowly Einar's eyes blinked half open. "T-tired."

They rolled him onto a blanket, dragged him to the tailgate, and each took two corners. They heaved and got his upper body up onto the wagon bed. "You climb in and pull." Huffing, they dragged Einar's inert body all the way into the wagon bed and wrapped him in quilts.

Kneeling beside him, Rune uncorked the quart jug of coffee. "Einar, hear me. I am going to lift you and pour some of this into your mouth. Drink it to help warm you. Can you hear me?"

Einar nodded, then managed to swallow once, twice.

When they pulled the sledge to a stop by the back door,

Knute and Leif were just arriving home from school. They leaped off the horse.

"What happened?"

"Is he dead?"

"Nei, you're just in time to help us carry him into the house." Between the four of them, they heaved and dragged the big man inside, where Gerd had laid a pallet by the kitchen stove.

"Put him there."

Rune knelt and pulled off Einar's boots and began rubbing his feet while Bjorn helped Gerd rewrap the quilts around him.

"Einar, can you hear me?" Rune asked.

A slight nod was a better response than nothing.

"Good." *Please, Father, save this man. Restore him to health both in his body and his mind.* Rune sucked in a deep breath. The fact that he was alive was a miracle by itself. *Thank you he did not die out there. I should have gone back earlier. Forgive me, please, and help me to care for him. Help us all.*

Slowly they warmed him up, using the hot rocks they had for warming the beds at night. Gerd checked his fingers and toes for frostbite, but only his nose and cheeks showed the white spots of being frozen.

"Is he sleeping or unconscious?" Signe asked.

Gerd shook her head. "Stubborn fool. Einar Strand . . . you—you . . ."

Rune caught the agony in her voice and on her face. "He's going to be all right." How he knew that was beyond him, but for some reason, he felt sure of his words. "Einar, can you hear me?"

Again the nod.

"Good. We're going to hold you up enough to help you drink coffee. It will not be hot."

Another slight nod.

Gerd poured coffee in a cup, laced it with cream and sugar, and knelt beside her husband. Rune slid an arm under Einar's shoulders and lifted. Bjorn dropped to his knees at his onkel's head and scooted so that his knees became a brace for Einar's upper body.

Rune blinked and sniffed at his son's actions. *Lord, how you have blessed me with my family.*

Gerd spooned the coffee into Einar's mouth and nodded when he swallowed. She looked to Rune and Bjorn. "Takk."

"Enough." Einar's gravelly voice was music indeed. They laid him back prone.

"I don't know how he hasn't more frostbite." Gerd set the cup on the table. "Could have lost fingers and toes so easily."

"Oh, the custard." Signe started to stand, but Gerd motioned her to stay seated so as to not wake the baby, who had slept through all the commotion in the sling around her mor's chest.

Gerd pulled the custard out of the oven and set it on the stove. "Leif, hand me a knife from the drawer." She cut into the custard. "Ja, it is done. This will be good for him to eat."

"Good for all of us. What a treat." Signe smiled at her husband and her boys.

Rune looked at his boys. "Let's get the chores done."

"I unharnessed the team and put all the horses in the barn," Knute said. "I gave them some extra grain too."

"Good, I forgot all about them." Shaking his head, Rune looked to Gerd. "Need anything more before we go?"

"Nei, you have done far more than he—we deserved."

"We are family, and families take care of each other. As my mor so often reminded us, God is in His heaven, and all is well." He smiled at her. "However, custard and cookies are good anytime."

"We will get the cookies baked." Signe motioned to the custard cooling on the counter. "We're halfway done. You all be careful out there."

"We will. And we'll put up the beds after chores."

Gerd frowned. "You don't expect Signe to go up those stairs yet, do you?"

"Nei, but soon." He smiled at his wife. "I will carry Kirstin up."

The next morning, Einar was sitting in the kitchen when the others returned from morning chores. Gerd and Signe were putting breakfast on the table.

Signe smiled at Rune and their sons. "Your dinner pails even have cookies today."

"Mor, this is Saturday. We don't go to school today."

Gerd and Signe stared at each other. Signe shrugged, her smile running into laughter. "I guess we forgot."

Knute grinned at his far. "So I can go out in the woods with you."

"No woods today."

They all stared at Einar, who was dishing up his eggs as if he had not spoken.

"What?" Rune looked to Gerd, who shrugged, but her eyes might have been dancing.

"You and me, we are going to Blackduck for the ceiling grate." Einar held up his bandaged hand. "You can pick out wood for a cradle for that baby, and we'll get lumber to close off that end of the machine shed so we can work out there at night or when it is storming." He went back to eating as if nothing had been said.

Rune felt his mouth drop open. He looked at Signe, who was staring at Einar as if he had sprouted horns or wings. Rune sucked in and blew out a breath. "You better get a list ready."

Gerd nodded. "We will. Now sit down and get to eating before Einar finishes off all the eggs."

Had the frostbite gone to Einar's head? *Thank you, Lord, for miracles do still happen. And this most surely is one.* Who ever would have dreamed of this?

He squeezed Signe's hand as he headed for his place at the table.

One Sunday, two weeks later, Rune loaded Signe and their three boys into the sledge, well fortified with blankets and hot rocks for their feet.

"Where are we going?" Signe looked around her. How wonderful to be out of the house on such a grand and glorious day. Blue sky, sun glittering on the snow, a crow calling from the woods.

"It's a surprise." Rune clucked, and the team headed down to the barn and then, instead of following the track out to the big trees, swung off to the right and across the field. White hats crowned the fence posts, and drift shadows blued the pristine white covering the ground. When he pulled the team to a stop, Rune pointed to a tall pine standing to their left.

"See that pine tree? That is the northeast corner of our five acres. Einar and I paced it off yesterday. There's a cleared area for the house we will build come spring. We'll cut the lumber from our own trees, just like Einar did." He turned to Signe. "We will have our home here."

"And still be here to take care of Gerd."

"Ja, and work with Einar. Bjorn, Knute, and Leif, we will all work five days each week for Einar because he needs us. The sixth day we will fell our own trees to build our home. And Sundays we will save for church."

Signe laid her head on his shoulder. "Church. A house of our own. A family. Just what we dreamed of. Someday."

"Our someday has already begun. I see promises of dawn every day when the sun touches the tops of the big trees, the smoke rises from the chimney, Kirstin fusses for her morning meal, and the cow bellows that we should hurry. And now we will have our own house too."

"The promises of dawn, I like that. And perhaps one day, someone else will come from the old country, and we can all build new homes here." She swung her arm to include the fields and the unlogged land before them. "All of us together. Family."

"Ja, God willing. Amen."

Acknowledgments

Starting a new series is always crazy-making, and UNDER THE NORTHERN LIGHTS is no exception. Part of the fun and the challenge was to begin sprouting a branch off the RED RIVER series, better known these days as the BLESSING series. Ingeborg's cousin Gunlaug in *An Untamed Heart*, which is set in Norway, has always pleaded to see her cousin again after all these years. I want to see the two of them together again too. *So . . . what if?* My favorite question to begin a new story, or continue an old one, leaped into my mind, ready for more adventure.

And so began this story, set in northern Minnesota near the town of Blackduck, where the huge white pine trees were systematically logged. Gunlaug's eldest son and his wife, Signe, and their three sons are brought from Norway at the behest of relatives Einar and Gerd Strand.

Many thanks to my agent, Wendy Lawton, for opening my eyes to a way of accomplishing this dream. She always knows how to dream big and encourage me. First readers Sandy

Dengler, who helps put much-needed evil in my novels, and Ellie Delgado are invaluable. I am privileged to work with Bethany House Publishers. Publishing books is indeed a team effort. Editor Jessica Barnes took over for my dear longtime friend and editor, Sharon Asmus, who got to go home to our Lord. Jessica had big shoes to fill, and she is doing well. So grateful. Through these years, VP of Editorial David Horton has become a dear friend, wise encourager, and a good question-asker when we come up with a new idea. What a jewel. Marketing a book takes several teams with all that can and needs to be done. Again, our team is superb. As are the folks at Baker Book House, who truly believe and do business as real Christians who seek God's will and wisdom.

The folks in Blackduck, Minnesota—especially Laraine Roach, a Facebook friend who read the manuscript and made valuable contributions, and the Historical Society, which sent me information, pictures, and answers to my questions. What great people. I hope to see them all in August of 2017 for a book release bash and thank them personally.

I am blessed to have the best assistants in the world, Opal and Cecile, who take care of things for me in many ways, from social networking to finances, along with galley reader, Judy. What a team I have!

I am so grateful to all those who pray for me. My first line of defense is my Round Robin writer-friends. We have been together since 1984, more like sisters than just friends. I have several families, my immediate family of two sons, Kevin and Brian, and husband, Wayne. Others include church family, our relatives, my Facebook family, reader family, and deep and wide friend family. We will all get to meet in heaven one day, and do we ever have a lot to talk about. Wayne has been in this since the beginning, filling so many roles in this writer business of ours. We've managed to visit a lot of places and many people, all part of the research it takes to make these books happen. Along with plenty of fun.

Who ever dreamed that our amazing God had all this planned from the beginning. To Him be all glory and honor.

Lauraine Snelling is the award-winning author of over 70 books, fiction and nonfiction, for adults and young adults. Her books have sold over 5 million copies. Besides writing books and articles, she teaches at writers' conferences across the country. She and her husband make their home in Tehachapi, California, with basset hound Sir Winston and their "three girls," big golden hens.

Sign Up for Lauraine's Newsletter!

Keep up to date with news on Lauraine's upcoming book releases and events by signing up for her email list at laurainesnelling.com.

More from Lauraine Snelling

When the women of Blessing decide to give Toby Valders a push to propose to Deborah MacCallister, their matchmaking scheme yields unexpected results.

From This Day Forward
Song of Blessing #4

You May Also Like . . .

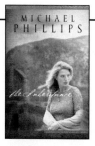

In Scotland's Shetland Islands, a clan patriarch has died, and a dispute over the inheritance has frozen an entire community's assets. When a letter from the estate's solicitor finds American Loni Ford, she sets out on a journey to discover her roots—but is this dream too good to be true?

The Inheritance by Michael Phillips
SECRETS OF THE SHETLANDS #1
fatheroftheinklings.com

Emily Carver is tired of moving from one mining camp to another and longs for a true home. When a handsome geologist arrives in camp, the two are drawn to each other but fight the attraction for different reasons. Will these broken souls allow God to bring healing to their hurting hearts—and embrace love?

A Treasure Concealed by Tracie Peterson
SAPPHIRE BRIDES #1
traciepeterson.com

In 1917, British nurse and war widow Evelyn Marche is trapped in German-occupied Brussels. She works at the hospital by day and is a spy for the resistance by night. When a British plane crashes in the park, Evelyn must act quickly to protect the injured soldier, who has top-secret orders and a target on his back.

High as the Heavens by Kate Breslin
katebreslin.com